THE

CAPRI

LETTERS

THE
CAPRI
LETTERS

Mario Soldati

TRANSLATED FROM THE ITALIAN BY ARCHIBALD COLQUHOUN

Alfred A. Knopf

NEW YORK 1956

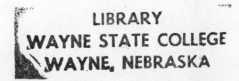

L. C. catalog card number: 55–10584
© *Alfred A. Knopf, Inc., 1955*

This is a BORZOI BOOK, *published by* ALFRED A. KNOPF, INC.

Copyright 1955 by ALFRED A. KNOPF, INC. *All rights reserved. No part of this book may be reproduced in any form without permission in writing from the publisher, except by a reviewer who may quote brief passages in a review to be printed in a magazine or newspaper. Manufactured in the United States of America. Published simultaneously in Canada by McClelland and Stewart Limited.*

PUBLISHED FEBRUARY 13, 1956
SECOND PRINTING, MARCH 1956
THIRD PRINTING, APRIL 1956

Originally published in Italian as LE LETTERE DA CAPRI,
Copyright 1954 by Aldo Garzanti Editore

THE
CAPRI
LETTERS

One spring morning in Rome last year I was passing through Via Margutta. I was on my way to a small film studio that is in one of those old courtyards between the slopes of the Pincio and Via Margutta—unexpected pools of quiet amid the confused mass of walls, stairs, railings, homes, and hovels.

Via Margutta lay half in sun and half in shade at the gayest hour of the day, eleven o'clock. Once midday is past, the atmosphere changes. It is true that the Romans linger over their lunches almost as if hoping to stop the clock and prolong midday till two or later. But eleven is always the gayest hour. I passed by the artisans' shops, the framemakers' and carpenters', a little mechanic's that had probably taken the place of an old forge, a wineshop, a laundry. Their workmen were also doing their jobs out in the street, which was cluttered with tools and with parked cars and motorcycles. And they were working happily, it seemed: striking noisily at the wood and tin, calling out to one another, one or two singing. As I walked along I slowed down a little as if to gather some of their joy in life before reaching the place where my own work was waiting for me.

Suddenly I heard my name called; I turned round and recognized, hurrying, almost running toward me, with his long, loose gait, holding a bottle of milk, an American friend of mine, Harry Summers.

It was some months, perhaps almost a year, since I'd last seen him. He had changed. His light-brown eyes looked tired and his face was paler than usual. He was uncombed and unshaved, as I'd never seen him before and never thought he would look. On his delicate, almost adolescent chin were scattered little blond hairs. Something seemed to have happened to him. We had worked together in an American radio organization during the war, and were friends; but not friends enough for me to be able to ask him, point-blank, what was the matter.

He came toward me in his usual affectionate way, smiling his usual melancholy smile, and put an arm round me for a second; I could feel the milk bottle against my back.

As we talked of how long it was since we'd seen each other, and I was explaining how my work had cut me off from my friends, and he how his had taken him on constant journeys to Paris, London, and New York, I noticed that even his clothes looked odd. After the war he had exchanged his elegant close-fitting American uniform for the dark-gray stuffs and double-breasted suits proper to his important new job. He worked at UNESCO, regularly in Paris, but he constantly visited London and Rome to organize exchange exhibitions of ancient and modern art between the United States and Europe. He had to visit important people and go to meetings and receptions nearly every day, like a diplomat.

So I was amazed to see him now in a pair of old flannel trousers, an open shirt, no tie, and a tattered pullover; a careless, neglected-looking getup that suited, however, the strange expression of his face. If I wasn't a close enough friend to ask him directly what was the matter, his clothes and the bottle of milk gave me an easy excuse.

"You're on vacation, I see."

"Yes, forever," he replied rather too quickly, and with a bitter little smile.

"What do you mean? Aren't you with UNESCO any more?"

"No, thank God! I've chosen freedom, too! I was tired.

Diplomacy's not my line. I only really like art history. In fact, I only really like Jacopo Torriti and Piero Cavallini!"

He had written unpublished monographs on these two thirteenth-century Roman painters, and had come to Italy to study them before the war.

"I've dropped everything. I couldn't take Paris any more. As someone, I can't remember who, once said, people there live as if they were going to live forever. Not as in Italy. Here death's always near, God willing! I no longer do anything now, or see anyone. Every day I go to Trastevere and study the Santa Cecilia frescoes."

"Aren't you happy then?"

"I'd be very happy indeed of course!"—he laughed bitterly again—"except for one little difficulty. I can't go on. Very soon my money will run out and I'll have to go back to America. That's why I ran after you as soon as I saw you. I wanted to ring you up, but I'd lost your number. You're the only person who can help me. You," he went on, laughing more than ever, fixing his big gentle eyes on me and putting a hand on my shoulder, as if, in his shyness, he pretended to be offering, not asking me for, help, "you're my man of providence!"

I was very fond of him. Yet I felt that little tightening of the heart ("Oh God, how shall I get out of this? What a bore!") which assails us when even our best friends ask us for help or money. In vain we try to transform the look of selfish irritation on our faces into an expression of affectionate sympathy. Our first words in reply to our friend's sudden request are always hesitant and uncertain. Does charity come naturally to anyone? Perhaps only to saints.

But Harry, who was as intelligent as he was nice, knew perfectly well that I was no saint; he noticed my embarrassment without surprise and went on with what he had been saying. He did not want to return to America at any cost. He wanted to stay in Italy. And to stay in Italy he needed money. I remembered that he was married and had two children. I asked after them, to gain time.

"Oh, the children are in America," he replied; "they're in Philadelphia with their grandparents. Well settled. I could go there too and work. There's always a job open for me as lecturer at B— University. But it would be the end, do you understand? The death of the spirit. I need to live here, among these stones, these people, this light." He looked around. Via Margutta at that moment was the best symbol of the old Italy and the Old World—old but alive.

I said: "Do you need money? But why did you leave UNESCO?"

"Too long a story. I'll tell you another time. Now you must help me earn more money."

"Why don't you write articles? Send things to an American paper?"

"I'm doing a bit of that. But if one's not a professional and already known, they don't pay much. No. Only you can help me."

"What do you want to do?"

"Whatever you want. You're a film-director. There must be thousands of jobs I could do in films—as actor, assistant director, script-writer, translator, dubber. I don't want much money."

He told me that he'd taken, very cheaply, comparatively speaking, a painter's studio near by; and with his free-lance articles, if I could give him a little work on the films, he'd be sure of making out.

"Come up and have a drink. Then you can see."

I looked at the time and refused with thanks; I was already late for my dubbing. As we walked on I explained that till my next film, which meant till next summer, I would be unable, even with the best of luck, to give him any work. Every place was taken, every job portioned out.

He was not convinced and came with me as far as the dubbing studio, still insisting. He could write scenarios. He knew the price of a good scenario; enough for him to live on in Rome for a year. I replied that to sell a film scenario was a very great stroke of luck; I myself, for instance, had never succeeded in selling one though I'd written at least fifty during my years in the film business. Even so, he might have a try, just because it was all a matter of luck; and I promised to give him all the help I could on my side.

Meanwhile we had reached the courtyard. In front of the doors and windows of the little studio the actors who were to do the dubbing and technicians in black aprons were walking about in the sun, smoking and chatting. Thinking that they were waiting for me, I quickly began apologizing for my late arrival; but the chief sound man laughingly told me not to worry. A power failure would keep them idle for another half-hour.

Harry took advantage of this to repeat his invitation; his studio was only a step or two away.

We went out again into Via Margutta and entered a doorway a few yards ahead.

After a dark, narrow, very long passage we went up some stone stairs with iron banisters and crossed a dirty terrace, flagged with loose, broken old bricks and hemmed in all round by the opaque windows of painters' studios and by balconies crammed with tomato and basil plants, belonging to small shopkeepers or artisans. A girl in her chemise, who was hanging out washing, looked at us indifferently. Along another passage, up another staircase, and finally we reached a courtyard closed on three sides by the usual little flats and the usual windows, but open in front to the high, thick, green mass of the Pincio. I had to pause and look for a second, in delight.

"How lovely!" I said.

"Don't you know these studios?"

"Others like them, near by. But I've never been here."

Harry squeezed my arm. "You see," he said, "if I had a boathouse in Minnesota on the lake, or a hunting lodge in the Wyoming forests, then I might like living in the States. But that university town! Philadelphia! Even New York! No, no."

He paused, then turned slowly and pointed to a small terrace just behind us and a little above our heads, reached by a narrow staircase of colored tiles.

"There's where I live," he concluded.

We went toward the stairs. But suddenly he stopped, squeezed my arm again, and gazed at me, smiling in silence. Then he glanced up toward the little terrace, hesitated again, and whispered:

"There's something I must warn you of. I don't know how to put it, but the woman, the woman you'll see now isn't—isn't a servant, let's say."

"Do you take me for an idiot? Then she's Italian?"

"A *ciociara*," he replied with his bitter smile. But this time it was almost a grimace. *Ciociara*—the word itself seemed to give him a painful pleasure.

As we went up the few tiled stairs, I was congratulating myself on having mentioned only his children, and not his wife, when asking for news of his family. I had met the wife two or three times, at British Embassy receptions, a year or two before. She was small and dark, not beautiful, but slim and very smart; a lock of hair over her forehead, in studied disorder; lively eyes; and an air, an expression in her whole person, of nervous intelligent refinement. I knew that she and Harry were always quarreling, and Harry had already then been talking of separation.

The woman who was not a servant announced herself, as soon as Harry opened the door, with a drawn-out cry of: "Harry!" (or rather " 'Arry," without pronouncing the *H*). "What about that milk! Be quick!"

"Here it is, my dear," and he quickly vanished behind a dark wooden partition that ran along one entire side of the huge room. It was a painter's studio, like all those in Via Margutta. A long, high window, beside the entrance, framed the view of the Pincio. On the left was the partition. The other two walls were crossed by a triangular balcony supported on big beams; one guessed at a double bed up there. Balcony and beams were painted black like the partition. The place was decorated in the usual style of bohemian Rome, a style that seems to appeal to the foreign intelligentsia. Sagging armchairs, a metal bedspring for a divan, tattered cushions, prints on the walls, heavy, overdecorated mock-Renaissance table and sideboard. Dust, dirt, and disorder everywhere. On the table, among bottles and plates, were books, papers, a typewriter, and a glass with a few flowers stuck in it.

Harry reappeared at once, leading the woman.

She was tall, strong, full-fleshed, with round hips and big, firm, jutting breasts. Her crow-black hair was pulled tight back, smooth and gleaming, on her small well-shaped head. Her eyes were big, pale green, and very beautiful. The body of a model; and a face just like a Cavallini mosaic. I at once had an impression, anyway, that I'd either met her or seen her somewhere before, and could not remember at the moment just when and where. But a second later it occurred to me that this impression might be due to her appearance, which was almost aggressively provocative, though at the moment, apparently, she was doing her best to look modest; it was the unmistakable look of a "professional" on vacation, trying not to betray herself, and thinking she'd succeeded.

She had a cotton apron round her hips. Taking a couple of steps toward me and pointing to her apron as she dried her hands, she said:

"Good morning. Excuse me for not shaking hands, I'm cooking."

"Martini? Pink gin?" Harry asked me, coming up to the table. He took up a bottle and looked at it against the light to see how much was still there. But just when he was about to open it, he stopped and turned to the woman with a sudden gesture.

"Excuse me, Dora, I didn't ask you. What are you having?"

"Oh, whatever you like, you know it's all the same to me. I don't understand any of your mixtures. You shouldn't drink 'em either, they're bad for you!"

"But why do you say that? You've drunk thousands of

Martinis in your time. You don't know how to make a Martini? Try!"

"What do you mean, try! I don't even know what it is"; then to me: "He's a case, your friend is! You tell him, he won't realize how simple we Italian women are."

"Harry knows that perfectly well," I said, "and likes them that way. But he's joking."

Harry was mixing the gin, laughing and looking pleased.

"Excuse the mess," began Dora again; "it's just a temporary place. But so central, only a few steps from Piazza del Popolo."

We drank a Martini. Harry reminded Dora that he'd talked to her about me a number of times.

"You don't know her," he explained, "but she knows you. She's often seen you. And your photograph in the film magazines. She's worked for you too, as an extra."

She named the film. Then I remembered where I'd seen her; but that, of course, did not change my first impression of her appearance.

Harry ended: "If you need extras, there are two of us now. Why don't you call on us? Or just on her, of course, if you can't use me."

As he said this he gazed at me smilingly. I gazed back for a second, straight into his eyes. I had sensed that he was in love with this woman. But in that second I sensed something else too. Harry was a noble character. If he was lowering himself to ask me for work in front of her, and indeed for her, and if he did so with every appearance of offering me his mistress, he was not urged to such an extreme only by need of money, but also by another, perhaps deeper impulse.

For the same reason I was certain that if I dared to court Dora, it would make him suffer and even, perhaps, arouse his anger. But I must admit that, even so, the ambiguity of the situation rather attracted me. And so did the woman on her own account. Slipping into the dangerous game, I began to hold out more hope now to Harry than I had before:

"I won't promise anything; but I can assure you I'll do all I can. Within a fortnight I hope and think I may have news. Give me your telephone number. Here's mine."

I got up, I had to go. This time Dora offered me her hand. Her big plump arms were bare. But her hand was small and her wrist relatively slim, ringed with a narrow watch-strap. She said good-by, even so, with a definite hint of coldness, without smiling, and thanked me for what I would do for them in a tone of conventional politeness.

"Thank you so much, but don't put yourself out. I have to leave next week. Harry has to leave too. And we don't even know where we'll be in a fortnight."

She seemed to be trying to correct Harry's ambiguous hints and say to me: "Look here, my dear sir, if you think you can fix up anything with me, you're mistaken. I may look easy, but I'm not; I love Harry." Or perhaps, more sincerely: "I've been easy and still am, behind Harry's back. But if I were with you too, my dear sir, who are a friend of Harry's, he'd be sure to find out some day. And that would be the ruin of me. For Harry is far and away the most generous of my clients; he gives me what none of the others has ever given me: a settled life."

Although I realized all this at once, or perhaps just because I did realize it, as I said good-by I held her hand and pressed my thumb on her wrist for that fraction of a second longer than usual which from a man to a woman or vice versa is always enough of an opening. She, alarmed, tried to show me that she resented my little pause; she turned her wrist round and freed herself of my pressure with a speed and violence subdued enough for Harry not to notice, but obvious enough to me.

"Good-by," she said at the same time, staring hard at me with her big green eyes, and prolonging the stare as long beyond normal as I had prolonged my pressure. "So pleased to have met you."

Harry accompanied me down through the labyrinth.

We had reached the last dark passageway before the street door when he stopped and in a few hesitating words asked me to lend him some money.

Yes, he certainly needed money. As certainly as he had gathered courage on seeing I was attracted by his mistress. But most certainly of all, I sensed that together with a need of money he was feeling an abject pleasure in asking me for it.

I hadn't enough on me and would have to make out a check. As I pulled out my checkbook and fingered my fountain pen in the inside pocket of my jacket, I was suddenly tempted to see Dora again and let her watch me in the act of giving money to her man.

"But I haven't a pen."

"I'm so sorry; you'll have to climb the stairs again," said he.

We ran back up them. And I was quickly punished. She was in the kitchen, where Harry joined her. With studied slowness I filled out the check on a corner of the table. Harry returned. And Dora did not reappear.

"Is it true," I asked Harry, handing him the check, "is it true that you are both leaving in a few days?"

"No, not at all," replied Harry with a laugh.

"Then why did she say so?"

"To make some excuse for my asking you for work; she's afraid of bothering you too much."

"So neither of you is leaving?"

"No. Dorotea would like to"—he lowered his voice. "She'd like me to return to America, and come with me. She can't understand why I should stay here and starve. She just can't understand it. And how can I explain to her? But she's dying to go to America. Maybe she doesn't love me, or her love is just part of that fixed idea of hers, to go to America."

"Italian women are like that," I observed.

"Italian women of her class, you mean."

"No, I don't think so; the others too."

"I don't understand. Like all other women!" concluded Harry, laughing.

Meanwhile Dora, or Dorotea, had not put in an appearance. I could not wait any longer. Disappointed, I made off, and then felt ashamed of myself at once; Harry's vice seemed to have infected me.

Although I longed to, I wasn't able to visit Harry and Dorotea again during the next few days. Harry rang me up a couple of times and said he'd followed my advice and thought of a film scenario. He was working on it now and would tell me about it as soon as we saw each other again. I encouraged him to write it, but avoided giving him too much hope.

Anyway, I thought, it was much easier and wiser to give him money personally, which was likely to be a dead loss, on the problematical sale of the scenario, than to try to find him some kind of job.

One Sunday morning toward the beginning of June, Harry rang me up and asked if I'd like to go to the sea with him and Dorotea. I happened to have nothing to do and was faced with a lonely day, empty of all except the gloomiest memories—abandoned ambitions, renounced desires. I accepted.

They came to get me in an old jeep. I got in front. Harry drove; Dorotea sat in the middle, wedged between him and me.

Her black hair was tied up in a red silk handkerchief, which made her face look stronger and her eyes greener; and her sun-suit, which was also red, with big yellow flowers on it, left her shoulders, back, and stomach bare.

What with the sun, heat, and wind, the smell of sea growing stronger the farther we got from Rome, the contact of her half-naked body, the weight of her arm on mine, the occasional pressure of her legs, and her mood, which today, I could not understand why, seemed light, jesting, and much more friendly toward me than the first time, I was soon in a state of fluttering agitation, swung between a very uncertain hope of pleasure and a quite certain knowledge of my duty.

When we were out in the open country and still twenty miles or so from the beach we were making for, Harry started to talk about the film scenario. He had begun to write it and had then stopped, overwhelmed by all sorts of doubts. He wanted to tell me about these doubts and ask my advice.

But Dorotea laughingly refused to allow him; today was

a holiday, she said; the sky was clear, the sun blazing, we mustn't discuss business; just think about a lovely bathe and a good lunch.

"I don't want to hear any mention of work! Life's good!" she shouted into the roar of the jeep. Her skin was naturally dark, smooth as a pebble polished by the sea. Two wide gilt bracelets spanned her wrists.

This time Harry seemed annoyed by her gaiety. And the more Dorotea laughed and chatted, the more silent and serious he became; with results quite opposite to what he probably expected, for Dorotea went on joking and turned more and more toward me.

"I feel lovely today! I feel I'd photograph well," she said. "Why don't you give me a little test, eh? I can act, you know. I'll show you soon on the beach."

"Of course!" I replied, drawn along by her mood. "With the greatest pleasure! I'm sure you're very good!"

Harry interrupted dryly: "Please, anything but that," and then went on staring silently at the road.

I could understand him, instinctively. I had guessed from the first moment that his passion was twisted and double-sided. Before, when she had been reserved, his reaction had almost been to offer her to me; today, when she was gaily provocative, he was definitely jealous.

We stopped after Tor San Lorenzo, halfway down the long, straight, deserted road between Pratica di Mare and Lavinio. Leaving the jeep in a lane, we took the parcels of food that Harry and Dorotea had prepared, crossed the big wild pinewood, and emerged on the beach.

This was deserted too, though it was Sunday. The cabins of Lavinio could just be seen in the distance; and here and there, but a long way from us and a hundred yards or so from one another, were a few bathing-shacks, so rustic and improvised that they made the place seem all the more like some wild island shore.

Harry, like nearly all Americans as soon as they get a chance, had taken on a methodical, Robinson Crusoeish air. He found some stakes scattered on the beach, collected them, stuck them in the sand, and put up the skeleton of a shack. He worked seriously, silently, forcing me to help him, while Dorotea, a short way off, lay face downward on the sand. He was remembering, for sure, the organized camping of his childhood in the Minnesota forests. But if he could also make me feel that his grave air was due to displeasure at Dorotea's excessive familiarity with me, and could pass it off as a severe and silent warning, then all the better.

So he ordered me to follow him to the pinewoods, where he pulled out a clasp knife and cut off a great number of branches. Then he loaded me and himself with them, and we returned to the beach.

Dorotea had got up and was yawning and stretching.

"I'm boiling," she said. "Now I'm going into the water. "Who loves me follows me!"

I said nothing, for I could see Harry looking at me and then at her, frowning.

"Go on, if you want to," he answered her. "We've got to finish here first."

We arranged the branches on the stakes, making a trellised shade. Meanwhile I was covertly watching Dorotea's tall figure moving slowly toward the sea. She had put on a light-green bathing-dress of elastic wool, which held and modeled the curves of her big body.

Taking my eyes off her with an effort, I said to Harry: "If you want to talk to me about the scenario now—"

"No, I don't feel like it any more. Not today. Today we must just enjoy ourselves. But I'll ring you up tomorrow morning, and we'll make a date. You've been so kind in helping me, I just wanted to show you I'd been working."

"If you need any more money, say so. We'll sell the scenario. And if not, you can give me back the money when you have some."

Wanting to clear away any misunderstanding between us, I stretched out a hand toward my jacket and took out my wallet. I was being obviously tactful in taking advantage of a moment that would probably not recur during the day; Dorotea was some way off and would notice nothing. I was offering him money, it was also obvious, so that even though he might not particularly need any at that moment, he could show me, by accepting it, that he was not offended.

He did in fact accept it, and once more gave me his usual sweet and melancholy smile.

"Thanks, you're a real friend."

It was a smile, a look, that he would no longer have given me in Dorotea's presence.

We joined her in the sea, then had lunch, smoked a cigarette or two, chatted, rested; but all three of us were now better behaved. We had each realized that if we had gone on as before, things would have ended badly. Dorotea was less provocative, Harry less touchy, and I more detached.

I did my best to detach myself, to tell the truth, and try to look elsewhere. But each time my eyes rested on her I felt I'd taken a flash photograph that I would develop when I was alone. And at home that night I took a long time to get to sleep. I could still feel the sun burning into my body, and when I closed my eyes in the dark I seemed wrapped in a golden glow of heat, sun, sand, sky, and sea all fused together. And in that golden glow the flash photographs developed one by one without my wanting them to. I saw Dorotea emerging from the sea, shimmering all over with innumerable drops of water, like precious stones on her brown skin. I saw her from the back, lying on the sand and leaning on one elbow in an abandoned and monumental pose; and it seemed as if, by a strange miracle, I was gazing at some French painting from the other side—an odalisque whom Delacroix had painted from the front. Or I saw her greedily munching at a leg of chicken or a slice of ham, feeding herself crudely and naturally; and I told myself sadly that I even liked her like that. Finally I saw her asleep, lying supine, slowly moving a leg. I saw her laughing, an emerald glitter in her eyes, moving a hand, waggling a ruby-nailed toe, which she was sliding up and down on the sand. . . .

Next day, by one of those sudden decisions not infrequent in the film world, I was told I would have to leave for Paris within a few days to collaborate in preparing the script for my next film. It probably meant an absence of about two or three months.

Toward one o'clock, as we had arranged, Harry telephoned me at the film studios. Without knowing why, I never mentioned my departure, though it was so imminent, and just said that I could not see him that day or the day after; then as I put down the receiver, I realized why I had said nothing about leaving; suddenly and almost involuntarily an idea had occurred to me.

4.

I knew that Harry spent every evening, between eight and ten, at the Press Bureau and stayed there some time gathering news for articles he sent, at irregular intervals, to his paper in New York. That was the time when I thought of paying a visit, without warning, to the studio in Via Margutta the last day before leaving for Paris, and trying my luck.

It was the journey that made me dare. If there was any danger of consequences, the parting would prevent them by cutting everything off short. And if I should feel too guilty afterwards, my remorse would be sweetened by distance and by the fact that I would not be seeing Harry for at least two months.

The ideal in a love adventure is to take one's pleasure, then cut and run. And he who can't always cut and run and is kept in one place by his work is apt to invert the terms. Cutting and running are no longer the consequence, but the cause of the adventure. He looks for an adventure only when he's leaving for other reasons.

On the other hand Dorotea really attracted me. That last time, by the sea, she had showed me she was not completely indifferent. I liked and esteemed Harry; so my plan was not a very pretty one. But what, I said to myself on the morning of the day, as I was assailed by honest scruples while shaving, what has a little flip, a short-lived pleasure, got to do with friendship and respect? I was not corrupting Dorotea. If it was not me, it would be someone else. In fact, I concluded, why so many others and not me?

I also, of course, thought over the arguments on the

other side. After all, renouncing Dorotea would not mean so much to me. Why then barter for such brief pleasure the long, if light, pains of remorse? Why break up my friendship with Harry, which was intact up to now?

But that was just why the thing tempted me. "That woman," I said to myself, "if you don't satisfy your curiosity about her, will always be between us two. Curiosity, not passion. Simply to save the friendship, in fact, you must, just the tiniest bit and for the very shortest time, betray it."

Finally, as any man knows, we're strong against strong temptations, but weak against weak ones. It's not worth while, we say to ourselves, being heroic about small lost opportunities.

How long it was, though, that June afternoon! And how long it took for night to fall at the end of Via Margutta!

In the warm blue air fell the last calls of the swallows, the cries of the children playing in front of the garage, the laughter of passers-by; it was an evening in the week of San Giovanni, when sin in Rome does not seem to exist any more, and the ancient pagan wisdom flowers again with the first breath of returning summer. The lights went on. The shadows lengthened. The eyes of the passers-by glittered. The occasional traffic in the narrow street, the cries and laughter and gestures and glances all seemed to be slyly, gaily hinting at the same time. If I still had any scruples, the last of them vanished without my noticing. And when I saw the tall silhouette of Harry come out of the front door, jump into the jeep, and drive noisily off toward Via Alibert, I lit a cigarette and moved forward without hesitation. The world's just there for the taking, I was laughing to myself.

I entered the main door and went upstairs. Silence, scarcely broken by the blaring of a radio, the explosions of a motorcycle, coming from near by, down in Via Margutta, but suddenly muffled by the thick walls. Darkness, lightened dimly by the reflection of some old lamp on the walls and the loose tiles. And the silence and darkness, as I wound up through the labyrinth of stairs, little courtyards, and passages, seemed to tremble as if there were something sacred in the air.

She came to open the frosted-glass door and at once smiled at me invitingly.

"Come in and sit down. Harry's gone out, but he'll be back soon." (I knew that was not true). "Sit down, do, please, I'm sorry it's so dark. The bulb in the ceiling has burned out this very minute."

In fact the only light came from a small red lamp on the table, set between the piles of papers surrounding the type-writer and a teapot and two cups balancing on more papers and journals.

Dorotea was very simply dressed, in a black skirt and a blue sleeveless blouse. Her big brown arms were bare to the shoulders. Her hair was gathered, as usual, at the nape of her neck in a big bun, gleaming and carefully combed.

She offered me tea and a slice of round flat cake, covered with little pearly bits of sugar, white, pale blue, green, yellow, and lilac, which made a most delicate color effect. It was thick, tasty, only slightly sweetened—delicious. One could tell it was some patriarchal cake, sure indication of an ancient civilized tradition.

"I made it," said Dora, laughing, pleased at my appreciation. "It's a cake they make at home."

"It's strange," I said. "I've been to Frosinone so often and never either tasted or seen it."

"What's Frosinone got to do with it?" she exclaimed with surprise.

"Why, Frosinone, the capital of the *Ciociaria*," I replied with some embarrassment, for the Romans always talk of the *Ciociaria* and its inhabitants with a certain contempt. "Don't you come from there?"

"No, not at all! I'm from Apulia. This cake is Apulian. We call it the *scarcella*."

I thought over Harry's mistake a moment, without astonishment. How often we make elementary mistakes about the people we love most and know best!

So she was Apulian. I looked at Dora. The delicate-colored little pearls of sugar and the taste of the *scarcella* explained, it seemed to me, and increased the fascination of her beauty, which had remained archaic, pagan, peasant, in spite of her provocative and professional modern air.

"I've come," I said, sitting down beside her on the metal bedspring, "to say good-by, as I'm leaving tomorrow for Paris and will be away some months." I exaggerated on purpose the length of my absence so as to justify the rather large sum of money I was intending to offer her. The ten-thousand-lire notes were all ready. I took them out and put them on the table without, of course, counting them, but in such a way that she could see at once more or less how many there were.

Dorotea frowned, as at my first visit, and did not move. There was an embarrassing silence.

"Excuse me for giving it to you like this," I said.

"Not at all," she replied shortly.

Yet I was sure she could be bought, and had prepared ready money, instead of a check, so that she could keep it more easily, without Harry knowing.

But now her serious expression disconcerted me. I could have sworn that, at sight of the money, she'd have taken on the usual careless, jesting manner of prostitutes when business arrangements are concluded. Instead of which she was looking straight in front of her and saying nothing. I didn't know how to begin. The silence was becoming painful. I began to talk about our trip to the sea, and how well she photographed, and the good, the great probability of my finding her a part in one of my films.

"As soon as I get back from Paris," I hurried on to say, longing to see her smile, "we'll arrange a little test for you, and you'll see, you'll see how well it'll work out."

Dorotea smiled at me. "Thank you; but I don't think Harry would like it."

"What! But it was he who said he'd like me to find you work!"

"He said it as a joke; he doesn't want it."

"But what's the matter with you today, Dorotea?" I said finally, going up to her, putting an arm round her bare shoulder and stroking it. "Why so sad?"

"I'm sad because I'm disappointed; I thought you were a real friend of Harry's, instead of which I see you aren't."

I had a flash of hope. Now she had talked, had hinted at the truth of the situation. My fears were unfounded. I'd made a mistake in tactics, that was all. My mute, over-immediate approach through that exaggerated offer of money had offended her. Dora had become serious only in order not to give in to me too soon, only so that I shouldn't think too badly of her. I should have given her more rope. A little sentiment was needed. I set about providing it at once:

"Don't be silly, Dora! What's my friendship with Harry got to do with it? Didn't you notice anything last Sunday? And yet I had the impression you did. Do you realize that since I've seen you, I've thought of nothing else? . . ." and so on, trying my best to avoid phrases that rang too false. And there was a certain truth in them, for I really was attracted to Dorotea, and really had thought of her for several nights. Without making any pretense of love I tried to tell her how I'd fallen for her suddenly and passionately.

No response.

Then I gradually raised the tone; bit by bit I became more and more tender and spiritual, embraced her, and when finally words failed me and my desire became urgent, tried to kiss her.

Suddenly she broke away and got up.

"No," she said, "I told you I don't want to. One can see you've never suffered from these things. I had a young man I was going to marry once. He left me and went off with one of my closest friends. I felt I'd die. And I swore that no one in the world would, because of me, go through what I went through. Particularly someone like Harry, whom I love."

"But Harry will never know," I observed weakly.

"It doesn't matter. It's I who don't want to. I wouldn't enjoy it at all. I'd be thinking, all the time, that I was doing something that would offend Harry, something that would hurt him."

She pronounced these last words very simply, looking me straight in the eyes.

I was angry.

"Then," I said maliciously, "you may do it with others, with any man who comes along, but won't with me because I'm a friend of Harry's."

"What I do is no business of yours. I love Harry and I need no one else."

Instinctively I put my hand on the roll of money which was still on the table where I'd left it. I'd have liked to take it back, or at least some of it. But suddenly I felt how mean the gesture was. I'd made a mistake, I must pay. Harry would be the gainer. That was just. So much the better. I drew back my hand, leaving the money where it was, and got up.

"Tell Harry to ring me up tonight. I'll get back late, but I'll be up packing my bags. Tell him to ring me any time, till he gets me."

I said good-by tenderly, kissing her hand lingeringly; and she let me do so, equally tenderly.

"Have a good journey!" she said as she accompanied me along the terrace as far as the little flight of stairs. "Send us a postcard from Paris! I've never been there, and have always longed to. . . ."

Harry rang me about three in the morning. I had finished my packing and was about to get into bed. He began by thanking me warmly for my loan and, adding this up exactly with what I had given him the last two times, told me that he considered the total as an advance on the sale of his scenario.

"Thank you," he explained, "not only for the money itself, though I really need that; but also because I shall now have seriously to get down to writing that scenario. If you don't sell it, don't worry. I have rich relations in America, you know; one day or another I'll be able to give it all back."

"One day or another, very soon, you'll get back to your own work again."

"I don't think so. I'm fed up with it all. I haven't told you anything yet, we haven't really talked. I've been leading this life for a year. You don't know. . . ."

He asked me the address of my hotel in Paris and said he would send me the scenario as soon as it was written. I might be able to place it more easily in Paris.

We said good-by very affectionately, and I thought about Dorotea again. When I'd left her and was hurrying down the stairs like a thief, then turned quickly from Via Margutta into Via Babuino for fear of meeting Harry, I had said to myself that, yes, perhaps she was sincere and honest and really loved Harry. Now I was not so sure. Her behavior might have been calculated. Or even a mixture of two, calculation and sincerity. I was perplexed, in fact, and still put out.

A few hours later, when the Paris train left the Termini station, it had passed out of my mind.

5.

My stay in Paris was prolonged beyond my expectations. The film of which I was supposed to do only the script there, and then shoot it in Italy, was actually put into production in the Joinville studios. Thinking I was lying, I'd told Dorotea the truth.

Toward the beginning of the second month, I received this telegram from Harry:

TOMORROW SUNDAY 9 AM GARE LYON ROME TRAIN PLEASE
COLLECT PERSONALLY FROM SLEEPING-CAR ATTENDANT CAR FOUR
TYPESCRIPT SCENARIO THANKS GREETINGS.

Why not by mail?

The attendant handed me over a thick parcel, carefully
packed and tied, and a letter.

"Mr. Summers," he explained, "told me to tell you that
I'm at your service if you need to communicate with him. I
leave for Rome again tomorrow evening at eight P.M. You can
telephone me at the Hotel Moderne, 3 rue Parrot. My name
is Borruso. I've known Mr. Summers for many years. We're
good friends. You can trust me. There's something about me
in his letter, too."

I looked at him in surprise, not understanding the reason
for all these precautions. He was a thickset dark man with the
look and accent of a Calabrian or Sicilian; he was unshaven and
had the pale, flaccid look of people who sleep little or badly,
the look that croupiers and newspaper compositors also have.

"When did you last see Mr. Summers?" I asked him.

"Yesterday morning at the Termini station, when the
train left. He wasn't feeling too well."

"Is he ill?"

"Yes, I think so. Liver. But that's not his real illness. Listen, I know that you're the best friend Mr. Summers has in
Europe." The man hesitated, took off his dark-brown cap, and
passed a handkerchief over his sweating face. "Can I offer you
a cup of coffee? I'll just be a few minutes, and get my things."

He climbed back on the train again. Meanwhile I opened
Harry's letter. It ran:

CARO MARIO:

Don't be surprised by the length of the scenario and forgive me for having made you come to the train. I thought you might be able to on a Sunday morning without putting yourself out too much.

When you read it you'll see why I didn't want to take the risk, however small, of its being lost in the mail. There's another reason too; this is the only copy, the original one, written directly on the typewriter for speed's sake.

The story is not finished, as you'll see. You'll find the rest on your return to Rome.

I've covered all these pages in less than three weeks, working with the greatest of ease from the moment that I gave up the idea of making up a scenario and decided simply to write the whole truth about my life during these last few years.

At the beginning I thought of drawing characters from my imagination and of a film subject that would in some way reflect my experience and problems. But I couldn't manage to get on with it. I never succeeded in combining all that's happened, from which I'm still suffering, with the plot I had thought up. I'm too tortured with it all and can't invent anything, or even mask my own memories and regrets. I can only confess. That's all.

So even the names, dates, and places—everything in my account is true. Just think it over. See what you can do about it. See if you think there's a film there. If you don't think it possible, it doesn't matter; I needed to describe, not only for a friend but for myself too, the events I've been thinking over and remembering ceaselessly; they've been weighing on me like a mountain, crushing me, for the last year. And describing them is the only relief. Thank you for having given me the chance.

Ti abbraccio

Tuo

HARRY

PS. FROM THE STATION. Borruso, the attendant to whom I've handed the manuscript, is completely trustworthy. I've known him since 1938. If you want to reply, please use him. *Don't mail.* I'm not sure of Dorotea, you understand; seeing me typewriting, she naturally thought I was working and became curious. She doesn't read English easily. But she does open letters. *Ciao.*

H.

Borruso got down from the train with his bag slung over his shoulder, a small suitcase, and a big parcel. He insisted on offering me coffee. We reached the buffet. He talked to me about Harry in a friendly, almost paternal manner, which didn't seem to me self-interested at all. Mr. Summers, he told me, was in a state of collapse—a nervous collapse after all his misfortunes. . . . Borruso thought I knew everything; I could not tell him that, on the contrary, I knew nothing as yet. Finally, after many hesitations, he revealed what was perhaps the real reason for his confidences. He had lent Harry, on various occasions, more than half a million lire. No one knew about this till now. I was the first. He believed Harry to be a man of honor. He knew about his position in the United States, his rich relations, and so on. And he didn't doubt his good will. But he, Borruso, had a family in Rome, a wife and four children; even if he did earn quite a little, half a million lire was always half a million lire.

I replied that I'd do everything I could to help Harry, and that I was sure he'd get his money back.

"You should persuade him to return to America," concluded the sleeping-car attendant. "What's he doing in Rome? Mind you, I may seem to be talking against my own interests. A creditor going so far away— But I repeat that I know Mr. Summers. As soon as he has the money, he'll return it to me. Now he can only get it if he returns to America. You see how I trust him? I'm thinking not only of my own but of his good. Don't you think so?"

I began reading the manuscript as soon as I got back to my hotel. I reproduce it here in its entirety, except for a few mistakes due to the speed of composition.

Harry's typescript

I think of Jane every day, every hour, I might say every minute. But to describe what happened to her, to me, to us two together, from the day of our first meeting till the end, I don't feel I can always follow chronological order, as perhaps, for clarity's sake, I should. For one particular moment, one second, in fact, is more present and alive to me than all the others; and it comes back to me continually, torturingly, pointlessly.

It was the moment of a single glance. In our room at the Grand Hotel, the day after our arrival in Rome, the last time. Her eyes, as she spoke over the telephone and I murmured quite unsuspiciously: "Who is it?" had an expression, for that second, which was dark, grim, turgid, an expression I had never seen on her and whose meaning just at that moment deceived me completely.

I had known Jane for five years. She had been my wife for

four, and was the mother of my two children. I considered her to be as perfect a wife and mother as I was an imperfect husband and father.

I had managed, or thought I had managed, always to hide my frequent little infidelities from her, and the vicious habit I fell back into each time I returned to Italy, of Dorotea.

It seems unlikely, but I had first met Dorotea through Jane, a few days after my first meeting with Jane myself.

It was in the summer of '44. Rome had been liberated on the 4th of June.

I saw Jane for the first time at a party, in a Roman villa requisitioned by a colonel who was a friend of mine. At once I felt an extreme tenderness, almost pity, for her. She seemed so small, fragile, and nervous, so intelligent and suffering, so much in need of protection; and I felt urged toward her from the beginning by an arid, sad, sincere, yet inevitable feeling, which reminded me of my affection for my mother and which had about it, absurdly, a bitter flavor of duty; not the sweet one of love, nor the intoxicating one of pleasure.

From that evening I saw her regularly with the calm and determination of a duty, or of a vice.

I liked to be with her, to describe to her my childhood, my family, my life; to tell her my impressions and ideas, take her to concerts of classical music; and I could even talk to her about my work as an art historian, and visit exhibitions and galleries with her, for she was cultivated and had a natural flair for painting. At no moment, though, during those first days, did I feel any desire to take her in my arms. Until one night, as we were driving in a carriage in the Borghese Gardens, and had been silent for some time, as if overcome by the suavity of the summer air, the painful thought occurred to me of how incomplete my feelings for her were. So it was not love yet! So she was not yet the one and only woman for me! Possibly I, too, felt that absurd impatience to force the hands of destiny which had urged some of my friends to marriage, to any kind of marriage, so long as it was soon. Like them I was also rebelling against reality. And following the strange virtuous feeling there was in my affection for Jane, I told myself that *it was my duty to find her attractive*. I glanced at her now out of the corner of my eye, without turning my head; and saw her at my side, leaning away from me against the back of the seat, her small, thin, nervous body, the image of weakness and unhappiness, quivering sadly with the movement of the carriage. Once again I realized that she did not attract me; but I realized too, in the same wretched second and for the first time, that the very fact that she did not attract me might, if only for a few brief moments, have its own attraction. The possibility suddenly opened in front of me in all its perversity and risk. The only women who have ever attracted me are tall, heavy, and coarse. Now I gazed at Jane's thin little body, at her scarcely discernible, barely rounded stomach; and I said to myself, yes, perhaps there was some enjoyment to be got out of her—the enjoyment of trying the very thing that did not attract me, and enjoying it *just because* it did not attract me. And now that I had released this spring, I suddenly found myself desiring her, desiring that stomach. With an acrid pleasure I turned toward her, squeezed her thin waist against me, and kissed her, almost biting, almost hurting her. Poor Jane!

But she didn't want to make love. She didn't want to either that night or any other night of that Roman summer; nor of the following year, 1945, when we met again in Paris; nor even that autumn, in New York, when we finally became engaged. She did not want to until after our marriage. We married in December '45 at Philadelphia. She was a Catholic and very religious.

Only a day or two after that evening drive with Jane I turned into a small *trattoria* in the center of Rome for lunch at about one o'clock and found her sitting at a table. She was lunching with an Italian woman, of overwhelming, flashy appearance, who seemed to be the center of attraction in the little room crowded with men.

I at once had the impression she was a prostitute, or, as the Italians used to say at that time (imitating our mixture of English spelling and Spanish pronunciation), a "segnorina." But while the "segnorine" were usually small and emaciated, with hungry, frightened looks, this one had an outstanding authority and, I might almost say, solemnity about her. Dorotea was looking round instinctively at all the men, smiling and winking at them continually. Every fleeting expression of hers, now serious, now ironic, made one think of bed, seemed to hint, now passionately, now shyly, of love. And in the height of her forehead, in the purity of her profile, in the glitter of her eyes, in the fall of her lips, there was something classical, decided, victorious. Every single glance of hers seemed to create between herself and the men around her a promise and a secret.

Of course I was astonished to meet Jane in a *trattoria*, and with a woman like that. We never met in the morning. I would go and get her at her hotel toward seven in the evening, we would dine out, and then spend the evening together, driving, dancing, or going to some party, till midnight. That evening she explained that a soldier had brought Dorotea to the hospital for a certain very simple treatment. And that Dorotea, in gratitude, had asked her out to lunch. She wanted to make her taste a real Italian meal. She had been so humble, Jane told me, so spontaneous in her invitation, that Jane had not felt she could refuse. But as I listened to Jane talking to me about Dorotea, I was in a turmoil; my whole thoughts were concentrated on Dorotea and how to find her again, and not on the likelihood of Jane's story.

From the very first instant I saw Dorotea (her dark, sun-burned neck and arms bare, in a silk dress with a white flower pattern, her eyes, teeth, bracelets gleaming, as she sat with her classic face and victoriously sensual look amid the gay chatter and warm shade of the little *trattoria*, into which a ray of sun shone through an open door, lighting up the glasses and napkins on her table and falling right on her feet, which showed under the tablecloth in black lacquer sandals and scarlet toenails), from that very first instant I desired her. I desired her with a quivering turmoil, a timid desperation, an absurd sense of my own unworthiness, which showed the part of myself still capable of reasoning that here was the woman of my dreams; had I been Italian I would have said a woman to my taste.

I sat down at the table and had lunch with them, forcing myself not to let Jane see how disturbed I was. The presence of Jane, facing me, elbow to elbow with Dorotea, increased the latter's fascination. Perhaps it was the almost schematic contrast between them of sacred and profane love. Perhaps it was also due to the difficulty of showing Dorotea how much she attracted me, and to the impossibility of making an appointment with her. But never again perhaps did Dorotea appear to me as desirable as that first time, when I knew nothing about her and was afraid of never finding her again.

But I did find her, very easily indeed, next day, by returning to the little *trattoria* about the same time.

And that evening I did not spend with Jane. . . .

6.

From that night till tonight—I'm writing this six years later—the only woman who's really attracted me has been Dorotea.

But I've always been ashamed of it. Not for a second have I ever deceived myself on her account. I'd realized from the first moment that she was a prostitute. And a prostitute she remained for me, even when I decided to live with her.

For years, at first, I always avoided being seen around in her company. And not only from fear that Jane would get to hear, but because I realized how obviously she looked what she was, and felt ashamed of being seen beside her, even by people who did not know me. Even today it's the same. With the difference that now I've reached the point of exploiting my own feelings of shame, and almost enjoying them.

Perhaps for the same reason, all these years from that first evening until a short time ago, my meetings with Dorotea were regularly spaced out, alternating with periods of absence. An exception was a journey through north and central Italy, on which she accompanied me in the spring of 1947, while Jane was at Capri with the baby.

As soon as I felt I could do without Dorotea I would stop seeing her, and return as soon as I felt I could not. Usually a fortnight, at most a month of deprivation was enough for desire to return. And if I happened to be in New York or Paris and knew I could not get to Rome at once, my desire would mount progressively and reach a sort of frenzy till the moment of our meeting and its satisfaction. Yet even at the height of this frenzy my judgment was still clear. Dorotea would appear to me then as a supreme good, a kind of divinity; and at the same time I still realized that she was just a very simple, vulgar woman, greedy for money. Her divinity, in fact, was not constant. It was not hers. It seemed lent to her by my desire.

That was the reason, perhaps, why up to a short time ago I never talked to Dorotea about Jane. I never told her, that first summer long ago, how important Jane was to me, and said I scarcely knew her. Nor did I ever tell her that I was constantly seeing Jane; nor that I had married her. I was afraid of giving Dorotea a weapon with which she could very easily, in the moments when I urgently needed her, have blackmailed me. I separated meticulously my life with Jane from my life with Dorotea, and carefully made sure that nothing, however unimportant, to do with one should have any contact, however superficial, with anything to do with the other. Every time I left Jane to meet Dorotea I gave Jane a perfect alibi. And every time I left Dorotea to return to Jane I took care never to betray anything of my married life. Dorotea never knew where my real home was in Rome. From Paris, from London, from New York, I always gave my office address.

If today, when it's all over, I think how detailed those precautions of mine were, I realize that they were not only due to my fear of Jane's getting to know about Dorotea or Dorotea about Jane, but to a deeper, more obscure feeling, due to the different kind of affection I had for one and the other; to my possibility of feeling diametrically opposed pleasures with one and the other, by persuading each of them (and almost persuading myself when I was with either) that I was only half my real self: with Dorotea, as I described myself to her and tried in every way to appear, a wild, irresponsible, fickle bachelor; with Jane quite the contrary—a staid husband, a tender father, true to duty, devoted to my work, moral, studious, and persevering.

But at first I did not attach much importance to my periodic urge for Dorotea. She was a beautiful woman, whom I liked to have every fortnight, and nothing more. The first few times, I used to invite her to dinner, either before or after, and spend an hour or two chatting and walking about with her too. But I soon realized that these were useless ceremonies; if before, a torment of the flesh; if after, of the spirit. I felt what Goethe called the pleasure of deception, and thought I could abandon myself to this pleasure every time I wanted to, with impunity; without the risk, that is, of the pleasure gradually becoming a habit. My life seemed clear ahead of me. I loved a woman worthy of my love, Jane. I had made her my companion, my wife, the mother of my children. Dorotea was a pleasant, but, I thought, just a superficial diversion; one that I could cut out at will; one in which I could therefore indulge without any fears or remorse; rather like smoking or drinking, habits we lightheartedly get into when young, certain of being able to give up at any moment; then a day comes when we would like to, and realize it's too late.

On October 15, 1944 Jane's hospital was transferred to France. It was our first separation since the day we'd met. The column of trucks left one evening for Naples, where it was to embark next day for Marseille.

Just before Jane left I went to say good-by to her at the villa on the Via Cassia where the hospital was encamped.

In the confusion of those last moments, inevitable in spite of the perfect organization of our medical services, Jane could not pay much attention to me; she was hurrying to and fro from one truck to another, carrying suitcases and packages of medicine; every time she passed in front of me she smiled at me sweetly, her eyes full of tears.

I too, sitting in my jeep, followed through a veil of tears the movements of her thin little figure, buttoned tight in its smart blue uniform. But my sorrow was strangely mingled with impatience; it was like a harsh and intoxicating cocktail of two ingredients that strengthen each other by their very mixing: one ingredient was sorrow at separating from Jane, the other impatience to be with Dorotea as soon as possible, finally to spend an entire night with her. This I had never dared to do till then, because from the very first I'd asked Jane to ring me, whenever she wanted, at any hour of the night, at my hotel, where it was well known I could not take women to my room. Jane, it's true, had never done this, but now that it had suddenly become impossible, I was filled with a strange sense of liberty. And my very suffering at seeing Jane leave without knowing when I would see her again gave a new flavor to the certainty of embracing Dorotea once more in a short time; in its turn this certainty, this sense of inevitable guilt, gave an added bitterness to my farewell to the woman whom I already respected as the future companion of my life.

In my agitation I got out of the jeep and began walking here and there among the huts, tents, ambulances, and departing trucks.

Suddenly I turned back; I thought I'd seen Jane through the little window of one of the huts. Yes, there she was. Telephoning. She was in profile and might have seen me. But I was outside in the dark, and she inside a hut lit up, if rather faintly, by an oil lamp. Then she seemed so intent, so absorbed in her telephone conversation. Whether because of the passionate vivacity of her expression (though it was her usual one, it seemed more evident as she telephoned now), or perhaps because I saw her in that weak light and she was standing on the tips of her toes to talk into the receiver, which was set too high for her, the fact is that she seemed smaller, more defenseless, more dear than usual, and filled me with tenderness and compassion.

How adorable my Jane was!

And how weak my spirit; how strong, on the other hand, my flesh!

But spirit and flesh were just words I used to myself in those moments of exaltation, smoking one cigarette after another, looking at Jane through the little window and thinking meanwhile of Dorotea, of the street, of the stairs up which I should soon be running, of the bell I should press with a tremor, and of the first embrace in the half-dark entrance hall as soon as the door was shut, her great body against mine; and imagining it all with spasms of impatience. Words! The truth, I now say to myself (now that that moment like so many other moments is irrevocably past), the truth is a different one; neither spirit nor flesh, but a kind of need, in love, to hate and suffer at the same time.

Finally she came toward me, laughing, adjusting a stray lock that had escaped from under her coquettish little cap. To whom had she telephoned? "To a priest," she replied, her confessor, to say good-by. Then I was holding her in a farewell embrace; and as I did so, I felt a strange lack and found myself comparing, without wanting to, her skinny, nervous little body and its schoolgirl air with the tall, heavy, soft one of Dorotea with its bitter strong scent. But it was not good-by yet. Jane was smiling contentedly because her work was over for the moment and the colonel had given her permission to travel a mile or two along the Naples road in my jeep.

We crossed Rome ahead of the column. It was already night. Perhaps for the last time we were seeing together the city where we had known each other, the city where we had spent a summer of love; the narrow, long, tortuous streets, the dark, heavy seventeenth-century palaces rising toward a black sky at which no one looked, the eyes in crowds which were almost Oriental, almost Semitic, but sadder and tougher; crowds formless, languid, and aggressive as the accent of their language and their dialect, but still redolent, in some way, of lost grandeur.

In the lights of the shops and the advertising signs, of the acetylene flares in front of the stalls, moved street venders, black-marketeers, beggars, guides, pimps, whores, urchins, gigolos. It was a whole world which Jane that evening, sitting beside me in the jeep as it moved slowly along, was seeing again and leaving; the warm world of Dorotea, I thought; and although I said to myself that I'd see it again, that in fact I'd be plunging into it within a very short time, it seemed that I too was leaving and saying good-by to it with Jane, and almost to be seeing it for the first time, as happens in the seconds before a parting.

We stopped high up, in the night breeze, on a curve of the road just after Ariccia. There were no trees near by. Around us at our feet smooth ground sloped away on every side toward infinity. Only in one small patch, down in the direction from which we'd come, could we sense the lights of Rome. Above was a dark-blue sky, glittering with stars. And the fresh breeze blowing on our faces had the flavor of the near-by sea.

I embraced Jane, pressed her to me, kissed her at length and with enjoyment. And suddenly, forgetting Dorotea for the first time in some hours, I longed to possess Jane as I had never longed to till then. Jane too that night, I think, would have liked it; at least, she had never been so near to liking it. But it was not possible. I had scarcely unbuttoned her blouse and my fingers were stroking for the first time her bony, delicate torso, her moving ribs under the delicate skin, and the firm nylon of her brassière, when suddenly we heard the rumble of the column passing over the Bailey bridge of Ariccia. Still mouth to mouth, we turned in that direction and saw the headlights of the first ambulances too near now, alas, for us to do anything but feel a sharp, sudden spasm in common.

And it was good-by, Jane, at once then, good-by, my love! She got into a car with some of her colleagues and vanished into the roar, noise, and dust of the long column. I stood there on the side of the road, by the jeep, stood there with no thoughts and apparently no feelings, watching it pass.

When the last Dodges were some way off, and their red tail-lights could no longer be seen on the road toward the south, where Jane had vanished without my knowing when I would ever see her again, I got into the jeep again and slowly, thinking of Jane all the time, set off back to Rome.

It was only after some miles, when I reached the first houses of Rome, I think, that I remembered Dorotea; and my first feeling was not of desire—no, not at all!—but of amazement at having forgotten her and at not feeling, for the moment, any more desire for her. I was free now, really free. I could hurry to her. She (I had telephoned to warn her) was waiting for me.

Yet I did not go to her that night. I was happy as I was. Happy in my love and my regret for Jane. My nerves were vibrating, taut, in a delicious jangle that heightened every sensation, and that seemed linked by some fluid to the column of trucks slowly traveling through the night breeze, under the stars, along the sea, toward Naples.

Coldly, sarcastically, today I tell myself that I loved Jane so much that night just because, that very night, she was going far away. It was a happiness in love which, for that moment, did not bind me to anything, not even to possess the person loved, as the person loved had just gone. I thought I was happy because I had found a wife; instead of which I was happy because my feelings (and perhaps also my feelings for Jane) freed me from the need to see Dorotea and were enough in themselves; I was happy because I was alone.

I didn't go to Dorotea. I didn't even telephone to tell her I wasn't coming. I passed in my jeep under your windows in Via Gregoriana, my dear film-director, and I saw your windows lighted. I stopped and shouted up to you. Giacomo N. was with you, and a Hungarian whose name I've forgotten, a colleague of mine at P.W.B. You were playing chess. Do you remember?

A game of chess. I didn't feel at all sleepy; I was regretful, and I was happy because I was sure of loving. A game of chess and the company of writers and intelligent men—it was just what I needed.

I came upstairs. You had some whisky. You had another

chessboard. I stayed—do you remember?—till dawn. When we were tired of chess, and also because the Hungarian was too good a player for us, Giacomo N. recited some poems of Heine in his warm voice. They were beautiful, certainly, and delivered well. But how as I listened could I distinguish their beauty from my own happiness? How distinguish the value of the friendships we Americans made in those months with so many sympathetic Europeans from the enthusiasm aroused in them and in us by the war, the victory, the liberation?

I went to bed feeling exhausted and serene, and confident too; I felt as if I were locking away a treasure for the night: and the treasure was Jane, the certainty of her love for me and of my love for her.

I dozed off still hearing the voice of N., which seemed to be rocking me to sleep:

Ach die Augen sind es wieder,
die mich einst so lieblich grüssten . . .

7.

How long did the spell last?

Oh, certainly, Jane's influence was much stronger from afar than it was near by. Even so, in the light of day, the shameful light of day, I at once had the disappointing sense of being slightly less in love than the night before.

A sunbeam was filtering between the half-closed shutters and lighting up the shadowed room; from outside came the lively hum of traffic mingling with the airy sound of bells and the shouts of street peddlers. *"Bottijaro! Bottijarooo!"* a gay voice repeated, gradually drawing farther and farther away until it was lost in the general din. I felt as if it were the title of some spectacle I was sure to find amusing, this announcement of a warm and beautiful October day in Rome. I looked at that golden streak of light, I listened to that confused music, and I knew that behind that sun and warmth and traffic, behind those voices, like the sweet tasty kernel of a big delicious fruit, was Dorotea. On the bedtable I found a sheet of paper on which, before falling asleep, I'd written out a telegram for Jane. I reread it, sad that I had not the courage to copy it out and send it. It read:

JANE MY LOVE WILL YOU MARRY ME WIRE ME AT ONCE WE WILL MARRY AS SOON AS WAR IS OVER LOVE.

But I sent another, identical one some months later. Then too it was in the first sense of loss and impulse after a separation. But I was not in Rome. I had left Jane the morning before at Saint-Pierre-d'Albigny near Aiguebelle in Savoy, had traveled all day, and reached Nice toward midnight. P.W.B., the information service on which I depended, was lodged in a big hotel, together with a number of other headquarters, so there was also a private post office in full working order. But above all I was in Nice, not in Rome; Dorotea was not there.

As I had driven farther away from Jane, during the long hours of motoring through the mountains of Savoy and the Dauphiné, I had thought of Jane with an intensity that grew with the distance between us. And as soon as I arrived at Nice, I'd hurried through the hall of the hotel to the reception desk, where there was a big P.W.B. notice, and sent the telegram.

So it was a telegram that it had taken me some months to send off, that was all. And what had I done meanwhile? Had I meditated, perhaps, on the decision I wanted to make? On the meaning and importance of marriage?

I must admit that I had avoided, as much as I could, thinking about it at all; as one avoids thinking about a tragic fatal event, or about the death of some old and ill person who is dear to us, which we know to be inevitable and want to retard as much as possible; to think about it, we feel, would be bad luck, would almost hurry it on; possibly, we feel, the only means to retard it is to pretend it will not happen, to forget it.

That is what I did, in those first three months. Though I thought of Jane every day, and wrote to her every day, yet I pretended not to realize that I would end by marrying her and that each of my letters, every word in each of my letters, was another step toward that fatal conclusion. But even that secret pretense was useless; any doubt, I felt, any reflection or reasoning would weaken my instinctive and unjustified urge to marry her.

I often asked myself afterwards, and still ask myself now, what was the deep-seated reason for such folly. For I have watched a number of my friends, American or European, reach marriage in more or less the same way; with the same blind stubbornness, and the same absurd self-condemnation. Is it cowardice, as soon as youth is over, to face the serious real life of maturity? Is it anxiety to put our energy to its hardest test, even if we exhaust it? Boredom with liberty and libertinage? Disgust with sex that no longer promises or gives anything new, but seems to repeat itself mechanically, automatically, the same every time, irresistibly leading us to vice?

I think it's something better and worse; at any rate, something more.

Man, I think, needs unhappiness almost as much as he needs happiness.

I see the anguished faces, hear again the hinting phrases, the short deep sighs of those of my friends whom I had left free and serene a few months before and now found imprisoned in their grim new determination.

I know quite well that my life may seem strange and exceptional, as you will gradually see. That is why I insist that at least this episode of my marriage is not so dissimilar to that of many men of my age and class in Europe and America. And yet marriage is obviously a public act; so then, surely, should be its motives. I have never found it difficult or unnatural to question my friends on this, and so have listened to revelations we can no longer call strange if they are common to so many. And I draw the conclusion that other sides of their lives, unknown to me, which for convenience' sake have been thought of as flat and ordinary, are probably as full of complications and deceit as mine.

In those three months, then, I was preparing, almost in spite of myself, for the decision to marry Jane; meanwhile I was visiting Dorotea at frequent intervals.

But every time I saw Dorotea, I found myself disappointed as soon as I ceased to desire her. Soon I was trying to retard the satisfaction of my desires artificially, simply in order to retard the disillusion. I even persuaded myself that this maneuver had a moral basis, a noble and affectionate purpose; I told myself that the reason I retarded and sometimes put off my pleasure was so as not to humiliate Dorotea. But at heart I knew perfectly well, I could see, that Dorotea did not mind at all. She had made her calculations. If one evening I would go no farther than taking her out to dinner and afterwards caressing her and making her caress me in the darkness of a movie, then giving her a thousand lire or so without going home with her, she knew she would earn more from me another night—usually the next night; but she knew too that I would not phone or see her afterwards for much longer than if things had gone naturally and, so to say, normally. No, it was not Dorotea, but I myself who was humiliated and even surprised every time by her sudden nullity for me the instant after we'd made love. It was such a strange phenomenon that it seemed almost impossible to believe, and every time I stubbornly, absurdly hoped it would not happen. What was the explanation?

While Jane was in Rome, I'd never spent a night with Dorotea. That was the explanation, I said to myself; my preoccupation about getting quickly back to the hotel, where Jane might ring me, prevented my staying quietly with Dorotea after we'd made love, and so from getting into touch, finally, with her soul; for she too must have a soul, however tiny, crude, and dim, lost somewhere in her great body.

And yet, when the first night did come (it was, I think, the night after the one of Jane's departure), disappointment was awaiting me again—a disappointment that, now I think it over, surprised me only because it didn't surprise me at all. That's not just a play on words, and I'll try to explain.

For the whole of the day before, and until the very last spasm of love-making, I had been deceiving myself. When I had awaked in the morning and through the half-closed shutters seen the sun and heard the confused sounds of Rome, in the afternoon when I telephoned Dorotea, during the evening when I took her out to dine in Trastevere and then drove slowly home by carriage, when I opened the front door and squeezed her soft waist in the dark hall, when we had finally entered her room, heavy with her warm, bitter, vulgar scent and had stripped naked and were finally lying skin to skin, all this time I had been deceiving myself that this agonizing, apparently limitless pleasure would in fact never end, but prolong itself in variations through the pauses and slackenings following each apex of pleasure, for the whole of that night and the whole of next day and—why not?—for the whole of my life. "Until this hour which is about to strike," I said to myself with absolute conviction, "until this night of love which is about to begin, which has already begun, I've never been able to make the test." Every time, up to now, as soon as I'd finished making love to Dorotea, I immediately began thinking of Jane—not thinking vaguely, but quite precisely, that I must get back to the hotel as soon as possible in case she telephoned me. And in my anxiety and preoccupation I had jumped out of bed, dressed, paid, said good-by, left, and hurried back to the hotel. So I'd never had a chance of making the test; of finding out if Dorotea's soul interested me, if I was capable of also feeling some tenderness for her; if my wholly physical passion for her could be tinged with normal humanity and friendship; if, in fact, I could manage to talk to her too. Because at first it was never a conversation, but on my side a kind of imploring and adoring monologue, even when I was offering her a cigarette or a glass of water; and what she said, on her part, was another monologue, the pronouncements of an idol, which to me sounded like some fascinating incantation, even if she only asked me for a glass of water or a cigarette. The pressure, meanwhile, of her leg under the table, or the point of her foot against mine, electrified those double mono-logues, as the hard wood of the prie-dieu or the marble of the altar transforms into an ineffable joy the suffering of the be-liever.

Nor was there any conversation afterwards. Just a few practical phrases, as short as possible; as if I wanted to cancel out the very existence of an idol.

"This time I'll only give you five thousand lire, because I haven't drawn my salary yet," or "Tomorrow we won't be seeing each other, because I'm going to Naples," or "Don't get up, it doesn't matter, I'll wash at the hotel," and so on. The idol, on her side, was no fool; she would lie smoking, motionless, on the bed, without saying a single word; and even if it was very hot, she would cover her naked body up to the neck at once, as if she had guessed my sudden longing for her to dis-appear.

But not that night. No, that night, I thought and be-lieved and hoped, pleasure would never end. I imaged endless combinations and attitudes for our embraces. As I sat silently by Dorotea at dinner, I repeated to myself all the mad phrases I would use in the darkness of her room, and conjured up in-exhaustible delights. I was so excited that I scarcely touched any food. And the few mouthfuls that I did eat I wanted to come from her; bits of bread or meat which I begged her to chew beforehand, a sip of water drunk from the side of the glass where she had put her lips. Dorotea, docile, smiling slightly, almost mysteriously, did what I wanted every time; without moving her head and with that slight fixed smile on her face she would give a slow circular roll of her big green eyes round the other tables, in case anyone should notice, then, quickly pop the food into my mouth.

When we were lying on the bed, naked and embracing, I felt, this time too, a great astonishment and almost a kind of fear at the happiness I was being granted, which, in spite of my constant brooding and desire, was stronger and more complete than anything I had imagined. Clinging to her flesh, squeezing her body, warming myself with her warmth, staying there for a time—an apparently endless time—motionless together as if we had really succeeded in fusing our limbs and losing the sense of each other's physical individuality, then moving into different attitudes in order to feel separate and different again and so have the joy of fusing once more, I in her and she in me, all this intoxicating, astonishing, mysterious game was repeated this time too.

Obscurely, I felt I was doing something forbidden, something that for many years I had thought I would never have the courage to do; and this courage also made me feel alarmed, surprised, and happy.

And this time too I thought that my happiness would never end. "It's for all my life," I said to myself, "for life and for death." At that moment I felt I'd like to have Dora make the most absurd, extravagant demands: for some fabulous sum of money I'd not be able to give her, but would get hold of somehow: or even marriage. I'd have broken off my engagement to Jane—to Jane, who at that moment did not matter to me at all, did not exist for me any more. I'd have done anything, given her anything then. It did not even for a second occur to me to offer her money or marriage myself first; for my sacrifice, however great, would have given me real pleasure only if it were inescapable—that is, demanded, imposed by her, and not dependent on my own free will. A real goddess, I told myself, should be very exigent.

But she said nothing that night either, except for the phrases I had taught or suggested to her.

And the instant that miraculous frenzy ended—in spite of all my spasmodic efforts to discover some secret method of continuing it—that instant everything was just as it had been every other time and always would be.

The only surprise, therefore, was that there had been no surprise.

This time, too, it had all been just self-deception, ordinary exaltation. Jane was far away on the high seas. No one would ring me at the hotel. I was absolutely free. But suddenly I felt, as always, sad, embittered, furious with myself, and hated Dorotea and her great brown body, soft and warm under my own. She disgusted me for the very things that up to a second ago I had adored; even her scent, which had intoxicated me a second before, I now found almost nauseating.

That night I discovered that the thought of Jane and the phone call had been only a secret and unconscious pretext, and that in the second following that supreme second something was inevitably released inside me, flew rapidly off toward distant memories; the prairies beyond Denver, Colorado; Pikes Peak, where I had been as a boy when my father worked at the mines; one night in the middle of the Atlantic, when I lay on the canvas of a hatchway, gazing in silence at the stars, with a cigarette and a bottle of whisky and the calm voice of a friend in the dark beside me. And I felt I was divided, inside myself, by two different opposing passions, and tortured by the need, which I still felt, to join them, fuse them, make one thing of them forever.

Such was this need of mine that that night (and many others after) I refused to admit defeat: remembering my exaltation the whole of that day and evening in the *trattoria*, I forced myself to remain by Dorotea's side and for the first time began talking to her with false sentiment and friendship. I told her, fully realizing I was lying, that I was feeling a new sweetness and tenderness for her, that in fact I was beginning to fall in love with her. Lying like that hurt me bitterly; and yet I did so in the hope that in time, if I went on pretending, it would turn out to be true. But as I talked, the tedium of pretending and the boredom of being beside her grew, until, suddenly exhausted, I stopped, and fell asleep.

I woke up a short time later. And at once I felt, as I did so, that I was different, was again, unexpectedly, what I'd been before. Physical desire, though still weak, had hold of me again. It depended on me, at that moment, whether I went or stayed. And going would not have been any great effort. My desire for Dorotea and for a good hot bath at my hotel were equal. But I wanted to try again: to stay and have another go, in the absurd hope that by doing so the miracle, which had not happened before, could happen then.

I stayed all night; saw the dawn, the sun in the slats of the shutters here too, and here too heard the growing sounds of the city and the calls of the bottle-man; but that sun, those sounds, those voices, had no spell for me now, only a nostalgia for what they'd meant to me the morning before, when they had still held the hope of love. Now they said just the opposite: disillusion, bitterness, love's impossibility. The sun shone, Rome woke, life continued; but I, on that rumpled bed, beside that splendid statuesque body which I'd so caressed and loved and which, though not desiring it any more, I still admired, I, gazing at that ray of sun in the shadowed room, listening to the sounds of the city, remained as I was, tossed, exhausted, between alternate waves drawing me toward slavery or toward liberty. Both in turn seemed either irresistibly fascinating or unbearably tedious; opposites that I would never be able to write, however much I hoped, and however hard and stubbornly I tried.

Very often the thought of Dorotea was itself enough to lead me toward Jane; or the thought of Jane to lead me toward Dorotea. I remember, for example, the Christmas of that same year in Rome.

Dorotea and her landlady had invited me to go with them to the midnight Mass in St. Peter's, and then come back home to Via Boncompagni for a small supper. I hadn't accepted though they'd pressed me. Mass and Catholicism would remind me of Jane. I preferred to be alone and think of her. Making the excuse that I was a Protestant, I thanked them and refused.

Christmas Eve came. Shortly before midnight I was going back to the hotel after having taken home Tem O'Rourke, a friend and colleague of mine whom you may remember. Tem lived beyond Sant'Agnese, on the Nomentana. I was alone in the jeep. At the corner of the Nomentana and the Viale della Regina I had to brake to let a taxi pass which had suddenly appeared from the right and was going in the opposite direction to mine. I was just able to glimpse in the back of the taxi a girl in American uniform, the same as Jane's. The face of the girl was also vaguely like Jane's. Although I knew that it could not possibly be Jane, who was in France and from whom I'd had a letter only that morning, the impression was so strong that I lost all wish to go straight back to the hotel. I felt nervous, upset, incapable of staying alone. I drove round the damp, cold, deserted Villa Borghese stepping without any hope and without any real intentions in front of the few prostitutes about. I almost telephoned to O'Rourke, to go back and see him. But by that time, I knew, he was already in bed with his mistress. Willy Osgood? Where was Willy at that hour? He'd told me: at a party of some Italian friends, and I'd forgotten who they were. And then I realized that I did not want Willy's or Tem's company, but only Dorotea's, whose image had been roused in me as if in irresistible contrast, by seeing Jane's image through the taxi window.

So I went to St. Peter's.

The huge church was filled with crowds and damp, with shuffling feet, whispering, and the muffled music of organs and choirs. The crowd was varied; part indifferent, part bored, part curious, part hypocritical, and part sincerely religious. But they all seemed religious at least in their mutual tolerance, however varied the reasons and the signs of their presence.

It was unlikely, if not impossible, that I would find Dorotea and her friend in that crowd. I began to wander round the great church, intending to go all over it methodically from entrance to apse and vice versa, first to the right and then to the left. On the altar of Confession, where Mass was being said, the glittering bunches of electric lights mingled with flames of torches and candles. The crowds of faithful, and of unfaithful, were in shadow. I walked almost up to the center of the nave, turning and looking round among the irregular groups of heretics interrupting and confusing the rather small queues of faithful, to see if I could find Dorotea.

I was lucky and did find her quite quickly.

As soon as she saw me she gave me a gay wave, which was certainly sincere. She hadn't expected to see me there, and realized that I'd come for her. She was pleased.

She was kneeling next to her landlady. Both of them wore on their heads white handkerchiefs folded in four. Over the lined and raddled features of that old procuress of a landlady the ornament was too simple not to seem incongruous. But it suited Dorotea very well. Her face with its classic lines, her strong direct glance, fitted the clean white triangle that fell over her forehead and seemed enough to transform as if by magic the "segnorina" of the liberation into a peasant woman of olden days, an artist's model of Corot's time.

I went back home with them, accepted their invitation to supper. I tasted the *scarcella*, a sweet cake that Dorotea had made with her own hands. And I did not regret having followed the impulse caused by the sudden similarity to Jane— or at least did not regret it more than at other times.

On Christmas Day I woke up at one o'clock in the afternoon, surprised to find myself in Dorotea's bed.

8.

The war was over. Toward the middle of July I joined Jane in Paris; and after some weeks of almost genuine happiness amid the very genuine euphoria surrounding us (rounds and rounds of drinks, amid crowds of friends, sitting on and on at little tables in the Champs-Élysées; nights wandering from cabaret to cabaret, dancing, drinking champagne; week-ends in little hotels along the Marne or in the forest of Fontainebleau), finally we began to prepare for our return to the States.

Our plans were definite: I would introduce her to my

parents; she would introduce me to hers; and we would marry as soon as possible.

Her family were Catholics. Jane had been educated by the Ursuline nuns in Philadelphia and never ceased to practice her religion.

It could not have been from religious scruples, however, that during our time in Paris, and before in Rome, and when I went to visit her in Savoy the last winter of the war, she stubbornly refused to let me complete the act of love with her. It could not be from religious scruples, for the kisses and caresses to which we abandoned ourselves every evening till their culmination of acrid, exquisite, and unnatural pleasure were as wicked and sinful, according to the Catholic Church, as if we had become lovers before marriage.

Jane was too intelligent not to realize this, and anyway I never really broached the subject to her. When I hinted at it, she seemed to be taking refuge in pretended scruples or modesty, making some mental reservation. On leaving the Ursuline Convent she had entered college. And there, with a college companion, a boy of her own age, she had already, as many American girls do, had the decisive sexual experience. But she had regretted it bitterly, and was determined now, she said, to distinguish our love from that passing adventure.

On my side I willingly accepted this explanation. I did not insist or try to persuade her to do what would, after all, have been merely natural. Perhaps I thought that by renouncing this final, crucial test, I would confer an artificial zest on a marriage the prospect of which secretly bored me; I would, I thought, at least get that attraction and novelty from the sacrament. For as I was firmly decided to marry in spite of and indeed against my own tastes, I was afraid that without the stimulus of that novelty I might weaken and change my mind before the fatal day.

So every evening, when I left her at her hotel or the door of her room, holding hands and gazing long into each other's eyes between tears and smiles before separating for the night, there was a bitter little voice inside me whispering the truth. And the truth was this: that if I'd really desired her I would not have been able to wait; and that the relative ease of my renunciation was a sign that my love was not, by its very nature, complete.

But that was just what I did not want it to be; that completeness was just what I tried, by every subtle unconscious means, to avoid.

When, for example, I returned to my hotel after that first night with Dorotea and thought of the long torment and desperate disillusion of the hours I'd just passed, I drew the conclusion that I loved Jane, and Jane alone; Dorotea was just an occasional caprice, however regular, a secondary pleasure, however strong, a vice like others, gambling, alcohol, opium, which can be harmful to bodily health if practiced without moderation, but make no changes in the aims we want to give our lives. And my only aim, I thought, was to see Jane as my wife and companion, Jane as the mother of my children. "Dorotea is just a vice," I said to myself sadly, "and nothing more." There was no danger of this vice engulfing me. At each orgasm the spell inevitably lifted, everything returned to the cold light of reason, and Jane became the source of that light. I also noticed that, as time went on, the intervals when I was carried away by the illusion of loving Dorotea completely became rarer and rarer and gradually shorter; always farther from the last orgasm, and always nearer the next. "It's just a physical thing," I told myself, "nothing more." And from that time I began to attribute dwindling importance to Dorotea. Even though the lack of her, in my long absences in America or France, made me suffer horribly, I felt I would be willing to try every means to rid myself of this periodic obsession.

In Rome or Paris I tried the brothels and streetwalkers; remedies of very short duration and totally contrary effect. A few hours afterwards, back would come the desire for Dorotea, and this time irresistibly; it seemed as if by trying an unknown prostitute instead of her, I had only prepared myself for her all the more. I remember one time; it was when I was in Paris with Jane, in the summer of '45. Late that night, after accompanying Jane to her hotel, I began thinking about Dorotea, who was, of course, in Rome and whom I could not possibly join that night. Hoping to quiet myself, I had stopped a passing girl on the boulevard and let her draw me along. A quarter of an hour later, as soon as I got out of her squalid little room, I jumped into a taxi, hurried to Le Bourget, found a military aircraft, and before midday had reached Rome, the mezzanine in Via Boncompagni, and was in bed with Dorotea.

The very brief pleasure given me by that poor girl had been followed by a deep disgust, and the disgust by a wild but decided frenzy. From Le Bourget I had telephoned to Jane, waking her and telling her that I had to go to Rome unexpectedly on business. My voice was trembling. Luckily Jane was half-asleep. I would never have been capable of the lie if that girl had not thrown me into such a state of agitation.

The winter before, as I told you, I'd made the trip in the opposite direction. From Rome, from Dorotea, to visit Jane.

She was at Saint-Pierre-d'Albigny, outside Aiguebelle, near the junction of the Arc and the Isère, where her hospital was encamped.

The night before leaving I had spent with Dorotea. And again I had persuaded myself, as I squeezed her to me in the big bed in her dark room, that I no longer wanted to leave Rome a few hours later. I had even deceived myself into thinking that I would never leave again. "I won't go," I said to myself as I stroked the thick brown skin of my motionless enigmatic idol, "I won't go; what is Jane compared to the pleasure I feel at this moment?" This was reality, this was life. The most honest thing I could do for my own sake, and for Jane's too, was not to leave, and never see Jane again.

But very soon, much sooner than with other, less silly hopes, it all ended as usual. And I was driving happily in the cold damp air of the winter dawn, happy and alone with the roar of the jeep as I urged it along the Via Aurelia toward the north. The sea was black, covered with white horses, the sky gray and high, the marshy maritime country bright green. How free I felt during that frenzied journey toward another slavery!

The valley of the Arc enclosed me between its rocks hidden in mist, veiled by rain.

From the windows of the little Hôtel de la Gare we looked out on the square in front of the station, calm and deserted under the rain. The food was highly flavored and delicious; the stove was hot: down in the big room below, the railwaymen were playing *belotte;* sipping an old brandy, we gazed into each other's eyes (Jane's sweet and brilliant under her short chestnut hair) and our knees under the table touched as if that light contact were our supreme pleasure.

What could be more different, more distant from Rome, from the sun, from Dorotea?

Certainly not the States, and New England least of all. For here at Saint-Pierre-d'Albigny in the unexpected charm of that cosy, muffled family atmosphere, in some way a forerunner of our future home at B—, Jane and I lived in harmony under the same roof together for the first time, and I began to believe in the possibility of a just, calm, bourgeois life, a life of peace and renunciation.

But it was a dream of sacred happiness even more absurd than the dream of profane happiness I had with Dorotea.

In Philadelphia I met Jane's family. They lived in Chestnut Hill, an airy and elegant suburb, in a big red-brick house surrounded by bright-green lawns, close-cropped at all seasons of the year, and tall rare plants. Her father, uncles, and brothers were all in the textile industry, and colleagues or dependents in some way of the famous house of Du Pont de Nemours.

When Jane introduced me as her future husband, announcing at the same time that we would marry before Christmas, I don't think I made a very good impression on them. Only Jane's mother, a woman sweet and optimistic by nature, was kind with me. The father, the brothers, and one uncle (she had three or four) who happened to be present that day, greeted me with polite, almost ironic coldness. But their irony was, through me, directed at Jane. They considered her to be a stubborn madcap, not to be thwarted lest this produce the opposite effect. Had Jane got it into her head to marry me? Perhaps to agree was the only way to make her change her mind. Opposition would only hasten the date of the marriage. They were certainly right. But they were incapable of hiding this secret hope and calculation of theirs. They said "yes," formally, to Jane, and held out their big bony red hands to me; but the eyes behind their gold spectacles, their thin lips, were smiling skeptically all the time, as if they were saying: "Go on, go on, children, go on, mad little Jane; be happy if you can; but we know perfectly well, and can in fact already see, that it will all end in tears."

The mother, on the other hand, had the same character as Jane's, passionate and stubborn, but tender and delicate, even subtle in her feelings. She was Catholic, the daughter of Irish parents, and had dedicated her life to two cults; music: and old Europe. But while a Steinway, which she played every day, was enough to satisfy the first, her journeys in Europe, which during her youth and the first period of her marriage had been a habit, in fact an annual rite, had later become rarer, shorter, and more difficult. Jane's father, a rigid and arid businessman, had never liked them; he adored his wife, but not what his wife adored. He had no sympathy either for music or for Europe. The first he forgave as a harmless feminine pastime, but he had not been able to take any part in her enthusiasm for the second.

"Good-by, my dear . . ." he would say regularly to his wife, the night before taking her to New York as far as the embarkation pier, "good-by for three months; amuse yourself! You know how sorry I am that business prevents my coming with you. But I'm sorry because I can't be near you, not for any other reason. I disapprove of this mania of yours of revisiting England, France, and Italy every year, when here in America, even without leaving our own United States, there are huge prairies, picturesque spots, wonderful cities, and almost entire peoples who are our brethren and whom you don't know. It's a real pity that you can't understand that. Now, if you wanted to visit this country, I might be able to come with you."

This was before the days of flying, and a visit to Europe meant, what with the journey both ways, an absence of two or three months.

As soon as Jane was of age, this farewell speech was made to mother and daughter together. Then one day, the mother, whether from inclination or deep conviction, or in order to have another, stronger reason for crossing the Atlantic every year, managed to conquer her husband's Americanism on an even more important point and to place Jane in a college at Montreux. Jane herself, it's true, had fought for this with all her might and begged for her father's permission. And perhaps he had finally consented to this enormity ("As if we hadn't first-rate colleges here! They're the best in the world! Why, girls come from Europe to Smith and Vassar!") because he had realized that his daughter was just exactly like her mother. It was useless to try to correct her—better to let her go to her fate. And he had consoled himself by concentrating on the education of his two sons, who, on the other hand, were like him. A few years later, in fact, he took them into his business.

Then the war came, and while Jane was in Europe with the armed forces, her mother, naturally, did not move from Philadelphia. As soon as the war was over she intended to take up her old habits. But the "old man," her husband, really was old now; and could not do without her even for a week.

Although I was as pure-bred an American on both sides as Jane's family were, I somehow gave them the impression of being a European; a good impression for the mother, a bad one for the father, brothers, and uncles. The few weeks I stayed in Philadelphia with Jane did not correct this impression. I was a perfectly good American. But to those people, simple in both their likes and their dislikes, I was European in my open-mindedness, European in my habit (for which I had to thank my parents, both Americans) of not considerating the States as the center of the world; European in the superior importance I attributed to the arts; European in my total incapacity to speak of anything, so they thought, which was not connected with painting, music, or literature.

They in their simplicity were right, I believe. I was, I am, European, in spite of being American by blood for generations.

The first to teach me this truth was my father. My father trained and lived as an engineer. He has never traveled outside the United States. But he's always been passionately fond of painting, and has always gone out every Saturday afternoon—he is now sixty-five—in all weathers and seasons into the country with his paintbox and easel.

At bedtime when I was a child and went to give my father a good-night kiss, I'd find him in his armchair, pipe in mouth, gazing, amid clouds of smoke, at the reproduction of some blue-green Pissarro or burnt-ocher Courbet. Courbet fitted in more with the smell and color of the pipe and tobacco. I would stand there a moment in silence, waiting for him to bend down and kiss me. But though he had seen me and heard me coming, he would say nothing for some minutes, but just put an arm round my shoulders and go on gazing (before my mother's voice called him and broke the spell) at the dreaming French landscape, which he held spread like an imaginary window on his knees; and as he gazed between half-closed eyes amid the pipe smoke, he would be tacitly inviting me to do so too. In the silence I could hear my father's calm breathing, feel the warmth of his body, smell the good tobacco near me;

from the dining-room and the kitchen beyond came the quiet sounds of my mother moving to and fro with the table things; and sometimes the background of silence and night was broken by the mechanical wail of a train passing not far off. The train gave me the idea of traveling. Late, alone in the dark, wrapped in the warmth and softness of my bed I would hear that wail in the night again. It sounded desperate, it was moving away, away into the darkness like a cry of anguish. . . . For what? I didn't know.

He would have liked to make me a painter, but contented himself by guiding me, from boyhood, toward a career as an art historian. When I had finished college, he sent me to New York University, where I studied under Loewen.

Professor Loewen at once advised me to specialize and suggested the Sienese painters of the fourteenth century. At the age of twenty-six I left for Italy, where I remained almost without a break, mostly in Siena, Florence, and then Rome, until a short time before war broke out.

When I returned to the States, my father had given up the work in mines and factories, which had become too heavy for him; and a company that recognized his outstanding honesty had given him a small job in a big factory in Chicago.

So to Chicago I took Jane to meet him and my mother. And finally we married; at Philadelphia, two days after Christmas, on the 27th of December 1945.

Jane was a Catholic, like her mother, and the religious ceremony was Catholic.

Then we went to Niagara Falls, purposely intending to have the ordinary conventional honeymoon of middle-class Americans. Both of us had been away from the States for two years before and during the war, Jane at college in Switzerland,

I in Italy studying. Now, on marriage, we felt a desire, almost a social obligation, to conform to the most banal American customs. It was, I may say, almost a kind of game for us, part boredom, part joke, part hypocrisy. We enjoyed mimicking and openly ridiculing the simple ignorance of our dear compatriots.

But the game did not last long. Loewen had a job for me, as assistant lecturer in the faculty of Fine Arts at B—, New Jersey.

My weekly lecturing hours were too few to require me, at first anyway, to live at B—; and as B— is not too far from New York, we could perfectly well have continued to live in New York, where we had taken a little apartment in the "village" while waiting for the beginning of the university courses.

Jane wanted to stay in New York; but I, either pretending or believing I was jealous, would not agree. And so, very solemnly, we began to lead a professional and family life in the closed, watchful, dull world of that small but important university.

9.

From the very beginning it came perfectly easily, almost naturally. All we had to do, though of course in rather more subdued tones, was to keep up the act we had started on our honeymoon—we were parodying, that is, models much less vulgar, though equally fatuous.

At Niagara Falls we had pretended to be a small business couple. At B— we tried to appear, even in our way of dressing, exactly as my colleagues and their wives thought that Professor Harry Summers and his wife should appear. This time unfortunately there was some truth in our act; we really were Professor Harry Summers and Mrs. Summers. I really did give lectures and tutorials, frequented the Faculty Club, and so forth. And so, from this basis of truth, gradually we found ourselves being taken in by our own pretense.

But now that I think it over, I begin to wonder if even behind that farce at Niagara Falls there was not a hidden germ, perhaps the first unconscious attempt at a serious, normal, and—for me—mistaken life. I begin to wonder if already then, and at Saint-Pierre-d'Albigny, and perhaps in Rome too the very moment I met Jane, I had not felt a desire for conformity, a nostalgia for bourgeois peace, a yearning for a settled family life, for children and a fixed job, an urge to weakness and cowardice, to renunciations of adventure and the vital instinctive life that was right for me and conformed to my deepest instincts.

The lowest passions have a guile of their own; for when they first assail us they try above all not to alarm, and take on a superficial air, the better to insinuate themselves. When repulsed by our reason, they begin to tempt our vanity. And we are so vain, so certain of being able to resist, that we are quite willing to deride them; we even pretend to have them, and parody them so as to congratulate ourselves on our own virtue. But as we do so, as we take this interest in them, we begin to feel them in ourselves, to taste their particular flavor, and slowly, unconsciously become used to them, until finally we find ourselves their slaves.

And a day comes when our reason too is suddenly turned inside out. The particular passion that we had always in the

past considered base or deceitful suddenly appears grand and true. "This is the light, this is the way," we say to ourselves with an extraordinary, if deceptive, sense of comfort. "We too are like all the others, like all other decent people. Normal. We have no more doubts. How restful! It's all so simple." All we needed was a little humility. And the moment we think ourselves humble, we're done, for humility is a virtue that one has only when one thinks one hasn't!

We thought ourselves humble, Jane and I did, the day the doctor told her that she was pregnant. Of course, we were prepared for the news, we expected it. But only then, as we were returning from New York, where I'd taken Jane to the doctor, and were driving through the long tunnel under the Hudson, did we seem to be a couple of parents like any other parents whose first baby would be born in a few months.

We were excited, apprehensive, and even happy. But I had at the same time a vague feeling of resignation, an intuition that I was being forced to accept a destiny which was probably not mine, that this was the announcement of a defeat whose terms and consequences were still obscure to me. I remember the curved walls, the shining, dirty white tiles, extending mile after mile, like a nightmare, toward the future; and the deafening noise, the speed, the other cars passing or overtaking. As I drove, Jane put a hand under my arm. I pressed it now and again, between the wrist and the elbow, that nervous, sensitive little hand, pressed it to feel closer to her, to communicate with her, to tell her something. What? That I loved her? No, not even that. That I was there, at her side, thinking of her; and I wanted her to know it.

Finally I broke the heavy silence, as soon as we got out of the tunnel and were mounting the heights of Hoboken, seeing once more the dark night, the sky, the lights of the boats on the distant river. I opened the little window for a mouthful of fresh air, and lit a cigarette. Then said:

"What do you think, Jane, ought we to tell the Pratts this evening?"

Michael Pratt was a young professor of archaeology who lived with his wife in a little house near ours. For the last four months we had been seeing each other every Tuesday, Thursday, and Saturday evening, alternately at our home and theirs, and playing bridge from eight o'clock till midnight.

Among the acquaintances we had made on arriving at B—, we had exercised our hypocrisy most on these Pratts. They were the most favorable ground.

Both of them were pleasant, kind, and completely void of everything, even of malice.

He was a tall, thin, red-skinned, blond young man, whose life seemed dedicated to the shape of his bushy mustaches, his collection of pipes, and the cut of his tweed jackets. These three occupations were enough to avoid disappointment in his only ambition: to appear English in spite of being American, and in spite of his pride in being American. His wife, to balance the scales, was not even vain. She was just completely silly. Bridge was the be-all and end-all of her existence. They had no children.

How pleasant they were, though, those evenings with the Pratts! Lullaby of long spring evenings round the green card-table! And almost the most agreeable part of them was my regret at the hours I was wasting there, at my neglected studies, my unanswered letters. Banished, during that timeless quiet of the game, were memories and desires, agonies and hopes. A shadow of passion (love for one's partner, hatred for one's opponents) lightly touched, also, the banal flow of those hours. The bottle of whisky and the tall glasses; the green carpet, the colored cards, Michael's tweed jacket, Mrs. Pratt's gray dress with its black and white dots, her small diamond earrings, her blond hair with its symmetrically set curls, and Jane's thin hands, her tiny wrists, one with a watch-strap, the other with a platinum and sapphire bracelet, which I had given her as a wedding present; reality, in fact, was reduced only to objects. Nothing existed apart from appearances. Nothing disturbed us any more. Finally we too were stupid, finally we too were happy.

But how were things between Jane and me?

There was, in me, a dumb, tenacious, desperate will to love her.

As I've already told you, Jane and I had never completed the physical act before our marriage. That happened at Niagara Falls. I wonder if I'd still have married her if it had happened before.

Disappointment? The word's too simple. I'd never hoped, or even thought, to lose myself in adoration of her as I did with Dorotea. As my affection for Jane was intellectual and sentimental, the act of physical love reduced itself with her to a mechanical function, in which sentiment and intelligence were uppermost without ever going farther, without ever fusing with that act. And so by a facile illusion the act of love with Jane seemed at first to be even more violent than it had been with Dorotea. I could lie to myself at first, and almost believe that I desired Jane more than Dorotea.

The truth, alas, was quite different. That detachment of the senses from the brain and feelings which afflicted me so much after making love to Dorotea, and which I overcame only in her absence and my desire for her, was permanent, endemic, fatal, with Jane.

But I was sure that Jane felt with me what I felt with Dorotea. The idea tickled my vanity; and so we achieved, each time, a sufficient degree of excitement.

When I was with Dorotea, I was lost in adoration for her, for her body. I never thought of myself, of my own body; or if I did think of myself, it was for brief moments and with a sense of unworthiness, almost of abjectness.

Jane, on the other hand, I would snuggle up to in the warmth of the bed, thinking not of her, but only of myself. Her thin, pink, nervous body, with its hot, dry skin, aroused no desire in me; my physical movements for those few necessary seconds seemed nothing but automatic vibration. I moved over her in the warm bed thinking only of myself, of how much Jane desired me, and even sometimes of myself as of a sort of distant emanation of Dorotea; and the thought— how complicated it was!—that Jane desired, without knowing it, nothing but an emanation of Dorotea intoxicated me for a second.

My pleasure was quick, morbid, sharp, almost painful, a sob of my body on that body, not, alas, dear to me, on that creature not, alas, divine. And at every second, every spasm, my brain was always free.

I would think of her, Jane; of how intelligent she was, how good she was, how much she helped and loved me.

Such considerations, while our bodies moved in unison on their own, brought me, almost every time, to tears. And I would light the light and try to gaze into her eyes to catch love there, at least. And as I gazed at her I would delude myself that I loved her too; that I myself felt, at that moment, an abandon of love, a fusion, or rather a confusion, of sense and sentiment. In that moment I said to myself: "I'm taking my pleasure with Jane's body; but Jane is also a person whom I respect, to whom I'm tenderly attached; so I love Jane in a way that's total and complete, in body and soul."

Poor me! I didn't understand that love consists just in the very impossibility of any such reasoning, in the very incapacity to distinguish between body and soul.

I would light the light and gaze into her eyes; gray-green between the half-shut lids they would gaze back at me: they seemed lost, tortured, in the intensity of pleasure, and to be saying: "You are God, I'm nothing. Do whatever you like with me, kill me if you wish!"

It was just exactly what I'd thought when, at the moment of crisis, I'd gazed at Dorotea. So my eyes, in those moments with Dorotea, must have had the same expression that Jane's now had with me.

But Dorotea's eyes I had fixed every time, surely, with even greater intensity and frenzy. Dorotea's round, green pupils, scattered with gold specks, had no expression. At least they had no expression that I could succeed in understanding. They seemed mysterious, severe, vaguely critical. If I tried, by some question, to find out why, I would discover that they hid no mystery, no reason for any severity or criticism. Perhaps Dorotea's eyes were what I wanted them to be. I loved them to be mysterious, severe, and critical. In any case, I loved them, dreamed of them, lost myself in them, and forgot everything. It seemed to me I could go on gazing at them endlessly without ever tiring. Which I did.

Dorotea's eyes! Now perhaps I myself had those eyes for Jane! . . .

Gradually I detached myself from her embrace, as late as possible, feeling I'd lied both to her and to myself. I had thought of making up for this by prolonging our embrace, without realizing that, by doing so, I was lying all the more and all the worse.

My arm, which I'd passed under Jane's back, was hurting me. But I only drew it away when it was almost numbed.

What was the point of all those efforts of mine? Love is like courage; no one can give it to himself. But I was certain that Jane loved me and had been made happy by me; I felt to blame and wanted at all costs to hide my coldness from her. I forgot that when pleasure is genuine it has no afterthoughts; one turns over on the other side and goes calmly off to sleep.

What was lacking in my feelings for Jane was natural desire, and the natural sweetness of satisfied desire. I did not want to confess this to myself, but forced myself to try to create both, in the foolish hope of succeeding.

Finally I would lie there, in the tortured and torturing bed, near her in body but far away in thought; and longing to sleep, the only real pleasure still remaining, which took so long—oh, so long—to come!

Again I heard, in the deep, empty silence of the American countryside at night, the gloomy wail of the trains. I remembered the nights of my childhood and the presentiment that tightened my heart then too, as it did now. But now childhood was far away; so was adolescence; and even my youth was almost over. In a few months my first child would be born. Was this life, then? Was I never to feel that peace, that just joy, to which I had a right, it seemed to me, as God had given me the will and capacity to imagine it? Ah, no, I felt confusedly, never. I would glimpse that light; perhaps I'd almost taste that sweetness; but I would never possess it. It seemed to me as if my future was enclosed by a leaden sky, pressed down by suffocating air. Down below, farther away, the train wailed again. No, I would never be happy.

But I could not resign myself to such a fate. I told myself that it was my fault: I'd made a mistake; if I'd had the courage to marry Dorotea instead of Jane, everything would have been all right. It was not a life sentence, I said to myself. It was only a mistake. An irreparable one, certainly, but still a mistake and nothing more. And in this thought I found my only consolation.

The bitterness, which I hid from Jane and almost from myself at night, would surge up again by day without my realizing it or being able to prevent it. The smallest incidents could cause it. A window closed or open, a piece of paper on the floor, a dish of food too hot or too cold, a delay on Jane's part in dressing to go to the Pratts'; I'd get impatient, become disproportionately angry. Yet I never linked this irritability of mine with the glooms of the night, I would not admit to myself that, perhaps through my fault, Jane was also becoming nervous and irritable. I had the explanation ready: we were beginning married life, and married life was like that.

It was worse at table. There were certain days when I could no longer bear to see her eat. I would keep my eyes lowered or look somewhere else. But if she was munching raw celery or an apple or a crust of bread, the sound was torture to me. And I would think of Dorotea, whose table manners were very crude indeed, and whose education had been infinitely inferior to Jane's. But the sight of Dorotea's mouth as she ate spaghetti with tomato sauce not only had never irritated me at all, but had, on the other hand, pleased me as something healthy, spontaneous, and animal.

One day Jane came home wearing a new dress. It was a loose, silk two-piece, one of those garments which we Americans call a "maternity dress," designed on purpose to hide pregnancy.

I neither liked nor disliked the dress. I glanced at it indifferently without saying anything. What suddenly irritated me, quite disproportionately, was Jane's phrase when, the next evening, as we were dressing to go to the Pratts', she said completely naturally:

"What do you think, dear, hadn't I better put on the *maternity dress*?"

I repeat, she said *maternity dress* completely naturally, without emphasizing the words or putting them in inverted commas, as if she too had now accepted all the conventions of the people among whom we lived, as if she too had become just an ordinary American woman.

Yes, her tone of voice irritated me. But I didn't say so. Instead I joked about the dress itself, comparing it to those of certain middle-aged ladies who go downtown in Philadelphia to play bridge in some big hotel. . . .

Scarlet with anger, she abused me, opened the wardrobe, tore the dress to strips, and finally broke into desperate sobbing. We didn't go to the Pratts' that evening; I rang up to say I had a headache. Late that night Jane was still weeping and still abusing me. Then we made it up and went to bed and things were a little better—a little less bad, that is—than at other times. I said to myself that if my sarcasm had so offended her, she must love me a great deal.

THE CAPRI LETTERS

The birth of a child, contrary to the hopes of parents who do not get on together and would like to, never solves anything. On the contrary, all it does is to hide, deepen, and complicate the differences.

Even so, during the last months of her pregnancy and the first after the birth, there was, perhaps because of the novelty, an apparent improvement in our relationship. Even before the baby was born we'd decided to call it Duccio if a boy, Donatella if a girl. Yes, Jane and I had Italy graven on our hearts!

Duccio was born on the 2nd of November 1946. We spent the Christmas holidays in Philadelphia, with her parents. Then we returned to B—. And toward April the petty irritations, the nervous states, the squabbles, had already begun again.

Then one evening I was called on the telephone by Loewen from New York.

"Harry, would you like to go to Italy?"

"When?"

"At once."

"But I've got a wife now, and a five-months-old baby."

"Take them with you."

"But what about my courses here at B—?"

"I'll take care of all that."

It was Loewen who had placed me at B—, and Loewen was now offering me a really responsible job. He had been asked to do it himself, and had neither the inclination nor the time. It was a matter of going all round Italy on behalf of the American government and checking all the works of art, sculpture or painting, place by place, monument by monument, to assess the exact extent and cause of war damage to the country's artistic heritage.

Behind the desk, cluttered with papers and reproductions, in his New York study, where I went to visit him next day, Loewen, small, dry, elegant, nervous, and kind, with his whitening blond hair, his clipped mustache, his pipe between his teeth, and his glittering eyes, seemed to me a kind of genie of my destiny; a modern magician who, with a gesture of his delicate, thin, pink hands, on which the blue veins showed in relief, with a smile on his thin lips, gave whatever twist he wanted to my life.

"Do you know what UNESCO is? A big organization in the U.N. Its base is in Paris, avenue Kléber. If you do your job well in Italy, and I'm sure you will, there'll be a post for you later in UNESCO. You don't want to die in New Jersey, do you?"

"No, Professor Loewen," I replied enthusiastically.

In his broken English, with its fascinating Jewish cum either Austrian or Alsatian accent, with both the German guttural and the rolling French *rr*, the little old magician then gave me numbers of personal commissions. I was first to go to Washington, to an office of the State Department, where I would be given all the particulars about the war-damage job. But I was also to be kind enough to find out a lot of other things for him too: where certain pictures from private collections had got to in the war; the state of certain frescoes; and the exact measurements of other paintings, measurements that were lacking in a catalogue he was about to publish which had been sent to him by Italian experts; finally I was to have reproductions made in color, on the spot, by specialist photographers and in certain specific conditions.

With growing enthusiasm I began to take notes; all these orders would be perfectly carried out. Yet as he went on naming the various places scattered over Italy which I was to visit, I was already thinking of Dorotea. Jane, even if she came with me, could not, with the small baby, follow me on that detailed pilgrimage. She would have to stay in Rome or Florence. Perhaps Dorotea could come traveling with me. I'd never written to her. I'd often wanted to, but had always stopped myself, fearing to give her something to blackmail me by. More than a year had passed. Would I be able to find her again? Did she still live in Via Boncompagni? I thought of our first meeting, after such a long absence, when I'd lost hope of ever seeing her again. I heard Loewen's voice running on like soft music, looked at his smiling face, but no longer took in anything he was saying. My mind was far away. I could see the Roman sun, the spring, the green trees on the Via Boncompagni, the busses passing, the shops, the bar beneath with its metal tables on the pavement, Dorotea's mezzanine; I could smell her heavy, vulgar scent. . . . Loewen soon noticed that I wasn't listening any more. He would make me out a memorandum with all details, he said. I was to come by and get it in a week, on my way through New York to take the plane.

That evening, at B—, Jane was happy. The telephone call of the day before had been too good to be true; she had not wanted to believe in it completely. But now there were no more doubts. We really were leaving. We really were going back to Italy.

I told her at once that I would have to travel extensively on Loewen's and the government's behalf.

"You can stay with the baby in Florence, or in Rome, or partly in Florence and partly in Rome, or in Siena, and I'll come and visit you every time I can, at least once a week."

"I wouldn't dream of it," said Jane in a firm voice and with a fixed look, as if she'd made up her mind a long time ago. "Not Rome, or Florence, or any other place. Duccio and I will live at Capri."

10.

Capri was scarcely the best place, particularly at that time of year, for a baby of six months. I'd thought this at once, as soon as Jane spoke. But I saw she was so decided that I did not dare, at that moment, to risk a quarrel. We were happy. Why spoil our joy? Jane had never been to Capri, she was determined to go there; and then I was really abandoning her for a couple of months; at least I could leave her free to choose where. And anyway I knew her so well; by contradicting her one achieved the opposite result. I kept obstinately silent. As soon as I got to Rome I telephoned, without telling her, to a woman doctor, Mrs. Jeans, who was to visit the baby; and I asked her advice.

Mrs. Jeans confirmed my fears. To take the baby to Capri was out of the question. The strong radioactive atmosphere would not suit it. Then at that time of year there was a constant sirocco, the famous "south wind," and one breathed in sand from the African deserts. But she said that I wasn't to worry, as next day, after she'd seen the baby, she herself would dissuade my wife from the idea.

As soon as I got to Rome I also made another telephone call without Jane's knowing. We'd only been settled for a few minutes in two rooms in the Grand Hotel; Duccio was crying, Jane was hurrying to prepare his bottle. I went downstairs with some excuse about the luggage, which had not yet arrived from the airport.

I remembered the number by heart. The booth enclosed me. My heart was pounding. Would I find her again? And would she still be willing to see me?

Through the glass sides of the booth I could see the lobby of the hotel; quiet, silent, with the usual English or American film extras. In a minute or two, perhaps, I would hear Dorotea's voice. The entrance hall, the drawing-room opening out from it through the big glass doors, the carpets, the chandeliers, the flowers, a page boy hurrying by, another sitting at a desk opposite me, all seemed to me solemn and significant, like the moment before a miracle. Everything was full of Dorotea, or of my yearning for Dorotea. In spite of my anxiety, I could not help noticing how a particularly intense emotional state enlarges in space and becomes concrete and recognizable. Bergson has analyzed this psychological phenomenon. But he does not really explain it. Perhaps, just as thought is only language, so passion is only space, time, touch, sense, matter?

It was not her voice. It was the landlady, the old woman, half procuress, so-called nurse, from whom Dorotea rented a room with the use of the kitchen. In practice the two women were intimate friends and lived together in common. I recognized her voice. And she too at once recognized mine. Dorotea was not at home at that moment; but she was here, in Rome, and still living there, thanks be to God.

"It's naughty of you never to have written, *signor maggiore*. We didn't even know if you were dead or alive. Dorotea's very angry with you, *signor maggiore*. Very angry! We've talked of you every day, *signor maggiore*. Dorotea thought she'd never see you again. But I always said to her 'You'll see, the *signor maggiore* will come back. When least you expect it, he'll come back!' We've had a bad winter, *signor maggiore*. Only the other day Dorotea and I went to the festa of the *Madonna del Divino Amore* and prayed for you to return. The Madonna has granted our prayer, *signor maggiore*."

Since the beginning of the conversation I'd had a lump in my throat. Now, absurdly, I was on the point of bursting into tears.

"When does Dorotea return home?"

"Who knows, poor girl? She works, you know. She does sewing for private families. Life's so expensive. You'll have noticed that too, no? All the prices've gone up. You can't make ends meet any more."

"What time can I ring up and be sure of finding her?"

"But what can I say, *signor maggiore?* Try ringing up tomorrow morning about midday, because she sleeps in the morning, poor girl!"

I'd understood everything, of course. She worked at her sewing till four in the morning.

"Would you like me to tell her to ring you? If you give me the number—"

"No, thank you, I'm only passing through Rome. I don't know how long I'll be staying. I may have to leave this evening. At once."

"Leave without even seeing her?" she exclaimed, and almost railed: "But then, excuse me, *signor maggiore*, what was the point of ringing up?"

"I'm leaving, but will be back—will be back for sure. Tell Dorotea that. I'm in Europe for some time. And then, possibly

I may not have to leave at once, now. I'll ring up tomorrow at midday, I hope."

The next day at midday was the exact time I'd arranged to take the baby to Mrs. Jeans.

Mrs. Jeans was an American pediatrician who had settled in Rome immediately after the war, foreseeing that the rapid increase of our American colony would soon guarantee her a large number of patients. Friends in common had talked to us about her in New York before we left.

Duccio had had a bad journey. He'd caught a severe cold and was refusing to eat. Mrs. Jeans did not find anything seriously wrong, but when Jane mentioned Capri, she forbade her to take the baby there, at least for the moment.

Jane refused to listen. With a stubbornness that astounded me and for which I could find no explanation, as soon as we got back to the hotel she took aside the head porter, the excellent Guglielmo, whom we already knew from before, gave him a good tip, and asked him the name of the best pediatrician in Rome, the "Guglielmo of child specialists," explained Jane. Guglielmo, that specialist among hotel porters, went to the telephone, stayed there a quarter of an hour, and finally succeeded in making an appointment for that same afternoon.

The "Guglielmo of child specialists" told Jane exactly what she wanted to hear. He smiled with superiority at Mrs. Jeans's veto. Capri, it was true, was perhaps not exactly the best place. But there was no need for exaggerating, good heavens! It was not at all inevitable that the baby would get ill there. He avowed, on his responsibility, that there was no serious danger in taking him there. He prescribed certain medicines, advised particular attentions, named a doctor at Anacapri, Dr. Cuomo, who was, it seems, particularly good with small babies, and wished Jane a good trip and a pleasant stay. Jane, as she thanked him, said she would be leaving the very next day. I'd never seen her so enthusiastic. And she had changed too since our arrival in Rome. Her cheeks were pink, her eyes glittering, she seemed to have a fever.

I too, alas, had a fever; I had not yet managed to telephone Dorotea! Which was perhaps why I didn't give much thought to Jane's behavior. That afternoon I went out alone to buy a car, which was indispensable for my travels and in which we would drive to Naples next day. I could have telephoned again. But I didn't want to risk not finding her and arouse meanwhile the suspicions of the landlady. Now that I was sure that Dorotea was in Rome it was better to make the most of my prudent silence. If the two women believed I'd left, they would not look for me in the hotels. To find me would have been so easy. A telephone call or two would have done it.

I don't know why I was so frightened. Dorotea had always been very discreet with me. She'd never given me the smallest trouble. Even when she'd asked me for money (which had happened very rarely, for it was always I who had offered it to her spontaneously), she'd done it with great tact, avoiding any possible hint I could construe as blackmail.

But her physical appearance was always in front of my eyes, and that was enough to alarm me. I saw her again, tall, heavy, imposing in her flashy clothes, a low-cut tailor-made or a white dress with red flower designs, her hair drawn back and gleaming, her forearms loaded with big gold bracelets, her long nails, her painted mouth and eyes, her patent-leather shoes, her aggressive walk, her brazen look; and I trembled at the thought of her getting to hear of my marriage and my wife's presence in Rome. I even feared the landlady, who, differently from Dorotea, was undoubtedly a really low and dangerous woman.

We left for Naples before nine next morning so as to arrive in time for the boat. And so I didn't telephone Dorotea that second day either. Telephoning from Capri was quite out of the question; apart from the fact that it would have been as good as giving Dorotea my address, Jane would have known all about it at once, and without Dorotea being the informer. At Capri there lived hundreds of idlers of every kind, vice, and nationality, people different from one another and each variable in himself, but all similar and constant in one irremediable defect—their physical and moral impotence; poor half-spent creatures who, finding no spark of life in themselves any more, busy themselves with the affairs of others even if those others are as dead as they. Seen from outside, their actions appear lively; sufficiently so at least to feed the last embers in their lives, curiosity and gossip. On the other hand the local Capresi (Capresi or Neapolitans established for some generations at Capri) stoke up the embers too. Indefatigably they carry twigs and branches thorny with malice, blow on the flames of envy, watch, point, laugh. This they do partly from financial self-interest, for the foreigners are their livelihood, but partly also from certain natural inclination; they themselves are decadent and decayed; gossips, spies, traitors, liars, actors, sophists, hysterical and tortuous; in fact, profoundly corrupt and unhappy like so many southern Mediterraneans.

The center of gossip was the little piazza, with its three cafés, crowded at every hour of the day; and among the principal sources of information were the post and telegraph offices. Prominent among the natives who were in the confidence of the managers of these two offices was a certain Don Raffaele, a former police functionary, a creature serviceable but servile, quick-witted but untrustworthy, to whom we had been recommended by our friend Guglielmo.

Now if I'd telephoned to Dorotea, Jane would certainly have known at once through Don Raffaele and the telephone office. I did not want to compromise by an imprudence that would anyway have given me only a very brief truncated pleasure the weeks of happiness traveling round Italy with Dorotea, which, after my long fast in America, I yearned for like a thirsty man for water or a starving man for bread. I decided to be patient.

Don Raffaele, warned by Guglielmo, came smilingly to meet us at the Marina Grande. He was a fine-looking man, between fifty and sixty, clean, well shaven, his long, white hair carefully arranged, and a certain British air which began with his blue eyes and ended with his flannel trousers, and which became suspect as soon as he began talking his fluent, inaccurate English, or simply when he just smiled his deceitful Mediterranean smile. Don Raffaele was very useful, but also—how shall I put it?—very exclusive. We had come to him. Excellent. He let us understand very clearly at once that from now on we could not refer to anyone else in Capri on any matter whatsoever. He would help, guide, and protect us. We must put ourselves in his hands. He took us round to visit some villas that were to let, and advised us, almost forced us, to make a definite choice. He sent us the maid, the cook, and the gardener, all three Capresi, who were indispensable for living with any degree of comfort in the villa, which was almost twenty minutes' walk from the piazza. The first night we slept at the Quisisana Hotel. By the afternoon of the next day we had already signed the contract and were settled in the villa.

"Villa Rubini" was writen on the entrance pillars; "Villa" on one side, "Rubini" on the other. *Rubini* in Italian means "Rubies." I never found out whether this was the name of the owner or a poetic name referring to geraniums, bougainvillaea, and other scarlet flowers that decorated the walls and front.

Don Raffaele got money out of us in every kind of way. The rent, the servants, the water for the bath, the water for the garden, the electric light, the tubes of gas, the daily supply of fish, all these and numerous other little jobs went through his friendly and exclusive organization and were the excuse for other little levies we had to pay, pretending to ignore them.

Anyway, I must admit, it was due to him that after a few days the household was in running order. But I could not make up my mind to leave Jane and set off on my tour, which I should already have started. This was one of the rare occasions when my duty coincided with a pleasure usually taken furtively, and my bad conscience kept on producing scruples to make me put my journey off. And these scruples had some foundation. Jane really was nervous, excitable, very thin, and she continually had that feverish air I'd seen in Rome. She would quarrel about trifles, on the slightest excuse. She was impatient with Duccio. At night, when the baby cried, she could bear it no longer. We must have a nurse. Don Raffaele crowned his labors: he immediately discovered in Naples a Swiss girl who specialized in newborn babies. And so, finally, Jane could take a little rest and I could begin my journey.

I left one morning by the five-o'clock boat. When I got up it was still dark. In Jane's sleepy and weeping embrace— No, no; I'm going wrong here. I do remember that dawn, three years ago. But at this point my story is getting confused and risks not being truthful any more.

I was about to describe my farewell to Jane, not as I saw it then, when I left her in Capri with Duccio and was filled with longing for Dorotea, but as it appears to me today.

Yes, Jane, as she embraced me, was sleepy and weeping. But can I say today that I noticed anything particular about that embrace at the time?

Can I say that, as I left the dark disorder of the vaulted little room and went to say good-by to Duccio, who was sleeping next door with the nurse, then walked through the cold blue air up the path toward the piazza, I had given any thought at all to Jane's behavior?

I was feeling emotional and remorseful. I was full of guilt. My own ambiguity tormented me, and I saw Jane only as a personified reproach, the torturing image of my own affection, the object of a passion that was different, but just as real as the one which had spurred me to disentangle myself from that pitiful embrace and was now urging me to hurry up the path, with long, quick strides, so as not to miss the boat.

The grip of her thin, nervous arms round my hips and back (as I bent over her in bed I could smell her slight natural smell, still like an adolescent girl's) had felt like a hair shirt that was punishing me and would, in memory, continue to punish me for my sin.

The narrow path went twisting up stone steps, between continuous walls of gardens and orchards. Indian figs, aloes, olives, mastic, and myrtle sprouted from the walls. I could hear the echoing of my steps, as quick as the beating of my heart. To leave Jane and Duccio like that (Duccio for the first time since his birth!) was almost a physical pain, a sharp weight on the chest. I longed for something to happen which would make me turn back—if only to see them both again, the two dear defenseless creatures who were my care and responsibility, linked together for me in the same tenderness— to see them again, be with them yet another day, and then leave once more. I longed to miss the boat. To miss the boat? But what on earth was going on in my mind? Was I mad? Not for anything in the world could I let another day pass without seeing Dorotea again. Since the week before, I had promised myself that for no reason at all would I stay away from her later than this very day. Miss the boat? Heavens, no! I looked at my watch and began running up the steps. And as I ran farther and farther from Jane I felt, with a pull at the heart, that, yes, my guilt was beginning to diminish; and that in a little, a very little time I would be suffering from it no longer.

When I reached the first house at Tragara I stopped a second, with closed eyes, to get my breath. A quiet voice near by made me start:

"Wake up early, today, *signor maggiore*, eh? Have sleep little?"

It was Salvatore, my gardener, in reality one of Don Raffaele's spies. He was looking at me from an open doorway, in shirt sleeves, a cut-throat razor between his fingers. The sight of his calm, at that moment, irritated me as if it were a malicious comment. And he had also used the infinitive form of the verb to help me understand Italian, which I understood and spoke better than he did himself. As for the *signor maggiore*, in a few days in Capri everyone called me that; for so Guglielmo, who had forgotten to warn me about it, had called me when he telephoned from Rome.

Muttering that I was going to Naples and didn't want to miss the boat, I began to run.

"The boat— *Nun currite, signor maggiore*—don't run— be another half-hour!"

"You filthy spy," I thought as I ran harder than ever, "you're saying that on purpose to make me miss the boat!"

In fact, when I reached the piazza the funicular which goes down to the Marina Grande had left that very moment.

The man in charge and a few idlers hastened to assure me that I could wait and would still be in time if I took the next train down; the boat would not have left. But I could see it down there in the port, like a toy on a spring which would be released at any moment; the water in the port was livid and flat as a sheet of glass; and the cold air, the mountains, the idlers on the terrace, everything around me, seemed motionless, lifeless, deceitful, hostile to my departure. I wanted to be in Rome before midday, so as to see Dora before she got up and went out. I must not lose that boat. I couldn't stand still, even for a moment. At the end of the piazza there was an old taxi waiting there for those who were missing the boat. The owner driver was a fat, dirty man, whom I had already noticed for his provocative and picturesque appearance, like that of a libertine of the later Roman Empire. Don Raffaele, usually benign toward the islanders, had accused this man of exceptional cheating and dishonesty and advised me never to use him. Without a moment's hesitation because of Don Raffaele's warning, I jumped into the taxi and told the fat man to drive me down to the Marina at once.

The fat man got in beside me. The taxi began winding down the hill. The man took the curves at high speed, jabbing into me with his elbow every time.

"Excuse me, *signor maggiore*."

"Of course."

"Going to Naples?"

"Well—to Naples, and on to Rome—then I have to make a tour all over Italy." I don't know why, perhaps out of liking for the fat man who was driving me so violently toward my goal, perhaps out of hatred for Don Raffaele, who certainly didn't like the fat man, I became more confidential than I usually was, particularly with Italians of the lower classes.

The fat man, of course, bridled with pleasure, and soon came up with another question.

"Will you be away long, *signor maggiore*?"

"I don't know, a month or two."

"And the signora?"

"What?"

"Your signora is staying on Capri?"

"Yes."

"That's good."

"Why?"

"The air, the Capri air, the sun, will do her good. She's got thinner, poor thin lady—uh, she's got thinner."

"What do you mean, got thinner?" I laughed, amused. "You've never seen her before! How can you tell she's got thinner?"

"Of course I've seen her! I remember her perfectly! It'd be three years ago, 1944, eh?"

Jane, I thought, as she told me herself, had never been to Capri before. So I didn't understand. After a second's silence and thought, I then pretended to remember:

"Ah, yes, 1944. During the war?"

"Of course! Capri was a rest camp. The signora was in uniform; so beautiful she was! She came here two or three times. For a week, or a fortnight. No one's recognized her now. But I'd driven her too many times. As soon as I saw her—*tracchete*, but it's the very same one, I says; I recognized her at once. I don't make mistakes like that, I'm very good at faces!"

In the first letter I wrote Jane I asked her why she hadn't told me the truth. She replied that she'd thought it would be easier to get my consent by pretending to be curious about a famous place she'd never seen than by giving me the true reason: her wish to return to a place she'd already known and loved. She had so longed to return to Capri that she had lied to me. She begged me to forgive her almost as if I had rebuked her in my letter.

At the Marina Grande, right where the taxi stopped at the entry to the pier, was standing Don Raffaele, elegant in honey-colored jacket and flannel trousers. On seeing me getting out of the taxi and, worse, saying good-by cordially to the fat man, he looked at me angrily, almost grimly. Only when I was a couple of yards from him did he regain his usual smile.

"Leaving, *signor maggiore*?" he said, taking my bag from my hand and walking with me toward the boat at the end of the pier.

I was afraid he might be coming to Naples too. I'd have had to accept his company and chat with him for the whole

crossing. I longed to be alone, to absorb myself uninterruptedly in my compassion for Jane as it gradually diminished,
and my desire for Dorotea as it gradually grew, and so prepare myself to enjoy my pleasure more deeply and completely.

I also feared that diabolic man's quick wits and extraordinary curiosity. If he made the crossing with me, he would
certainly manage to suspect my state of mind and guess part
of the truth.

I was on tenterhooks as I walked beside him toward the
boat. I longed to ask him outright if he was coming to Naples
or not. But I held myself in. Possibly the question alone would
be enough to arouse his suspicions and decide him to come.
Luckily he remained on land. Soon his figure, turning slowly
back along the pier with the *Maresciallo di Finanze*, lost all
its threatening meaning, became nothing but a lightish
splodge, a spot on the island rising, vast and black, with its
walls of rock against the sky.

The sky's color was uncertain. It was impossible to tell
whether it was clear or covered with a network of clouds.
Either the sun was behind the clouds or it had not yet risen.
There was scarcely a ripple on the gray slaty sea as the boat
swung into the open bay.

I looked at the cold, black island. Somewhere on its convulsed and rocky flanks it contained Jane, the sleeping Jane.

Yes, I was freeing myself for a time from my affection
for Jane and Duccio, from a whole area of feelings, and leaving them there, enclosed and as if buried on that island.

I tried to imagine what I'd have felt if I were leaving
Dorotea instead of Jane. Or if—why hesitate? why not write
down this thought too, which I had that morning?—if Jane

were dead, and afterwards I'd married Dorotea, and it was my wife Dorotea, Dorotea the mother of my son, whom I was leaving at Capri, while I went off on business.

As I imagined this I felt a tenderness flooding over me, fusing as never before with passion, leaving me vaguely empty and disappointed at the very thought. Then the sun appeared, and in the sunlight was Naples, yellow and rosy, now very close, welcoming, all around me.

I hurried to the Excelsior garage, where I'd left my car, and set out for Rome.

I can't remember that drive; I don't know, I think I must have driven very fast, I can only remember that the more I pressed on the accelerator, the slower the car seemed to go. I kept looking from the clock to the kilometer stones, the kilometer stones to the clock. Every second I waited for the next stone to appear was an agony; and the interval seemed to get longer and longer between the moment when I finally saw it and when it had flashed by.

How would I find Dorotea again? What would be her action, her gesture when I reappeared? I didn't think, I raved. Again and again I returned to the same visions, as in the delirium of fever. I talked to myself in a loud voice. I muttered, I shouted the absurd words, the mad phrases I would use to her, and, above all, those I'd never use—though perhaps I should have—because I hadn't the courage.

I felt an intense need to smoke but did not light a single cigarette during the whole journey, perhaps so as not to slow up even for a second (I might miss her by just that second, she might have gone out, and I felt I'd go mad if I didn't see her that morning), or perhaps simply to avoid any slackening of tension, any loss of my voluptuous obsession.

I stopped the car under the window of her room, on the mezzanine floor. The shutters were closed. I looked at the time; five minutes to noon. Perhaps she was still sleeping, as was her habit. I entered the house door, went up the dirty stairs, just exactly as I'd imagined so many times during those bitter nights at B——, without any hope that imagination would some day become reality. I rang the bell, the landlady appeared.

"Oh, it's you!" she almost shrieked.

"Is Dorotea in?"

"Yes," she said, "she's asleep."

"Don't wake her, please," I asked her, at once lowering my voice. "Don't wake her yet. I'll wait for her to call you."

Now that I was there, and that Dorotea was a few yards away, behind that door at the end of the passage which I recognized and could see with my own eyes, I wanted to prolong as much as possible the joy of waiting when one knows one won't wait in vain.

"All right," said the landlady, laughing. "You can take her in the coffee yourself. It's almost ready. In a few minutes it'll be noon. She always wakes up when she hears the sirens. Do you know that we'd stopped expecting you, *signor maggiore*?"

I followed her into the kitchen, and when it was ready I took up the little tray with the cup of coffee and the sugar. On tiptoe I went up to the door, turned the knob, entered, shut it behind me.

The room was in half-darkness, the air warm, almost suffocating, impregnated with her scent.

Dora was asleep, her great brown torso rising naked out of the sheets to below her breasts. She was sleeping calmly, on her right side, turned toward me. One arm was under the pillow, the other folded in front of a breast, its wrist loaded with the usual gold bangles.

I stood there motionless, with the coffee tray in my hand, looking at her. The windows were shut, the noise of the city muted.

Then the sirens sounded and Dorotea began, slowly, to move. She opened her eyes, yawned, saw me, rubbed her face, laughed, and said to me calmly:

"So here you are, you rascal? You *have* taken a time!"

I went up to her and whispered: "Dora—"

I stopped. The tray with the little cup was tinkling in my hand.

"Trembling, eh?" she laughed. "And suppose I told you I don't want to make love with you any more?"

I think I must have blanched; perhaps she even thought I was going to faint, for she hastened to reassure me:

"But no, you silly boy, what do you think?" and with a great violent gesture she flung back the sheet and showed herself to me naked, ready, as always.

I hadn't moved.

She stopped me in time.

"Just a second. How American you are, my boy! Coffee first. And it must be hot!"

11.

I took Dora with me. Although I'd thought of doing so from the moment Loewen had suggested the tour through Italy, at heart I had never really considered it possible. First of all I was convinced I would never have the courage. Then,

I knew by experience that for the first few days after my longing for Dorotea was satisfied, rather than any desire for her returning, I preferred not to see her at all; and as I had to leave Rome the day after my arrival from Capri and go straight to Tuscany, where I was to begin my tour, till the last moment I could have sworn I would be leaving alone.

Instead, I took Dora with me. It was a sudden decision, due perhaps to anger, certainly not to surprise, at finding myself disappointed once again after nearly two years away from her; it was a reaction similar to the one that had urged me in the past stubbornly to prolong my nights with her, in the searching hope of perpetual pleasure; it was an extreme attempt, a bet I made with myself, thinking I would never have such a favorable chance (a business journey, Jane immobilized with a small baby) of discovering, by living with Dorotea for several weeks, if nature had really denied me the capacity for married happiness.

The thought of having at the end of the journey to break a link that might meanwhile have become a delicious habit did not worry me at all. On the contrary, in that case I would return to my tenderly bitter life with Jane, comforted by knowing once and for all that I was not condemned to do so by fate, by a forced and therefore undeserved renunciation, but by a free, almost heroic choice.

I wanted, in fact, to try living with Dora; to see if I would become fond of her; to see if she would become fond of me; and above all to see if this fondness, new in our relationship, which had always and only been of another kind, would smother that primitive fire.

It's useless for me to describe the details. Here is the result of the experiment at once: what happened, or what seemed to have happened, to me and Dorotea while we were living together.

Dora, though continuing to make love with me exactly as she had always done, with the cruel and almost mysterious impassivity which was just what I most liked in her, became fond of me; that is, she began to worry about my health, and try to be useful to me in various little ways: ironing my handkerchiefs, packing my suitcases, preparing my bath, looking at the menu in restaurants, advising me about the best and most nourishing food, carrying, as I went round the churches or museums, my album of reproductions, a book, the camera; going out in the morning, while I lay in bed, to buy the newspapers for me; finally, evenings when I was tired and we stayed in the hotel, filling my pipe for me with great care—all things that Jane had never done.

At each of these attentions I, on the other hand, felt a growing sense of discomfort and irritation, a strange intolerance, almost a shame at being too happy. This state of mind ceased only at night, and when I had put out the light. During the day, while Dora was with me, being helpful, respectful, and affectionate, I had a feeling—I don't know how to put it to you—a feeling, well, of being hemmed in on every side, of being suffocated, of being enslaved; a slave not of my own slavery, because I gave the orders and did whatever I liked; but a slave, which was much worse, of her slavery. I was no longer, in fact, free; night and day, in one way or another, either because she was beautiful or because she was now also good, I found myself being forced to show her my reactions. Very soon this became an insufferable torture, worse, perhaps, than I felt with Jane, whose company, though it gave me little pleasure, did at least leave me alone in a sadness I could not confess.

What had I to blame Dorotea for? Nothing. She had accepted my invitation with surprise, humility, enthusiasm. She was never presuming. She thought of herself as a prostitute and nothing else. And if, in spite of my irritation, I continued to trail her round with me, after Tuscany through Emilia, Lombardy, and the Veneto, it was only because at night in her deep humility I was certain to find what I sought.

But why that shame of feeling too happy? Why did I feel that the deep calm in which I was living for the first time was wrong in some way? Was I perhaps thinking of Jane, of Duccio, of the vows I had taken before the Catholic priest? No, definitely not. Jane and Duccio, except for the few minutes during which I wrote or telegraphed to them every two or three days, were canceled from my thoughts, did not exist for me any more. It was not that I believed myself guilty. It was not remorse. It was just the opposite. I felt I was living rightly, I felt I was living truly, and the sensation was disagreeable, almost intolerable, as if I could not breathe.

At night in the calm of a little hotel, in some small provincial town, after a hard day's work under the June sun driving over miles of bad roads to photograph a ruined church or visit a dusty little museum, noting down the director's pathetic list, checking, arguing; after evening had fallen at last; after a good bath, even if the water was cold; after a dinner that was always and everywhere excellent; after a quiet walk in some dark leafy lane or along old ramparts; after a brandy at the table of a little café, holding hands like two young lovers, as some little orchestra played sweetly among the trees and the street lamps; after all that, in the calm and silence of the little hotel Dorotea would make me completely happy. And yet I'd say to myself: "Is this all? Is there nothing else? Really nothing else?" Every desire, natural or acquired, seemed to have left me. I felt empty, dispirited, diminished. Yes, above all diminished. Reduced to being just myself. A spot. A nullity.

And gradually I began to feel this unpleasant sense of being diminished by day too, when I surprised myself in some instinctive act of tenderness for Dorotea, such as an urge to caress her in public, or look at her, or smile at her so that she would smile back, or squeeze her hand, or put an arm round her waist. She would respond, docile as ever; and that, without my being able to say so, vexed me.

Once, at luncheon, she insisted on my eating a couple of raw eggs with pepper and lemon as well as the dishes I'd ordered; *due uova all'ostrica*, as they call them in Italy. She insisted, gazing at me fixedly, with obvious meaning. The idea, the look, the smile, made me pleased and angry at the same time. Angry, almost furious, just because I was pleased. So I could satisfy her as she satisfied me? It was the first time she had shown any sign of it. And this was another disillusion for me. She was no longer an idol. She was just an ordinary woman.

Finally I cut it all short. I'd never told her of Jane's existence or of being married. Every time I had to write, telegraph, or, much more rarely, telephone, to Capri, I did so with extreme caution so that she should know nothing about it. In hotels we would take two separate rooms, not next to each other, though we slept together. My terror of being blackmailed by Dorotea was now quite unreasonable, and perhaps this was only an unconscious stratagem on my part to keep my desire alive.

After the Veneto, my program was to go on into the Marches; but I had to make a visit to Rome, where I was expected by Mr. H. L. G., whom you've met, an important functionary at UNESCO. It was now settled that in the autumn I would go to UNESCO in Paris. Mr. H. L. G. was passing through Rome and wanted to see me. That was the time, as you may perhaps remember, that I lunched with you at Cinecittà together with H. L. G., who wanted to visit the studios.

We were supposed to stay in Rome only two days. I went to the Grand Hotel, Dorotea to her own place. I was very busy with H. L. G. and we did not see each other during those two days. It was understood that on the morning of the third day we would leave together for Ancona.

Late in the afternoon of the second day I accompanied H. L. G., who was returning to Paris, to the airport at Ciampino. The plane left rather late, and toward dusk I found myself alone on the great flat stretch of land between Rome and the Alban Hills. It was early in July. In the vast, deep, cloudless sky glimmered the first stars. The distant housefronts of Frascati were still lit by the afterglow of the setting sun. There was a sweetness in the air, a languor that made it absurd to be alone. Even the big silvery planes maneuvering about the runways, one silently gliding in to land at that moment, seemed part of the enchantment. I telephoned to you, I remember, and asked you to come out and dine with me in some little open-air place in the hill towns. You weren't at home, were still working, and no one knew when you would be back. I went to the bar and drank a couple of whiskies, wondering what to do next. The idea of returning to Rome and dining all alone in the gloomy restaurant of the Grand Hotel, and probably finding myself forced to talk to some American acquaintance whom I couldn't avoid, did not attract me at all. I hesitated and finally, as it was getting dark, rang up Dorotea. What about our dining together? Then, instead of leaving at dawn as we'd arranged, perhaps we might drive through the coolness of the night, which would be much pleasanter. We could sleep till the afternoon at Ancona, and then have a bathe. Was there a good beach near Ancona? There must be.

Dorotea replied that she very much wanted to come; but, thinking she wasn't going to see me, she'd made an engagement. She was dining in a *trattoria* with her brother-in-law, who had to talk to her about certain family matters. I lost my temper; it was the first, perhaps the only time I ever treated her badly. Perhaps I was letting out in that way the ill humor of the past month. Dora was very distressed. She would have put the appointment off if she could, she said, and seen her brother-in-law another time. But now it was too late to warn him, he had no telephone and lived a long way off. He was expecting to meet her at the *trattoria*. By that time he would certainly have left home, and she herself, when I rang, was just on the point of leaving too.

"If you'd like to come with me—" she finally said hesitatingly, "I'll introduce you; he's a good person, a family man. He works for the cinema, as a fire specialist—you know, every time there's any fire or smoke or fireworks to be arranged, they call him."

Dora had never told me she had a sister.

"I'd never told you because my sister died years ago. He's

married again. He has four children, they're at the seaside at Ladispoli. Will you come? Do, if you don't mind. We're at the Osteria della Pesa, in Trastevere, Via Garibaldi."

"I'll come and get you," I said angrily, feeling I could not bear to spend the evening alone, and no desire at all to meet this brother-in-law.

But she would not let me call for her. She'd already called a taxi, she said. She was late. With a sudden decisiveness that surprised and pleased me, she repeated the exact address of the *trattoria* and rang off.

As opposed to Jane, whom I trusted completely, everything regarding Dorotea made me suspicious. As I returned to Rome, I thought it all over and decided that this brother-in-law wasn't a brother-in-law at all and that she'd wanted to reach him at all costs before I did, so as to warn him of her lie. And now, naturally, Dorotea's lie began to interest and excite me. I at once got the idea, with a mixture of fear and hope, that this was some low creature, a kind of *souteneur*.

He was a pale, fat, bald, hairless man, with a big nose and two blue, watery, gentle, yet astute eyes. He was dressed with a certain elegance, but wore no tie. He was very agreeable. He had the air of a pimp and might also be an old *souteneur*. Sitting with him and Dorotea at a table where I saw them at once among all the tables full of clients, at the end of a long courtyard enclosed by the high red walls of ancient tumbledown houses, was also a young man; he was a tall, handsome, dark young man with gleaming curly hair and singularly gentle lively eyes; he wore no jacket, only a silk jersey, which showed his well-made torso; he had a gold bracelet and a watch with a gold band on his wrist, a heavy gold ring on one finger, and a gold chain with a small medal on it round his throat.

Dorotea saw me from afar and made a sign to the two, as if to say: "There, he's here." The two men jumped to their feet; the old one, the brother-in-law—real or false—took a step or two toward me through the tables, doing his utmost, by gestures, bows, and smiles, to be ingratiating.

He was certainly a pleasant fellow. As he ate with gusto, offering food or wine with even more gusto, praising and criticizing ceaselessly, telling little anecdotes about his work on his last film or banal little jokes, he was smiling with enjoyment at the dinner, at spending the evening with us, as if he wanted nothing more in all the world. He showed the sinner's kindliness and humility. The young man was very much more reserved. He scarcely spoke at all, ate moderately and with studied composure, as if not to make a bad impression on me. He was a friend of her brother-in-law's, Dorotea explained at once, and he too worked in the cinema, as a small-part actor. I realized that the youth had seen a dazzling combination in me: I was a gentleman, an intellectual, and, what was more, on top of all that I was also an American. From self-interest, or more probably from simple vanity, he was anxious to make a good impression. That was why he ate and spoke so little. But he was apt to make an unnecessary show, at least with me, of the hand with the bracelet, watch, and ring. Every time Dorotea or I or the brother-in-law put a cigarette to our lips, he hastened to extract a lighter, also of gold, which he snapped under our noses with a great show of that hand. Or if he smoked himself, he held the cigarette with the hand arched in mid-air, almost so that even those at the other tables should admire it. It was a beautiful hand, certainly, as far as a man's hand can be beautiful; but nothing justified that repeated, incessant exhibition of it.

At a certain moment the brother-in-law—let's call him that—with a wink at Dora and me, began poking fun at the young man in a jolly way.

"*Figlio bello,*" he would say, "but of course you don't understand the first f— thing about wine. Excuse my language, *signor maggiore,* you understand Italian perfectly, I know, so we must be careful what we say."

I laughed with amusement: amid the shouts and laughter of the other customers, the clank of cutlery, someone singing rhymed couplets from table to table with an accordion, the summer night, and this company warm with vulgar humanity, I felt relaxed, finally freed, without any regrets, from the last prejudices that still clung to me from old New England, and plunged into a pagan world where all reality has soaked in sin and forgiveness. How different from those evenings with the Pratts!

"You see, *figlio bello,*" the brother-in-law went on to the young man, who was smiling and trying to take the twitting as unconcernedly as he could, "you don't understand wine any more. You're degenerate. Don't you see, *signor maggiore,* what he does? He puts ice in it! Why, with all your little film jobs, and playing up to foreign ladies, and all your whisky, gin, martini, '*hello, gimme a drink*'—isn't that how you say it in English, *signor maggiore?* Well, you've spoiled your palate. And I hope it's only that!"

I listened, and meanwhile tried to imagine what were the real relations between Dorotea and those two, and between those two among themselves. At first, perhaps because of that vaguely ambiguous air they both had, and considering their difference in age (the brother-in-law was about fifty, the young man twenty-five), I had thought that the two were more than friends. But when the older man began poking fun at the other so cordially and jollily, without the slightest hint of acidity, I realized I was on a wrong track. It was with Dorotea that one or the other, or perhaps both, had relations. And I did not—I confess it quite willingly because it's true—feel any jealousy at all.

While I was jealous of Jane (jealous perhaps just because I did not love her, or did not love her enough, and felt that I could not give her all that she may have wanted), I had never been, at that period at least, jealous of Dorotea. It was part of Dorotea's nature, of her very fascination, that she went with other men. I never thought of giving her anything but money. She, the idol, would have despised any other gift from me; I'd have been disappointed if she hadn't. So I did not dream of claiming any rights over her. I had no longing for her to be faithful to me; I thought that finding out about her lovers would leave me indifferent, or even stimulate me. Later, when my vanity came into play, things became more complicated and everything changed. But at that time that was the way I felt, and I'm not ashamed of it; nor am I ashamed of writing it. And anyway, if one thinks it over, nothing is more unjust and more ridiculous than the way custom—above all, in France and Italy—condemns the betrayed husband or lover. No man is considered ridiculous for loving a woman who is married or tied to others; well, he *desires someone else's woman* no less than does the husband or the lover, who continues to love his wife or his mistress even when she betrays him, or perhaps just because she does betray him.

The brother-in-law talked on and on. The young man went on smoking, to show his hand. Dorotea looked at me from time to time with strange, cautious, scrutinizing glances; she didn't want me to realize it, but she was trying to guess what I was thinking.

And I was thinking that I would leave her that night. Why? From jealousy?

On the contrary. Meeting those two, suspecting they were perhaps her lovers, had fanned, not quenched my passion. But just because this drew my link to her closer, it seemed to me that I could now interrupt it for a time without harming it. If I had interrupted it before that evening and just left her after the gradual cooling off of the last month, I would have been afraid of losing my taste for her forever. Instead of which I wanted to leave her that very moment; while I found myself desiring her again as I had in the very beginning, and while I felt certain I'd desire her in the future and during separation, till I went to her again.

Dorotea was scrutinizing me. She was intelligent, and understood something of what was going on in my mind. For example, she'd understood perfectly that I'd realized those two were her lovers, and that it did not worry me. At the same time, I'm certain, she also read in my face the secret, sudden decision I'd taken to leave her. But she did not take the final step; she did not manage to guess (how could she have?) the subtle reasoning that persuaded me to leave her. She did not know how to conciliate the opposing feelings that agitated me and that I, on the other hand, had ended by conciliating in my own way. She thought that, mingled with my pleasure at meeting her lovers, I also felt annoyance. She feared my vanity and the prejudices due to my education. She was regretting having introduced me to them.

What would have happened if she had understood everything? If, conscious finally of her power over me, she had risked the grand melodramatic gesture, the cruel farewell that one used to read about in French novels and see in German films? If she had got up with the self-possession of a treacherous woman, taken the handsome young man by the arm, and gone off, saying calmly: "We'll see each other tomorrow, Harry, as usual," or even: "Look, I can't leave tomorrow morning after all. Come and call for me in the afternoon at six. There's no use your ringing me before. *Ciao*"—how would I have reacted?

Oh, I don't think I would have rebelled. Those words, or worse, were precisely what I most longed to hear. No, I wouldn't have rebelled. Perhaps I'd have loved her for the whole of the rest of my life.

But she was not a treacherous woman.

She was rather a good girl, all told; worried about her future and how to rub along from day to day.

The time came to go. I offered to take them back to the center of Rome; and left them, all three, at her front door, saying someone was waiting for me in the hotel. My idea was to show Dorotea that I wasn't jealous.

But Dorotea became suspicious. She took me aside. The other two, with quick discretion, moved away a few yards.

"You said you wanted to leave now so as to travel while it's cool?" she whispered. "Do you still want to? My bags are ready."

"No, thank you, Dorotea," I said hesitantly, "I really have an appointment now with that man."

"But you told me he'd left."

"Not with that one, with another one I met later. I may not be leaving tomorrow morning either."

"How am I to know?"

"I'll ring you. Tomorrow morning. Not before ten anyway. So sleep sound."

And I kissed her hand with ostentatious correctness, as Italians do to married ladies; I intended to let her understand, if she could understand, that she was her own mistress.

"Do whatever you like," I added in a whisper, trembling and hoping she would understand.

She didn't understand. She looked disconcerted and glanced toward the two for a second; then, instead of leaving me, came up closer, almost touching me with her whole body, and enveloping me in her cheap scent.

"What's wrong with you?" she breathed. "Are you annoyed at my introducing you to my brother-in-law?"

"Good God, no!"

"Or the other one?"

"You're dreaming. They're so nice, both of them. I've had a wonderful evening."

I broke away, walked up to the two men, and bade them a cordial good-night.

Then I went straight to bed. But I couldn't get to sleep. After an hour I got up, dressed again, packed my bags, went downstairs, and handed the porter a telegram to be delivered in Rome next morning. The telegram told Dora that I'd had to leave unexpectedly for Paris by a night plane. We would see each other on my return, in about a month. I thanked her.

I did in fact leave that night; but by car, for Ancona, to my work.

12.

Before crossing the Apennines, I took in more gas at Foligno. While I was waiting at the gas pump, I glanced at the map. There was a choice of two routes: one, to the right, through Tolentino and Macerata; the second, to the left, through Nocera, Fabriano, and Iesi. The first was a bit shorter, but also narrower. The second wider—and it passed through Iesi. The name of the little town roused a memory in me of a woman in an icy winter during the war, and farther back in the past of the same woman when I was still a youth, during my first journey to Italy, just after I'd left college.

Of course I chose the road through Iesi. I wanted to go through that town once again, up the wide, straight main street, past the yellow-gray palaces gloomily lining it, to the little piazza with the church, and see again, as I passed, a house, a doorway, some windows on the second floor, catch the echo of a thought, a dream, an unappeased desire I'd once had.

She was called Checchina. When I came to Rome for the first time, toward the end of 1938, it was long, of course, before the days of Fulbright scholarships. Scholarships then scarcely paid one enough to lead a decent life. But I was twenty-four and so happy to be in Italy!

I went to live in a *pension* in the Corso d'Italia, with some people called Cottich, from Trieste. The maidservant was from the Marches, from Fontanelli, near Iesi. That was

Checchina. She was twenty-one. Dark, tall, slim, with a perfect body and gentle, refined, almost finicky manners. In Italy maidservants can be distinguished at once when one sees them in the street. Checchina, when she went out, seemed like a middle-class young lady, a secretary in an office.

She attracted me at once. But I was chaste then. We Americans, especially if we are intellectuals and from New England, are not at all like you Italians. Today perhaps things are changing a bit. Then—that is, until the Second World War —many of us even married without ever having had any decisive sexual experience beforehand. At college, if one went out with a girl friend in the evening, it was to the cinema or, if one had any money, to the theater and afterwards—if the girl lived in a hired room outside the university (we boys all lived at the college, because it cost less)—one drank lots of Martinis to give one courage, and then we would caress each other in every sort of way; but we practically never reached the extreme conclusion. And so though I courted Checchina, gave her as many tips as I could afford, and after some time even gave her little presents in kind, all I dared to take in return were a few light caresses when she brought me my coffee in the morning. I thought I had all the time in the world, and every day put things off till later. Meanwhile I liked chatting to her. She talked such beautiful Italian, so clean, without the slovenliness of the Tuscans or the aggressive sag of the Romans. One of your authors, whose name I can't remember, has written a book on the Italian language called *The Gentle Language*. Here, in Checchina's mouth (delicious scarlet lips without a touch of lipstick, and tiny white teeth), here was Italian that was really *gentle*.

Meanwhile war was getting nearer. The Consulate called

all Americans in Rome and advised them to prepare or at least to begin considering having to leave at a moment's notice. Many left at once, terrified. Others like me, who adored Italy, refused to believe in the threat, or took refuge in wishful thinking, and remained.

Thinking it over now, I'd say that the possibility of leaving should have made me get to grips with Checchina. And yet I didn't. The danger of war had almost the opposite effect and I went on as I had before; my caresses became even less expansive. She used to tell me every little thing about her family and her home at Fontanelli. They were peasants; the sisters worked at Iesi, in a china factory. We became friends. There was a tenderness, a curious confidence between us. And, at least on my part, a constraint, a timidity, a scruple that I couldn't manage to shake off.

One night, when I got home about eleven, the household was asleep. I walked in on the tips of my toes, as usual, so as not to make any noise. A long passage led to my room. I didn't even put the light on, because the passage was lit by a glass door that led to the bathroom. Over this door there were rubber curtains, which let the light through, but prevented one's seeing inside. But they weren't up that night. The *pension* was being cleaned out at the time, and perhaps the curtains had been taken down for washing. Instinctively I stopped in front of the glass door and looked in. That was the time when, after her day's labors, Checchina would take a bath. And I could see her quite clearly through the opaque greenish glass. She was lying in the bathtub, almost motionless. I could see the black splodge of her hair, the small oval of her face, without distinguishing the features, the slim body in the water, and that other, smaller black spot.

I stood there looking at her, holding my breath, giving furtive glances to right and left from time to time, for fear someone from the *pension* would come out of one of the rooms. I stayed there till Checchina got up and began washing herself. Then very slowly, taking advantage of the splashing to cover the sound of my steps, I went on to my room.

But that picture remained in my mind and I did not undress.

Taking off my shoes, I stood listening behind the door. I was waiting to hear Checchina come out, then follow her and join her in her room before she locked herself in (for she would certainly lock herself in). I certainly couldn't risk knocking at her door, as her little room was next to that of the Cottichs.

Unfortunately, at the same second that Checchina left the bathroom I heard the front door opening; a certain Nakim, an attaché at the Egyptian Embassy, came in at that very moment. This Nakim had never been a person I liked; at table he always led the conversation on to politics, and afterwards I would regret having talked to him, so unpleasant did I find his views. He was a pro-Fascist and anti-Bristish; he avowed great respect for America, and was always trying to show the differences between us and the English, which made me more annoyed than ever.

How I'd have liked to kill him that night! Not only had I to renounce Checchina; but a few minutes later, as, resigned to this, I was about to lie down, I heard a knock at my door. I jumped to my feet, in the absurd momentary hope that it might be Checchina. Instead of which it was he, the Egyptian; he put his ugly features through the half-open door and, his big lips open in a mellifluous obscene smile, gave me appalling news. Hadn't I heard the radio? Hitler had entered Poland, Chamberlain would declare war next day.

I embarked from Naples a few days later. Before leaving I gave Checchina a really big present, which I had difficulty in getting her to accept. Then at the last moment I called her to help me finish packing and gave her a kiss, just a single kiss. She cried. I could taste the bitter tears mingling with the fresh peasant flavor of her mouth. I squeezed that slim, strong, pliant body, that waist so narrow that I could reach round it with my hands. She kissed me with her eyes closed as if she were drinking some new liqueur; and arching her back with a violence I would never have suspected of her, she pressed her belly against me, offering herself to me.

But when, a few seconds later, we loosened our embrace, she was, of course, grateful to me for not having gone farther. She smiled at me, her eyes full of tears, and excused herself.

You will laugh at me, perhaps. But I've been cynical enough in other parts of this account, I think, to be allowed, now, a bit of sentiment, even of sentimentality; and to be believed. For you must believe in her purity. Just as she had offered herself to me with fear a second before, now she thanked me, without regrets, for having respected her.

When I returned to Italy with the army, as soon as Rome was liberated I looked for Checchina. The Cottichs had returned to Trieste, the *pension* had passed into the hands of others and now called itself Pensione Shelley. No one knew anything about the maidservant.

The Marches were liberated in the summer of 1944. I thought of Checchina sometimes, particularly when the bulletins mentioned Iesi and Fontanelli, where, I supposed, Checchina had returned for the duration of the war. But I was

THE CAPRI LETTERS

very busy and could not leave Rome; and I'd already met Jane and Dorotea.

Checchina was a distant, youthful, almost literary idyll. I thought of her as a character in some romantic tale. Sometimes, though, the memory would flash back of her naked body in the bath as it had appeared to me through that green glass; and I would remember the thrust and abandon of her farewell kiss; and my desire for her.

In November or December of that same year '44, before I went to France to visit Jane, P.W.B., on which I depended, told me to accompany three Italian journalists to the front, so that they could write articles for their papers.

First we visited the so-called Gothic Line, the Fifth Army front; then we turned back to Foligno and over the Apennines toward the Adriatic, where the Eighth Army was then operating.

By pure chance, we happened to stop at Iesi for the night. The hotels were all requisitioned, and full. Two of the journalists put up in the huts of the headquarters of the Italian troops, then mainly transport troops, fighting with us. The third journalist and I found a couple of rooms in a private home, an apartment on the second floor, in the main street, which crossed the whole town. There was a small plate on the door, with a name on it that I've now forgotten, but which that night, as I sat there at the gas-supply point, I remembered perfectly as soon as I saw Iesi on the map. It was some modest, ordinary little Italian name, ending in *ini*, *elli*, or *etti*. How I wish I could remember it now, for if I did I'm sure it would help me to describe the little apartment, clean, poor, redolent of avarice and dignity, behind that name and door! Gleaming red floors of small hexagonal bricks; little rooms furnished in the style of the late nineteenth century, with the chairs and sofas in white covers: fireplaces with vases of artificial flowers inside glass domes; high iron bedsteads, heaped with heavy coverlets and knitted white bedspreads. The electricity had not yet been restored. Signor—the owner, whose name I cannot remember, was a strong, tall, rather bent old man, bald and red-faced; he gave the journalist and me each a candle, carefully fixed in blue enamel sconces. We paid in advance because we had to leave early the next morning. The furniture, the decorative objects, the mementos, were all properly arranged and clean; but it was appallingly cold. The owner, who was going round the house wrapped in an overcoat and woolen scarf, said that he did not heat the place because it was too expensive.

We went out to dine, then came back to sleep. That little apartment, with its order and its iciness, had fascinated me. The truth is that, from the first moment of my entering it, I'd thought of Checchina. And now, when I slipped into bed between the rough sheets and lay gazing at the little room by the gentle light of the candle burning on the night table, I told myself that Checchina was certainly not far away, that Fontanelli was only a mile or so from Iesi, and that if I'd gone to look for her that evening, perhaps she would now at this very moment be lying in that bed with me. It was so cold that I could see each breath rise in a slight cloud and then dissolve in the dim light. I thought of Checchina's body beside me between the rough sheets. She must be twenty-seven by now; and I was thirty. Six years had gone by!

I woke up before dawn. And went out at once. To Fontanelli. I wanted to see Checchina again, or find out what had happened to her. Of course, I did not mention this to the journalist. All I said was that I had to go to the Town Major or the car pool, I don't remember which, and made an appointment to meet him at exactly eight o'clock in front of the Italian headquarters.

A quarter of an hour later I was at Fontanelli in my jeep. I remembered Checchina's surname. I can remember it even now, but won't write it down; it was the same surname as that of a great Italian philosopher. The difficulty, as happens with us too in some small villages in the Middle West where immigration has ceased, that nearly every family in Fontanelli had the same name.

But on going into the tobacconist's and stopping for a moment's chat with the excuse of buying cigarettes, I traced Checchina without any difficulty. She was there, alive and well, and about to have a baby. She had married the year before, when the Germans were still there. Her husband was a fine young fellow, they told me, who now drove trucks for the Allies. I was uncertain whether to see her or not, and was also afraid of giving her a shock in her condition. So I decided to leave. I asked the tobacconist to give her warm greetings "from the American student of Corso d'Italia."

But I had just turned the jeep in the muddy road, pitted with deep cart tracks, outside the village, and was heading toward Iesi, when I heard gay shouts behind me. There was Checchina, with a red handkerchief on her head, running toward me. I jumped down from the jeep, my knees trembling.

She was pregnant, certainly. But what a delight it was to see her again! Her look, her smile were just the same. She had changed in only one thing. She'd always been lively and intelligent, but now she was also at ease.

"How are you, Signorino Harry? How good of you to

come! Do you know that as soon as the Allies began advancing toward here, my mother kept on saying: if only Signorino Harry'd come this way! I was just going toward the Iesi road to look at the trucks passing by! I really was! First I learned to distinguish the Americans from the English and the Poles. Not many Americans pass this way. And this will make you laugh: the ones there were nearly all seemed to look like you!"

"It's the first time I've been sent to this front, or I'd have come to see you before," and I added in a light tone, using the formal third person and avoiding any hint of sentiment, from respect for her new condition: "I haven't forgotten anything, either. How often I've thought: what's Checchina doing?"

"You know, you haven't changed at all. . . . You've become more of a man, of course! But perhaps that's the uniform. . . ."

She was at ease, pouring out rapidly, happily, her beautiful limpid Italian, in a tone that in spite of its simplicity was almost worldy, almost smart. Perhaps she was overcoming her shyness in this way, hiding her emotion and surprise. Perhaps there was—who knew?—also a touch of vanity in her attitude; some women had come out on the steps of the nearest houses and were standing there looking at us from afar; Checchina must be pleased at their seeing her in the company of an American officer, one, perhaps, she'd already talked to them about.

"Come along, Signorino Harry," she said finally, taking me by an arm, "come to our home and have some coffee with us. I'll introduce you to my husband. He's still asleep because he only just got back with his truck late last night. But he'll be getting up now. Or perhaps you don't like coffee and milk?

You'd prefer a glass of aquavite? We make it ourselves, it's really pure!"

Looking at my watch, I told Checchina that I was expected back in Iesi and was already late. I thanked her warmly, but really couldn't come; I'd be back, I said, as soon as I could.

She looked very disappointed and sad at my leaving at once.

"If only I'd known," I said, as I climbed back into the jeep, "I'd have brought you something for the baby. . . ."

I had some cans in the jeep, the usual military rations, jam, pork and beans, Spam. I hesitated a second. But she did not seem to be in want. And the present, the usual one all our GI's gave to Italian girls, might, it seemed to me, have offended her.

I said good-by, wished her luck, and started off. At the corner I turned and looked back. She was still standing where we had said good-by and had taken off her red handkerchief and was waving it at me.

Of course I didn't return. I had behaved myself. War, contrary to what is generally thought, makes people more humane. The surrounding horrors, death and slaughter, produce beneficent reactions; they prevent confusion of feeling; they get things into proportion in men's hearts. The smile of a bride has a meaning then. But perhaps it was just that I was younger. I had not yet been corrupted by my passion for Dorotea and my marriage to Jane.

I didn't return. Sometimes I thought of Checchina; she would come into my mind at night before I went to sleep, and I'd tell myself that the next day I'd try to remember to go into some shop and buy clothes, toys, presents for the baby, make up a good-sized package and send it off to her. But then I was lazy and forgot, as we are always apt to be lazy and forgetful when we have only to be kind.

And now here I was in the summer night on the road to Iesi again. In a short time, before reaching the town gates, I would see a sign on the right, with an arrow: *"To Fontanelli."*

I saw it, slowed down an instant, looked at the time, half past three, and went on. Another three years had gone by. Was Checchina still there?

Driving into Iesi, I thought of her, and remembered her not as I had seen her that morning, a wife, soon to be a mother, but as she had been years before, in Rome, when I'd held her tight in my arms. I felt again, with a nervous impact that nearly took my breath away with sudden desire, the surge of her belly against mine. At that moment I passed in front of the house where I'd spent that night in the war, thinking of Checchina, years ago, and stopped almost involuntarily at the door.

It was not yet four o'clock. The blue light of dawn was already spreading over the long, deserted street. The asphalt was smooth and clean. (The war had ended long ago.) At that moment all the street lamps went out. And the ancient prospect of palaces and houses seemed intact, in that ghostly light, like scenery on an empty stage, seen by muted daylight filtering through a window.

I got out of the car. On one side of the door, set in a stone pillar, were the names of the various tenants, beside their respective bells. I found the name at once, for I still remembered it then. But I didn't ring. I went and sat in the car again. Was I mad? Had I seriously considered ringing at that hour? And at the bottom of my heart, without reasoning, but just as one fumbles through the depths of some old drawer without looking in, I found Dorotea, my disillusion of the evening before and of a whole month with her, my disappointment that Dorotea was not all that I had foolishly hoped her to be, my hatred of myself. I wanted another woman, today, now. I wanted Checchina. I knew that I could have Checchina at any moment of my life when I really wanted her. But I realized that to persuade her to come to a hotel, one of the little hotels in Iesi, would be a criminal thing to do. And although I was selfish, corrupt, and a sinner, although I was a coward too, I was not a criminal.

The day now beginning was a Sunday. It was quickly growing lighter. The whitening light was showing up the limpid prospect of houses more and more clearly. A ray of sun, at the end, touched the church and the tops of the highest buildings. No one passed. Shut up in the car, I dozed away for a time, waiting.

I was waked by the ringing of bells. There were a few passers-by now, people going to the first Mass, perhaps. I wandered up and down the main street in search of a bar. They were all shut. I went to the railway station and drank a cup of coffee, then back to the main street, to the same doorway, and looked up at the windows on the second floor; they were still closed.

Finally, at half past seven, I rang the bell. The street door opened by itself. I climbed the narrow stairs between enclosing walls. On the landing of the second floor was standing the owner of the apartment; older, more bent, wrapped in a woolen dressing-gown. I tried to remind him who I was. Hopeless; he couldn't remember. During the war so many soldiers, English or American, had lodged there. Now, he said, he no longer let rooms. His wife was dead. He lived alone, was pensioned off; he'd been the clerk of the magistrate's court. I said, without caring how odd it must have sounded, that I wanted to spend a day, just a single day, in Iesi; that I would be leaving for Ancona before midnight; that I'd come from Rome, been driving all night, was dead tired and needed to rest; that I'd been waiting below since dawn, in my car, so as not to disturb him; and that I didn't want to go to a hotel because I'd liked his home so much, particularly that room (I pointed it out to him, from the landing, through the open door) where I'd slept one night in November 1944.

He looked at me in amazement.

"No, I'm not mad," I said, trying to give as serene a smile as I could, "I'm just a sentimentalist, a romantic. I'm an artist," I even added. "A painter. You must excuse me."

"I am sorry, *signore*," he replied with a movement almost as if to push me toward the door, "but I can't. It's Sunday. I don't cook myself, you know. The woman who works for me doesn't come today. And the room isn't habitable. There are no sheets, or blankets, or anything."

I said that it didn't matter, I could sleep perfectly well on the mattress. Finally, as I talked, I took out the money I had in my pocket, some ten-thousand-lire notes.

"I'll give you ten thousand lire," I said to him, avoiding saying more not because I wasn't prepared to pay more but only because I feared that an even larger sum might arouse his suspicions, with opposite results.

The poor old man, whose monthly pension was perhaps only slightly more than what I was offering him for a day's

THE CAPRI LETTERS

121

rent, gazed, almost in spite of himself, at the big note I was holding out to him, and stood there motionless, undecided, his eyes half-shut.

"Here's my passport," I then said with a sudden inspiration. "Look at the photograph. Examine it. I'm an American citizen. And please keep it. You can give it back when I leave."

I handed him the passport, and with it the ten-thousand-lire note.

"But it doesn't say 'Painter' here," he observed. "Here it says '*College Teacher.*' That's not the same thing, it seems to me."

"Yes it is, because though I'm a painter, I teach art history at a university in America."

"All right," he said then. Trembling slightly, he folded the bank note and put it in his pocket, then moved ahead of me to his front door and opened it wider for me. "If you'll wait a moment, I'll get you some sheets and blankets."

I protested that I didn't need them; but he insisted, and went out, dragging his feet in their slippers. He returned at once, and then tried to make the bed up for me himself; but I thanked him and refused to allow it.

Once alone, I went to the window and threw it open, for the room smelled as if it had been closed a long time. Leaving the shutters open, I glanced down into the street, which was now getting more animated, then threw myself on the bed. When, how soon, could I decently appear at Fontanelli?

I set off toward eleven o'clock. Before that I wandered all over Iesi, trying to find a shop open. I wanted to take some presents—toys, clothes—for Checchina's child. This time I must not arrive empty-handed. Only confectioners' were open. I bought a cake and a box of candy.

When I reached Fontanelli, people were just coming out of Mass. So as not to be conspicuous, I'd left the car outside the village. But everyone, I realized, noticed at once that I was a foreigner and looked at me curiously. I'd been silly; my car would soon be noticed too, and my prudence arouse more suspicions than ever. So I turned back to get into the car and park it openly in the square in front of the church. But before I'd reached the end of the village, a woman caught up with me and stopped me by saying in an undertone: "You're looking for Checchina, aren't you?"

"That's right," I replied in surprise. "How did you know?"

"Weren't you here once, one morning during the war? As a soldier? An American, in a jeep?"

"Yes, I was, but you—?"

"Oh, it's nothing, I just remembered. I'm a friend of Checchina's. Checchina has always talked about you. Even since the war, even nowadays."

"How is Checchina?"

"She's very well. She's had another baby. There are two of them now, two little boys. They're all doing fine. Come, and I'll take you to Checchina's home. She'll be pleased to see you."

We turned off by a side street, and then into a lane of beaten earth, between gardens, vineyards, and a few new houses with red roofs and green shutters, looking like a cross between farm cottages and little villas. Finally the woman, who'd been walking quickly and silently ahead of me, said: "She's here," and pointed to a house rather larger and more pretentious than the others; surrounded, as the others weren't, by iron railings and a small garden. "Wait here. Checchina'll soon come, you'll see."

"But perhaps she's busy. Tell her I'm sorry to disturb her. If I could have warned her—"

"Don't worry. She's with the children. But I'll look after them, for a minute or two," and her big rosy face with its two sharp, lively, intelligent black eyes smiled at me knowingly and kindly.

A few seconds later Checchina appeared at the door. She was slim, her hair carefully done, and smartly, almost townily dressed in a pretty coat and skirt of sky-blue, with a big white flower in the buttonhole. Sunday, of course; perhaps she'd just that moment returned from Mass.

"Signor Harry!" She ran toward me so impetuously that for a moment I thought she was going to embrace me. "I always knew in my heart of hearts that I'd see you again! Thank you for coming!"

"But how did your friend here recognize me?" I said, calling her by the familiar *tu* without realizing it, while the time before I had called her *lei;* and also without realizing it stretching out my free hand and touching her elbow and arm.

Checchina then, lowering her eyes and blushing, explained: "It was I who saw you, Signor Harry!—from far off as I came out of Mass; you were in the middle of the piazza, and I recognized you at once, yes, at once. I felt such a thrill, but a lump in my throat too. I didn't dare go up to you in the middle of all that crowd. So I sent my friend. You know what a village is like. They're very simple here, with narrow little minds, and think the worst at once! Last time you came it was wartime, and everyone talked to the Americans. And I was just going to have my first baby then. Did you know I've another one now? He's eight months old. If you could see how adorable he is, Signor Harry!"

She no longer called me *Signorino*.

"How good of you to come—" but suddenly she was silent. I remained silent too. It crossed my mind that I perhaps ought to tell her I was also married, and also had a baby now. But I was afraid if I did I might compromise the real purpose of my visit, which was not, I'm afraid, just sentimental this time. So I said nothing. We looked each other straight in the eyes, standing there in the July sun, in the rustic Sunday silence, a silence delicately touched, rather than broken, by the quiet clucking of hens, the wail of a child (perhaps from the house? perhaps one of hers?), a bell tolling the midday Angelus from a distant village.

"Checchina," I said, putting a hand on the back of hers, and the contact was as sweet as the sweetest kiss, "Checchina, I'd like to be with you a little longer. . . ."

"I'm sorry," she murmured, lowering her eyes again as if she had not the strength to resist my look. "I'm sorry I can't ask you to come into the house this time, Signor Harry. My husband's not here. He left this morning with his truck for Foggia. I'm alone with my mother and the little ones. And, as I've already said, it's a tiny village. They'd gossip at once."

The husband wasn't there? When was he coming back? Then she could get away for an hour or two? To Iesi? Did she never go to Iesi? Yes, sometimes, and usually, as a matter of fact, on Sundays. Sunday evenings. She would put the children to bed, leave their grandmother at home to look after them, and go off to Iesi with her woman friend, or her husband if he was home, to the cinema.

So it *was* in the cards. I gazed at Checchina, almost trem-

bling with excitement and pleasure. Motherhood had broad-
ened her hips, so that her waist, which had always been narrow, seemed very much narrower. Her breasts were not big,
but high, jutting, round. Her mouth, her look, showed at that
moment a deep happiness from the union of desire and hope.

I gave her the exact address of the house and explained
everything. I'd be looking at the street from behind the shutters, watching out for her. At exactly eight o'clock she was to
walk up and down in front of the street door. Then I'd see
her and hurry down to open it without her having to ring
the bell. I didn't want the old landlord to notice her visit; he
might have objected. Then, after handing the packages of
sweets for the children over to her and just resisting the temptation to squeeze her waist for a second, I hurried away before anyone should appear.

I ate at a *trattoria*, then slept soundly for the whole of
the afternoon, lying naked in the dark little hot room, on a
sheet I had thrown over the mattress. Now I was sure.
Checchina would be coming at eight. In an hour or two, after
all these years, she would be mine. Never, I felt, had I been
so happy as I was lying there. And I realized that my stubborn
determination to be with Checchina in that very room was not
madness. That late nineteenth-century room, with its dignity, its severity, its modesty, was the most suitable scene and
background for the loss of a young mother's honor; it seemed
to promise, almost to guarantee, pleasure. Anywhere else the
sacrifice of Checchina's virtue would have meant much less to
me.

The two serious-faced photogravures of husband and wife
in their huge, carved gilt frames, the iron bedsteads with
their brass knobs, the carved walnut mirror, the marble-

topped washstand with its big china basin and jug, the opaline carafe and glasses on the mantelpiece, the dusty glass case through which one could only just see the imitation flowers inside, the fringed, embroidered felt and plush, the white linen dust covers on the chairs, the luster holy-water stoup without any water in it, and the prie-dieu at which no one, perhaps, had prayed since the last century—everything in that room, even the smell of age and dust, seemed to need, almost to call for, a breath of profaning vitality.

I awoke long before eight, already excited, even exasperated by waiting, pleased at finding that I'd ceased to long for Dorotea, rejuvenated as if by a miraculous cure by the thought of Checchina.

I couldn't stay still. From prudence, to avoid being noticed, I decided not to go out. And I could scarcely endure the waiting. I was as excited as an adolescent before his first love affair. Up and down the room I went, lying down on the bed, getting up at once, tidying the covers and sheets with great care, then a few minutes later throwing myself down on them again.

At half past seven I began looking out of the window to watch for her arrival. The sun had not yet set; but the street was already completely in shadow and crowded with people meandering slowly, chattering, in their best clothes, along the gaily lit shop-fronts; it was the little town's Sunday parade.

Suddenly I caught sight of her. She was wearing a black suit and carried a bag in her gloved hand. She had stopped at a window almost opposite the main door and was turning to glance hesitantly up at the house. I hurried downstairs, opened the little door in the big street door a fraction, and waited in hiding. After a few seconds a hand in a white cotton glove pushed at the door. Checchina entered and was in my arms.

We tiptoed silently up the stairs. I was afraid of seeing the old landlord appear; it would have been dangerous or at least embarrassing. But perhaps he was out. Finally we reached the room. I locked the door. Then I embraced Checchina, flung her on the bed, kissed her, tore off her clothes.

"How long," I muttered, "how long I've been thinking of this moment! How many years, Checchina! My Checchina! Mine, mine, mine!"

She was smiling, with her eyes shut and an expression of extreme happiness on her face. But I was gazing at her, gazing at her as if to penetrate her with my eyes as well. And that constant never-changing smile of hers seemed to have something ironic, superior about it; her closed, stretched, well-cut lips, raised at the corners in that smile, looked like those of certain archaic Greek or Egyptian statues.

How short a time the spell lasted!

After a few minutes, perhaps after a few seconds, I found myself holding a sweaty, panting woman, smelling of cheap eau-de-cologne, with a flushed, dissatisfied face. And then I looked round the room, which, contrary to my plans, I hadn't remembered to look at from the moment I'd entered it with Checchina; and the old room had no meaning any longer, was just a collection of poor dusty relics.

"Checchina," I said after a long silence, "do you know I'm married too now?"

She started and looked at me as if I'd wounded her deeply, treacherously.

"Yes, Checchina. A year and a half ago. I've an eight-months-old baby too."

For some time she did not speak. She stroked my cheek. Then said. "Is she American?"

That seemed to console her a little.

"You've done right," she said, calling me *lei* again. "I've often thought you ought to get married. . . . Are you happy?"

"No, Checchina."

"But does she love you?"

"Ah, yes! She does that!" I exclaimed with certainty. "And at heart I love her too; but it's another thing."

"I know," she said with a sigh. "I love my husband at heart, too. Perhaps in the same way you love your wife. But it's—like a mother's love."

"That's just it, Checchina."

Then began a long, agonizing aftermath of this adventure which I'd not been able to resist. I had nothing to say to poor Checchina any more. I felt nothing, or seemed to feel nothing, for her any more. In a few seconds I had completely consumed, burned up, a desire that had lasted nine years and, perhaps because of that, had seemed at one moment important and inexhaustible. Darkness gradually fell over the room. Checchina did not leave. She couldn't; she was afraid of being recognized as she came out of the front door, of even finding herself face to face with someone from Fontanelli (many came to Iesi from there on Sunday evenings). She intended to wait till the parade was finished and the main street almost deserted; then to half-open the little street door and, before leaving, have a good look to see no one was passing. Then she would go to a certain cinema, where the friend I had met that morning was waiting for her, and return home with her after midnight on the last bus.

I was hungry and felt like going out right away. But of course I could neither say so nor let her realize it. I dressed, walked up and down the room, smoked, talked now and then, trying hard to hide my disillusion, boredom, hunger, and even sleepiness. Checchina lay stretched out on the bed, half dressed, leaning on one elbow, and perhaps guessing my thoughts. At one moment she asked me for a cigarette. She very rarely smoked, she told me, and held the cigarette clumsily, laughing at herself. And meanwhile the minutes passed slowly, more and more slowly.

Whenever I said anything, the subject seemed to die on my lips, and I would try to find another one to follow on, and not succeed right away. Dorotea rose irresistibly in my imagination again. I longed to be with her. And yet I compared my present disappointment with the disappointments I'd felt every time with Dorotea too. Those had been different, much less serious.

With Dorotea I was the only one who suffered. To see Dorotea immediately after we had made love, lying there calm and indifferent and dropping off to sleep almost at once, relieved me of every responsibility, if not toward myself, at least toward her.

Now, on the other hand, I felt disgusted with myself. I looked at Checchina, still tender, still anxious, as she gazed at me across the room from the bed, and I felt what a shallow, selfish wretch I was.

Finally, just before ten o'clock, after making sure from behind the shutters that the parade was completely over, she got ready to leave. Before putting on her coat she insisted on embracing and kissing me violently, lingeringly. She had on an embroidered chemise, of shiny pink silk, and was probably very proud of it. Perhaps she hoped that I would remember her like that, as a licentious, sophisticated mistress.

Then she gathered up her bag and took out a small packet of tissue paper; it contained a little gold chain with a medal of Our Lady of Lourdes.

"I've brought it for you to remember me by, Signor Harry," she said. "The medal is blessed. I know you're not a Catholic. But it will bring you luck all the same. I don't ask you to put it round your neck. Keep it where you like, in your wallet, or a pocket. Just promise me you'll keep it."

Touched, I promised. In the dark room, by the light from the street through the slats of the shutters, I saw that Checchina's eyes were full of tears.

"Or even," she said finally, making a great effort not to cry, "if some day you really don't want to keep it, don't give it to anyone but your wife. Will you promise me that too?"

"I promise," I said, and added, instinctively, that my wife was a Catholic.

Through the closed shutters, I saw her come out of the street door and walk rapidly off, without turning back, without looking up, watched her vanish from my life forever.

After going out for a meal I left at once for Ancona and reached it before midnight.

At the hotel was a telegram, waiting since the night before. It was from Jane. She asked me to come and get her. She had to leave Capri as soon as possible because Duccio wasn't very well. Nothing serious, she assured me. But the doctor had advised a change of air.

13.

In Paris we rented a furnished apartment in Auteuil. Every morning I would drive to UNESCO avenue Kléber, lunch in the underground cafeteria or some little restaurant in the quarter, and return to Auteuil about six in the evening. An official's life; a high salary; little work; endless boredom. I was in control of a section, with an office on the fifth floor, secretaries, and twenty dependents or so. From my office windows I looked out over the smoky, silvery roofs of Paris; the alternating sun, mist, rain, and wind; the avenues, black or green according to the season, furrowed out among the gray houses, to the distant gilded dome of the Invalides. Yes, it was sweet, Paris! What was it, in that vivid air, in that ever-varying sky, in those silvery lights, that seemed to veil one's memories and restrain one's desires, to still the longing for different, distant places and make one content with one's own fantasies?

Rome always urged me toward sin; America toward chastity; Paris toward a compromise with both.

Duccio, fortunately, had nothing seriously wrong with him. He was only run down and nervous, from a climate that did not agree with him. When, interrupting my tour for a few days, I had reached Capri straight from Ancona, I found Jane, too, looking very tired and nervous, I thought; she blamed herself for having insisted on Capri, regretted it, and wanted to leave at once. She was even ready, if I agreed, to return to America. I sent her to Switzerland, to Sierre in the Canton of Valois, a village halfway up the mountains, which was ideal for Duccio at that season of the year. Then I went back to my work again and quickly covered the Marches, Abruzzi, and the whole of southern Italy, where there had been less destruction. I finished my tour at Palermo toward the end of August, sold the car, and took a plane to Rome. There I stopped only for a single night, which I spent with Dorotea, whom I had not seen since that last visit; and next day I went on by train to Milan and thence to Sierre. By early in September we were already settled in Paris.

Jane was sad, but calm. The mountains had done her good too. Every day, when I came home, I found her busy with Duccio. She had sent the Swiss nurse away and now did everything herself, including the cooking. All the help she had was a woman to do the heavy work and look after the baby when we went out in the evening, and in the morning when Jane went to church. This was a new development. Jane had always been religious, but never practicing to the point of going to church every single morning, as I saw her doing now. When I asked for an explanation, she replied that when she'd been alone at Capri all that time, seeing no one except the servants, she had found herself returning naturally to her old childhood habits of prayer, meditation, and the sacraments.

Perhaps, she said, Duccio's illness had also frightened her; particularly one terrible afternoon, some time before she'd wired me from Capri. Duccio had had a violent stomach-ache, suddenly gone purple, and seemed on the verge of death. It was the day of San Costanzo, the great Capri *festa*, so the two servants had been given a holiday. The Swiss nurse had twisted her ankle two days before and couldn't walk. There wasn't even anyone in the villas near by; they'd all gone to the piazza to see the procession. The air resounded with explosions of fireworks mingling with a continuous, obsessive ringing of bells, and bands playing religious hymns. She had had to run herself, her heart in her throat, as far as the village to get the doctor. The pharmacist's was shut. The doctor was out; he'd gone to the *festa* too. How could she possibly find him amid all those crowds, that noise and confusion? When she asked if anyone had seen him, someone said he had, and pointed in a direction to which she rushed off, jostling her way with difficulty through the crush. But when she got to the spot, she found the doctor was no longer there. Meanwhile time was passing and Duccio was dying. Finally, almost at nightfall, she came across Don Raffaele, who assured her he'd seen the doctor take the bus for Anacapri a few minutes before. Then Jane took a taxi (the fat man's) and tried to catch up with the doctor. But the old car had broken down halfway up the hill. It stopped, as often happens, at the steepest point just under the great rocky wall of Anacapri, where there's a little white statue of Our Lady of Lourdes in a grotto just above the road. As the fat man sweated around the car, Jane had instinctively prayed to the Virgin and promised Her that if nothing had happened to Duccio meanwhile, she would take the sacrament again and return to all the religious practices she'd given up long ago.

She had found the doctor on the little piazza of Anacapri, returned at once to Capri with him, and hurried to the villa. The nurse was standing at the door laughing. It had been nothing after all. A few minutes after Jane had left to look for the doctor, everything had passed over. Duccio had begun sucking his bottle and then gone calmly to sleep. Later the nurse, worried at not seeing Jane return, had sent off a messenger to her with the good news, a little boy, the son of a fisherman. But obviously the child had not been able to find her in the confusion.

Jane had then set herself this problem: "Have I," she'd

said to herself, "got to observe my vow even if Duccio was already out of danger at the moment I made it?"

But she had reflected that time, like space, exists only for us humans and not for God, nor for the saints in heaven, among whom the Virgin is nearest to God. She had considered that a miracle can also be granted in answer to a prayer made not only hours, but even years and centuries afterwards? The essential thing was that the person praying should not know *at the moment of praying* that the miracle had already happened.

After this dubious logic she went back in her memory over the desperate agony of those hours. "When one loves," she explained to me, "and then suddenly fears or even just considers the possibility of the person one loves dying, it's then we feel our complete nullity. What can we do? Change the course of destiny? And so our love urges us to hope, believe, and pray. 'God! O God! Please don't let my baby die!'"

And at that moment, as the thought, the possibility, of our Duccio's dying recurred to her, even as a pure hypothesis, an illustration of what she'd been saying, she was suddenly overcome again and began trembling and, I'm sure, mentally praying once more.

I listened to her and, though I did not pray myself, understood her, felt moved like her. Yet a very strange reflection occurred to me at the same time. How was it, I said to myself, that the idea of Duccio's death, and also of my father's and of Jane's, touched me with such immediate anguish; and yet I could consider with perfect indifference the possibility of the death of Dorotea?

My love for Dorotea may have been different, perhaps opposite, yet I certainly loved her. I loved and desired her above every other creature in the world, and was grateful to her for the happiest hours of my life. By what defect, then, by what monstrous twist in my heart could it be that the news of a disaster to her wouldn't, I knew with certainty, worry me in the least? I, who sometimes suffered agonies if anything happened to retard by a few hours, or put off till next day, an appointment with her, would have renounced her very life without any sorrow, or regret, or even unhappiness. On the contrary, in fact, the certain knowledge that Dorotea was no longer alive, that neither journey nor money nor scandal could ever bring her back, would have given me some kind of peace. At last I would no longer desire her, no longer love her. It wasn't the thought of her dying that would persuade me to pray, I concluded, but if anything that of her living. Why? Was I really as selfish as all that?

Many other times I've asked myself this question, and never have I found an answer. The more I think it over, the more confused I get, the more I feel that I understand nothing about myself.

As a result of her new-found piety Jane now began to hint that she would like to see me converted to Catholicism too. She persuaded me to read the novels of the most advanced and broad-minded Catholic writers, such as Greene and Mauriac; and she would sound out my impressions and doubts, try innumerable arguments on me.

But by now, through my long stay in Italy and my studies too, I had become so deeply imbued with the rites and myths and habits of Italians that I felt almost Catholic already; and I could see no need of any official consecration of my conversion, nor of practices such as penance and Communion, in whose esoteric value I had never believed anyway. I disliked, too, the wordly and snobbish side of the business. In these last years, for us Americans and for Anglo-Saxons in general, Catholicism has become too fashionable. Finally, there was the faint but affectionate memory of the religion of my childhood; of certain Sunday mornings in Denver in the snow and frost, of the choir in the Presbyterian church where my father and mother were regular attenders; to betray the innocent memory of that cold, gracile faith seemed to me not only pointless but impious.

So I would blandly evade Jane's repeated attempts, and above all refuse to enter into those religious discussions which she tried to start almost every day, after she'd been told by a Jesuit priest who was her assiduous adviser in Paris that the keys of curiosity can also open the gates of Faith.

But nothing could arouse my curiosity that dreamy autumn, I don't know why; perhaps it was laziness, the inertia into which I was forced by my new job, the regular, monotonous life, the long mornings and golden afternoons in the solitude, warmth, and comfort of my office at UNESCO. I had begun smoking a pipe again, and would start it up in the morning. It was a corner room and had a large window looking east and a bay window looking south and west, so that there was always sun on a fine day. The smoke of the pipe would fill the sunny room with a cloud that surrounded and enwrapped me, cutting me off from the whole rest of the world. I would sprawl deep in my armchair. A huge, massive desk in front of me formed a barrier to the rare appearances of my staff, who seemed veiled and distant through the smoke. On the desk were a few papers and reports, some photographic reproductions, a book or two. I would pretend to read and write. In reality I did nothing at all. Within the first few days I'd fallen gradually but rapidly into a profound habit: once I'd dealt with my scanty mail in the first hour of the morning, I would slip off into endless daydreams, abandon myself to sweet obsessions, round one fixed and central figure —that of Dorotea. Never, as far as I can remember, had I so caressed, watched, studied, loved, and thought of Dorotea as in that period. And I was happy and almost assuaged by my dreams, so that I forgot the reality at the origin of them.

Can thinking of a pleasure possibly be stronger than the pleasure itself? Those who've been through what I've been through know that it's not only possible, but logical and normal.

Any sexual pleasure, even the liveliest, is in reality always interlarded with unpleasant little details, extraneous sensations that do not fuse with it, however much it may apparently overwhelm them, and they may be canceled out by purifying memory.

The final sexual act itself favors onanism; it does not free one, it exhausts one, and so prolongs desire to the infinite. We think we will succeed, next time, in imagining, materializing, the object of love better than we had the time before; and the goal, the final reserve of all such fantasies, is the reality of the sexual act, in which we can still hope.

Sunk deep in my chair, behind my desk, I would draw out a photograph of Dorotea, the only one I had of her, and contemplate it. It was a snapshot taken at the sea, on some beach near Rome, Ostia or Fregene; a back view, in bathing-dress; she was turning her eyes to the camera, with a saucy look.

I gazed at that photograph so long and so intensely that

I came to attribute an intrinsic value to it; as if it were much more important than the goddess it represented (who was far away and unreachable) and had become a fetish in itself worthy of my devotion and capable in some way of rewarding it.

Then I'd tire of this fetish. It would become meaningless to me. Putting the photograph away in a drawer for another fortnight, I'd find it more rewarding to think of Dorotea with the help of only memory and imagination. I would see her in dresses that the most *haute* of *coutures* could never have created for her; loaded with more jewels than any rajah had ever given his favorite odalisque; or naked, with just the jewels.

Her jet-black hair, gleaming, fine, naturally wavy, and quivering slightly at the roots, particularly on her forehead; her high, broad, imperious, almost flat forehead: her big green eyes, glittering with gold flecks in the shadowed sockets, where the skin was slightly wrinkled, exquisite promise of vice; her round cheeks, her full lips, her strong and very white teeth; her shoulders and arms like a statue's; her back a vast smooth brown surface that I could gaze at endlessly, tirelessly, as at a sea lying calm under the sun, enveloping with one look the strength and softness of the waist; the big, hard, heavy breasts, the swelling hips and thighs, the velvety belly, and under the belly

> *Une riche toison qui, vraiment, est la sœur*
> *De cette énorme chevelure,*
> *Souple et frisée, et qui t'égale en épaisseur,*
> *Nuit sans étoiles, Nuit obscure;*

the round knees smooth as pebbles ground by a torrent; the straight legs, big but proportionate; the slim ankles; the compact feet.

The only part of her body corresponding to her ankles was the hands: they were curiously small, not thin, but almost narrow; and when I held them, they seemed to shrink and lose themselves inside mine, which engulfed them as if possessing them completely.

From æsthetic curiosity (which was also a natural result of my profession) I was continually searching through the history of art for any possible incarnations of Dorotea.

I would look through books, monographs, collections of photographs, and always end by poring over Roman paintings of the decadence, among the ancients; among the moderns, Andrea del Sarto, and even more over Sebastiano del Piombo.

The worthy expert who has taken over my job at UNESCO will surely never understand why our small, all-purpose library and collection of photographs should include everything written about Sebastiano del Piombo, and a complete series of photographs of his works.

I found a big reproduction of his *Portrait of a Woman*, which is in the Berlin Museum, put it in an old frame, and hung it up in my office directly facing my desk. But these rapt musings were seldom very satisfactory and only led me to others considerably less serene and simple; to imagining, that is, my future meetings with Dorotea, each different from the others, each novel, complicated, and strange, yet each lifelike: future meetings, future acts and attitudes in love-making; future days spent with her; and sometimes I liked to think of my whole future life dedicated to her.

I thought, for example, of getting her to Paris without

Jane knowing, and settling her in some little hotel. When I left UNESCO, at the end of my office hours, the idea of going home at once, of cutting off that free play of fantasy in which I'd been immersed for so many hours, repelled me. And although I knew perfectly well that I would never have the courage to get Dorotea to Paris, I would go round looking for a hotel for her.

The Left Bank: evening falling; and me wandering round in my car, still dreaming. I would stop in front of a *bistro*, enter, and slowly sip a *fine* while I gazed at the sign and windows of some squalid *hôtel meublé* on the other side of the street, where, I thought, I could settle Dorotea. . . . Often I'd even take this game to the point of entering the *hôtel meublé*, visiting a couple of rooms, asking the price, fixing one for the day after next. I would confirm by telephone. The name? Mademoiselle Corradi, I'd say—Dorotea's surname! And seeing the filthy old man writing "Mlle Corradi" down on the slate, I would feel a tremor of joy, as if I were watching her miraculously beginning to materialize.

I reached a kind of calm, almost happy dream-state. Perhaps Jane saw on my face signs of this dream life so apart from her and suffered from it. But she could say nothing to me, unless some little incident, otherwise without meaning or danger, suddenly crystallized our mutual incomprehension. Then we would quarrel in harsh, bitter terms and torture each other like a long-married couple. The reason, or pretext, might be the choice of a dress she was about to put on; or a toy to buy Duccio; or how to spend the evening, hesitating between a concert, a *boîte*, and staying at home.

It was on one of those cheerless evenings, as we were driving toward a *boîte* in Saint-Germain-des-Prés and entering the leafy shade of the boulevard Raspail, that she turned to me and, with a bitter smile touched with sudden sincerity if not with affection, made an unforgettable remark: "Don't you realize, my dear, that we are both living in hope that the other will die?"

I denied it hotly in speech and thought. But it was true, alas! Oh, yes, it was true! Why, at that very moment, during our very silence, which had lasted since Auteuil, I had done nothing but conjure up, if not desire, a peaceful life with Dorotea, should Jane be no more.

Jane would return insistently to the problem of religion. She never despaired of converting me. And I might perhaps have ended by yielding, or at least agreeing to meet the Père de Lalande she talked so much about, if my constant habit of daydreaming had not saved me from other more serious deceptions.

At night, almost always, we were reconciled. But by now even the embraces that seemed to placate us were lies, on my part at least. Dorotea was in my thoughts all day; from thinking about her my senses had become used only to her. As I embraced Jane in the dark, I found myself always imagining, though the real sensation was quite different, that I was embracing Dorotea. This was the only way I could still love. And from the remorse and disgust that followed my brief and imperfect self-deception I took refuge in the solitude of sleep.

Did Jane guess something? Did she feel how far from her I was? I would deny this to myself; it was so much easier.

Then at a certain moment I began writing letters to Dorotea. Of course I didn't post them; I was too afraid of blackmail. I wrote them, reread them thinking that I'd post them, then shut them in an envelope on which I'd put a stamp.

Then I would go out, to the nearest post office, and hesitate a long time in front of the box. After which I would return to UNESCO and lock the letter up together with others in a drawer of my desk. When I went to Rome, I thought, I'd give them all to Dorotea, for her to read in my presence. Then she would know how much, how ardently, I'd been thinking of her. After which, of course, I would take them back and destroy them.

What did I say to her in those letters? Everything that I had imagined in my distant solitude. Praise of her beauty, confession of my love, the absurdest desires, the maddest projects. I told her that I'd like to abandon Jane and Duccio and dedicate my life to her; serve her like a slave; sleep at the foot of her bed like a dog; endure any humiliation, exaction, or cruelty from her with delight; adore her like a goddess; stay with her till death. "Strip me of everything," I said to her, "except the capacity to see and be seen by you. Let me wallow in my own squalor, for my squalor is the consequence of your splendor." In one letter, I remember, I told her about another dream I'd often had, utterly absurd though it was; that not only I should serve her, but also those I loved most, Jane and even Duccio. Jane could be her maid, and Duccio her maid's son, whom she, Dorotea, kept in her home from charity.

Such were the follies I thought up and wrote down, those and others that I can't even describe, none of which I would ever have tried to put into practice. Thus I was able to convince myself that I was doing no real harm to Jane and Duccio. They were just idle abstractions, I believed, symbols, harmless fantasies; and the letters were ritual scribbles, private erotic stimulants, nothing more. But I felt a need to write that mawkish but irresistible nonsense and see it written down in front of me. How pitiful, squalid, and absurd I should find these letters if I happened to read them again. Luckily I'm almost sure I've destroyed them, or if not, hidden them so well that I can't even remember where.

There was another habit I'd got into at that period—of not being able to pass a jeweler's window without thinking of Dora; often I would stand there for a long time, gazing at gold, pearls, diamonds, bracelets, rings, necklaces, earrings, as presents for her. Sometimes Jane was with me. And she seemed quite pleased to pause in front of those windows too. I would stare silently. And Jane, beside me, would stare silently too. Perhaps she was thinking that I was choosing some jewel as a present to her. . . .

A friend of mine whom you don't know, a North Italian called Comba, one of those Piedmontese Catholics who might well be a Protestant, noticed one day, as we were walking along the faubourg Saint-Honoré, how apt I was to linger in front of jewelers' windows. When we reached the rue de la Paix and were at Cartier's, I felt I had to give him some reason for these lengthy halts. I was thinking, I told him, of a woman with whom I was in love.

"You're deceiving yourself, my dear fellow," exclaimed Comba then; "you believe you're thinking of her. But you're morally impotent, really: all you're thinking of is a new way of rousing your own excitement. I don't know who the woman is you mention, and don't want to know. But if you really loved her so intensely, you wouldn't feel any need to give her expensive presents. A flower, any memento would be enough. The less, in fact, the present was worth in terms of money, the more it would be worth in terms of love. The ancient

Romans, or rather the Romans of the decadence, were like you; they used to hang garlands on Priapus, and sometimes on the part of their bodies of which Priapus was a symbol or divinity."

That was a long time ago, and so many things have happened since. Yet even now I can't decide whether Comba was right or not.

Anyway, after some months of living like that, of endless brooding shut in my office with the photograph or the image which I managed to evoke of Dorotea, writing letters that I never posted and so to which there were never any replies, of gazing at jewels I wanted to give her but never bought, I began to find this fantasy world insufficient.

I decided to telephone Dorotea and hear her voice, if only for a few minutes. But ashamed of being possibly overheard by my staff, through whom I would have had to put the call, I waited till one o'clock, when everyone had gone out to lunch, and then asked the exchange directly for an urgent call to Rome.

The minutes passed and the call did not come through; I was on tenterhooks, too, at the thought of not finding Dorotea at home. That was just the time she usually went out for a walk in Via Veneto and a glass of vermouth with some friend.

But all went well. Once again, after all those months of separation, I heard her low, rather raucous, warm, sweet, calm, decided voice.

"*Quando te decidi a famme 'na visita?*" ("When are you going to make up your mind to visit me?")

The Roman accent, which irritated me in anyone else, coming from her gave me a thrill of pleasure as if I were caressing her bare thighs, her warm, brown, smooth, full flesh.

"I'm always thinking of you," went on my goddess's voice; "why don't you write me a nice letter?"

"I'm very busy, Dora, I haven't the time."

"And suppose I asked you to. I want a letter from you, 'Arry."

I want. Hearing that *I want*, I felt a kind of flutter, a stab of pleasure in my heart. *I want.* It was the first time she had ever demanded anything of me. In a flash I was asking myself: why? And in a flash answering myself: she has no money, is going through a bad time, and wants a letter of mine to blackmail me with.

So, "No," I replied promptly. "I haven't time to write to you. I'll ring up again."

"When?" replied she, even more promptly.

"The day after tomorrow," I promised. "*Ciao*, Dora my lovely, I'm always thinking of you too, every day, every hour."

"You're a big *pallonaro!*" (which in Roman dialect means storyteller, fibber).

"I swear to you, my lovely; every day, every hour."

"It's not true or you'd have written to me."

"I *have* written to you, as a matter of fact."

"Liar! I haven't even had a postcard!"

"I've written you lots of letters, but never mailed them. They're all here in a drawer. When we meet I'll show them to you and you'll see."

"Silly boy!" she said gently. At that moment the exchange warned me the first three minutes were over, so she ended: "Then I'll expect your call the day after tomorrow at this same time. *Ciao*, 'Arry. Thanks for the call. *Ciao*."

I put down the receiver, and in an instant realized that

those three minutes of telephone conversation had meant more than all the months of daydreaming. In a flash I saw my long-drawn-out slide toward madness.

I could still hear her voice; again and again I repeated to myself: "I want . . . *pallonaro* . . . liar . . . silly boy!"—living, true words that had really been spoken by another human being and not invented by me, who had anyway not been able to in all those months! I felt swept by the flood of real life, carried away by the healthy shock of reality; and suddenly, too, so tired of my own vice that at that moment I felt I never wanted to think of Dorotea again; I found myself looking with new eyes at my study walls, at the faces of my staff returning from lunch. That afternoon I got through some real work, and left for home at five.

During the drive I told myself that I would ring up Dorotea again within forty-eight hours and then try to make a quick visit to Rome. I must bring things to a head. How? By leaving Jane and going to live with Dorotea? That never even crossed my mind. I just wanted to get back into contact with reality, and so rediscover the balance I'd lost for so long. My work at UNESCO was a sham; I was losing initiative after initiative, doing the bare minimum necessary to deceive my superiors into thinking I was working. My own personal studies I had completely abandoned. A monograph on eleventh-century Roman painters and mosaicists, for which I'd gathered material during the summer in Italy, was stuck halfway through the first chapter. And finally my behavior to Jane was unforgivable. That vice of daydreaming about Dorotea and living intensely in those dreams all the time had distilled a subtle poison of dissatisfaction, of resentment at my own unreality and impotence; instinctively I had turned on the person nearest me, on Jane; without knowing it, I was blaming her every moment for not being Dorotea. The primary cause of all my bitterness, I had thought, was Jane; so I had revenged myself on her.

This could not go on. From my very affection for Jane, I had either to go to Rome or to find another woman, in flesh and blood, to take the place of Dorotea. In order not to torture poor Jane any more, I had to be unfaithful to her intermittently in the flesh and not just continuously in thought.

In this new state of mind I reached home, and as so often happens in life when one has made a decision that involves another person as well as oneself, I found Jane with news that deranged and indeed overruled any plans of mine.

She was expecting another baby. Till now she had hidden every suspicion of this from me because she herself, she said, would have preferred it not to be true at that moment. One reason for this attitude of hers was that Duccio was still small and needed a lot of attention. So she had not said a word. But now she'd been to the doctor that day and there was no more doubt about it: her pregnancy was almost in its third month. She intended to leave for Philadelphia with Duccio before Christmas. Père de Lalande, on whose opinion Jane now depended for every move, had also advised this. The new baby would be born about April or May.

Thus a period of separation opened up before me; I would be living alone in Paris for some months, and be able to see Dorotea, be with her, as much as I liked.

But plans that seem more desirable than anything else in the world when they are unrealizable are apt to lose their urgency, even their glamour, as soon as they become possible.

So when I was left alone in Paris and could at any moment have gone to Rome, or brought Dorotea to Paris, I began putting off both decisions from day to day. I also formed another habit; every morning, toward noon, I rang Dorotea from my office; and every night I tramped the Champs-Élysées on the boulevards, ending in bed with some prostitute, nearly always a different one. I did not want to lose Dorotea, or rather I did not want to lose my desire for Dorotea; and at the same time I tried to free myself of her by satiation and variety, by searching for one who suited me more than the others and who at least rang a temporary change on my obsession. Thus I met Ivonne, called Vonie, a fat, small, violent southerner from Montauban, nice, but very grasping and very avaricious, as, I am afraid, alas, nearly all French women are.

I met the laughing Simone, from Marseille, a specialist in net underwear and black stockings, who seemed to have come out of a lithograph of the nineties.

And Mamai; and Lisa; and Danielle; and Monique. Rather nervously, at least for the first time, I would follow each one up her rickety wooden stairs; and with each, in her squalid room, I would feverishly pull her zippers, in the hope that this was the lucky time, this time the miracle would happen, and I'd find the goddess who would make me forget Dorotea.

What was the point, I ask myself now. Even if I'd found her, what was the point of substituting for Dorotea another woman like her, who could never be the companion of my life? But perhaps, absurdly, that is just what I was looking for: a woman like Dorotea who at the same time was like Jane.

Every morning I telephoned Dorotea. After the first few times I had nothing much to say to her. Yet I still went on.

This daily telephone call had immediately become another rite, a superstition. I could not live without hearing her voice.

I would ask her what the weather was like, promise to think of her and to send her some money.

At the end of February I went to Rome in connection with my job and stayed there a week. I had a room at the Grand Hotel; but I slept in Via Boncompagni, at Dorotea's.

On my return to Paris I took up my former life: every night I walked the boulevards in a state of idiotic anxiety; after a day or two I began to telephone again to Dorotea.

Donatella was born on the 9th of May, in Philadelphia. Early in July, Jane left the babies with her mother and a good nurse and joined me in Paris; she was to stay a fortnight or so and accompany me to Rome, where I was to receive a decoration conferred on me by the President of the Italian Republic in recognition of what I had done for the recovery of works of art damaged in the war.

This journey was the occasion, if not the cause, of all the harm that followed.

14.

At the photographers' flashes that assailed us as we came down the gangway from the plane at Ciampino, I turned and moved aside, instinctively, so as not to cover the V.I.P. behind us. But there was no V.I.P. there. The photographers laughed and shouted:

"It's you we want, *signor maggiore.*"

"And your wife!"

"Signora, please, just a moment, smile!"

Jane, who was in front of me, backed up a step on the gangway and clung to my arm, smiling confusedly.

I turned round again, but for another reason. "God," I thought, with a sudden stab of fear, "what if the photo appears in tomorrow's papers in Rome, and Dorotea sees it and so finds out I'm married!"

Persistently I refused to be photographed. There was no reason to be, I said, covering my face with my briefcase; I wasn't an important person; I'd merely done my duty; I was touched and grateful to the Italian press, but I really hadn't foreseen such a welcome.

No, I certainly hadn't foreseen it, or I'd have done everything to avoid it. The reporters laughingly tried to take us even so, and anyway a flash photo must have been taken at my first appearance on the gangway, before I could hide. What was I to do now?

I went up to one of the photographers and asked him not to give the photo he had taken to the press. Taking care that Jane should not notice, I took him by the elbow, squeezed it hard, and asked him when and where I could see him.

Two hours later, leaving Jane in the hotel, I was at Publifoto, in a little office on a mezzanine floor in Piazza Barberini.

The photographer was called Gandolfi; he was a small, rotund little man, with a black mustache and very lively eyes. With meaning smiles I hinted at why I really didn't want the photographs to be published: a love affair, women, the Roman papers go everywhere . . . trying to suggest in this way that in some city in Italy other than Rome there was a woman who should be kept in ignorance of my marriage or at least of this visit of mine.

As I talked I made a gesture to reach for my wallet. Gandolfi laughingly stopped me in time, without taking offense; it was quite a small matter, he said, and he promised to destroy the negatives and see that his colleagues who had photographed me did the same.

I left, not entirely convinced. It had all seemed too easy. On the other hand, to insist on guarantees from Gandolfi might, I thought, have been either offensive or dangerous. Offensive if Gandolfi was a decent person; dangerous if he was not, as my insistence might tempt him to blackmail. In these doubts, I glanced at him a second as I left; his astute and smiling features were open to both interpretations.

Next morning I examined the papers apprehensively. None of them had published the photograph. I heaved a great sigh of relief. But when, a little later, I went down into the lobby and passed Guglielmo on my way out, he murmured to me with a bow:

"My congratulations, *signor maggiore*."

I turned round; Guglielmo was smiling kindly, bending toward me from up behind his desk.

"Congratulations for what?"

"For your photograph, of course! And the Signora's too!"

I made an effort to control myself.

"I haven't seen any photograph," I said, trying to appear indifferent, and even a little curious. "Where was it published?"

"In the *Rome-American*, of course, *signor maggiore*! Wasn't it brought to your room this morning?" and he handed me the paper, pointing to the photograph. There was also a caption with my name and Jane's showing clearly, and a short article on that cursed decoration.

I'd looked very carefully through all the Italian papers and sent out for them specially. But I had not thought of the American paper in Rome, which the hotel usually sends up to its American clients on their breakfast trays.

Gandolfi had kept his word. He had prevented the photographs being published in the Italian papers, believing, naturally enough, that I would see to the *Rome-American* myself. I tried to soothe myself at once. The *Rome-American* is read almost exclusively by Americans and English. Dorotea probably didn't even know of its existence.

I spent the morning at the Ministry of Public Instruction. They told me I would be presented next day to the President of the Republic, who would himself solemnly confer the decoration. At one o'clock I went to get Jane at the hotel and took her out to lunch in Piazza Navona. I didn't even consider seeing Dorotea this time. That business of the photograph had taken away all desire to.

So there I was in Rome with Jane again, as four years years before. In the memory and natural evocation of the first flowering of our love we passed some of the calmest, happiest hours we had spent for a long time. The heat, the vast sunny piazza, the welcoming shade of the *trattoria*, the gay freedom of Italian manners, the fresh food, the cool yellow wine, and that sea breeze called *ponentino* which never fails to come up toward two in the afternoon and to circulate throughout the city even on the most torrid summer day, everything seemed to reconcile us for a moment to our destiny; once again we accepted, loved life. It was a state of mind that was certainly pagan, but just as certainly religious.

A sense of how brief and provisional it was contributed to this *détente:* I had embraced Jane again in Paris only three days before after the months of separation due to Donatella's birth, and now, at the end of the week, she had to leave for the States again, as Duccio's nurse was due for a month's holiday. The seat on the plane was reserved; Jane was leaving again on Saturday. The direct air route had just opened between Rome and New York.

Maybe we were happy together then just because we knew that another separation was soon ahead; but what is paganism if it's not a religious sense of *carpe diem*?—living every day of our lives with pious, humble enjoyment as if it were the last?

We took a taxi back to the hotel. A sweet euphoria from the wine and heat and sun enveloped us. We stripped naked, threw ourselves on the bed, and made love naturally, thoughtlessly, as boys and girls do—or as people think that boys and girls do; perhaps it was the only time in our lives we ever did so.

The sun had just set when we awoke. We opened the windows, which we'd closed because of the heat; swallows were flying with long, lacerating cries, passing and repassing, almost touching the windows, in the blue air over the gardens of the Baths of Diocletian. Looking toward the Piazza Esedra and the railway station, one could see, if one strained one's eyes, the sky full of their swirling little black shapes.

Jane was standing beside me, in silence.

"We're not worthy of this peace," I was thinking, and, without realizing it, heaved a deep sigh.

At that moment the telephone rang. Jane went and took up the receiver. It was someone who did not speak English. Jane, perhaps because she didn't know Italian very well, seemed to hesitate as she replied. Anyway, she was talking in a very low voice. It was a big room, I was still by the window, and the sound of the traffic prevented my hearing what she said. All I caught was the word *letters*. Thinking Jane was in difficulties because of her Italian, I came away from the window to help and crossed the room toward her. She was pale. She made an instinctive gesture with a hand toward me, a gesture for me to keep away, and her look—

Well, my dear Mario, here I'm back at the beginning of my story.

Jane's look at that second, at the telephone, in the room in the Grand Hotel, as I came up to her and whispered, unsuspectingly: "Who is it?"—that look of hers is with me now and always will be; somber, grim, tragic; a look I had never seen on her, and whose meaning I mistook at the time. It disturbed me; to me it seemed severe and accusing; on seeing it, I had at once thought, with a catch at the heart and a certainty as absolute as if I'd heard it with my own ears, that someone, there at the telephone, had revealed my secret to Jane. Who? Perhaps it was Dorotea, or a friend of Dorotea's whom she had put up to blackmailing me—that so-called brother-in-law of hers, or the young man with the bejeweled hand.

With a trembling hand I took the receiver from Jane's trembling hand and said loudly into it: "Hello."

A man's voice replied.

"Ah, it's you, *signor maggiore*?"

"Yes, who am I speaking to?"

"I was saying to your wife just now—"

"Who am I speaking to, please?" I repeated, making an

effort in front of Jane to transform my fear and shame into the impatience and indignation proper to an honest person who receives an anonymous telephone call.

"So that's how it is, is it?" went on the voice in a jeering, threatening tone, without answering my question. "That's how you forget old friends, eh?"

It was an Italian voice, with a vulgar southern accent, either Roman or Neapolitan. With the stupid, irritating habit of Italians of the lower classes when they talk to a foreigner, he was using the infinitive of the verb; they think they are making themselves more easily understood in this way, while all they achieve is the opposite.

I looked at Jane. She had moved back to the foot of the bed; she was pale, and still had that accusing look, those great somber eyes of one seeing a horror for the first time; something in whose existence she till then had not believed.

"Will you tell me, please, who I'm speaking to?"

"You know, *signor maggiore*, it's not a nice way to behave. Just said the same thing to your wife. It's not nice to come to Rome and forget old friends like this. . . . And yet we've been together! Even at dinner! And have friends in common, very very intimate friends. . . ."

I put down the receiver. I was sure now; it was someone on Dorotea's behalf, who had seen the photograph in the *Rome-American*. Perhaps, now I'd put down the receiver, the person would not dare ring again, at least for the moment. I turned to Jane and tried to smile at her.

"Some idiot amusing himself, perhaps a journalist. . . ."

But Jane had gone into the bathroom without saying a word.

Thank God, I thought. I could not have borne to see her

in front of me with that look. A second or two of it and I would have confessed everything to her. I lit a cigarette and slowly began dressing.

When she came out of the bathroom, and then for the whole of the evening, she avoided meeting my eyes; and I meeting hers. Neither of us said a word about the telephone call.

But now there was an embarrassment, a reticence between us. Silences kept on falling that evening at dinner, even in the middle of a conversation. Afterwards, luckily, we had to go to a party at the Doolittles', in the Via Appia Antica; there were a lot of people there; we danced, talked, drank till two in the morning. Also there was W. K., a Hollywood actor who, following the fashion, had come to spend the summer in Italy. We gave him a lift back to the hotel. And when we were alone again, we were tired, had drunk a good deal, and criticized the party, the Doolittles, W. K., and everything and everybody we had seen.

Next morning, according to arrangements, I went to the President of the Republic, and Jane went with me.

That afternoon, I had decided to myself, I would try to see Dorotea and either frighten her into silence or pay for it if necessary. I cashed a big traveler's check and put in each pocket one of two equal rolls of ten-thousand-lire notes. In this way, if I could get away with half, I would not run the risk of having to increase the price up to the entire sum of notes I had in my pockets.

I arranged through Guglielmo, who understood such things, to be warned, in Jane's presence, that I was expected at seven for an urgent message at the press office of the Embassy.

I went out at ten to seven, telling Jane I would be back late to dinner, after nine.

From the Grand Hotel to Dorotea's was only a few steps. But after walking up the Via Veneto as far as the corner of the Excelsior, I could not face turning into Via Boncompagni at once. I wanted to get my ideas in order, to think over what I would say and not say, and so on. I went on to the Porta Pinciana, crossed the Corso d'Italia, and walked about in the public gardens of the Villa Borghese. "Above all," I thought, "I mustn't mention either the photograph or my marriage right away. Although at the bottom of my heart I was certain Dorotea was responsible for the telephone call, I thought it would be better to have proof of it, in her own confession, before blaming her explicitly. And then—even though there was little chance of the telephone call not originating with her, it was my duty to take the chance into consideration: firstly from an elementary respect for Dorotea, with whom I'd never in all these years had occasion to find fault; and secondly for my own convenience. If, in fact, Dorotea was not to blame for the telephone call, it meant that she did not yet know of Jane's existence; and then I myself, with my bad conscience, would have revealed it to her.

It was dusk when I came out of the Villa Borghese. Suddenly, just as I crossed the Corso d'Italia and began going down Via Piemonte toward Via Boncompagni, something changed in me. Till then, about this matter of Dorotea's possible blackmailing and the best way to deal with it, I had been behaving or preparing to behave with the cold caution and wisdom of an old European libertine, not like a young American intellectual. Suddenly, at the first steps I took in Via Piemonte, I realized it was not like that at all. At that point the pavement runs by the railings of a private garden. And there, one Saturday about two in the afternoon, in September or October 1944, I had stopped a long time with Dorotea. I remembered her light black-silk dress, her bare arms —it was still very hot—her shiny leather belt with big copper studs. Jane was waiting for me at the hotel with other friends; we were to lunch together, and then go out to Lake Bolsena for the week-end. I was late, as I'd wanted to see Dorotea and explain that I would not be able to see her that night or Sunday. I had hurried to Via Boncompagni and met her on her way out for her usual walk in Via Veneto; I'd not had the courage to make her go upstairs again, and began to talk and explain as I walked along by her side. Of course, I was terrified of being seen by any of my colleagues who knew Jane, or even by Jane herself; so, taking Dorotea under her cool, plump arm, I had turned with her into Via Piemonte, where there was less danger of chance meetings, inevitable in Via Veneto. I remembered how I'd looked round as I went up Via Piemonte, terrified at the appearance of every American uniform, and trying not to let Dorotea notice my glances; and this feeling of apprehension, mingled with the nearness of Dorotea, the contact of her bare arm and tall, soft thigh, her vulgar scent, and a gripping return of desire, was not at all unpleasant; in fact, the risk of finding myself face to face with Jane, who might be passing there on her way to her apartment from the hotel, seemed to increase my pleasure at being with Dorotea. So I had prolonged our conversation, which should only have lasted a few seconds, for half an hour, perhaps more. I remembered Via Piemonte gradually becoming deserted in the late midday Roman hush, and how, stopping in the patchy shade of the little garden beside the gate, I had gazed for a long time into Dorotea's green and gold eyes; how, not being able to kiss and embrace her then and there as I wanted to, I began describing to her, in a low voice, without gestures or movements but in minute detail, all the fancies crowding into my head about what I intended doing with her, in bed, the day after next. And I remembered how, as I'd talked like that, so strong was my desire and my need to put it all into looks and words and the contact of a hand, that I'd suddenly felt as if my breathing and heart had stopped. Dorotea's face, and the building in the sun on the other side of the street behind her, seemed to quiver and veil themselves in a light mist; silently, with dry lips, I looked dazedly at the deserted street. . . . Oh, why couldn't I give up my life to this woman? Why was she one of the women whom they'd taught me to consider bad? I didn't know. All I knew was that if she hadn't appeared just that to me I should not have wanted to give up my life to her.

Passing now by the same gates and remembering that distant moment, I realized, as I squeezed the two rolls of bank notes in the pockets of my jacket, that though I thought of myself as cautious and sensible, I was really mad, for I was both afraid and yet longing to find that Dorotea was responsible for the telephone call and to be blackmailed by her now, blackmailed for the biggest possible sum, much, much more than I had in my pockets!

I feared it and wanted it at the same time; and wanted it just because I feared it. I glanced at my watch. Eight o'clock. I began to hurry, almost to run. Perhaps I'd miss her by a matter of seconds. I thought of flinging myself at her feet, imploring her forgiveness, saying that I understood her resentment at my not having rung her up, or told her of my arrival in Rome, or confessed about my marriage; and of offering her, as an inadequate provisional reparation, all the money I had on me.

In this state of mind, which thinking it over today I would consider *exalté* and almost mad, I hurried down Via Piemonte. As through a haze I saw two cats following me, boys playing, an old man sitting smoking in a doorway; ordinary things that at any other moment would have had no particular meaning; then they seemed symbols of free, happy animal life, urging me irresistibly onward. I turned down Via Boncompagni, reached the doorway that I'd never entered, even in my calmest moments, without a quiver of trepidation, crossed the lobby, slowing down so as not to arouse the suspicions of the porteress, who could see me from her little window, and started up the dark stairs.

The mezzanine floor and Dorotea's front door were already visible from the first landing. Just as I reached it, I stopped short in my tracks. Opening that very door and coming out was Jane. She glanced instinctively down in my direction. I prayed she had not recognized me in the darkness. She turned back toward the interior of the flat and shook hands through the half-open door. I rushed headlong down the stairs; but instead of running toward the entrance lobby, to reach which I would have to cross a patch of courtyard where I could easily be seen from the stairs, I kept straight on toward some cellar gates. They were closed. I flattened myself against the wall near by, in the darkest corner, and waited. Jane's steps could be heard coming slowly down; a moment later her thin legs, her slim, straight body came into view; as she reached the ground floor she stopped, looked around as if searching for something or somebody, and finally, instead of going on toward the entrance, turned hesitatingly toward the back of the stairs and the cellar. She caught sight of me in the dark, came down a few steps toward me, and when she was sure it was I, said in an anguished whisper:

"Harry, what are you doing here? There's no point in your going up to see that woman, I'll tell you everything myself. . . ."

I was struck by how gentle her tone was in spite of the anguish in it.

Going up toward her, not daring to look her in the face, I muttered: "You see, Jane, I—"

"Don't say anything," she exclaimed, taking my arm in a strange way, with the gesture of one needing support or defense. "Don't say anything now, please. I've a horror of scenes in the street, Harry. Let's go to the hotel. I'll explain everything to you. Come on, let's go, please."

She was imploring me.

Why?

On the way we never said a word. She was immersed in her thoughts, I in watching her. Mentally reconstructing what had happened, I too was pleased not to have to speak at once; convulsively I prepared my defense. So Jane, I thought, there was no doubt about it, must have followed me; or perhaps she'd had information from someone, from the same person who had telephoned the day before; or perhaps Dorotea had telephoned her personally, giving her name and address, and she had come, seen Dorotea, talked to her, and now knew everything. Her gentle manner did not reassure me, it terrified me. What would Jane exact of me? She was a practicing Catholic now; divorce didn't exist for her; she had often given me her definite views on the matter. Then would she exact a promise from me never to see Dorotea again for the rest of my life? The sternest judge could not have found a worse punishment. I would try to get out of it, of course. But would I be able to? I knew Jane, how decided, precise, obstinate she was. And I at once began preparing my defense. I'd been with that woman once or twice, I'd say; just once or twice, not more. And anyway she herself, Jane, had introduced me. Didn't she remember? Years ago, in the summer of '44, in a *trattoria*. I'd run into her afterwards by chance. Naturally I would not confess that I had returned to the *trattoria* in the hope of meeting her again. I'd run into her by chance one night, after Jane had gone to France and left me alone, all alone in the sensual, sinful atmosphere of Rome! And I'd been with her once or twice, for ten minutes at a time, never more; just a weakness of the flesh, yes, a passing infatuation; men are men, and even Americans, when they live a long time in Italy, become like Italians, the best of whom, as Jane must know, even if they are married men, consider going with prostitutes as no serious sin. . . . And what if Dorotea had told her about our journey through northern Italy in the spring of '47? I would deny it, firmly deny it. Dorotea was lying, I'd say. And anyway, I thought to myself as I searched my memory, what proofs could Dorotea have given her of that journey? Names of places, dates? She could have got these from me, on one of my visits to Rome. No, Dorotea could have no proof that I'd been with her any longer than I needed to confess.

We reached the hotel. As soon as we had shut ourselves in our room, Jane, in the same imploring tone, asked me not to switch on the lights.

The windows were open to the gardens of the Baths of

Diocletian; it was almost night, but the buzz of traffic came up noisily. Jane took off the jacket of her light suit and closed the window. Then she sat down, not near me and not facing me, in a corner of the sofa.

I felt that the moment for confessing and asking forgiveness had come.

Gathering up my strength, I said: "Jane—"

But she interrupted me at once.

"Don't talk, Harry, please! You don't know anything. I implore you not to talk and not to say anything to me now. First you must listen to me. Don't think I don't feel guilty. Oh, only God knows how much I've cried and prayed. Prayed that this moment should never come. Prayed that you, your position, your career, shouldn't be damaged by my unforgivably light behavior. Light? Guilty, guilty, guilty for what I've done, and guilty for never having spoken to you of it. But Père de Lalande told me that it was better so. And certainly it was better so, better that you should never know; if only what's happened now had never happened. Let's hope it's still not irreparable, that those letters—you see, I don't even dare to ask for your forgiveness. I don't dare—you're so good!"

And so saying she flung herself down on her knees, with her head in her hands, shaken by convulsive, desperate sobbing.

I got up, knelt down beside her, and gently stroked the short hair on her bony little head.

"No, I'm not good, Jane," I whispered to her at once, touched by her tears, though with no inkling what she meant about her guilt or letters or my career. "I've things to blame myself for too. Even you know nothing about me. And what could *you* have possibly done, my poor love?"

Certainly, at that moment I was so surprised and touched by her tears that I felt an overwhelming shame and an impulse to confess to her, for the first time and without in any way diminishing its importance now, all about my relations with Dorotea.

But Jane was crying too much to hear what I said; or she may have been feeling herself so much to blame that she attributed it to kindness, affection, or an attempt at forgiveness on my part. She, I realized at once, needed, far more than any forgiveness of mine, the outlet of confession. She felt as if a mountain were on top of her, crushing her; a mountain not perhaps so much of facts as of thoughts, of dark agonies and long solitudes, and she wanted to unburden herself of them not so much to get away from them as to understand, accept, and—who knows?—perhaps enjoy them. She wanted to talk to me because she felt obscurely that only with me could she talk frankly, in detail, lingeringly, about sins which, perhaps, she had never committed sufficiently completely. Certainly she could not confess like that to Père de Lalande, while continuing, in a certain sense, to sin. She could to me.

So when she had calmed down, she took up one of my hands, kissed it, and said: "Thank you, Harry, for being so good to me, I don't deserve it. I must admit that when that swine telephoned yesterday, and I saw your look, and from it realized you'd guessed or at least suspected the truth; and when tonight, as I left that woman's, I saw you at the bottom of the stairs and realized you'd followed me, I thought I'd never have the courage to talk to you about it. But now I see you are so good, such a friend, a real friend—"

In spite of my curiosity, I said hesitantly: "If you want to wait till later, Jane, when you're feeling calmer—"

"No, Harry, now. Be patient. I must tell you everything now. Not only for my own sake, but for yours too. Tomorrow we'll have to act, do something, find the letters again. That swine who has them can do something. He was threatening on the telephone. He can be a danger to your career. And it's my fault, my fault! Oh, Harry, will you ever be able to forgive me?"

"Yes, Jane," I replied gravely, "I'm at fault too. Whatever you've done, you're already forgiven. Now tell me."

15.

Anyone who has felt—and who has not?—what it's like to discover the infidelity of a woman one has thought faithful, even if one has not been faithful in return, knows that the pangs of jealousy, varying in degree according to the circumstances, are mingled with another torturing sensation: that of finding oneself deceived about a person with whom one has lived, day in and day out, over a long period; the stunning humiliation of suddenly seeing her as completely different from what one had always seen her. In those brief seconds of revelation we seem to be watching a cruel metamorphosis taking place under our very eyes. Even the lines of her face, so familiar till then, her look, her actions, the shape of her body, the movement of her hands, her gestures and walk, become in a flash different, new, mysterious; we don't recognize them any more, they no longer belong to us. She has smiled, we think, at pleasures we shall never know; her eyes have gazed at another man with an expression we have never seen; her hands have quivered in tender caresses we have never felt on our own body, as the body, the reality that provoked them, was different. And in the same anguished second in which we feel all this, there rises in us, unconsciously or not, sometimes suppressed by our own vanity and prejudices, sometimes freely and irresistibly, a new desire for her. We want to possess at once this new creature whom we have just discovered and who, perhaps wrongly, seems at that moment to be the one real, mysteriously unknown partner of our lives; we want to know this sudden new apparition at once to the very depths and conquer our shock in a convulsive embrace.

I too felt something of the kind as Jane, returning to the corner of the sofa and almost crouching there, withdrawn into herself, began to tell me her story, without looking at me. I gazed at her with anger and surprise, as if I were looking at some hostile stranger with whom, however, I was intimately linked. For though at that moment she needed my affection and understanding, she must certainly have hated me secretly in the past, and still do so, in a way, for the part of that past which she had not repudiated.

But leaving aside vanity and prejudices, from which I was certainly not immune, the obsession of my own guilt was so strong, the fear of being forced to reveal my own infidelity so recent, that they restrained whatever reactions I felt—jealousy, pain, pardon, or sexual attraction.

For ten minutes I had walked along by her side in the lively Roman twilight from Via Boncompagni to the Grand Hotel, preparing a credible mixture of truth and lies to attenuate my confession; I had entered that room a few minutes before, almost breathless with shame at myself; I had glanced at Jane's last expression with trepidation, without daring to raise my eyes to her, whom I saw as virtue incarnate, the personification of the conscience about to accuse and judge me. And then, just as I was about to open my lips and make the tremendous effort to talk to her about my guilt, she had burst into tears and made a similar effort, raised another incubus as heavy as my own. Where I'd expected to find an objective justice which, however terrible, could also console, I had found myself suddenly faced with a mirror. If I hated Jane for what she'd done and was about to describe to me, I could not help hating myself even more, who had confessed nothing so far. If I forgave her, I forgave myself.

And when I let myself be carried away by the temptation to find her attractive for her novelty, for her guilt, I began to think she would also find me attractive in the same way as soon as she knew about Dorotea. We would love each other not for ourselves, but almost for others. And here I grew confused and drew back, as if sensing a monstrous tangle, which anyway wasn't even real. . . .

. . . But what have I written? I reread the last phrases. Fine phrases, fine words: *grew confused, drew back, tangle, unreal.* . . . They seem just words and phrases. Their hypocrisy, it occurs to me, is sure to be accepted at once by hypocritical readers who don't want to be disturbed, and by you too, my dear Mario; it's a hypocrisy that hides vanity, prejudice, and cowardice most of all.

Why? Can't, for instance, the love between a prostitute and a man who lives on her be a real love? What, then, is their humble, frank, mutual acceptance? What is the courageous spectacle they openly give of their own abjection? To proclaim degradation means to recognize a moral hierarchy, a height from which to fall. They need not even repent to achieve forgiveness; the humiliations of their daily life are enough: the segregation to which they are condemned by the majority is enough; the judgment of society is enough.

By this I don't mean that Jane's and my duty was to change our way of life and become a prostitute and a pimp. Everyone does not only what good, but also what evil he can.

Our only duty was not to deceive ourselves. By birth, education, and culture Jane and I were conditioned to hypocrisy, to lying to others. Our duty was not to lie to ourselves in the secret of our own hearts. For we had something between us that made hypocrisy essential: our children, the basis of society.

Our duty was to recognize, each in the secret of his own heart, our deepest instincts and their similarity to each other. We should have envied, she and I, the abjection of prostitutes and their companions. Possibly—who knew?—only by such public abjection would our disquiet have been stilled. Only by being humiliated before all the world could we too have come to love each other with that complete love which seemed to have been cruelly denied us. One pays for everything, and in order to have one thing has to lose another.

"Harry," Jane was saying meanwhile, "in 1944, just after Rome was liberated—not more than a month after that evening we first saw each other at Colonel Rehm's party—you met the woman I've just been to see in Via Boncompagni. It was I who introduced you to her. She's an easy woman, a prostitute, I think. But you're sure to have forgotten her. You can't possibly remember. . . ."

She described the meeting in the *trattoria*, going into details that she thought might help me remember. I did not know what to say. But what could I say? Could I choose that moment to tell her that since the very next night after that meeting in the *trattoria* Dorotea had been my mistress for the last four years? I was in anguish. Perhaps my expression deceived her, for she made more and more efforts to describe the *trattoria*, the luncheon, the date, and Dorotea herself, until I, with a vague gesture of pain, which she perhaps took for impatience and severity, said that, yes, I did remember and she could continue. And Jane continued:

"That woman, who is called Dorotea, is the only person I know who knows—the young man I loved. I wrote him letters, Harry, letters from Capri, when we came back to Italy two years ago, and he swore he never received them. I believed him. But last night, on the telephone—"

"Who was it on the telephone?" I interrupted. "Was that him?"

"No, it wasn't his voice."

"Are you sure?"

"Absolutely. It was a voice I didn't know. It mentioned the letters at once."

"It didn't to me," I said. I remembered clearly that the voice had not mentioned letters.

"Of course," Jane hurried on. "Of course I didn't say anything to you about them. Letters are the weapons of blackmail. The only proof. Without the letters I could always deny it all to you and then buy them off him. Or I could confess everything to you, as I am doing; and he could use the letters against you too, by threatening a scandal if we didn't pay him."

"But who is this person who has the letters? Him? Was the person who telephoned acting for him?"

"I don't know, I don't know, Harry," she said between her

tears. "That's why I went to see Dorotea. Dorotea's absolutely certain it's not him. Dorotea, you know, is a decent woman, a woman with a real heart. But she could be mistaken."

"But you," I observed, "if you've written him letters, and known him for so long, you must have some idea of his character. Is he the sort of person who's capable of doing this?"

"No, I don't think so. At least I'd never have thought so, never. . . . But when one's guilty, Harry, one doesn't see clearly into others—least of all into the person linked to one's guilt. Perhaps—probably—almost certainly—I may be accusing him falsely. But I'm not really accusing him, Harry. I know nothing about it. I've failed in my duty toward you, Duccio, and Donatella. I'm afraid something terrible may happen. We must pay up. Buy back the letters. Dorotea says that Aldo is sincere and has never received them. Otherwise, if he had, he would have told her. They see each other often. And she says Aldo can't possibly have had anything to do with the telephone call."

"But where is he? Why doesn't she go and see him? Wouldn't that be simpler, meanwhile?"

"He's not in Rome, he's in Milan, and it's not a thing that can be dealt with by telephone or letter."

"But what's in those letters, Jane? Why are you so afraid? Love letters, romantic phrases—I can't say the idea's pleasant, but why are you so afraid?"

"No, no, I was mad when I wrote those letters. Don't ask me anything. I'll tell you at once; tell you everything. You'll think I was in a state of exaltation, obsessed, mad. I must tell you everything."

"But if it's true that he's nothing to do with it and hasn't ever received the letters, where are they now?"

"I have a suspicion."

"Who of?"

"Be patient, Harry. I must tell you everything first."

"But don't tell me why. Just tell me who; whom do you suspect?"

She was silent and sat there more hunched up and drawn into herself than ever. To confess this name seemed more difficult than anything else. She had told me and repeated her lover's name almost voluptuously, it seemed to me. But this name, of the person who at the bottom of her heart she suspected of having the letters and blackmailing her, she couldn't say. She sighed deeply, sobbed, looked tortured, and was silent.

"Is it a person I know?" I said to help her out.

She did not reply.

I repeated my question, and added: "Tell me, Jane. If I have to take action, I must know the name. Do I know this person?"

Finally, between sobs, she breathed: "Yes."

After another silence, during which I saw what an agony she was in and asked myself in surprise for the reason, she confessed: "Don Raffaele."

Pride had been more difficult to conquer than morality. To confess her intermediary's name was more difficult than her lover's. Anyway, what did I know of this Aldo? I couldn't just despise him out of hand. But Don Raffaele I knew well, unfortunately. I could see again his hairless face, his mock Anglo-Saxon correctness, the vulgarity of his every act and gesture, his mellifluous smile, his shifty eyes. How on earth had that low creature Don Raffaele entered Jane's life? I was amazed and disgusted. For a moment, at the name of Don

Raffaele, I had forgotten my own guilt and Dorotea and her landlady and the friends I'd met that evening in the *trattoria*, who were certainly no less vulgar than the middleman of Capri.

"Why Don Raffaele?" I asked.

"Because the voice on the telephone . . ."

Jane could not repeat to me exactly the words she thought she'd heard in that childish Italian which had made her go pale. But the person on the telephone, she thought, had told her that her letters had never been mailed.

"And I," concluded Jane, "had given them to Don Raffaele to mail."

"I don't understand," I said.

"I know, it's complicated, Harry. And difficult for me to explain. Anyway, it's an old story. For me, and what I feel about it now, it's a story that's been over a long time. Oh, I'd hoped that it was over altogether. That you'd never hear anything about it, or have to suffer from it. And if it hadn't been for those letters, that's what would have happened. I first met Aldo in Naples, in February 1944."

"Before me, then?"

"Yes, before you, six months before."

"Why didn't you ever tell me?" I asked, involuntarily taking on the judge's role. But it was she who wanted me to be her judge. I noticed that my questions and apparent severity seemed to console her in some way. It was exactly what she needed. That was why she had spoken to me. I began to sense that she wanted to confess in detail that distant lapse of hers, which had perhaps never been complete enough, just in order to relive it again in some way—in the only way she now had the courage to relive it. I felt a great compassion for her, and my look and voice were sad. Willingly she mistook this sadness for severity.

"I've never told you anything, Harry—because from the first moment I saw you and knew you, you've always been so much above me."

"Jane, don't say that. If you only knew, I'm certainly a worse sinner than you are."

She smiled. I could see she didn't believe me. Should I have interrupted her? And talked myself? Confessed everything, on the spur of the moment? Disillusioned her forever about me?

I swear that I was silent not from cowardice, not for my own sake, but for hers. At that moment I felt, with a certainty which, I admit, I don't feel now, just what my duty was. And I felt I was making a bigger sacrifice then by keeping silent rather than talking. It was my duty to continue to pretend, at least for the moment, that I was, as she said, so much above her.

"From the very first moment I met you, Harry, I saw you, I don't know, as a sort of living reproach for my relations with Aldo, a call and a hope to free myself of them. I think I loved you just for that. For you carried me up with you into your world, among your pictures, studies, thoughts, where everything is beautiful and pure. . . ."

"Jane, Jane, my dear, beautiful sweet . . ." I said, tears welling up irresistibly from the sense of my own unworthiness. And I embraced her and held her to me in a wave of overwhelming tenderness. "Why this martyrdom," I thought, "why do we want to be angels and can't? Only death," I felt, "can bring an end to it."

But the law of life is that everything must be paid for;

that to every height there is a corresponding depth; that the most divine of feelings must inevitably alternate with the most bestial; and that the spiritual urges farthest removed from the tyranny of the flesh evoke as counterbalance the instincts from which we thought ourselves to have been freed.

"I met Aldo in Naples in February 1944," began Jane again, after our long, tender embrace, when we were once more far apart, she in her corner of the sofa, I standing by the window. "I was working at the Camaldoli Hospital, the biggest and most modern in Naples, which had been requisitioned for the Allied forces. It was a bad moment in the campaign. The front was on the Garigliano, and the bridgehead at Anzio. Hundreds of wounded were coming in every day. We were working very hard. The big square in front of the hospital . . ."

As Jane spoke, I saw Naples during the war again. My memory flashed back to that particular atmosphere of confusion, vitality, and adventure, in the city which was the liveliest in the world in normal times and which Gobineau had even then called a human ant-heap, now stirred to frenzied chaos. And I remembered that square in front of the hospital. What a place! Swarms of people. Traveling stalls. Merry-go-rounds, shooting-galleries. Open-air barbers. Children like flies everywhere. Unemployed and refugees of all kinds and ages. Civilians and American, British, Indian, Italian, Negro soldiers in a tangle of language and gesture. Traffic of canned goods, cigarettes, women for the soldiers. Black market of everything, for everyone, by everyone. And our military police carried away in that human sea, completely impotent to establish any kind of order, limiting themselves simply to controlling the most dangerous abuses, the drunkenness of our GI's.

Without Jane having to tell me, I also realized the state of mind she was in when, after her work was over, she came out on that square and had to cross it on her way to a few hours' necessary distraction in the city.

After the long hours of nursing, after seeing ghastly suffering and sometimes death, after the agonizing strain of operations, after the shrieks and groans of the wounded, after the nauseating smell of dressings, there she was out in the pure air, under the blue sky, in a climate that in February is already spring, and with the sun, the Naples sun, shining over everything.

"One morning I came out about eleven o'clock. I was off duty till six in the evening. Edith, whom you may perhaps remember, was going with me. But she always took much longer to get ready than I did. What the fate of a lifetime sometimes depends on! If it hadn't been for that little defect of Edith's, I'd never have met Aldo. I was longing to get out and breathe pure air, and told Edith that I'd wait for her in the square below and asked her to hurry.

"It was a wonderful day. I was in a jacket and skirt, without an overcoat. How well I felt—strong and happy, in a mood for amusement, and thinking of Capri. Till a few minutes before, as I dressed I had gazed from the window of my room on the top floor of the hospital at the distant shape of Capri, gray between sky and sea. I'd never been there. But Edith and I would perhaps be going within a month, when our fortnight's leave was due. We had to write in the leave roster which rest camp we were going to, and we had naturally put Capri. That day, meanwhile, we intended going down into town, lunching at a restaurant by the sea, eating *frutti di mare*, then going out for a row in a boat. As I waited for

Edith, I was walking up and down in front of the hospital. Every now and then I would close my eyes and feel the sun on me.

"Standing still, in the sun, amid the crowds, right at the corner of the building, was a young man. As I went up and down from the main entrance to the corner and back, every time I reached it I could see him clearly. I was forced to look at him, and he looked at me.

"He was tall, very tall for an Italian, and very muscular, though his height made him look slim. He had short brown curly hair; regular features, with the round adolescent lines of certain ancient statues; light, almost yellow-looking eyes; and full lips. He attracted me very much at once. He was dressed well, too well, as flightier Italian men dress, with studied, almost feminine elegance.

"I remember well how by the third or fourth time I passed near him on my walk, I'd ceased to feel annoyed at Edith's lateness. Instead I found myself glancing worriedly at my watch, for she would be arriving at any moment now. But she was still late. And now every time I walked toward the young man our eyes met with a smile, a slight one on his side, a scarcely perceptible one, perhaps, on mine. I glanced again and again at my watch as if to let the young man know that I was waiting for someone and that our smiles, on both sides, only alluded to my embarrassment at waiting.

"But suddenly I felt a longing to talk to him, if just for a second, about any futile subject. Going toward him, I pulled out a pack of cigarettes, put one to my lips, then as I reached him, turned round and began searching ostentatiously in my bag and pockets for matches, which I pretended not to find. He came up to me at once, his left hand outstretched; it was a big hand, with a gold ring, a gold bracelet, and a watch with a gold strap. Flicking a lighter, he said something to me in English."

There was no doubt about it, then. I had met the young man too that evening in Trastevere. He was a friend of Dorotea's, it couldn't be anyone else. I didn't remember his face; but his hand, how could I forget that?

"He spoke English with a strong Italian accent, but more or less correctly. I don't know what we talked about—the lovely day, Naples, the war, Capri. A few embarrassed words, between long silences. I was beginning to get worried. What if one of my superiors, entering or leaving the hospital, should see me talking to an Italian, particularly one of such dubious appearance. At the same time I could not stop gazing into his laughing yellow eyes, and I realized that if Edith did not arrive I wouldn't have the strength to break away."

You, as an Italian, must remember particularly one of the oddest sides of our occupation, odd for you Italians, but so normal for us Americans that no one even commented on it. But you must certainly have been struck by the fact that, while American soldiers hadn't the slightest scruple or hesitation about associating with Italian girls, of every kind and with every purpose, from frenzied coupling with so-called *segnorine* to the most correct sentimental relationships with girls of good family, yet it was unthinkable for the WAC's and all the women serving in our army as nurses, typists, or secretaries and so on to have even the last kind of relationship with Italian men—not to mention the first!

Naturally, as with all spontaneous manifestations of a point of view or deep-seated customs of a people or an army, there was no rule forbidding an American girl to be seen in public with an Italian man. There was no need for such a law, for it was no crime, but simply a thing that never happened, which was inconceivable could ever happen.

In Naples, in Rome, and later in Milan, I often went to parties given by the best families, aristocrats who were often related to English or Americans. We would dine, dance, and spend the evening exactly as if we were in the most formal and boring drawing-room of Mayfair or the East Side. It would be full of Allied officers. But never once did I see a single American girl. The problem never even came up. It just did not exist.

There was no theory behind this. If you had accused any girl in the American forces of avoiding Italian men because she considered them outcasts, she would have either just laughed or thought you silly. Before and since the war there have been cases of marriages between American girls and Italian young men, particularly if the latter are of good family. But none at all during the war. On the other hand, during the war and since, there have been lots of marriages between young American men and Italian girls.

So I realized at once it was the flavor of forbidden fruit that had tempted Jane. In this too her behavior reminded me of mine, for though our GI's risked nothing in being seen with *segnorine*, it was considered rather careless behavior for an officer, particularly with a *segnorina* as showy as Dorotea. In any case a passing escapade was admitted, not a continual affair.

"Finally Edith arrived, very much surprised to see me with an Italian. I said good-by more coldly, in Edith's presence, than I'd have liked, and never even gave him my hand. But for quite opposite reasons I looked him in the eyes also more fixedly than I'd have liked. As he said good-by, he introduced himself with a ceremonious little bow:

" 'Gentilini.'

"I went off with Edith, hoping never to see him again.

"Perhaps the hope was not sincere. Perhaps when we're being tempted and trying to overcome the temptation, we never are sincere. Oh, Harry, I felt very strongly that that handsome, vulgar young Italian attracted me for all the things in life I most despised. But at the same time I felt that the violence of my temptation was linked in some way with this contempt. What was I to do?

"I hoped never to see him again.

"But next day, as I was changing to go out, I found myself, almost unconsciously, preparing an alibi with Edith. I told her that as soon as we got down into the town we'd have to separate, as I was going to confession. In Naples there was a church of the Marist fathers, who are French or at least speak French. Edith isn't a Catholic; she was to let me go alone, and we were to meet later at the restaurant. I did actually intend to go to confession. Next day was the first Friday of the month, and I intended to go to Communion as usual. But can I sincerely say that, deep in my heart, I hadn't kept a dark corner for the chance of meeting that young man again?

"Which was in fact just what happened. As soon as we were out in the square, I looked round instinctively, in the blinding sun and confusion, for the figure of Aldo. I saw him at once, though, artful like all Italians, he was not waiting near the gate where Edith had met him the day before, but much farther away, beyond the corner where I'd seen him before he came up and talked to me. He saw me at once too and let me know it, not by any greeting, but by taking the cigarette out of his mouth and standing still, looking in our direction. Yet Edith also saw him at once. He really was too showy. Or perhaps he attracted her too. She pointed him out to me with a touch of malice in her tone:

" 'Jane, look who's down there! Isn't it that handsome Italian you were talking to yesterday?'

" '*That handsome Italian*,' those were her exact words. And, terrified by my own reactions, I realized that though Edith's malice hurt me, it also flattered my pride. The strongest of the mixed emotions agitating me, as I crossed through the crowd on my way to the city, was pride at having set eyes on such a handsome man and pleasure at my own desire for him. This desire was so strong and new in me that for the moment at least it alone seemed enough to fill me with joy.

"At that moment I had no ideas, no plans. I had seen him again for a second, among the crowd, in the sun. That was enough for me. If a Mephistopheles had appeared at my side, invisible to Edith, and whispered in my ear: 'Jane, do you want that young man to follow you?' I'd have replied: 'No, why should I? I'm happy to have seen him again, and want nothing else.'

"But yes, there was a Mephistopheles near me that day. Only he was also too artful to show himself. He took on the guise of a street vender, one of the innumerable street venders who thronged Naples in those months when all the inhabitants of the city seemed to go round from morning till night selling something. He was very small and thin, bent, almost hunchbacked, dirty, unshaven, with sunken cheeks and a pair of eyes glittering like diamonds. In his long, dry, filthy hands he had some postcards or amulets, perhaps both, I can't remember. At the turn of a narrow street, where it was difficult to pass between a fence on one side and an open-air booth for fried food on the other, he planted himself in the middle of the passageway in front of us and forced Edith and me to stop. Disconcerted and revolted by him, we refused to buy anything. But while he insisted and I turned instinctively to look for another way through, I saw Aldo in the distance, high on a flight of stone steps by which we ourselves had just reached the narrow street; the street was in shade, the stairs full in the sun; for a second I saw Aldo standing motionless amid the crowds surging up and down.

"He had seen me. He was following me with great care. This time he made me a sign with a hand, which no one, even Edith, however, could see among the gesticulating crowd. Anyway, she did not notice anything as she was too busy giving money to Mephistopheles to let us pass.

"My heart was beating hard now. I'd been sure that Aldo would follow me. But he might have lost me in that dense crowd and labyrinth of narrow streets. And at one and the same time I was hoping and fearing that he would lose me. I didn't know which I wanted more, really. I was in torture. That was the only time I turned round. I left things to chance, or fate, or Providence—at that moment I no longer knew if I had a faith still or not.

"When we reached the church, I said a hasty good-by to Edith and confirmed our rendezvous at the restaurant we'd been to the day before. I hoped at least to enter the church before Aldo, if he was still following me, could see where I was going. I knew that if he managed to get near me I would never have the strength to avoid talking to him. All I had the strength for was to run away, vanish, and pray.

"After saying good-by to Edith, I hurried up the steps of the church and then, as I raised the heavy leather door-curtain, glanced back. No sign of him. With a sigh of relief and disappointment I went in.

"The church was very dark. I went to a side chapel, where the lamp of the Holy Sacrament was burning. It was empty. To call a priest to hear my confession, I should have gone into the sacristy. But I needed to pray beforehand. Kneeling down, I prayed desperately to Our Lord, to the Sacred Heart of Jesus. . . . Next day was His day; and His image, by a moving coincidence, was on the altar before which I was kneeling. The lamp burning there was not electric; it had a real flame, quivering in a heart of red glass. And my heart quivered with that flame, and prayer came spontaneously to my lips:

" 'Jesus,' I said to Him, 'You who suffered so much in the Garden of Olives, You know what I've felt since I've seen that young man. And You know that my anguish isn't just ridiculous. If I described what I feel to Edith, she would certainly laugh—be shocked and laugh. But You, oh My Lord and God, who forgave the Magdalen, You won't be shocked. Tell me, O Lord, what I should do if I see that young man again, if he follows me again and tries to talk to me. I don't love him, O Lord, I know that my passion for him is shameful and sensual, like his beauty, which is pagan and diabolic. Must I continue to flee from him? But the more I flee, the more I desire him. Even now I feel desperate and unhappy and full of regret at having hurried into this church so that he shouldn't see me; perhaps at this very moment he's looking round the little square outside and into the neighboring streets, never suspecting that I've entered this church. Have I done right, or wrong? If I've done right, why do I feel regret? Why does Your peace not descend on me? If I've done wrong, why don't I feel sure I've done wrong? Why have I such contradictory doubts? My Jesus, O Lord, O Sacred Heart of Jesus, I put my confidence in You.'

"Scarcely had I finished this prayer when I felt I was no longer alone in the chapel. I was leaning over the prie-dieu, holding my face and muffling my sobs in my hands, and my fingers and palms were wet with tears. I raised my eyes a little—enough to see beside and very near me, to my right, the body of Aldo. I recognized it from the jeweled left hand, which was at that moment settling slowly, gently, by the fingertips, on the edge of the prie-dieu. He was standing by my side. All I could see was his body, broader than I had thought, and his hand.

"The pleasure I felt was so intense that I remained motionless for a long moment, my face in my hands, as if continuing to pray. But I was not in fact praying. I was kneeling with eyes closed, happy, suddenly emptied of everything. He was there, beside me, his body was there: that was enough for me."

16.

To a judge?

No, not even to a witness. Jane, without knowing it, was telling her story to an accomplice.

How often I'd felt the same anguish! With only one difference. I'd never prayed. And what use had prayer been to her?

Rather than placate, it had refined her agony. Rather than resolve, it had complicated her problem. Prayer, therefore, had had the opposite result to the one conventionally expected of it.

But might not this extreme torment of hers, this refinement of pain and pleasure, possibly have been one result of it? A contrast nobler and truer than mine?

"Finally I raised my head," went on Jane, "and began to dry my tears, I said nothing because, I repeat, I was thinking of nothing. I had no plans, ideas, or even desires. And I believe that if Aldo, too, had remained silent, I would have stayed there in that church, kneeling near him, for any length of time. But he spoke.

" 'You're crying?' he murmured. 'Why are you crying? I'm so sorry!'

" 'Go away!' His words had been enough to break the spell. 'Go away!' I begged him. 'Away! Go away at once, leave me alone.'

" 'But why?' and instead of going he knelt down at my side, touching my arm and grazing my cheek against his. I looked ahead of me, at the altar. But he looked at me and said in a low voice: 'Why do you want me to go away, now that we can talk in peace?'

" 'We're in church! Aren't you ashamed? I've come here to pray!'

" 'Ashamed? What of? Don't you know that I love you?'

" 'Don't talk nonsense. You scarcely know me.'

" 'Has one got to know people to love them? You know one hasn't. I love you. I've loved you from the first moment I saw you. I'm a student. Will you marry me?'

"Oh, Harry, you know how these Italians are. They're

so sure of themselves. They look one in the eyes. And if they see a reply, a smile of sympathy in a woman's eyes, they think they've been authorized, even invited, to continue. But we, who don't consider our personal feelings so important, and don't believe that we have to follow our instincts so unhesitatingly, and aren't used to confusing sincerity with innocence, we're taken by surprise.

"I should have smiled at that absurd proposal. Instead of which I was perturbed. Of course, I wasn't stupid about it. I realized at once that this young man was only talking about marriage so as to make a favorable impression on me, convince me at once that his passion was serious, and so obtain a more immediate favor. And if, by a chance as absurd as the proposal, I had agreed to marry him, he would have had nothing to lose. He would have brought off a master stroke— *'fatto il colpo,'* as they say in Italian. But I was so perturbed that, disregarding these considerations, I did actually think of it as a real possibility. What, marry that vulgar, effeminate Italian? It would be like giving my soul to the devil for the whole of my life.

"I realized that I was tempted, desperately tempted, to say yes and surprise him. He knelt there, smiling and calm. But I had hell inside me.

"Suddenly I jumped up, terrified. Escape was the only chance.

" 'Good-by,' I said, and hurried out toward the door.

"He reached me in the middle of the church, took me by an arm, and stopped me. I'd have liked to tear myself free, but two old women were looking at us, and I didn't dare. And the pressure, the contact of his hand, had weakened my will at once.

" 'This way,' he said gently, leading me toward a side door instead of the central one where I'd come in. Before raising the curtain into the lobby, he went up to the stoup and offered me holy water.

"I looked at him in amazement, hesitating as if faced with a sacrilege and the devil in person were offering me holy water. But his expression as he did so was so simple and conscientious, almost childish! I grazed his damp fingertips, turned round, genuflected to the altar, and went out.

"In the dark lobby, as he let the heavy curtain fall behind me, I tried to open the door to the street. But it was closed with a massive chain. Before I could touch it, he was near me, embraced me, held me tight to him, and began to kiss me.

"I hadn't had much experience. My flirtations could be counted on the fingers of one hand.

"Anyway, this was something completely different from everything I'd known till then. I'd never thought one could be kissed like that. In those seconds I realized that till that moment I'd been just a little girl. So a kiss, I said to myself, can be a rough, strong, and savage thing. My head was whirling; I seemed to be fainting; the world around, Edith, friends, mother, home, war, ideas, tastes, everything I'd lived with till that moment, all collapsed, were canceled from my consciousness, no longer existed for me. All that existed was the particular flavor of that mouth, its infinite changing variations, each as precise and logical as so many concepts which, however, needed no words for expression as each had its meaning in sensation. Animals, I suppose, must think like that."

"Jane," I said to her at this point, thinking bitterly of Dora's kisses, "Jane, why didn't you marry him instead of me?

I believe it was your duty to marry him and no one else."

She raised her eyes to me, perhaps for the first time since she had begun talking, and seemed to be seeing me through the distance of her memories.

"My duty? Perhaps—" she replied, and in the tone of her voice there was a deeper bitterness than mine, regret at a chance lost forever, memory of a fatal cowardice. "But I didn't see it as my duty, quite the contrary. My duty. . . . Perhaps you're right, Harry; only you used the wrong expression," and she concluded with the glimmer of a smile even more desperate than the sadness that had dominated her till then. "One ought to say: it was my duty not to do my duty."

"Exactly, Jane."

"But how could I know that then? If I'd never seen Aldo, and some friend of mine had praised his looks and described them to me minutely, I'd have felt only disgust and repulsion; in fact, if I thought a minute, he seemed to unite in himself all that I've most loathed all my life, from childhood. He was Italian, and although I loved Italy I've never had any respect or sympathy for Italian men. He was handsome, and I've always felt cold toward handsome young men; since college I've always gone for intelligent companions, not good-looking ones. He was vulgar, and the slightest suspicion of vulgarity had always been enough to destroy any man's attraction for me. When people talk of love at first sight, they usually mean it's just the result of long preparation and happens when we meet someone by chance who corresponds to our tastes, culture, and education, or even, according to some people, who resembles our father or someone we've loved in childhood; an apparition, in fact, for which we were already prepared.

"For me, nothing could have been falser. Or, if you like, nothing could have been truer the other way round. Aldo was exactly the opposite of everything I'd ever loved and dreamed of. You know, Harry, how I've always loathed jewelry on hands—not only on men's hands, but even on my own. Before you gave me this bracelet, you know that I'd never worn one before. Even a wrist-watch irritates me, you know. Very often I've carried mine in my bag. At first, you remember, I couldn't even get used to my wedding ring. Those metal watch-straps, those identity bracelets which became so fashionable during the war among our soldiers and which everyone wore, have always disgusted me, I don't know why.

"Well, that left hand of his— How can I explain to you? It became a fetish, an obsession with me. I could never look at it without being disturbed. And when he went out of my life, it was the thing I most remembered about him.

"I wanted to go to an analyst. Père de Lalande told me it was useless and would only make things worse. When the devil succeeds in tempting our flesh and nerves in such a way, against every argument of our reason, he can't be defeated even by prayer, but only by our trying to think of something else, by distraction. Père de Lalande even advised me not to pray. For by praying, he told me, I would go on thinking of my temptation more than ever, without wanting to.

"I understood this by myself that day, saw it clearly even in my anguish as he kissed and hugged me to suffocation in the darkness of the lobby. At one moment I felt lost. I was being embraced and kissed by the devil in person, to drag me down into hell. I must do something, anything short of flight. For I realized that a violent reaction now would only have the opposite effect, and link me to him forever. So I fell back on cunning and suavity; not only with him, but with myself. 'If I tear myself out of this embrace,' I thought, 'and tell him I don't ever want to see him again, I know perfectly well that next day I'll suffer so much and the temptation will be so strong that I won't be able to conquer it. And I'd look for him among the crowds at the hospital entrance, and do all I could to meet him again.' So I used cunning.

" 'Listen,' I said, drawing out of his arms slowly, caressingly, so that he did not try to prevent me, 'listen. It's very difficult for us to see each other in Naples. I'm always with my friend as you saw yesterday and today. And at all costs she mustn't ever notice anything. She wouldn't understand. Also, I'm very busy at the hospital. But in a month I'll have two weeks' leave—'

" 'In a month!' he whispered sadly. 'In a month the war will be over! And you, if you don't want to marry me, will go back to America! I love you and am ready to marry you. But I realize that you must get to know me before accepting me. And how can you if we aren't together a little? In a month!'

" 'No,' I said, 'the war won't be over. It'll last a long time yet. In a month I'll have a two weeks' leave, and will go to Capri. . . . Couldn't you come to Capri? There we'd be freer, we might be able to see each other. . . .'

"He smiled with pleasure. I asked him why.

" 'Because I'm not living here in Naples,' he said. 'I'm living at Capri. I work as an interpreter with O.S.S., with Colonel Livingstone. I come to Naples nearly every day. But I'm living at Capri. Tomorrow they'll give me a uniform.'

"We left the lobby and walked slowly across the church again toward the main entrance, my arm in his. This coincidence about Capri should have calmed me, instead of which

I began to worry, though only slightly, all over again. I had wanted to leave with the possibility, the hope, of seeing him again; not with the certainty. In fact, when I'd told him that the chief obstacle to our continuing to see each other in Naples was Edith, I had not mentioned that she would be coming to Capri too. But I found some peace in the thought that, after all, no one was forcing me to go to Capri. In a month, if, as I hoped at that moment, the temptation had passed, I could choose some other place."

"Instead of which——"

"I went to Capri just because I thought I'd overcome the temptation. Since that day I had never seen him at all. He had not come to the square any more. Within a few days I'd succeeded in putting him out of my mind, in almost forgetting him. I'd had a moment of madness, I said to myself. And I left for Capri with Edith, without any hesitation and feeling quite sure of myself. Père de Lalande says it was the devil who made me so calm and certain and even made me forget the physical appearance that had tempted me. The devil knew that the only sure way to get me to Capri was to take away all my fear of sinning and even my memory of that sweetness. . . . The strange thing, I observed to Père de Lalande, was that Aldo himself never appeared during that time, as if he'd known and been in agreement with the devil. But this too was quite by chance. Colonel Livingstone had been transferred and the new commanding officer left Capri much more seldom and, when he did, never took his interpreter with him.

"I caught the boat with Edith one morning in May. My heart was light. I swear to you that I'd forgotten everything. I enjoyed the sea, the sun, the pure air, chatting with Edith, discussing everything we'd do at Capri during our two weeks.

Edith wanted to paint and had brought her paintbox with her. I had brought a lot of books and wanted to lie about in the sun for long hours and get sunburned. We wondered whether the water was warm enough for us to bathe. That's all I was thinking about. Later on we went into the saloon as we suddenly felt rather chilly and hungry. We went on talking at a table in the bar, eating sandwiches and drinking vermouth. Suddenly we felt the boat slowing down and looked out.

"The island lay in front of us, huge, high, against the sun, an unexpectedly disagreeable sight.

"I felt a tug at the heart. In those contorted lines, in those convulsed and colorless shapes, I felt something sinister and hostile. And now Aldo had appeared to me again. After a month of not thinking about him, he now reappeared against the cold dark background of the island. I saw him again in detail, his face, his look, his body, and all that I'd thought I'd forgotten.

" 'Aldo is up there,' I said to myself, looking toward the soaring peaks and the little scattered houses. 'Aldo is up there, and without Edith knowing and without knowing it myself until this moment, I am going to him.'

"That same evening I saw him in the piazza. As he had warned me, he was dressed in American uniform, like so many Italians who worked in our offices. Yet as soon as he saw me, he was extremely discreet. I was with Edith, sitting at a café. And he was at the café opposite, with some American officers. As soon as he saw me and was sure that I'd seen him, he put on his sunglasses, either so as to be able to look freely toward me, or so that there'd be less risk of Edith recognizing him. I was grateful to him for his prudence. But if I wanted to be with him, how was I to set about it? And then, *did* I want to be with him?

"I was in a turmoil, torn between fear and desire. Fear of not being able to meet him without Edith knowing or some American seeing us; and fear of committing sin. The first fear helped the second. The difficulty, the impossibility almost, of being with him persuaded me that my sin would be all the more serious.

"Edith, luckily, had turned her back and could notice nothing. I had also put on my sunglasses. And that evening all I did was look over at the tables of the café opposite, observe his every gesture, even from a distance, and enjoy the thought that we were both on the island and that tomorrow, the day after, one of those days, there'd be, perhaps, a chance for us to meet naturally.

"Finally Edith looked at her watch and said that it was time for us to go. We were staying at Anacapri, in a Danish lady's *pension*. The *pension* was deserted; we two were the only guests. But the Danish lady had asked us to be punctual for dinner and the bus was leaving in a few minutes.

"To reach the bus, which was at the end of the piazza beyond the church, we had to pass right in front of Aldo. I was afraid Edith would see him. But I also wanted to prolong to the last my pleasure in looking at him. I told Edith I wasn't hungry; that it was so pleasant at that café, in that cool air, with our Martinis in front of us; that we had been living by the clock for more than a year and now we were resting; the Danish lady might be worried, but it didn't matter; if need be we could take a taxi. Edith, smiling, surrendered. But just at that very moment I saw the American officers with Aldo get up and move away, and he, naturally, moved too. He lagged behind and kept on looking in my direction until he vanished under the arch toward Tragara.

"I returned next day. We got into the habit of coming to that café for *apéritifs* twice a day. At midday and evening. And every time I saw Aldo; and every time he saw me. We could not go on like this. An anxiety, a kind of mania, was rapidly growing in me, and even prevented my sleeping; it was taking away my appetite, all pleasure in my stay. Edith, worried, asked what was wrong with me. I told her that I didn't feel well. Perhaps the Danish lady's food did not agree with me. Finally, one day, I suddenly realized that a week had already gone by since our arrival on Capri. Another week and we would be leaving. I was sitting at the usual café when this suddenly occurred to me. And Aldo was there in his usual place. As if urged by a spring, I got up, before I'd even thought of what to do. But I was determined to speak to him.

"Edith, who was reading in the sun, asked where I was going. I found an excuse, I don't remember what—oh yes, I'd seen a pair of sandals I thought of buying in a little shop in one of the side streets. As I said this, I trembled at the idea that she might get up and come with me. But she didn't move and went on reading. So fate was on my side!

"Encouraged, I crossed the piazza toward the café where Aldo was sitting. As I walked straight toward him (both of us were still wearing our sunglasses), I looked fixedly at him and he looked fixedly at me. Still looking at him, I passed very close, almost grazing him. When I reached the little street by the church, I turned an instant and saw him getting up; he had understood.

"I almost ran up the little street, and when I'd reached a spot that was out of sight of the piazza, I stopped. A second later Aldo was there, holding me in his arms. There was no one about, luckily. But I tore myself from him violently and walked on again, explaining as I did so how he was to see me."

"You had already thought it all out, of course!" I observed to Jane, with involuntary sarcasm.

"Yes, Harry, but only as a sort of game," she explained, readily, sincerely.

"A dangerous game!" The ironic remarks came out without my wanting them.

"You must believe me, Harry!"

"I believe you, I believe you." And in fact I did believe her, and do still believe she was sincere. But I added: "And how does that change matters, anyway?"

"It changes matters because everything seemed to happen naturally, independently of my will. I know quite well that I'm just as much to blame. I'm not looking for excuses, Harry. I only want to tell you it all, as it really happened.

"I'd thought everything out, twisting and turning it all in my imagination at night, in my room at Anacapri. I heard the wind among the olives, opened the window, went out on the terrace, looked at the olive groves pressing close against the house all around, and the big bougainvillaea with its lilac flowers climbing up to my terrace; I gazed at the night, the starry sky, the lights of the fishing boats in the deep darkness of the sea; and that fixed idea allowed me no sleep. I'd thought everything out as if it could happen; yet thinking, firmly, that it never would.

"Now, in that little street I had no time to change that plan. Even if it was not the best, I had no time to think of another. I told it to Aldo. Then, asking him to wait before he followed me and if possible to return to the piazza by another way, I said: 'Till tonight!' and hurried away.

" 'What about the sandals?' said Edith when she saw me.

" 'They weren't my size.'

"Aldo was to come after midnight, as soon as the colonel, who went to bed at any time and sometimes very late, had left him free. The Danish lady went to bed about ten. Edith, luckily, had a passion for sleep and went off early that night too. By half past ten I was locked in my room. It communicated with the bathroom, but the bathroom communicated with Edith's room by another door. The keys, thank God, all worked.

"I'd told him to take a car, but he couldn't reach me before half past twelve. I tried to pass the time by writing a letter home, reading a book, an illustrated magazine. Impossible. Never in my life had I felt in such a state. I tried to distract myself. But my thoughts kept on returning to my meeting with Aldo, which would take place in two, three hours, that night anyway. Very soon, I think, I got into a state not far from madness. Up and down the room I walked, my feet bare so as not to make a sound. I looked continually at myself in the glass, combed and uncombed and recombed my hair. It seemed difficult to breathe. I opened the window, went out on the terrace, came in again. I'd never felt such a sensation of acute physical suffering mingled so deeply and inextricably with delight, and I could find no peace.

"At one moment I felt a need to sob and shout out loud. It was like a fit. I was afraid not to be able to dominate it. I let instinct guide me and did what my body told me. I stripped naked, lay down on the floor, and began to twist about like an animal. Eventually I found myself lying quite motionless, face downward, on the smooth, cold tiles; I'd taken my watch off and put it down on the floor in front of me. My eyes were fixed on the dial as I lay there quite still. It was my small wrist-watch, the one I still have now. It has no second hand. So time even seemed to have stopped for the watch too. 'Suppose it's half past eleven,' I said. At the thought that he might come as late as two in the morning or later, I felt I'd never have the strength to wait.

"In the half-darkness of the room (I'd covered the bedside light with a scarf) my eyes strained to watch the progress of the hands. And their progress was endlessly, torturingly, slow; as if one second after another was being torn from me, lingeringly, agonizingly, rackingly drawing me farther and farther away from the object of my desire. Drawing me away? Yes, how can I explain? My desire was growing much more quickly than the time I still had to wait was lessening. After a quarter of an hour lying face downward on the floor, an hour and three quarters seemed infinitely longer than two hours had a quarter of an hour before.

"When now I think over that terrible night, I'm convinced I was ill. That young man, however much he attracted me, in no way justified such a state of mind. I was gripped by madness; like the stories one reads in the papers about a peasant one night axing to death his wife and children, for whom he'd always shown love. That is why, you see, Harry, I feel I can tell you everything. It's as if I were talking to you about another person. I *was* another person. Why, otherwise. should I have chosen a man I despised?"

I said nothing, but thought of myself and Dora, and I knew that Jane was mistaken. Not lying. She thought she was telling the truth. But I knew that our nature sometimes seeks in love the very negation, the annulment, of ourselves. And it's no illness. On the contrary, it's an urge to understand all the part of reality which we usually refute, a desire to be like others, a need for normality.

"I don't remember any more what other follies I abandoned myself to while I waited. All I remember is that the more time passed, the more I suffered. The delight that had been mingled with torture at the beginning, gradually lessened until it vanished altogether. Toward one o'clock I even began to hope that he wouldn't come after all; all I wanted was to know. It was agony. I yearned for it to finish in any way at all.

"From half past twelve onward I stood out on the terrace, against the wall, in a corner from which I could see the entrance gate. No keys were needed. He only had to push it. I'd explained everything. I fixed my eyes on this little gate at the end of the path through the orange trees; fixed them so long and ceaselessly that the muscles of my neck and face ached. It was as if it depended on me; as if, by continuing to fix my eyes on it, I could, by the obstinacy and strength of my gaze, conjure up Aldo's figure from one moment to the next.

" 'Now,' I said to myself a number of times, 'now I'll count up to nine; and after nine he will appear.' I counted, feeling certain. Counted. As I counted I gradually slowed down. But still I felt certain. I reached seven. Eight—

"Nine. Nothing had happened. A warm wind was blowing in gusts over the olives. There was no other sound. The Danish lady and the maid slept on the other side of the house, Edith on the corner next to my room; not even she, if she'd been awake, could have heard that gate open or anyone walking up the graveled alley.

"I didn't look to see if there were stars. I didn't look out to sea at the lights of the fishing boats, as I had on other nights when I'd thought of him and only of him. I gazed fixedly at the gate. And without, now, even thinking of him any more. I only thought of what I was looking at: the gate. As the gambler who has put everything on a single number looks only at the roulette wheel and where the ball is going to stop, without ever thinking of the money he wants to win. I was mad, Harry. Don't you too think I was mad?"

"Yes, I know, Jane," I said without wanting to, "I understand you. I've felt something of the kind too."

"You can't have!" she exclaimed, almost shouted. Once again I realized that no confession on my side was possible that night. Perhaps she would not even have believed me. She would have thought I'd invented it, out of pity for her. At all costs she wanted to feel she'd sinned; as if, with the passing of time, she'd almost begun to doubt the reality of her own memories.

"Suddenly I heard a step," she went on. "A light, distant step on the concrete path that leads down between villas and gardens from Anacapri. It sounded like someone barefoot, a local.

"I held my breath, still gazing at the little gate. What if it was him and he'd made a mistake, and went on down the hill? I'd explained everything to him clearly. But the path went on. Farther down there were other villas, other gardens, other gates. The step grew nearer, gay, light. It couldn't be him. I resigned myself beforehand to its not being him. Perhaps it was some fisherman on his way down to the sea, to draw up his nets. It couldn't be him.

"For an instant a figure passed by the gate. A girl. How I hated her! I realized that, subconsciously, I'd still hoped it was him. I could have killed her! She was surely returning from or going to meet a lover. I hated her for that too. Finally, perhaps from the next-door villa, I heard a gate creak. Silence returned. And from time to time little gusts of wind, the olives rustling.

"How long did I stay there, standing still against the rough wall, of which my back now knew every dent and sharpness? What time was it now?

"I hadn't brought my watch out with me. I'd been silly enough to hurry out on the terrace impulsively, without thinking of it. Now it seemed impossible for me to go in for it, to leave my observation point even for a second.

"There was the gate, white amid the black leaves of the oranges."

17.

No, she did not wait for him in vain. And he came back the following nights, every night of Jane's last week on Capri. He would arrive toward one o'clock, clamber up the bougainvillaea, and leave before dawn.

Neither the owner of the *pension* nor Edith noticed anything. Only once was Jane afraid. One night he told her he was free next day; the colonel was going to Naples and there was no work for him to do. He suggested to Jane that they should meet at a given time at a deserted spot beyond the Marina Piccola; he would come for her in a boat; if it was a fine day, as it probably would be, they could bathe together. Jane refused. Then when dawn was breaking and the moment came for him to leave, he threw himself on the bed, determined to stay and sleep there. Jane, terrified, had protested angrily, but she'd had to yield and keep him there the whole day, till the next night, hidden in her room.

She locked herself in. The difficulty was never to let in Edith or the maid. Pretending she had a violent headache, she said she had to rest and didn't want to see anyone. Edith, one of the many times that she came to knock, had even asked her if there was anyone in her room, as she thought she'd heard voices.

Jane had waited until Edith went down to Capri; then she'd gone out, locking the door behind her again, and hurried down to the kitchen to get some sandwiches and wine.

Edith, on her return from Capri, had knocked at the door again and found it very odd that Jane would not let her in. She was worried, she said. Finally the sun set, night came, and as soon as possible he left.

Jane had told me about this rather comic episode, she said, only for one reason: that it made Edith suspicious, and this had very serious results.

Much more serious than Jane thought herself! If it hadn't been for that suspicion of Edith's, I'd never have met Dorotea.

On the last night, Jane thought it would be unwise, after what had happened, not to accept an invitation to accompany Edith to a party given by some officers they knew.

So she said good-by to him the night before. And at his insistent demand, for he said he was very much in love and still wanted to marry her, she agreed to see him again, but only in Rome. It was known that Rome would shortly be liberated and that the hospital would be transferred there at once. Jane told him to write to her when she reached Rome, and gave him the military address of the hospital. Then they said good-by.

Jane realized she had been weak to give him her address. But at that moment, she assured me, she was cured. She longed to leave Capri and for everything to end. She'd given him her address as the only way of avoiding his bothering her. Otherwise she was afraid he'd come and look for her at the Camaldoli.

The parting, on Jane's side, was cold and disillusioned. When finally she saw him walk away down the alley for the last time, go through the gate and disappear, she heaved a great sigh of relief.

The last day she spent with Edith, and in the evening went with her to the party. They dined in a *trattoria* with the officers who were their hosts, who afterwards, as was their habit, took them on a round of visits to drink whisky and dance with friends. Jane was pleased to find herself among Americans again. Perhaps from reaction, or perhaps because she'd realized during those nights spent with an Italian that her tastes and preferences had not changed, she felt a need, a hope to meet an American who could attract her in another way; in the way in which I attracted her when she met me in Rome a month or two later.

Toward midnight they found themselves in a luxurious villa at Tragara. She had scarcely entered, in a euphoria of whisky and company, when at the end of a corridor, through a series of open doors, she saw Aldo, in a white kitchen, taking ice out of the electric refrigerator and preparing drinks. She'd found herself in his colonel's house. Aldo saw her at once too, but did not greet her and went on with his work. Jane was certain nothing would be noticed. What about Edith, though?

Just afterwards, in the drawing-room, Jane instinctively tried to turn her back on the door to the passage. Edith, on the other hand, was facing it. So it was from Edith's expression that Jane saw Aldo had come in with the drinks; Edith started, went up to her, squeezed her arm tightly, and whispered in her ear: "Jane, your friend from Naples!"

"Which friend?" exclaimed Jane.

"Yes, look, *that handsome Italian!*"

Jane looked and denied it before she had time to consider if this was wise. No, Edith was mistaken. They were alike—very much alike—but it was not him.

Edith insisted. But Jane did not give herself up for beaten. Later, however, when she and Edith happened to be talking to separate groups of officers, she suddenly noticed Edith looking at her. And it was not a friendly look. No, it was a hurt, surprised, inquiring look.

Aldo was moving round the drawing-room, but only to bring more bottles, glasses, and ice or take away used glasses. He took no part whatever in conversation, was not introduced, and returned to the kitchen each time. In fact, he was acting as a waiter, even if officially his duties were those of interpreter.

Never once did he raise his eyes to Jane or make her the smallest sign. Jane, of course, particularly after having discovered Edith's suspicion and secret hostility in that glance, was in agonies. Finally the time came to leave.

As they went out through the garden, Edith came close up to her, looked back at the villa, and said in a low voice: "I don't understand why you deny the evidence."

"Go and ask him yourself, then," Jane had replied rather sharply then. "You'll see."

She was sure now that Aldo would back her up. It was Edith who wouldn't. Edith asked nothing more about Aldo, and never mentioned the matter again. But from that moment Jane realized she could no longer count on her friend.

A month or so later, Rome was liberated. As soon as Jane got there, she received a letter from Aldo. He made an appointment to meet her on the terrace of the Pincio, by day. Throwing prudence to the winds for once, Jane went. Away from Aldo she had gradually been gripped by the need for him again, by her madness, her illness for him. These alternating states of mind, said Jane, psychoanalysts call cycles.

Illness? No. But I understood so well! Even if the physical and social consequences made it more serious for a woman, how could I not forgive her?

It so happened that Edith was driving through the Pincio in a carriage and saw her with Aldo. This time there was no doubt. Jane thought of an explanation: she would tell Edith that in the Pincio she'd run into the young man from Capri, not the one from Naples. But they were arm in arm at that moment. The explanation was not very credible.

Edith surprised her. When they met that evening, she said nothing about it. But from that moment she began to treat her with slight coldness, and every now and then gave her one of those strange glances in which Jane saw not only indignation and reproof, puritan Anglo-Saxon prejudice, but also un-conscious envy.

Some weeks later Jane was sure she was pregnant. In spite of her repulsion and horror, and though all her deepest ideas were against abortion, she never for a moment considered anything else. But the only person she could apply to was a medical officer in their unit, and this doctor was Edith's fiancé. Even if he said nothing, it would have been impossible to hide everything from Edith.

She had to act at once. After a night of anguish she told Aldo. He introduced her to Dorotea. Dorotea, with her landlady, who was, or said she was, a nurse, took her to another nurse, and the latter did the job.

It was in this very period that Jane met me. Reacting against the despair and fear through which she'd passed, against her remorse and her fear of the future, she had attached herself to me as to a guardian angel.

Even so, she never entirely ceased to see Aldo as long as she stayed in Rome. At intervals, succumbing each time after a hard struggle with herself, she went to visit him in some furnished room; sometimes at night too, perhaps after she had dined with me and while I myself did not dare visit Dorotea lest Jane telephone me at the hotel.

"That evening you left for Naples, when you were to embark for France next day," I asked Jane, suddenly remembering, "when I came to get you at the camp, and I waited while you went to and fro on your work, at one moment I saw you telephoning. You told me you'd rung up a priest, your confessor, I think, to say good-by. Was that true?"

"No," said Jane, bowing her head. "I did have a confessor, an American Jesuit priest. The one who afterwards sent me to Père de Lalande in Paris. But I'd already said good-by to him the day before, at the Gregoriana. That call was not to him."

We remained a long moment in silence. I thought again about that night, the departure from the hospital, the confusion of ambulances and trucks. I remembered my sorrow at having to say good-by to Jane, and my impatience, so strangely linked with that sorrow, to be with Dorotea. I saw Jane again at the telephone in the booth, scarcely visible through the dirty cellophane window, far away and almost unreal. She was talking on and on into the telephone without knowing that I, outside, could see her though I could not hear what she was saying. Never as at that moment, in spite or perhaps because by going away she was leaving me entirely to Dorotea, never had she been so dear to me, seemed so destined for me. Now I discovered that the truth was very different. It certainly made me suffer.

Yet I felt that I had no right to complain, except from vanity. For Jane had lied to me; but at heart she had not deceived me. She had only betrayed me in so far as she had betrayed herself, and in this betrayal I was her accomplice. Her guilt had taken her one day to Dorotea, and that had led to my guilt. Just a bitter consolation? More, I think. She had telephoned; I'd thought she was telephoning to a priest. She was telephoning her lover. But I, as I had looked at her and thought of her as mine, had thought also of Dorotea and superimposed Dorotea's image on hers; so was I not one with her in the same deceit? And had not Jane, really, been nearer to me, more faithful to me, more mine, just because she was at that same moment as divided within herself as I was?

No, the more I thought it over, the more I realized that Jane and I were fatally united, joined and confused in good as in evil; and that so are all human beings in one way or another: the betrayers betrayed, and the betrayed betrayers. Everyone, shut in his own egoism, thinks one day that he has a right to debase himself, to indulge some low instinct that he thinks does not harm his neighbor. But he is mistaken: that low instinct is never harmless; it propagates, it multiplies, it reacts. Sin seems, in fact, to be regulated by the same law that regulates virtue: and perhaps sin, no less than virtue, is a form of love.

She said: "Harry, I've lied to you about something else; hidden something even more serious from you. At Christmas, the last Christmas of the war, I was in France, you in Rome. Well, that Christmas I came to Rome and spent two days there without your knowing it, and never told you. I took advantage of a short leave I'd been given and a plane taking two doctors from our hospital to Rome, and left Saint-Pierre-d'Albigny to meet you. I wanted to give you a surprise and spend Christmas with you.

"But, once in Rome, I was gripped suddenly by the temptation to see him again. There was something desperate, extreme, about that temptation. Even though you had not asked me yet, I knew that we would marry once the war was over. 'Well,' I said to myself, 'I want to see Aldo again and be with him for the last time. Then I'll go back to France, then to America, and it will be over forever.'

"I rang him as soon as I reached the airport. He was at home. I went straight to him, before I'd even gone to the hotel. I stayed with him till nightfall. It was Christmas Eve. Aldo had to dine with friends and couldn't get out of it. We made an appointment for next day, and he left me alone. I went to the hotel.

"In spite of the time (it was past nine) I telephoned the Jesuit priest at the Gregoriana. I was tormented by remorse for what I'd done. I wanted to confess, to go to midnight Mass and take Communion. The priest said that the church was closed at that hour and he couldn't see me. I insisted. Then he told me that one of their priests, a German who spoke excellent English, was going to say midnight Mass at the German nuns' of Blessed Paula of Mallinckrodt. He gave me the address, and said he'd warn the priest and telephone the nuns."

"Do you remember the address?" I asked Jane.

"Why? I don't remember it exactly, but it was near the Via Nomentana. Why do you want to know?"

"Because I saw you that night, Jane. You took a taxi, didn't you?"

"Yes," she said.

"Just before midnight?"

"Yes."

"I was in the jeep. At the Viale della Regina crossroads I saw you for a second, in a taxi. I saw the American uniform and thought then it was a girl who looked like you. How could I imagine you were in Rome? That night I went to a Catholic church too, to St. Peter's."

I said no more.

We did not dare look at each other.

If only I could have spoken! But how could I? Later, a day or so later, I would tell her everything. At once was impossible.

"At the convent I found the priest, who heard my confession. Then I went to Mass. It's a small chapel. On the benches to the left were the nuns, ten or twelve of them. On the right the guests, a few German families resident in Rome. The nuns sang while the priest said Mass. One, an old, thin one, played the harmonium. She had the most beautiful hands I've ever seen, white as wax, so slender and delicate.

"All the nuns sang in chorus. They sang their Christmas hymns. One or two of the tunes were the same as ours. They sang in sweet and trembling voices. Their faces were alight with happiness and faith. When they looked at the altar, they saw what I could no longer see: their childhood, the loveliest hours of their childhood, which were not lost for them. They had remained faithful to their loveliest memories. And now these memories, perhaps of distant Christmas nights in Bavarian villages, returned to them intact. Their hearts still held what they had believed and hoped and loved. They had renounced the world. But they had kept the best that the world can offer: the union of body and spirit.

"I realized, watching them, how mistaken it is to think of nuns as women who mortify their senses. No, they sublimate them. They were praying and singing, I saw, with a transport of their whole nature. And when they got up from the benches and began walking slowly, erect, their hands joined, their gaze fixed ardently on the altar, to receive Communion, I saw that in them was fulfilled the supreme act of love.

"I asked myself at that moment if it wasn't my duty to follow their example—not, that is, to become a nun, but to marry Aldo. To throw away my life, as they had thrown away theirs. To trust and love one single being to the utmost, with my whole self. To sublimate my senses too. Was Aldo unworthy? Why was he unworthy? What human creature is unworthy? Unworthy of what? Of me? I knew quite well that of the two of us it was I who had sinned; I who was betraying him, and you, and myself, by dividing myself between him and you. Had he not said many times, and even repeated a few hours before, that he was ready to marry me? I used to laugh when he said this to me. Well, he might be self-interested; the marriage would raise him up socially; but if there was any possibility of salvation in him, if there was a seed of decency (and why shouldn't there be?), it was my duty to tend that seed and make it flower.

"Just because I did not feel I had the courage for this, I cut my appointment with him next day, and never even telephoned to warn him. In the evening I took the plane back to Nice, disappearing, I thought, forever from his life."

"Jane," I said with deep understanding, "Jane, it's true; now I'm sure; it was your duty to marry him."

"I forgot him. Or I thought I'd forgotten him. What with the end of the war, Paris, the return to America, our marriage, a new life, and then Duccio. But already at B— in the long hours I stayed alone at home while you were lecturing or at the library, I had begun, bit by bit, to think about him again. I did it as if there were no harm, no danger in doing so, you understand? As if they were just idle fancies. And gradually, instead, they became an obsession. I thought about him continually. That's why I was so nervous. That's why I was determined to come to Capri. You were right, the climate wasn't good for Duccio. But I was mad again, as I'd been before. I wanted to see him again at all costs, at Capri. It was at Capri that I'd always imagined myself meeting him once more. It was at Capri that I wanted—how can I say it?—to put my dreams to the test, to convince myself if I really loved him or not. I felt that I'd have no more doubts now. It would be either yes or no. And if it was yes, I was determined to tell you all and go against my religion, against everything; to divorce you and marry him.

"That at Capri. But meanwhile I telephoned him when I got to Rome. He hadn't lived there for a long time, they told me, and hadn't left an address. I still had the number of that woman, Dorotea. I rang her. She did not know, either, where Aldo was just then. But she assured me that she'd be able to trace him through a relation of hers. If she succeeded, what, she asked, was she to tell him? To write to me, I replied. Where? To Capri, I said. And then I suddenly thought that his letter might arrive when you were still there. It was then I made that mistake, that great mistake, Harry. Oh, I realized what I was doing. But it was stronger than I. There happened to be a piece of paper on the bed-table as I was telephoning. It was the piece of paper on which Guglielmo had written addresses for us in Capri, particularly the name of Don Raffaele, to whom we were to apply as a trustworthy person to find us a house. I asked Dorotea to tell Aldo to write to me in a sealed envelope, and put the envelope inside another one addressed to Don Raffaele. Aldo only knew my maiden name. Anyway, I told Dorotea everything, even that I was married."

"But what about your letters?" I asked.

"Once at Capri—I hate telling you this, Harry. You see I've told you everything else. But this is what I'm most ashamed of. Well, I've sinned and I must pay for it."

She was silent an instant, her face buried in her hands, as if gathering up strength. Then she began again:

"At once, on the first day, at the Quisisana, as soon as I found myself alone for a moment with Don Raffaele—you had gone to the piazza or somewhere—perhaps to buy some papers—I talked to Don Raffaele. He would be receiving a letter, I told him, and he was to give it to me without your knowing."

"But what excuse did you find?"

"I invented some story about having been divorced before marrying you. And how my former husband, who was now in Rome, wrote to me every now and then. And how I preferred you not to know. There, I've told you everything."

"But what about your letters, your own letters?"

"Aldo's letter arrived when you were still there. If I want to imagine what hell must be like, I remember what I felt that day. You were with me, in the living-room of the villa. It was sunny. Don Raffaele came in with his greetings, his bows, as usual. He handed you a list of expenses he'd incurred. You put the list on the table, and as you read it and pulled out your wallet and counted out the money, he winked at me behind your back. Just like this. I was in hell at that moment. Don Raffaele was the devil."

Jane had winked, imitating Don Raffaele. As she did so she went pale. I too felt a shiver at seeing her. And then, immediately afterwards, a great compassion. What was it that forced a creature so noble, with a mind as open and clear as Jane's, to such baseness, such self-torture?

"You know what everyone used to say about the post office at Capri. Probably they were exaggerations. But this led to another temptation of mine, part of that other, bigger temptation to which I'd decided to abandon myself. I wanted, yes, absurd as it may seem, I wanted to put myself in Don

Raffaele's hands. Either fearing or willingly believing that the post office would open my letters, as soon as you left I handed Don Raffaele a letter in an unaddressed envelope. He was to write the address himself. The post office knew his writing and would certainly not open it."

"And so, for Don Raffaele, this first husband of yours is an Italian. But do you think he never opened the envelopes?"

"I'm afraid of having understood what was said on the telephone only too well. I'm afraid that they were never sent. When I saw Aldo later, he swore he'd never received a single letter from me. And till yesterday, till the phone call, I'd always believed he hadn't told the truth."

"But why should he lie? Why tell you that he hadn't received them if he had? For what purpose?"

"I thought—I don't know—that my letters were so absurd and mad that he'd not had the courage to reply, or hadn't replied from simple laziness and didn't dare confess it to me."

"Where were they addressed to?"

"Where he'd told me, in his only letter. To the Hotel Excelsior in Rome."

"Was he living at the Excelsior?"

"I think so."

"Do you remember how many there were?"

"Six. Some of them very long ones."

"And what did you say to him?"

"Everything I felt and hoped in those days. I told him how I was waiting for him, and why I was waiting for him. All the maddest ideas that passed through my head. If I'd not been able to write those letters, if I'd not had that outlet, I really think I should have gone mad."

THE CAPRI LETTERS

"But didn't it ever cross your mind that by doing so you were putting yourself entirely in his hands?"

"Yes, it did. But don't you understand? That was just what I wanted, to put myself in his hands. The danger was part of the pleasure I felt in writing them."

"You didn't think of me, or Duccio?"

"I did think of you. But I was ready for any solution, however extreme, however shameful. I told you, I was ready to divorce you and marry him."

"Did you write that in the letters too?"

"No. That was the one thing, perhaps, that I didn't write. Because I'd decided to see him again before I made up my mind. I wasn't sure that when I saw him again I'd love him as much as I wanted and believed I did. I could have written him a letter a day. I could have lived writing to him. But he never replied. The last fortnight I didn't write any more. Duccio began to be ill. I said to myself that the Lord wanted to punish me; that I was living in a state of mortal sin, a sin of thought and a sin of desire; that I could not go on like this.

"And by now I despaired of seeing Aldo at Capri."

18.

The *festa* of San Costanzo, patron saint of Capri, is on the 14th of May. Preparations begin a long time ahead. From early in the month, in the lonely sirocco-laden afternoons, Jane began hearing the irritating explosions of firecrackers and the interminable ringing of monotonous bells. The baby would give a jump at each explosion. If he was asleep, he would wake up and never go to sleep again. If he was eating, he would push the bottle away and refuse to suck it any more. There seemed an atmosphere of disquiet and anticipation, not only on Jane's part as she waited for Aldo, but in the season itself, the exhausting weather, the entire island preparing for the *festa*.

Jane was still obstinately waiting, but at the bottom of her heart she had lost hope and was feeling she had damned herself for nothing.

Then came the day of the *festa*. Already in Paris, to explain why she had returned to the intense practice of her religion, she had described to me what had happened that day; her sudden terror at a colic of Duccio's, her anxious search for the doctor among the crowds in the procession, and her vow to Our Lady of Lourdes. She had described everything, however, except the most important part. The real reason for her vow she'd kept back. Now, sobbing, she asked me to forgive her and told me the truth.

"For the last two weeks, as he didn't reply, I'd stopped writing those mad letters. I had renounced any hope of seeing Aldo, though I still thought about him. Whenever I met Don Raffaele, I felt a deep loathing for him. It was a loathing mixed with anger for having put myself in his hands so uselessly. And I felt, as I saw him, a torturing regret for having dirtied myself so in the hope of a pleasure I'd not even had. There was no consolation, no compensation at all. I was getting the worst of everything. Duccio was really beginning to suffer from the climate, ate little, slept badly. So that had been a useless risk too. I began now to think of the date of your return, which was drawing nearer, almost with impatience. But that date would also mean the end of all my dreams; and I could not resign myself to that. Was this really to be my fate? After long months of desire, after all the fantasies, which had recently become detailed, precise, definite, would I really never in my life meet Aldo again?

"I used to leave the villa and wander round Capri like a madwoman. I'd go on along deserted paths toward the point of Tragara, beyond the view of the Faraglioni, beyond the last isolated villas. I'd wander over the yellow, short dry grass, among the great porous rocks scattered about, and stretch out on one of these warm, rough rocks, lying there motionless a long time, looking at the deep-green sea and the sky, or covering my eyes with a handkerchief and a straw hat, when I would see a warm, shapeless yellow darkness.

"I would lie there expecting him by some impossible chance to arrive at that moment at that very spot. He had climbed the path I'd used and now, having seen me from above and noiselessly crossed the grassy field, come up behind me and was embracing me before I'd even seen him.

"Again, like that first time I'd waited for him on the balcony in the *pension* at Anacapri, I counted up to nine. But this time the calculation was much more absurd!

"I'm ashamed to tell you these things. But I don't want to hide them from you, so that you can measure the state of hysteria and folly I'd reached.

"As that first time I had seemed to find some comfort in the roughness of the wall I was leaning against, so now I found it in the jagged surface of the rocks. Lying on them, my body began after some time to hurt in various parts. And the pain was almost a pleasure. For my body, by suffering, made me feel I was no longer alone.

"One day when I got home from one of these walks, I

had the idea of continuing to hurt myself in some way. This need to suffer physically was an integral part of the waiting and the desire which were my life. It was a small consolation. I thought up ways of making myself suffer. I felt a kind of need to be squeezed, crushed, suffocated.

"At night, when the servants had finished their work and left and the nurse and Duccio were asleep, I went down into the garden, took a thick rope that was used to hang the washing on, cut off a long piece, and then, locked in my room, tied it round my waist two, three times, as hard and tight as I could, so that it almost took my breath away. I imagined it was him gripping me like that with his hands. And I went to bed suffering, but at least happy to suffer, and fell asleep.

"Another day I walked up to the *pension* at Anacapri. I went over the path he had come that night on his way to me. There was the little white villa among the dark leaves of the orange trees, and the bougainvillaea with its lilac flowers clambering up to the terrace outside my window. I went in. The Danish lady was much older and more wrinkled. She made a great fuss over me. There were no guests, except for an elderly spinster, a writer. I asked to see my room. Everything was exactly as it had been. The light wood furniture, the curtains, the cretonne covers, the trinkets, and the air, the light, the smell, the sounds from outside, of the country, of the wind in the olives. Certainly when Aldo appeared I'd come back here with him. I did not tell the Danish lady that I was married; I told her that I was on Capri for a few days, alone in a hotel. And that if I should stay longer, I might perhaps come to her.

"But this was in the first days, when I was still calm, still certain that he would reply to my letters and come.

"Afterwards my days gradually became more and more restless, agitated, frenzied. I'd go continuously up to the piazza, wander among the café tables, the groups of foreigners and tourists, in the hope, every time, of seeing him. Or I'd meet the funicular, which came up immediately after the arrival of the Naples boat, and scrutinize the faces of the passengers with tireless anxiety. Don Raffaele was always there, with his ambiguous smile, and his exaggerated and obsequious blackmailer's greetings. His presence seemed to persecute me. When I met him returning home toward one in the afternoon in the deserted sunlit path, even before I asked him he would throw his arms wide and with a gloomy look say:

" 'Nothing, signora, nothing yet. . . .'

"I would force a smile and say: 'It doesn't matter, Don Raffaele. No importance at all. Thank you, good day.'

"But then, a few steps farther on, I would stop in front of a little wooden gate that opened in the white wall of a villa.

"It was the villa (I seemed to remember, but I was not sure) where I had gone that last night of my stay in Capri during the war, the villa of the American colonel, with whom Aldo then worked.

"I would stop in front of that little door of old faded, cracked green wood, and it seemed to me, absurdly, that Aldo had left a trace of himself on it, his name carved with the point of a penknife on its rough surface. ALDO, I sometimes seemed to read there, ALDO, ALDO. I don't know why, but if I could have discovered his name for certain, written by him, on that old bit of wood, it would have comforted me almost as much as his arrival at Capri. Perhaps I was suffering so much because I was living entirely in imagination and desire.

In spite of the letter he had written to me from Rome a month before, I began to doubt whether he really existed; and I needed some external object that could prove it to me.

"My eyes searched until they ached trying to decipher the squiggles on the door, partly made by age and weather, partly by human hands that had really scratched names, dates, and phrases there. How was it possible, I said to myself in my folly, that Aldo hadn't written his name there too? But then, was I absolutely sure this was the colonel's villa? I had come with Edith, that far-off night, and after lots of highballs—how could I be sure?

"Finally the *festa* of San Costanzo arrived. The day before it, the nurse, as I already told you in Paris, had twisted her ankle badly going down to the Marina Piccola and couldn't walk. The two servants, who had asked me a long time ahead, were on holiday till the day after.

"Toward three in the afternoon—for the last two hours bells had been ringing and rockets firing uninterruptedly, while from afar, brought by the gusts of wind, could be heard the choir of the procession or the band intoning religious hymns—as I was lying on the bed, shut in my dark room and trying in vain to find sleep, which I never even found at night, suddenly I heard the nurse call out in a terrified voice: 'The baby's sick!'

"Duccio was puce-color, his eyes staring, his whole body rigid. He didn't seem to be able to breathe.

"I took him in my arms and shook and called him. But he didn't seem to hear or even see me.

"With the nurse, who understood children and their illnesses, we tried everything—water, slaps, holding him face downward by the feet, artificial respiration.

"Finally he came to. Although his color didn't change, he turned his eyes toward me and recognized me. He did not cry or smile, but fixed me with his open, sad eyes, with an expression of intelligent suffering. A conscious, adult expression. For his eyes expressed not only suffering, but a human surprise at having to suffer. They looked surprised and hurt. 'Why didn't you tell me, Mamma?' they seemed to accuse me, those eyes. 'Why didn't you tell me I could suffer like this?' And suddenly his little hands began to claw at the empty air. Then jerkily, in spasms, they trembled.

"I looked the nurse in the face and realized then there was no hope of its not being serious. She could not walk. So I ran outside. There was a telephone in the villa next door. But the house was shut. I rang the bell. I called, shouted; no one there; they were all at the *festa*. Then I ran as fast as I could up the path toward the piazza.

"I didn't meet a soul till the piazza. When I reached it my heart was pounding in my throat. Crowds were jammed into every cranny; people were standing on the chairs and tables of the cafés to watch the procession, which was just about to pass. The bells were ringing continuously, reverberating among the narrow walls. Firecrackers were exploding very near; the din was deafening. I began to push through the crowd, toward the pharmacist's at the end of the piazza, squeezing my way between the bodies in the fetid, stifling air. Everyone was crushed up on top of one another, men, women, locals, tourists, foreigners, trying to see above the shoulders of those in front, applauding, laughing, shouting, moving about. It seemed incredible this could be a religious festival. Before reaching the pharmacist's, I caught a glimpse of Don Raffaele at a window above the café on the corner. I called him with a shout and asked him if he'd seen the doctor.

"'There he is,' replied Don Raffaele from the window, and he pointed toward the church on the opposite side. 'There he is, on the steps of the church!' Then, noticing my confusion: 'I'll come right down, signora!'

"I plunged back toward the church, but could only move very slowly. Don Raffaele had reached me before I'd got more than a few steps. Continuing to push ahead as best I could, I told Don Raffaele that Duccio was ill, very ill; while I tried to reach the doctor, why didn't he go to the pharmacist's?

"'The pharmacist's shut today, signora!'

"Don Raffaele tried to encourage me ('Don't let yourself worry too much, keep calm, babies get all sorts of little ill-nesses!') and helped me on by going ahead of me and clear-ing the way.

"But when we reached the steps of the church, the doctor was no longer there.

"Don Raffaele asked everyone. No one had seen him. Then he began protesting, rather frantically, that he'd seen him with his own eyes at the very spot where we were stand-ing, only a few minutes before. Everyone around continued to deny it, and Don Raffaele to protest.

"Finally a woman admitted having seen him. Yes, it was true, Dr. Cuomo had been there by her side up to a second before and had gone off in that direction, to the left, crossed the piazza toward the funicular. The woman, a local, and Don Raffaele talked very rapidly together in dialect, with much gesticulation, and I could scarcely understand anything they said. Above all, I couldn't understand why the woman kept on talking after telling us the direction the doctor had gone. She wasn't talking about anything else; in that stream of words I could constantly make out: '*Dottore, u dottore, u Dottor' Cuomo.*' And I couldn't understand why Don Raffaele went on answering and questioning her without a pause. Surely the only thing to do was to follow the doctor and try to find him. I took Don Raffaele violently by an arm, pointed in the direction the woman had pointed, and asked him, please, to follow the doctor at once.

"But no. Don Raffaele made me a sign for me to keep silent, just a moment, another moment. And went on talking in dialect with the woman.

"I looked round, bewildered, thinking of Duccio and his surprised, hurt, imploring eyes. Wedged tight in that crowd and heat and noise, watching the Children of Mary in pale blue enter the piazza at the head of the procession, hearing their tremulous shrill voices over the shouts and applause, I felt helpless to do anything, anything at all, to save Duccio, and suffered as I have never suffered in my life.

"'Don Raffaele! Don Raffaele! Please!' I shrieked, pushing him hard with both hands.

"'Keep calm, signora, keep calm,' he replied, turning round quite unperturbed. 'What's the use of agitating yourself like that?'

"'But the doctor's gone off in that direction!' I shouted again, pointing toward the funicular.

"'No, he hasn't. It's his wife, who was here with him, who's gone off there. The doctor, on the other hand, has gone to the house of a woman who's having a child, and this woman here was just explaining to me where this other woman lives.'

"'Is it far away?'

"'I don't think so.'

" 'Let's go at once!'

" 'But wait. This woman here hasn't explained it quite clearly. I haven't yet understood exactly where it is.'

"He began to talk to the woman again, and she to explain and make quick gestures, right, left, up, down, which were meant to indicate turnings and other turnings, ascents, descents, steps, arcades, paths.

"At that moment the band, which had entered the piazza after the Children of Mary, suddenly broke into a first triumphant, lacerating crash.

"Behind the band came eight men in long red robes held in at the waist by rough cords, shouldering on two poles the wobbling gilt statue of the patron saint. I looked with loathing at the saint's rosy features and childish eyes; with loathing at the three old priests, smothered in gold, who followed the statue, looking tired, bored, and indifferent to all the noise, chatting among themselves or exchanging every now and then a glance or a phrase with some near-by woman in the crowd; with loathing at the little boys violently swinging their censers and scattering clouds of rank incense; with loathing at them all.

"And there, while Don Raffaele at my side was still talking to the woman and getting her to explain exactly where to find the doctor, while the band, which had stopped a few yards from us on the steps of the church, was repeating at full strength and without a pause the chorus of its triumphal march, there beyond the line of fat canons in capes and ermine following, equally profane and repulsive, the little boys and the three priests, there, in the front row, in a group of smart-looking women, stood Aldo.

"Even at the very first glance I had no doubt it was he.

"There he stood, in his beauty and his youth, amid the crowd, in the Capri sun. A blue jersey with short sleeves. The hand with the gold bracelet. He laughed as he looked at the procession. One arm round a girl, he was talking animatedly to a fat, painted, bejeweled old woman standing by him on the other side. And suddenly the deafening noise of the band, the banal repetitive chorus, were no longer unpleasant: in an instant they had become lovely, truly triumphant music.

"I forgot everything. So he had come. But he had not come for me, evidently. He had come with friends. With women. That was why he hadn't written any more. Even so, the pleasure and surprise of seeing him there alive in front of me again a few yards away were so strong that I felt no disappointment, no jealousy of those women. They were part of his triumphant appearance. They were a kind of court which was his due and which suited him very well.

"How long did I stand there like that, gazing at Aldo? Don Raffaele's voice shook me as if out of a dream. I had completely forgotten Duccio. Don Raffaele told me that he was hurrying off to get the doctor. I was to wait there.

"But I did not wait there. As soon as Don Raffaele had gone into the crowd, I, quite without wanting to, without realizing it, as if I were hypnotized, forgot all about Duccio again. And, as the procession was ending, I crossed the piazza and went up to Aldo.

"He saw and recognized me without any embarrassment, as if he was expecting me. He must have been expecting to see me, in fact, as he knew I was on Capri. With perfect assurance he introduced me to his two women friends. The youngest was, at least so he said, a film actress. And the fat old one was even a celebrity, a famous radio and variety singer—a name that of course I didn't know or have forgotten. The younger one was pretty but insignificant. And anyway I realized at once that she was not Aldo's friend, but the old singer's, whose guests they were. The singer, on the other hand, seemed to me to be a woman of character—brash, gay, violent, and authoritative. She was having an affair with Aldo, there was no doubt about that, and almost seemed to me in love with him. And appearances (only appearances because I never had any wish to make inquiries) were not exactly in Aldo's favor."

Jane's story interested me. But it made me want to prevent, all the more, any blackmail with the letters; to find out who had telephoned, and what this Aldo was really like.

"Do you mean to say," I asked Jane, "that the singer gave him money?"

"I don't know anything about it, Harry; but that was certainly the impression I had, seeing them together."

"But didn't he work? What work did he do? Was it true he was a student?"

"I don't know for sure. As to work, I think he only worked in films while waiting to pass his exams. I don't think, anyway, that he earned much. Dorotea told me today that now he's in Milan in a review."

"What about the letters?"

"As soon as I could get a minute alone with him in the confusion of the crowd scattering after the procession, and the singer and her friend were walking a step or so ahead, that was the first question I asked him."

"Well?"

"He said that he'd never received them. At least he denied it firmly at once. Why, he asked, shouldn't he have replied? I'd sent them to the address he had told me in his letter: Hotel Excelsior, Rome. Why on earth hadn't he received them? I suspected Don Raffaele of holding them back; but at that moment there was Aldo finally alive beside me, and at the same time the thought of Duccio, for whose sake I would have to leave and perhaps lose Aldo. In the anguish of these two strong contrasting feelings I forgot to worry at all about the fate of the letters. Anyway, we joined his two friends at once. Aldo was going with them to the Quisisana for tea. I hadn't the strength of mind to leave them. So I went with them. What would Don Raffaele do when he returned to the piazza with the doctor and didn't find me? My anxiety not to leave Aldo and my fear of losing him struggled with my anxiety and fear for Duccio. In this uncertainty I managed to achieve, at least in appearance, that calm which Don Raffaele had advised in vain. 'This doesn't matter,' I tried to persuade myself; 'Don Raffaele and the doctor, not finding me in the piazza, will certainly think I've returned to the villa and go straight there; then the doctor will see Duccio at once and prescribe the necessary treatment.' But my calm was only apparent. Sitting at tea with Aldo and the two women on a terrace at the Quisisana, I was in torture at having to talk, joke, and make myself pleasant while Duccio was suffering, perhaps in danger, perhaps— But then I looked at Aldo opposite me. His face had never seemed so beautiful. I was immobilized in that armchair, incapable of getting up and hurrying off as I should have liked to. I was full of desire and remorse. I was happy but desperate. I felt infinitely ashamed of myself; but this shame, I realized, was the consequence of my complete subjection to the creature facing me at that moment, who seemed almost divine; so my shame also gave me pleasure—in fact, increased my pleasure. I felt guilty, guilty at the moment of committing sin. But I felt this sin to be inevitable, right, even beautiful. Can you understand me?

"The sillier and more fatuous the jokes between Aldo and the two women became, the more I tortured myself with the thought that, in those very moments, Duccio was suffering and looking round for me with those eyes of his which so far understood no words but only faces, his mother's above all; this thought seemed to give my infatuation value, to make it infatuation no longer, but real love. This was what I wanted, I said to myself. In the three years that I'd been separated from him, in the long months of solitary daydreaming in America, and finally here at Capri morbidly waiting for him and dreaming about him, had I not prayed for just such a supreme moment as this, for a crisis in which I would prove to him, and still more to myself, that my love was stronger than all I held dearest? And now fate, or God, had offered me this moment, this crisis. Finally, at the risk of Duccio's life, whom I loved more than anything in the world, I had been given this cruel chance of showing how serious my feelings were.

"You see, Harry, these things are clear to me only now, I notice, when I tell you them. In fact, it's by telling them to you that I make them clear to myself. At the time, and even afterwards, they were just a confused mass of anguish and emotion.

"The singer and the girl had decided to make a short trip before nightfall to Anacapri, where they'd never been. They went upstairs to change and I remained alone with Aldo for a quarter of an hour. That was the moment when

I could have told him about Duccio, and escaped. But he knew nothing of my marriage as yet. Stupidly, from fear of losing him, before confessing everything, I wanted him to make love to me again. I wanted it at once. I said so, without looking at him, but without hesitation. He seemed very touched by my desire, which he said he had already noticed. But he was sorry it couldn't be at once, as it would put out his two friends.

"When, then?

"Tomorrow, he said; the other two would have left and he'd try to stay behind. Or he'd go with them as far as Naples and then return. No, that night, I replied, still without looking at him, that very night or never again for the rest of our lives. That very night? He tried, without hurting my feelings, to persuade me to put it off; to make me understand by hints that he was in a party, a guest more or less of the singer and the other girl, and that he couldn't possibly leave them alone that night. What would happen, I asked, if he did leave them alone? They'd be offended. Well, what did that matter, I said, strong in the knowledge of the far worse harm I was doing to myself for his sake. But they'd be so offended that they'd drop him, he explained, they'd never want to see him again. Then I said that if he didn't come with me that night, he would never see *me* again. Still he hesitated. He was silent, and in the silence I thought of Duccio. I saw those little hands again, waving about, shaken by that strange quivering. How much time had passed? What had happened meanwhile? When would I kiss those little hands again? Finally Aldo spoke. He said yes, he'd come tonight. Where, though? To Anacapri, I said, to the Danish *pension*, as before. I'd already been there, it was easy to arrange. I'd wait for him in the path, in front of the gate, at ten. At midnight, he begged. All right, at midnight, I agreed. It would give me more time with Duccio. At midnight.

"I raised my eyes then and looked at him, and saw his gentle yellow eyes gazing at me with desire, but also with uncertainty, almost alarm. How could I be sure of him, I asked. I would go all the way up there. How could I be sure he'd come?

"He could not think of any answer or any proof to give me, and just repeated that he would come and I was not to worry. I was worried, I replied. His word wasn't enough. I wanted a proof. He looked around in bewilderment, then glanced at his watch. 'He's afraid,' I thought, 'of his two girl friends returning.' But it wasn't that. He'd had an idea. He slipped off the gold-mesh strap with the watch on it and handed it to me with a boyish gesture:

" 'There, it's all I possess in the world. Take it. Put it in your bag so that no one sees it. If I don't come, you can keep it forever.'

"I gave a harsh laugh, to revenge myself in some way for the continuous thought of Duccio and the sacrifice I was making. What, I asked with a laugh, did his gold bracelet matter to me?

" 'I know you're rich,' he said then, 'but for me this is worth a fortune. Look at it carefully. It's an Audemars et Piguet. The mechanism alone is worth two hundred thousand lire. With the case, and the strap, which is solid eighteen-carat gold, it comes to more than half a million. I'd be mad not to come. You wanted a proof? I couldn't give you a bigger one.'

"I felt malicious. I'd already given him my soul. What

did anything else matter? I was holding the watch in my hand; I weighed it, looked at it, and then said laughingly:

"'Who knows! I may not be sure of you even now. Perhaps if you tell that singer everything tonight, she may give you one in diamonds.'

"He wasn't offended, poor boy. He dropped his head sadly and whispered again in a still lower voice: 'Don't worry.'

"He had got a little older. For him ten years seemed to have passed, not three. His body was still a youth's, but his face, though its cheeks were still full and firm, showed a line or two here and there, and his eyes were ringed and almost tired.

"The two girl friends reappeared, the fat old woman and the thin young one, powdered, repainted, freshly sprayed with Mitsouko, one noisy, the other simpering.

"We went into the piazza. The outing was to consist in hiring a car, driving to Anacapri, stopping five minutes to look at the view, and then coming straight back.

"I said good-by. There was no reason now for me to stay with them; I could hurry home, feeling at the same time sure of not having lost Aldo. But some strange force seemed to be holding me back and making me linger. I could not tear myself away or take my eyes off Aldo. Having said good-by to them once, I went along with them to the car—the fat man's taxi—and stood there, hesitating, as they got in.

"We said good-by again. The singer, cordial and lively, noticed my hesitation as she gave me her hand. Why didn't I come too, she asked. And seeing I did not refuse at once, she drew me, almost hauled me inside, by my hand which she was still holding.

"I was mad and unnatural, I said to myself as the big motor swung up round the first bend toward the cliffs of Anacapri. Why was I here, sitting squeezed between two over-scented women, getting farther and farther away from Duccio? A mother! What a mother I was! No, no, I wouldn't renounce my motherhood; to draw Duccio to me, kiss him, feel him alive between my hands, alive— For the first time I seemed to realize what it would be like if Duccio had died meanwhile. No, the idea was not absurd; it was quite a natural possibility. Lots of children die at that age, particularly if they are delicate. Duccio wasn't delicate, he was strong and healthy; but he had suffered a lot from the climate. Would I find him dead on returning home? Oh, what could I do to save him?

"I could pray. Finally, for a second or two, I prayed with my whole soul. But was I in a fit state to pray? How long had I been in mortal sin? Not just an hour or two, not just since seeing Aldo at the procession; but since the day I'd reached Capri and begun waiting for him; since that evening at B— when you returned from New York after visiting Loewen and announced that we were going to Italy, and I decided to myself that I'd come to Capri, and told you so; and long, long before that too. I had slipped gradually into mortal sin by letting myself brood, first as a kind of test or game and then more and more seriously, over the memory of those distant hours I'd spent with Aldo at Anacapri; and by imagining other, endless, equally distant hours with him, in an improbable, almost unthinkable future. Could I pray? Would my prayer be worthy of reaching Our Lord? No, certainly not. That would make things too easy. So I didn't dare pray any more. The only thing I could do was concentrate on my own unworthiness to pray.

"At that moment the car reached the last and steepest slope on the climb. It slowed down, spluttering, then after a yard or two stopped.

"Just above that very spot, up among the rocks, in a niche like a small cave, there is a statue of Our Lady of Lourdes, surrounded by votive lamps and ex-votos. The driver of the taxi, the fat man, suggested we should get out and walk on for the last short lap of the climb, while he tried to start the engine again.

"In the gray light of dusk the sheer cliff towered high above us, a vast black mass in which only the little blue and white statue of Our Lady could be discerned, gently lit up.

"Aldo and the two women were not looking in that direction. They had gone to the parapet and were gazing down over the precipice at the colorless glassy sea and the distant lights of Naples. Then, joking among themselves, they began walking on up the road, as the fat man had suggested.

"I stayed behind a few seconds. I gazed up at Our Lady, then at the tall, slim figure of Aldo drawing farther away up the white road, arm in arm with both women. Yes, I could pray! But I must pay in some way for doing so, too. Pay so that my prayer should be answered and obtain the grace that Duccio should live. Our Lady, whom I was now gazing at intensely, had given me the idea and the courage. Yes, she had also given me the courage.

"I had a second, just a single second, of hesitation. Looking at Aldo as he walked away, I felt in that second that I was losing, forever, not only him, but something much more important, something of myself, what exactly I did not know. In that second I realized I was as if suspended on a thread. My whole life was at stake. Suspended where? What stake? I didn't know, I knew nothing. But as I asked myself the question, I had already decided.

"I'd already made my vow. If Duccio lived, I would renounce Aldo forever."

19.

"Shortly afterwards, when we'd got back into the car and were driving round the lanes of Anacapri, the singer noticed that Aldo was not wearing his watch. I said at once that I had it, took it out of my bag, and handed it back to Aldo, who looked at me questioningly. We'd had a bet, I explained to the singer; Aldo had lost and given me the watch as a pledge.

" 'But Aldo,' observed the singer, still jokingly but giving us both a searching look, 'Aldo, to get his pledge back, must have promised some compensation. Why doesn't he carry it out?'

"I said that I didn't want any compensation. I wasn't interested any more. And on getting back to Capri, I bade the group a final good-by.

"I found a way of muttering quickly to Aldo that I'd been joking; he was right, it was much better we shouldn't see each other that night.

"At a run, and praying to Our Lady the whole way, one Hail Mary after another, I set off home. The nurse was standing at the door with Duccio in her arms. Duccio was perfectly well, had been perfectly well only five minutes after I'd hurried to call the doctor; he'd eaten his usual meal and then gone off to sleep. The doctor had come with Don Raffaele and said it had been a violent indigestion with absolutely no consequences. But what had happened to me, the nurse asked. She had been terribly worried. . . . .

"I couldn't reply. I was sobbing with happiness, kissing and embracing the laughing Duccio, and could think of nothing else.

"I could think of nothing else for two days. Busy with Duccio, every now and then the thought of Our Lady came to my mind and I mentally thanked her.

"On the morning of the third day, as I was getting ready to take Duccio down to the Marina Piccola, the maid came and told me a gentleman had called who wanted to see me. She had not understood the name.

"I went downstairs, thinking it was perhaps Baxter, the English musician I'd met in the piazza before you left and who'd come to tea two or three times since. Instead of which it was Aldo.

"As soon as I saw him, I wanted him at once with all my strength; but no longer with all my heart. How can I explain? Well, he was no longer a god to me. He was a vice. An irresistible vice, perhaps. But nothing more than a vice."

"Well, what did you do, Jane? What about the vow?"

"I broke the vow. I broke it without hesitation, that very night."

I looked at her in amazement.

"Without hesitation? How could you? Why? Our Lady had listened to you. Weren't you afraid?"

"No. Because by then I had persuaded myself that the vow no longer had any importance. You know, I had been certain I'd return home and find Duccio seriously ill. To leave him that night, and go up to Anacapri to be with Aldo *while*

Duccio was in danger—that's what I had renounced to Our Lady. That was the vow I'd made, so that Duccio should live. Nothing else. Going with Aldo now meant nothing any longer. It was a pleasure, yes, but a pleasure that no longer had anything—how shall I put it?—anything final, anything absolute about it. It was like fresh water, I felt, compared to what I'd have felt if I'd not made the vow, not given back the watch, and gone to Anacapri that night.

"To go to Anacapri that night, if I hadn't made the vow, meant—you realize?—asking you for a divorce and marrying Aldo. And it would have been a momentous, a tremendous decision, even if, before carrying it out, I had gone home and found, as I would have found, Duccio in perfect health; for I would have been carrying out a decision made at a moment when I was still fearing for Duccio's life, after having tried to pray, and above all after having had the inspiration of the vow."

I reminded Jane of what she herself had told me in Paris when she had talked about her vow, though she had left out the essential part. I repeated, I thought, her very own words: "If God exists, there doesn't exist a before or an after for Him. Everything is contemporaneous for Him." So I considered, myself, that she was bound to observe her vow.

"That's what Père de Lalande told me, too. I tried to defend myself with him, not because I thought I hadn't sinned, but to explain that the sin I'd committed in breaking the vow was infinitely less grave than the sin I'd have committed if, after being inspired to make it, I'd not carried it out that night and gone to Anacapri. That would have been the really mortal sin. The sin that one can commit only once in one's life. The sin for which one can despair enough to go to hell, or repent enough to become a saint. I didn't commit that."

"You must be pleased, Jane, you didn't commit that."

"I am pleased. But sometimes I have a doubt. A strange, torturing doubt. That maybe that sin was necessary. Now, for example, now that I'm afraid for you, now that Don Raffaele is blackmailing us with my letters. . . . Wouldn't it have been better if I'd committed that ultimate sin and we'd been divorced? You'd have nothing to fear now."

Next day Jane was to go to Ciampino to catch the direct plane for New York. We canceled the reservation and made one on a plane leaving from Paris three days later. Then we went down to Capri. It seemed obvious that only Don Raffaele could have the letters, and that the telephone call had been made by someone he knew.

Early next morning we left Rome in a hired car. We were in Naples by ten, in time for the boat. By noon we were disembarking at Capri. Don Raffaele was at the Marina Grande according to his usual habit. He was walking up and down the mole with the head of the *Guardia di Finanza*, waiting for the boat. He saw us at once and came toward us, waving both arms and smiling his broadest smile. But soon he noticed we had no luggage. We told him we were leaving the same afternoon. He seemed surprised and disappointed.

"What? Not staying? It's a crime! To come to Capri and not stay at least a night? Eh! Eh! Eh!"

"We came simply to talk to you, Don Raffaele," I said seriously. His expansiveness exasperated me. I did not want to seem too alarmed. Nor to find myself drawn into any familiarity. So the sooner we came to the point, the better.

"To talk to me? What an honor! I am completely at your service. Tell me, tell me, *signor maggiore*."

"Where shall we go?" I said, turning to Jane.

"Would you like to come up to the piazza? Will you allow me to offer you a vermouth? It's my turn this time."

"I must talk to you about a certain matter, Don Raffaele. We have no time to lose. Can we come to your house? Perhaps that's better." I thought, of course, that he was keeping the letters at home, and once he had accepted the sum I intended to offer him, I didn't want to lose any time laying hands on them.

"At my home? Oh, *signor maggiore*, you must excuse me. But it's so far away for the signora, poor lady. You'd have more than half an hour's walk. I should be most honored to receive you in my poor home, of course, *signor maggiore*! But it would be too much bother for you, believe me. We can talk at the café. Why not?"

"It's a delicate matter, Don Raffaele," I said, looking him in the eyes.

But he, usually so observant and attentive, this time did not seem to notice how meaning and sharp my glance was.

"A delicate matter?" He shut his eyes a second, as if thinking. "We can go to the Quisisana, on a terrace. What about that?"

"Not even there, Don Raffaele. Please understand me at once. I must talk to you without witnesses. In a private place."

"Very good. Come to the Town Hall, then. There's no one there at this hour."

"To the Town Hall?"

"But yes, I see you don't know. Forgive me for talking

about myself. But I'm Mayor now, Mayor of Capri. I have been for the last six months. My fellow citizens were good enough to trust me. Now, please, you first, signora. . . ."

So saying, he motioned us into the funicular station, then stopped me hurriedly as I went toward the ticket booth.

"Please, for heaven's sake! You're with me. No one who's with the Mayor pays for his ticket. Eh! At least you'll grant me that."

During the trip on the funicular, we talked about the season, the number of foreigners, the water problem on Capri; then he asked after the baby; and Jane, in spite of her inner repulsion, was so dominated and carried away by his emphatic cordiality that she found herself replying in the same tone and giving him news of Duccio, even telling him of Donatella's birth, and so on. Meanwhile I was looking at this man with whom in a short while I would be having a shameful, sordid struggle. I studied his hairless face, his thin lips, his shifty, smiling gray eyes, the slight wrinkles at the corners of his mouth—the subtle skeptical mask that he'd inherited from generations of courtiers, traders, servants, and priests, down through the ancient Mediterranean world, through Phœnician, Greek, Alexandrian, Italic, and Spanish civilizations, till it reached this vulgar being who wore it, without ever taking it off, as the most powerful weapon in his armory. And I calculated, as I looked at that mask, the resources of his centuries-old cunning against the improvised resources of my own. How would I defeat him? How expensive would my victory be?

He knew all about us; there was no doubt of that at all. He knew that Jane's family was rich. He knew that we lived in Paris. He knew about my job at UNESCO. I had not mentioned it to him, but it seemed obvious in his attitude, noticeably more obsequious than his usual one to me the year before.

I looked at Don Raffaele, saw him laughing, joking, complimenting Jane; and then I stopped listening to him and desperately began turning sums over in my mind. A thousand dollars? Two thousand? Five thousand? Ten thousand? I had my checkbook in my pocket. My deposit account at the American Express in Paris would not be enough, I said to myself; Jane would have to ask her father for more. Perhaps we'd be able to get hold of some of the letters with a first sum down. But how much would it cost to get them all?

Nothing was changed in the piazza. Except that, because of the blazing heat and the time of day, the foreigners were all sitting on the shady side, and the café facing them, in full sunshine, was completely deserted. It was so hot that everyone was sitting at his table motionless. Half-naked men and women in dark glasses drank tall iced drinks with slow, cautious movements.

We crossed the piazza, entered the little Town Hall, and went up to the second floor. Don Raffaele had the key. He ushered us into a big, bare study, dark from closed shutters.

"If one doesn't shut them, the heat's killing," explained Don Raffaele. "Will the Signora allow me?" and he took off his jacket. Then he sat down on his mayoral seat, behind a big desk piled with papers, and waved us to two plywood chairs on the other side.

Before speaking, I screwed up my courage and indignation. I looked at Don Raffaele once more. Sitting in his armchair, in a short-sleeved gray shirt, he was drying the sweat on the nape of his neck with a handkerchief. Above him on the whitewashed walls were photographs of the Pope and the President of the Republic; higher up a crucifix.

"Don Raffaele," I said, "let me go straight to the point without any preamble. My wife has told me everything."

The slight attentive smile that had remained on Don Raffaele's thin lips till then fell away at once. He looked at Jane and then at me for a moment with an expression that was serious but calm.

I went on: "I know that last year, while she was here at Capri, my wife received a letter from her first husband. A letter that was sent to your address, Don Raffaele, and that you handed to my wife. My wife did not intend to deceive me, but simply to prevent my being worried. At the same time, to avoid the chance of the post office opening letters that she intended to write to her first husband—"

"Excuse me for interrupting, *signor maggiore*. It's quite true, unfortunately, that in the past the Capri post office was not to be trusted. In fact, I was the first to tell your wife so. But I'd like to say, just as sincerely, that since I've been Mayor of Capri, that's all changed. That dreadful, that appalling abuse, which violates one of the primary and most elementary privileges of a civilized nation, is ended at Capri, *signor maggiore*. You can tell that to everyone—to all your fellow countrymen. It was the first action my administration took. Although, as you know, the postal services don't depend on local administration, but directly on the state, as soon as I was elected Mayor I went to Rome for that very purpose, at my own expense, and managed to stop the leak. For the last six months the post office of Capri has been as secret as the post office in Washington. Excuse me for interrupting you, *signor maggiore*. Now do please go on."

Go on? I could no longer find words to go on. Though there was no logical link between this unexpected emergence of Don Raffaele as reformer of post-office morals and my hesitation about what sum to offer him for the letters, I felt, as he said "stopped the leak," this hesitation growing by leaps and bounds; and with it, alas, the first sum I'd intended to offer.

Don Raffaele must certainly have calculated this effect; that was why he had interrupted me with so many fine phrases and so much parade of morality.

He was Mayor. He had reformed the post office. So the price of the letters would be much higher than I'd thought.

As I said, I found myself incapable of going on. Luckily, Jane now began.

"Don Raffaele," she said, "I've told my husband everything. I've told him, that is, about the six letters I gave you to put into other envelopes, address, and mail."

"Very good, Signora," said Don Raffaele.

"How much do you want for those six letters?" I cried suddenly, jumping to my feet and banging my fist on the table.

Terrified, Don Raffaele shrank against the back of his chair.

"I don't understand," he stuttered, "I don't understand what you mean, *signor maggiore*."

"Oh, you understand perfectly well. Don't act the innocent. How much do you want for those six letters? I'll offer you a thousand dollars. All right?"

"But, *signor maggiore*, willingly—willingly, with all my heart. And without any thousand dollars. But I posted the letters!"

I was standing, bent over the table, over Don Raffaele, who was looking at me and shrinking back more and more terrified. I am very tall, and I dominated him.

Gazing at him in the eyes with all the hatred I could muster, "Don't tell lies. *Basta!*" I shouted. "The letters never reached their destination. You know that perfectly well. Who was it rang us up in Rome the day before yesterday? Someone sent by you. So, *basta!* How much do you want? Are a thousand dollars too little? Say so. At least have the courage for that!"

I realized then that Don Raffaele was trembling; trembling, panting, and pale with terror.

"Excuse me, *signor maggiore*," he said imploringly, "calm yourself, I beg you. Let me get up. . . ."

Leaning with both hands on the arms of his chair, he raised himself, trembling all over, turned toward the wall, looking up, and extended his right hand toward the crucifix.

"There, *signor maggiore*," he exclaimed, almost in tears. "I swear it on the crucifix. I swear on the crucifix that I enclosed the six letters—you say there were six, and I don't deny it, but I just can't remember how many there were. I enclosed them, without reading them, in other envelopes, and in my own hand wrote some name I don't remember; but the address was the Hotel Excelsior at Rome. I sealed them and mailed them. That's all I knew or know. I repeat, I swear it on the crucifix. May my little niece, who's sixteen years and four months old and is the only person in the world I love, for my wife never gave me any children, may my little niece Costanza die at this moment if what I've told you is not the pure and simple truth."

As he spoke, he was looking now at the crucifix and now

turning to glance over his shoulder and watch the effect his words were having on us. Finally he lowered his arms and went back to the desk, drying his tears with his sweaty handkerchief, still gazing at me in terror. I was silent and looked at Jane. She was sitting with her head bowed, also silent.

After a long pause:

"You mustn't behave like this," went on Don Raffaele in a low voice, stretching out a timid hand toward me, then going on in a humble, almost paternal tone. "Listen to someone who's lived a good many years more than you have. Calm yourself. Don't let yourself get worked up like this. There are so many misfortunes, so many sorrows in life. But compared to, say, a serious illness, the incurable illness of someone one loves, some member of one's family, what are your troubles, or even your scandals? Nothing, believe me, nothing. . . . I'm old, my wife died of cancer. Seven years of torture. Those are the real misfortunes of life, *signor maggiore*. Thank Heaven and the Madonna that the Signora is well, that you are well, and that your babies in America are well. And as for the rest—try to settle that calmly, collectedly, without getting so worked up. Really, *signor maggiore*, a person like you!"

A lump I couldn't check was swelling in my chest and throat. I held out a hand to this man I had so unjustly, so basely calumniated, held it out with extreme timidity, for I needed him to shake it.

"Forgive me, Don Raffaele. I've been a madman. Forgive me. Will you forgive me?"

"Forgive? Forgive what, *signor maggiore*?" exclaimed Don Raffaele, clasping my hand in both his. "These things are just dramas—sentimental dramas, they happen to everyone. One loses one's head, one no longer knows what one's doing. Then it all blows over and one doesn't even remember what it was all about. Of course, of course, with all my heart, *signor maggiore*."

"Forgive me too, Don Raffaele," said Jane, who had got up and come to the table and now also held out her hand.

"Oh, that's enough about forgiveness!" replied Don Raffaele, getting up, bowing, taking Jane's hand and kissing it. "What am I, Jesus Christ? I'm the Mayor of Capri, and as Mayor I'm very severe and never forgive anyone anything! If refuse is thrown on the pavements and not in the iron receptacles I've had put at every corner, it's a fine! If foreigners make too much noise at night and waken people sleeping, it's a fine! If the bathing costumes of the lovely ladies on the beaches are—you understand, eh?—not quite those laid down by the law, it's a fine! Fines, fines, fines!"

He broke into loud laughter and led us outside for a vermouth.

"Are you going back to America, *signor maggiore*? By plane?"

He knew nothing about Paris, nothing about UNESCO, nothing at all. Our bad consciences had attributed to him a vast network of information and a diabolic power that he did not possess.

Having drunk our vermouths, he bid us a jolly good-by. It was almost two o'clock. He was late, he said, and his little niece was waiting for him at home. In fact, he'd even realized that, convinced though we were of his innocence, we still associated him with our anguish and the mystery of the letters and would be pleased to see him go.

He went. And from that moment, from then till the end,

everything went well between Jane and me. We moved down to the Marina Grande right away and lunched there, to be sure of not missing the four-o'clock boat.

That night we slept in Naples, where we had left our luggage. Next morning we took a through sleeping-car for Paris.

We thought about Don Raffaele and felt reassured. The letters? The scandal? "Let's wait and see what happens," we said to each other. "Whoever has them, if he wants money, will be sure to ask us before publishing them. It was silly to get into the state we were in."

I was almost sure now that Jane hadn't properly understood the conversation on the telephone. I tried to reconstruct the words that could have caused the mistake. Tortured by remorse, obsessed by the idea of blackmail, Jane herself might have been the first to mention letters. And the person, whoever he was, might have said in his artificially childish Italian: "Letters? *Mai sentito*." As if to say: "Letters? Never heard of them." And Jane could have thought he'd said: "The letters? They have *never been sent*." *Sentito*, sent, *spedite*. "The letters have never been sent." Then she had immediately thought of Don Raffaele. What about that?

I explained my ingenious theory to Jane. Complicated and improbable though it was, it anyway helped to calm us.

What had most impressed and reassured us was the extraordinary humility of Don Raffaele, of that wily, money-grubbing man who was certainly guilty of innumerable low deals in his life and yet had not reacted or been indignant when he was, for once, wrongly accused, but had taken the accusation almost with resignation and used fear as his only defense.

That's what Italians are! Humble with a humility that may reach cowardice, wise with a wisdom that may reach betrayal; always human, never heroes, and sometimes saints.

Don Raffaele, who had seemed diabolic to us from the first moment we had met him, had revealed himself in those last five minutes as almost saintly. Yes, he'd done a saint's work!

In the sleeping-car I talked to Jane soothingly about these things. All that had happened seemed like a bad dream. Evening fell. The train was climbing up the dark mountains and drawing near the frontier. We did not put on the lights. Through the windows in the open stretches between tunnels, as we coasted along the rocky sides of the mountains, blew the pure air of the Alpine night. Lying on my bunk I could see the black crests of the mountains against the dark-blue sky and brightly glittering stars.

I had forgotten everything, even Dorotea, and found myself loving Jane.

I was happy. Why not admit it? Why not admit, in life, such sudden changes and contradictions? Why try at all costs to find a logic where there's only mystery and perhaps a higher logic that escapes us and we cannot understand?

I was happy. Happy with Jane as I'd been with Dorotea, and even more.

I don't remember what I thought, what, exactly, I felt. I only remember being happy in that train.

And so, because of that, Jane's first words immediately afterwards hurt me, filled me with disappointment and bitterness. I had thought she was happy with me, like me. But no.

Immediately afterwards Jane said gently, caressing me:

"We both love each other, Harry, I know. We love each other with a real love. But what a pity, Harry, that we don't also love each other when we make love!"

At that moment the train slowed down as it reached the last station in Italy. The black outline of the mountains, the sky, the stars, slowly stopped moving, fixed and framed themselves in the little window. I heard the steps of the railwaymen or rare travelers, scattered voices, a call, a far-off cry, a whistle. Then the silence of the mountains at night, and the rush of waterfalls. A clock from the village rang out eleven. And I repeated Jane's words to myself, had already committed them to memory as a condemnation: "What a pity that we don't also love each other when we make love!"

For her, then, from that point of view, I was little more than fresh water. Fresh water—that expression was hers too.

I did not reply. She was lying on top of me. Her face was buried in my shoulder. I pressed it to me and felt its bony little features as part of me. I did not deny what she said. Or reply. I just looked at the mountains. And listened to the waterfalls.

The funny thing was, I could not help reflecting, the funny thing was that Jane might be mistaken. Perhaps she had felt happy too, and from natural pessimism had not noticed this happiness so near her. Or was I, from natural optimism, just opening a ray of hope to my own vanity?

But, I went on reflecting, my happiness with Jane just now was due, I suspected, to this being the first time I'd made love to her since she'd confessed to being unfaithful. And I wondered if one day she too, when she'd heard my own confession, would be just as happy. . . . But it would be absurd to tell her about Dorotea that night. Jane was leaving for America next day. On her return to Paris in September I would tell her everything, calmly. But I wanted to tell her something at least that night; instill some kind of suspicion; if only so that she should not torture herself too much, should not feel herself too much to blame toward me. How much more unfaithful I had been! And not only with Dorotea, but with so many other women. Then among others I remembered Checchina. And with Checchina the little gold chain, and the medal of Our Lady of Lourdes—the very Madonna to whom Jane had made her vow—which poor Checchina had made me promise to keep or give only to my wife.

I looked for the chain, which I always kept in the inside pocket of my wallet, took it out and handed it with its medal to Jane.

"I'm also guilty toward you," I said. "When you get back to Paris I'll tell you everything. This medal of Our Lady of Lourdes was given me by a woman, an Italian woman, I went with while you were in Capri. I'll tell you about it."

Jane frowned. "Why should I keep this medal?" she said. "I don't want it."

"Do keep it, please," I insisted. "Then when you look at it, you won't feel too remorseful. Anyway, she was a very decent girl."

"Why do you say was? Is she dead?"

"No. But I don't think I'll ever see her again. Yes, she was a decent girl. Your Aldo is a decent boy too, at heart. The evil, Jane, is never in others. It's always and only in ourselves who desire it."

She did not reply at once, but looked at the chain. I saw

that she was thinking intensely of something and had not the courage to say what it was.

Finally she murmured: "Aldo wears a chain like this round his neck too!"

She put it round her neck and, perhaps carried away by this new thought, began to kiss me passionately. I remembered then Checchina's last words when offering me the gift, to persuade me to accept it: "It'll bring you luck, you'll see."

And that time, perhaps, Jane was happy too.

She seemed happy till the last moment, till the last kiss I gave her, at Orly airport, the following night.

Farewells at airports are the worst. One is separated at the very beginning, while still in the same place, by uniformed bureaucrats who herd the departing passengers along low fences, by plate-glass windows, through narrow corridors, like beasts being led to the slaughter.

I waited outside, in the night, looking at the big Constellation in which Jane was to leave. The propellers were turning for a test. But the travelers had not yet been allowed out of the buildings. There they were, at last, a group of distant, lost-looking human beings, who seemed to me to be walking reluctantly, as if urged by invisible executioners, toward the monster that was to carry them over the ocean. In vain, through the darkness and distance, I tried to make out Jane's little figure from the others. But, hoping that she could see me, I raised my hand and waved.

The little group climbed up to the plane. The steps were drawn away. Once more the propellers of the four motors whirled, one after another, for the final test. Then all four together. And the plane began slowly turning on its own axis.

It was moving slowly, but in a few seconds, inexplicably, it had already vanished into the darkness, toward the center of the runway.

I got into my car, and drove away from the airport toward Paris. Half a mile farther on I stopped and got out. I looked toward the airfield. There was a confused sound of engines. Here and there I could see searchlights. Where was Jane's plane?

A few minutes later I thought I could make out its shape, gray in the black night, gaining height. For a moment two lights, one red, one green, going on and off alternately, appeared in the middle of the sky. Then nothing more.

There was just a sound of engines getting fainter and fainter; suddenly I noticed the tremendous screech of crickets, filling the country night.

It was very hot. The sky was covered with clouds. Not a star was to be seen.

HERE HARRY'S TYPESCRIPT BREAKS OFF.

20.

I must declare at once, as a man in the film business, that Harry's story undoubtedly seemed to me full of suggestive ideas and possibilities, but that to obtain the financial backing even of the most civilized and broad-minded producer, it would have to be thoroughly worked over.

As soon as I had read the typescript, I wrote to Harry and told him this, adding that his story had really impressed me. Could he hurry up and finish it and send me the ending at once? In a couple of months, on my return to Rome, I would certainly have some definite ideas to discuss. We would try to work out a film scenario from it together.

Not that I had much hope of ever being able to make a film with characters whose psychology was so complicated and exceptional, not to say unbalanced. All I hoped for was to sell the scenario, as there was a chance of casting a famous American actor and actress, and so netting a couple of million lire for Harry.

But I did not write and tell him about this last minimum plan of mine. I did not want to discourage him from finishing the story. Nor did I write to him about all the contradictions and absurdities I seemed to have noticed in the events he had described, which made me doubt at times if they were true. How, for instance, had they possibly let that mysterious telephone call so upset them as to go off to Capri and attack Don Raffaele in that absurd scene? But above all I could not understand the phone call itself. According to what Harry had written, the person, when telephoning, had made vague threats, *but had not asked for money.* So why all the fuss?

As for the character—let's call him that—of Don Raffaele, I was certain that Harry and Jane had exaggerated both ways; first in thinking him too diabolical, and then too saintly. The truth certainly lay between the two. Don Raffaele was not capable of blackmailing as they had first feared, but neither was he capable of that deep humanity and humility which had so roused their enthusiasm later. Very probably Don Raffaele, realizing he had to deal with two people whom he must have considered unbalanced, had calculated it was useless to be angry, prudent to be amiable, and in any case wise to get out of the dilemma as soon as possible with a few well-chosen words. I agreed that he didn't have the letters. But these were Americans, and in his position as the new Mayor of Capri the important thing was that at all costs they should never doubt his integrity in the future and never pass on the smallest suspicion to anyone else. That aim he had fully achieved, with his swearing on the crucifix, his tears, and his gentle meekness.

But where had the letters got to? Was it in fact true that the young man had never received them? Hadn't he been responsible for that telephone call? I was not so optimistic about this as Harry and Jane were.

And what had happened afterwards between Harry and Jane? What had made Harry leave Paris and his job on UNESCO to go and live in poverty with Dorotea in Via Margutta? Had he and Jane been divorced after all? Harry, when I'd seen him, seemed to be linked to Dorotea for life and death, and a desperate, ruined, drifting man. What had happened?

After some time I confess I began to wait for the end of Harry's story with real impatience. Every evening, the first thing I did when I returned to my hotel from Joinville was to ask the porter if a package had arrived for me; or a letter, or a telegram telling me to go to the Gare de Lyon as last time.

But Harry did not even answer my letter. I wrote to him once or twice again, each time without result. So two months passed, and when, at the beginning of September, I returned to Rome, I went to Via Margutta at once.

It was with a certain trepidation that I climbed the dirty stairs. No, I wasn't thinking any more of that attractive Apulian. I was thinking of Harry and his life, about which I now knew everything, up to a certain point. Everything. But not about Dorotea, who still, after a long, detailed account, remained mysterious for anyone who read it, because she was mysterious to Harry himself.

What sort of woman was she, at heart? Venal or generous? Did she love Harry or was she with him only for what she could get? It was difficult to answer this just on the basis of Harry's confessions; difficult because it was clear that Harry, without knowing it, did not love Dorotea for what she really was—whatever she really was—but loved her for what he imagined and wanted her to be and was stubbornly, idiotically determined to represent her as being: evil, selfish, cheap, cold, and domineering.

There was something similar here to what had happened with Don Raffaele. Harry did not watch Dorotea with any passionate desire to find out what she was really like, but with a longing to identify her with the absurd, overwhelming mythical impression roused in him from the very first by her physical appearance.

The real Dorotea, humble, prosaic, and easygoing, did not correspond to the myth that Harry had made of her. But this difference confirmed the myth for him, rather than destroyed it. Incapable and unwilling to see his goddess as she was in reality, Harry transformed the continual disappointments she gave him into suspicions, full of mystery and fascination. If he noticed, for example, on some occasion that she was not so evil and imperious as he had dreamed her to be, he did not deduce, as anyone else would have done, that she was meek and easygoing; but that she had not, on that occasion, wanted to show herself evil and imperious, as according to him she certainly was. *She had not wanted to.* And the reason for her not wanting to was inexplicable and more fascinating to him than if she had wanted to. Her domination over him was limitless and inexhaustible, because it was fed not by her real qualities, nor even by his own illusions, but by the very disappointments he continually felt.

In fact, if by some absurd chance Harry had found another Dorotea, and this Dorotea had really been the evil, stupid creature that he adored, in a very short time he would have ceased to adore her. Being, as he was, a decent intelligent man, he would in a very short time have found himself revolted by the tough hardness, the squalor, the boredom of a woman who was *really* evil and *really* stupid. No, he could continue to be with Dorotea only because Dorotea was completely different from what he thought her.

That was my interpretation. But I had deduced this from Harry's manuscript and was anxious, naturally, to confirm it from reality.

I passed by the painters' studios, crossed the little courtyard with its old tiles, and rang the bell on their door.

I waited a long time; then rang again, in vain. They must be out, I thought, and went away. I returned late the same afternoon, with the same result.

I was determined not to telephone. I wanted to surprise them. Even so, I decided to that night. I rang them at eleven, at midnight, at one. And then in the early morning. The telephone gave the disengaged signal and no one replied.

Then I returned to Via Margutta and, after having tried their studio once again, went down to talk to the porteress. Harry, she said, had left about twelve days before. She could not tell me where for. He had told her nothing, and left no address. I asked after the "Signora." The porteress knew nothing about her. She had vanished the same day too. So they had gone off together? The porteress could not tell me. The only certain thing was this: Dorotea and Harry had been seen together till the last moment, and had got into a taxi together, with their luggage, at the front door in Via Margutta. In a taxi, I asked, not in the jeep? Harry had not got the jeep any more, he'd sold it more than a month before.

I went to the Foreign Press Association, where I knew Harry worked. They told me they had not seen him for some time, they had heard he'd left for the United States.

Then I remembered Borruso, the sleeping-car attendant who had lent Harry half a million lire and had left me his Rome address. Borruso was traveling and would be back in a few days.

When I finally saw him, he told me what he knew. Harry had returned to the States to settle there. Before leaving, he had been to see Borruso and given him back the money; he had sold the jeep, he told him. He was returning to America and taking up his post again as university lecturer. But he had not given Borruso his address either. I tried to get Borruso to say, without mentioning Dorotea, of whose existence I presumed Borruso to be ignorant, whether Harry had left alone.

"Alone. Yes. Why? Of course. Who do you suppose he'd have left with? He was alone here, I think. . . ."

"I suppose so," I said. "Anyway, he'll have gone back to his wife in America."

Borruso looked at me in amazement.

"To his wife? Had he married again? I didn't know that."

"No, to his wife, the first one, the same one."

"The Signora Jane?" Borruso said then. "Didn't you know she's dead? She died in a plane accident. Two years ago. Do you remember that plane which left Paris for New York toward the end of July? The one that fell into the sea near the Azores; there was that boxing champion on board, too. . . ."

So Jane was dead. The whole of Harry's story took on a different meaning now. I went back home and reread parts of the manuscript—above all, the part about Jane, her last journey from Naples to Paris, and the little medal of Our Lady of Lourdes.

I had scarcely known Jane, and only seen her two or three times, years before. All I felt at the news was the pity one feels for all the unknown people who live, suffer, love, and meet a sudden horrible liberating death. But her impetuous, tortured character, her thin little figure, lived before me in Harry's pages. My imagination was assailed by the ghastly seconds she must have been through before she died. Whom had she thought of, I asked myself, in those seconds? Her children, Harry, or Aldo, or all of them together, in a spasm of extreme doubt about the meaning of life? What is death? And how can one explain that, though one day sooner or later, either slowly with knowledge and preparation or in the horror of a single ghastly moment, all human beings have to experience this supreme and most inevitable of all torments, yet they still go on while they live constantly inflicting minor torments on one another, just as if they did not have to die at all?

It was a long time before I had any news of Harry.

Finally, early in February of the following year, I got a letter from him. It read:

Long Island, January 30, 1951

CARISSIMO MARIO:

After such a long silence, my first duty is to ask you to forgive me. No, I don't consider that the events which have recently turned my life upside down and forced me to do just what I least wanted and least foresaw can justify my laziness. I admit that I could, and should, have written you a line, or at least wired you in Paris, to tell you about my marriage to Dorotea and my return to the States with her.

But I realized that you did not know about Jane's death, and just as I'd never had the courage to tell you about it before when I wrote you that long account which I sent you in Paris, so now I hesitated and put off from day to day the heaviest confession of all.

A week ago, finally, I wrote a couple of lines to Signor Borruso asking him to do a small commission for Dorotea. And I've just had his reply. He tells me that he has seen you and, by chance, told you about the accident.

It happened on the 28th of July 1948, near the islands of the Azores.

From that day, for more than two years, I've felt Jane's death was my fault. And only now, when Dorotea has taken her place, even with the children, in a way I could never have foreseen, am I beginning to feel I was accusing myself wrongly; and to find, not peace—which I've never had—but at least a little serenity again. Possibly what I'm suffering from now is a new illness, an illness that I'd never felt before, at least not till this moment: boredom.

I loathe the States, and long for only one thing: to return to Italy. I'd use any excuse. Dorotea, naturally, wants to stay here. That doesn't matter to me at all. I'd have no hesitation in leaving her here with the children, as she'd like it. And I'd come alone. I need, please understand me, I *need* to return to Rome. At least for a short time, three, four months—can't you find me some excuse? I assure you I'd need little, very little money. Thirty thousand lire a week would suit me perfectly. The important thing is not the money, it's the *excuse* for coming, a job on a film, working on the script, dubbing, whatever you like. But it must be a real excuse, of course; one that corresponds to a real job, however insignificant.

I can ask for a holiday from the university when I like. I'll say it has to do with my studies. Loewen, in spite of my UNESCO scandal, still continues to protect me. No, I'm not afraid of losing my job here. And Jane's parents, who, as I think I told you, are rich, give us an allowance that's more than enough to keep the children and Dorotea. For Jane's parents have seen a lot of Dorotea now and got to know her; and they have a surprising admiration for her and boundless confidence in her. In the mess I've made of my life, at least this has gone well. As you can imagine, it was the last thing I'd expected. It never even crossed my mind.

So do try, my dear Mario, and see if you can work this miracle and send for me. On my side, I'll try to take up my story where I interrupted it, finish it as soon as possible, and send it off to you. I'll make two copies, so that I can send it through the mail without worrying. When you got the first part in Paris, you wrote me two or three enthusiastic letters. You told me that with some cuts and modifications you seemed to *see* the film. And that there was also a chance of placing the scenario, as there were parts in it for two famous American stars. I hope you still think this. You added that you were anxious to know the end; also because, in a good script, the most difficult and important part, anyway the one that most strikes the rather unimaginative minds of producers, is always the end.

Now, I don't know if the end I'll send you will also be a good one for the movie too. I'm very much afraid not. But I can't, alas, do anything but describe the truth to you, as I did in the first part.

Do please reply at once. I need a word of encouragement from you.

> With warm affection,
> *Tuo vecchio,*
> HARRY

ps. You are free to reply whatever you like now. Since Dorotea's been in America she's been so happy that she does not give me the least bother. She's busy all day long, looking after the children and the house. The kitchen gadgets drive her mad (with delight). She's learned to drive a car, is taking English lessons, and doesn't read my mail any more. But, oh, what a bore America is! H.

The same day I received this letter, Borruso telephoned to give me Harry's address. I thanked him for his kindness, saying that Harry had written to me too. Then Borruso told me that next day he was sending, by a friend in T.W.A., a small package to America which Harry had asked for. If I wanted to write or send something myself too, he would be pleased to help.

So I sent a few toys to Harry and Jane's children. But what was in the little package that Harry had asked for, which, I knew, was for Dorotea?

I went to Borruso's home to take the toys, and my curiosity was satisfied at once.

The little packet contained those multicolored pearls of fine sugar, probably impossible to find in the whole of America, which Dorotea used to scatter over her famous *scarcella*.

21.

The continuation of Harry's typescript reached me about two months later.

CONTINUATION AND END OF HARRY'S TYPESCRIPT

I interrupted my story at the point where I should have had to tell of Jane's death. Her death marked a pause, a sort of great vacuum, in my life. On reaching that point it was natural that I should no longer have the strength to continue writing. The fact, the crime, was still too close to me. I say "the crime" because last year, while I was writing my account in Rome, in Via Margutta, I thought of Jane's death as a murder I'd committed.

If, in fact, I had not participated, so morbidly and guiltily, in Jane's scruples and remorse, I would never have let that telephone call upset me so, would never have agreed to our going to Capri to see Don Raffaele; I would have calmed her down and persuaded her to leave from Ciampino by the direct plane for New York on which I'd made a reservation for her some time before. But I hadn't a clear conscience. Without knowing it I was associating and confusing my own guilt with Jane's guilt. And just as when I'd thought it was Dorotea blackmailing me I had hurried, almost with enjoyment, to meet things half-way, arranging those rolls of ten-thousand-lire notes in my pockets, so later I had left for Capri in a state of excited expectation, hoping to find Don Raffaele a real rogue.

I had given Jane the little medal and chain of Our Lady of Lourdes. . . . The news reached me through the evening papers. When I came out of the office the newsboys on the Champs-Élysées were calling out about the fallen plane. Here I'd like to note down faithfully, minute by minute, hour by hour, what I felt from that moment till I was certain of her death. First my suspicion, for a second or two, that I'd mis-understood what the newsboys were shouting. Why should it be Jane's plane and no other? Then another suspicion, against myself—that for a fraction of that second I had actually hoped for Jane's death, so as to be free of her and able to marry Dorotea. Meanwhile I had bought the papers, hurried to the American Express, rung up Air France, our Consulate. Des-perately I tried every source of information. I refused to resign myself to the truth. For three days and three nights I did not sleep or touch food. I just smoked and drank. Finally there was no more doubt. I wired my in-laws in Philadelphia. Luckily Donatella was only a few months old, and even Duccio not yet two.

But what is the point of giving a detailed description of those days? Even if I wrote hundreds of pages, I could never undo what had already been done. Jane had vanished. Jane was dead. I would never see Jane again. Death, from that moment, hasn't frightened me any more. Or rather, yes, it still frightens me; but when I think of it, I think of Jane. Of Jane, who has already taken that step, already known those last seconds. And, I think, how can I not accept the same myself? Whether another life exists or not, whether Jane and I will meet and recognize each other again or not, in both cases death has been more familiar to me since that moment. I think and talk of it more willingly than I ever did before, because it has taken Jane. And sometimes I feel it's quite impossible we shouldn't see each other again. When I've drunk half a bottle of whisky, Jane is there, at my side, invisible, waiting for me. It's just a question of time. Of years, days, perhaps of hours and minutes. It doesn't matter. She's there waiting for me, and I'm pleased she is.

Often I've dreamed (if by some absurd chance I really believed what I'm about to tell you, I would not have the courage to tell it), I've dreamed that she was dead and in hell; but that by some obscure design of the devil and some inscrutable divine permission she had returned to the earth for a few days or a few weeks. Jane was dead, Jane was in hell, and yet there was her body, her face, her glance, her movements, even her dresses here on earth. I know that she comes from hell and will return there. Desperately I embrace her and hold her to me. This happens in the street, at the corner of the boulevard Saint-Germain and the rue des Ciseaux, near an Italian restaurant where we used sometimes to go and dine, and in the same district as the hotel I was living in, where I slept as I had this dream. We used to leave the car on the boulevard, at the corner of the rue des Ciseaux. Now it's dark, too, it's night. The shabby old shops are closed, with their wooden shutters and iron bars. And it's on the pavement there, after I'd got out of the car, there, a few yards off, that I meet Jane. I hold her to me and then look at her. Her cheeks, which when she was alive were always pale, but with a healthy, dry, nervous pallor, now have a strange, terrifying flush. They're red, as if burning. And *I know* what that red flush means, *I know* where poor Jane comes from. Her eyes glitter. She looks at me and says nothing. But her eyes are full of tears, and glitter in that ghastly way as if they no longer love me or anyone else because those eyes have seen and still see the place which they will see forever. And yet she is here, now she's walking along beside me, giving me her arm. And she seems to be stricken with some horrible, incurable illness, of guilt—above all, guilt. Hell is all in this idea of guilt. She had wished it. And even now, with that red flush, that glittering, desperate look, fully conscious though she is of the eternal misery to which she has condemned herself, yet by a monstrous contortion of her own will she still wishes it. She wishes it, and cannot avoid wishing it. And just as she has no more love for me, so I have almost no more pity for her. And this lack of pity is a martyrdom to me. I pity myself for not pitying her.

"Jane," I say, as we move together toward the Italian restaurant, "can nothing at all be done? Is everything decided? Really decided forever?"

She looks at me and doesn't reply. . . . Oh, how red her eyes are with crying, with horror, with hatred, with despair! My heart is gripped by pain. So it's true, I say to myself, that God is just, even to the point of hurting us? Even this final hurt? Of torturing one of His creatures eternally? Have we been wrong in hoping for His mercy? I look at Jane, gaze into the eyes gazing desperately into mine, and feel I can't pray to this God any more. The only thing that I can do is love Jane, love Jane in spite of everything and in spite of this God; love Jane because she is mine, my chosen one. I know how good she is. I know how gentle she is. I know that deep in her heart there is innocence and charity. Why is it that God allowed her to be judged not for what she was, but for what she'd done or thought in some moment, long or short, of her life? And now how is it that He allows her to return to earth, with her body, at the corner of the boulevard Saint-Germain and the rue des Ciseaux? What is the purpose of this miracle? Is there any hope for her?

And I asked, talking to her, with her arm in mine: "Jane, my love, is there any hope?"

But Jane looked at me with those grim, somber eyes, the same ones I'd seen when she had talked on the telephone in that room of the Grand Hotel at Rome; only now they also had that horrible glitter. Those eyes looked at me, and she did not reply. Was there or wasn't there any hope?

And the worst was that in my dream I would suddenly find myself doubting if I really was dreaming; "because," I said to myself, "this isn't possible, Jane is dead, the plane has crashed, it's lying deep in the Atlantic near the Azores, so her body can't be here on the boulevard Saint-Germain at the corner of the rue des Ciseaux, and nothing I see and feel and touch is true and I'm just dreaming." But at that moment a car passed on the boulevard or someone whistled gaily, and in my dream I felt that I was not dreaming. It was true. It was all inexplicably true. Jane was there in her body, and must, MUST return to hell. But why had she come? So that I should know? And what had she really been guilty of? What was the sin for which she had lost her soul?

In my dream I thought, without ever saying so to poor Jane, that she had been guilty of sinning with Aldo; first her fornicating with Aldo; then the long daydreaming about him, the sin of desire; and finally the sacrilege of not carrying out her vow, and her adultery. But when I awoke—I jumped up in bed, damp with sweat, my heart beating hard, my eyes straining in the darkness, and lit the light in terror. I was alone in my little room in the hotel in the rue des Saints-Pères, a small cozy hotel whose owner and servants and many of whose clients I had known for a long time. Yet even so, when I awoke from those horrible dreams, I'd feel alone and realize that I could not go on living like that without some company for the night, someone whose naked body in bed would chase the devil from my room. I thought of Dorotea. Not because I desired her any more then. But only because she, with Jane, was the woman I'd known best.

When I woke I would sigh with relief at having dreamed it all. My eyes were wet with restrained tears. I'd think of Jane again, as I'd seen her in my dream, and then break down and sob without restraint. Yes, I did pity her then; for that short, bitter life of hers. How was it possible, I would say to myself, that God had condemned her? No, he couldn't have. Even if that wasn't her real sin. For Jane's real sin was different. Now I thought it over again, awake, I remembered. It was the sin of which she had accused herself at the end of her confession to me; the sin of believing too much in evil and too little in good; the sin of not having married Aldo; the sin of not having resisted the temptation to make that vow, and of not having gone to Anacapri that night with Aldo. Well, if that was her sin, why not have pity on her? Why not forgive her? Christ had forgiven the Magdalen, who had loved and enjoyed before she had suffered. Why had He not also forgiven Jane, who before suffering had been afraid of loving and enjoying? Was not her fear, her restraint, her shrinking, her retreat before love, was not all that a form of love too?

And I got out of bed, and for the first time since my distant childhood I prayed too. I prayed for mercy on Jane, for mercy on myself and my children, mercy also on Dorotea, mercy on all human beings.

It seemed impossible that God would not grant this mercy. I was alone. And if, when I put out the light again, it seemed to me that an invisible and evil presence was hiding beside my bed, a demon whose red eyes I was suddenly afraid of seeing (perhaps the Jane who had appeared in my dreams was not the true Jane, but a demon who had taken on her semblance), if I heard a creaking made by him, and almost felt him breathe on me, saw his subdued grin, then I would start praying again.

"O Lord," I would say, "forgive us our debts as we forgive our debtors. And deliver us from evil. Amen."

It was many months before I began to want a woman again. After what you know of me, after everything I've told you, I can feel you don't believe me, and suspect me of hypocrisy. Let me, then, be absolutely frank. I admit that the expression may seem ambiguous, lending itself to a mental reserve on my part. But you must take it literally. For many months I did not want a woman—but that does not mean I did not have one. I wanted to want one—let's put it that way. I wanted to bemuse myself, to exhaust myself. And I only partly succeeded. I took up an old habit. At night I went walking up and down the boulevards on the prostitutes' beats, and very often I just gave them money without asking anything in return except their company, for half an hour, in some squalid *bistro*, over a glass of Armagnac.

I felt no need to make love. All I needed was company. And the only company I could endure was that of prostitutes. Why? Who knows? Every falsity, every convention, every superstructure bored me. I wanted the truth. And it seemed to me that I could find it only in the unpretentious humility of those women, above all when they were neither young nor beautiful. They thought me mad, some suspected me of impotence, others of degeneracy. I did not bother about disproving it. What did it matter? I let them think what they liked of me. It was enough for me that they agreed to keep me company, listen to my desultory remarks, my half-confessions, and answer my questions about their lives, their tastes, their past, and their plans for the future. Among them, I would also find the greatest variety of character and opinion. There were the bitter ones, the skeptical ones, the despairing ones, the rebellious, the subversive ones. And there were also the ingenuous ones, the happy, confident, conforming, conservative ones. All of them, however, had kept one great illusion, whether they still hoped or had by now despaired of realizing it: the illusion of the power of money. Not even on this subject did I bother to contradict them. Anyway, how could I have dared to? How could I have dared explain to them that money, in whatever way one may possess or obtain it, is always paid for by the loss of something alive, if only by the loss of suffering? If I had presented this argument to them, I would have offended them, and uselessly too, because they would not have understood me. They were too much in the race to see the winning-post.

Money! The money for which they had sacrificed their lives, I, too, as Jane's death drew slowly farther away, found myself beginning to desire again. But I began to desire it only in order to lose it, or rather to have it taken from me.

The first symptom of recovery that I noticed in my slackened will to live after the months following Jane's death, months of nightly remorse and terror, and of daily indifference to any form of activity, the first symptom of life (perhaps also because it was linked to Jane's death) was this: I remembered her letters from Capri. Where had they got to? Who had them? And I began thinking about them again.

It was very unlikely that Jane had misunderstood what was said on the telephone. With a great deal of effort I'd managed to build up a possible case for a mistake. But I'd done this above all to calm Jane. And it was too complicated a hypothesis; thinking it over calmly, it didn't hold.

The letters! Whoever had them (Aldo or anyone else) could still use them for blackmail. At this suspicion, this idea, I felt a slight stir and fluttering of the heart, as if I had touched a spot, the only spot still living and capable of feeling in my numbed body; I felt a temptation to pleasure deeper and more titivating than the pleasure itself, and one that I had deluded myself I was free of forever, not having tasted it for so long. Those six letters of Jane's! I began to tell myself that my duty was to recover them, not so much to defend myself and my children from a possible scandal as to prevent an insult to her memory. I must confess, however, that, mingled with this sense of duty, I also felt a strong curiosity; and that even this curiosity was not simple, but mixed with pity, jealousy, envy; there was deceit, perhaps, in my desire to know just how far poor Jane's folly had gone, some promise of obscure enjoyment from reading them, as if I hoped to perpetuate and perfect her sin.

But that, of course, is my analysis today, two years later. Then all these instincts were fused in one single urge, and I felt it shut blindly inside me, getting livelier and stronger every time I thought (and gradually I found myself thinking more and more) of the existence of those letters.

THE CAPRI LETTERS

268

Until one day this slow, continual burgeoning of imagination and exaltation suddenly bore fruit in an impulse that seemed to me natural and unexpected. I left for Rome.

It was nearing Easter, and I surprised Dorotea, toward noon, with an apron tied tight round her strong hips, a handkerchief on her head, her hands covered with flour, her face and lips unpainted, her eyes without their usual bister. She had an astounding classical beauty, such as I'd perhaps never seen in her before. She could not give me her hand, but raised her arms and spread out her elbows for me to embrace her. I did so, without either foreseeing or desiring it. And the contact of her strong body, the smell of her scent, the sudden memory of joys I'd not thought of for so long, made me forget on the spot the only purpose of my journey.

Dorotea was mixing flour for the *scarcella*, the sweet rough cake I had tasted at other times, which she made every now and then during the year; at Easter, she told me, it was a rite in her part of the country. She would not interrupt her work. I followed her into the kitchen, sat down on a straw-seated chair, and, forcibly distracting my attention from the unexpectedly seductive sight of her gay, robust, but age-old and beautiful movements, began to tell her why I'd come. In order to reach Aldo and the letters, I had, of course, to begin from the beginning, and tell her what I'd always kept hidden from her —my marriage, and my wife's having been the same Jane she had known.

As I talked, Dorotea, kneading the dough on the table, almost had her back turned to me. I noted, with amazement, that she showed no surprise at what I told her. She went on working either as if she was not listening or as if I was telling her nothing new. It was so strange that I was forced to interrupt myself.

"What's the matter?" I said to her. "Haven't you understood?"

"Yes, of course; go on," she said in a tone of indifference, kneading away, it seemed to me, with more violence and speed than ever, "go on, come to the point."

I had in fact begun with a studied preamble. Before I came to my revelations I'd told her that I had to ask her for a great favor; that this time, as she may have already guessed, my visit had no other motives, but that I would be extremely grateful to her all the same and prove it.

"Come to the point," she said, without looking at me, still kneading away; her tone, I realized now, wasn't simply indifferent, it was resentful. "Perhaps," I thought, "she wants to show me she's offended, or she really is offended, at my having hidden from her that I was married and a father." I rose to my feet, went up to her, put both my hands on her hips, and murmured:

"What's the matter, Dora? Are you sorry that I've been so deceitful?"

She turned slightly, scarcely pausing in her work, and smiled at me sweetly, almost maternally.

"What on earth are you thinking? How silly you are! You never deceived me, because I've always known it. Even before you married I knew you were engaged to her. I knew everything. What did it matter whether you told me or not? I knew her well, poor little thing, she was so good."

"You've heard about the accident too?" I exclaimed, in amazement.

She stopped working. Turning toward me, and looking me in the eyes, she said seriously and simply: "Of course, the *Messagero* published the names of the victims, didn't it? In fact, when I first saw your surname, I thought it must be you. But then I saw it said you'd gone to Paris with her from Italy the day before, and seen her onto the plane, and that she only happened to take that plane by chance, as she should have left from Rome. Is that true?"

"Yes, it's true," I said.

"Poor little thing. Three or four days before, when you were both in Rome, she'd come to see me. She was so sweet, so refined, so smart. You know, Harry, I was really sorry. Sorry for her, and also for you. Do you know that I cried all that night, and couldn't sleep? Ask the Signora. . . ."

She nodded toward the other room, to indicate the landlady.

I looked at Dorotea almost with the same astonishment with which I'd looked at Jane when she had first confessed her guilt. Only this time my surprise was not painful, but downright admiring. So Dora had always known, and always kept silent, and pretended to believe what I had said about myself. And I'd been determined to hide my marriage from her for fear of her blackmailing me. She must also, without any doubt, have guessed the reason for my long, stupid pretense; but she had not reacted and had had the tact and grace to accept what I had said.

All that was extraordinary, almost too much to believe, if I'd not had the proof, here, under my own eyes. I looked at Dorotea, and seemed to see her as a new being, with a mind full of nobility and delicacy in a body—but even her body, now, was different. And had lost all its spell for me; or at least all the spell of pleasure, vice, and sensuality that it had had until a moment before.

I asked myself if this was not just a personal transitory impression; or if this good, maternal, judicious, homely side, which I'd already in the past suspected to lie under Dorotea's professional appearance and habits, was not her real and deepest nature.

She had returned to her kneading again. And I looked at her and was silent, and felt a great calm, a great sadness, and no desire for her any more. My thoughts returned to the letters. These, in fact, were the only things capable of moving me now.

Very seriously I asked Dorotea about Aldo. Could he possibly have them? If she was not absolutely certain he hadn't, she must say so; I didn't care what sacrifice I'd have to make, even of a lot of money, to lay hands on them.

Without hesitation, and with complete simplicity, Dora replied that she was sure Aldo did not have them and had never received them. And she explained to me why he'd never received them. She hadn't been able to explain to Jane because Aldo had been in Milan at the time and Dora had only seen and spoken to him about it afterwards.

When Aldo wrote to Jane at Capri, he told her to reply to him at the Hotel Excelsior in Rome. He had given her that address partly because he was ashamed of his own, a squalid rooming-house; and partly to impress Jane and make her think he was now a well-known film actor and frequented the smart world of Via Veneto. In reality he was an extra and sometimes got a job as a dancer in revues. As he was a good-looking young man, he also, from time to time, had a profitable affair with some actress or singer. Now, Aldo was aware of his hold over Jane. He would have liked to profit by it, possibly even to succeed in getting her to divorce me and then marrying her. But all this was just in words, or not even in words, only in his imagination. For though Aldo believed himself to be sly, cynical, and calculating, and always promised himself to bring off a master stroke some day, in reality he was a nice, rather shy and rather lazy boy, who'd never been tough or persevering enough to profit from any situation by carrying it through to the end. And so, though he had given the address of the Excelsior in perfect good faith—that is, with the worst intentions —he'd not even had the courage to enter the Excelsior lobby, face the porter, give him the necessary tip, and withdraw his correspondence.

"Why, if you try the porter of the Excelsior, you may still find the letters there," ended Dorotea.

After two years? It seemed impossible. Anyway, I went straight back to the Grand Hotel and, promising a handsome tip, told Guglielmo to make the necessary inquiries.

Before dark all six letters were in my hands. I hurried to the airport and returned to Paris. And I even forgot to telephone Dorotea to thank her.

22.

Taking my eyes off the little porthole, through which I could see the dear old city of Jane's life and mine drawing away in the golden dusk below, I looked at the six envelopes in my hands. No trace of any tampering or resealing. They were all perfectly sealed, and a little yellow at the edges. So that voice on the telephone had not mentioned letters after all. Jane, in her anguish, had misunderstood.

I deciphered the dates on the stamps and arranged them chronologically. Then I opened and read them, one after another.

Here they are, copied down word for word, alas, as they were written; mad, tragic, shameful, but perhaps more ridiculous than anything else. I would not have been so cruel as to copy them out and send them to you, had I not considered that in doing so I was being much crueler to myself than to poor Jane's memory. In fact, the letters I had written to Dorotea from Paris were even more silly and more absurd than these. And besides, I was guiltier than Jane, for I had also been a coward. I had never posted them!

(1)

Capri, April 6, 1947

ALDO, MY LOVE:

Thank you! First, before telling you all the things I want to tell you and must, thank you, thank you! Your letter is in front of me. From the moment I got it—the happiest, most intense, most alive moment of my life since that last time I saw you—from the moment I got it I've been living with your letter. I never tire of reading it, looking at it, feeling it, kissing it. Now I know by heart the shape of every word, and the curves and lines that you traced out with your hand, thinking of me.

Thinking of me. You were thinking of me. Of me who aren't worthy of your thought pausing on me for a single second. Because you are so superior to me. And I'm so guilty toward you.

Yes, this is my deepest feeling toward you. Of my guilt. Guilt aggravated by my having let so long go by without doing my duty—which is to throw myself sobbing in the dust at your feet and beg you to forgive me.

I do it, I do it now. There, I've thrown myself naked on the floor, as I did when I waited for you in the Danish *pension* at Anacapri; I'm crushing my breasts against the cold tiles; in front of me are these sheets of paper on which I'm writing. I feel a duty to write to you from this position of humility and pain.

My love, I haven't been granted the grace, the good fortune, the happiness of seeing you since that Christmas Eve of 1944. You'd made an appointment for the next day, do you remember?—at noon on Christmas Day, at the Café Picarozzi at Santa Maria Maggiore. We were to lunch and then spend the whole day and that night and the day after together. With a mad presumptuous gesture, I rejected all this happiness which you in your great goodness were offering me. I insulted and offended you basely; and my hand is trembling as I write to you. I did not come to the appointment, and as if that was not insult enough, I didn't even telephone to warn you, ask you to forgive me, tell you I was leaving, and say good-by. I owe you—oh, not explanations. There isn't any justification (as you can well understand) for my folly, my pride, my mistake. But I must tell you what my silly reasoning was—the absurd consideration that prevented my seeing you again. Here it is in a few words: that Christmas afternoon you, by your goodness, your beauty, your greatness, had made me so happy, filled me with such joy, transported me to such a paradise, that at midnight Mass I heard a voice in my conscience telling me clearly to accept your proposal of marriage and join myself to you for life, for life and death, to become your faithful wife and life's companion. It was an immense honor you did me, wretched me. And yet I was so impious, so *suicidal*, as not to have the courage to do it. That's why I didn't see you and left without telephoning you. Because at that moment I couldn't have just had a passing contact with you of any kind, big or small. It was all. Marriage. Or nothing at all. Do you understand?

Now that all has changed. As you will have heard from Dorotea, I'm married to an American, a fine good man, but I don't love him, or rather yes, I do love him, but as if he were a brother, a son, a father, a little of all three together; but I don't love him as a husband or as a lover, no, no, not for a single second do I love him as a husband, a lover, a man. And I've had a baby. A baby who, together with you, is the being I love most in the world.

I expect to see you at Capri, soon, very soon. My husband leaves tomorrow and will not be back until the end of May or the beginning of June. So we have two long months of happiness ahead of us. You see how presumptuous and how silly and selfish I am. When I say happiness, I'm only thinking of myself. Will you be happy? Will you still love me? Your letter was very sweet and kind. But I don't know if you love me still as you did once.

Well, I'll be frank. Even if you don't love me, I shall be happy when you come to Capri and deign to take me in your arms again. If you knew how much I have dreamed about them, those arms, those shoulders of yours!

How could I expect you to love me when I was so mad and criminal as to refuse your offer and break the appointment, an appointment for life, in order to marry a man whom I deeply respect but do not love?

I expect nothing, Aldo, my Aldo, and forgive me for daring to call you "my." I expect nothing. All I do is beg you to come soon to take possession once more of your servant and slave,

JANE

PS. If by any chance you can't leave as soon as you get this letter, write a couple of lines, just a couple of lines, to me at once, to tell me you are held up, so that I don't suffer too much. I adore you, I kiss your hand. The left hand, you remember? My master's hand. I kiss it, kiss it, kiss it, Your J.

(2)

Capri, April 11

LORD AND MASTER OF MY LIFE:

For three days, since I've been awaiting your reply in vain, I feel I'm going mad. I need, you understand, I need to see at least your writing.

Your writing is like you, because it comes from your own right hand, the companion to that master's hand.

This morning I was waked at five by my baby crying. There is a nurse to look after him, and so I didn't have to worry. But at once I thought of you and could not get to sleep again.

My only consolation, my only life, is in writing to you. This is the second letter I've sent you. But if you knew how many I've written and never sent. I've been writing to you for more than a year. In America there was a period when I wrote to you almost every day. Then I burned them all.

I've waited here for the mail—that is, for the person whose address I gave you (here it is again in case you've lost it: Maresciallo Raffaele Criscuolo, Capri, is enough)—till Don Raffaele could have got here after the mail's arrival. But in vain. And then I've sat down to write to you, my love.

Aldo my love, why don't you write to me? Why not? What have I done?

I realize I don't deserve anything. But if only I had a line, a single word from you. You can't be so cruel. Yes, I know and repeat again that I'm guilty toward you, and so toward myself.

Guilty for having forgotten the real joy you had given me. But why do you want to punish me like this now?

I wonder if perhaps you don't write to me because you've already left or are leaving on your way here, and so don't think it worth while.

Morning and evening I go to the piazza and meet the funicular from the boats. I look for you there.

Perhaps you'll arrive today. Who knows?

But if you haven't left yet, and are held up, write to me.

When your letter arrives, I'll kiss every word in it. You know, I read your first and only letter over and over again. They say that people's writing shows their character. And I see your character, your wonderful character, in the shape of your words; I like the way you write the vowels, the *o*'s and *a*'s, so round, caressing, embracing. Every *o* and *a* makes me feel you here in person, enveloping me with your body. But I like your signature most of all. Your signature where, as if on purpose, there is an *o* and an *a*. But the *l*'s please me too. Your signature is like yourself. It's alive, warm, calm, affectionate, beautiful. Aldo. Aldo.

I kiss your signature, I kiss your right hand, I kiss your left one most of all.

I'm yours, waiting every second for you.

JANE

(3)

MY MASTER!

It's eleven days now since I wrote to you the first time, replying to your dear, sweet letter, which I always keep with me, and put under my pillow when I sleep, and reread again and again to give me courage. Eleven days and you haven't replied yet. This is the third letter I've written to you. You'd opened my heart to a great hope. Why do you want to make me suffer so now? Up to a point I realized it's right. It's right that I should suffer and wait. It repays in a way my heavy debt to you. It's right that I should wait for you and suffer as I do suffer without any sign of a reply from you, because in that way I can get a clearer idea all the time of the great mistake of my life. If you are silent for that reason, if you're holding up your visit so as to punish me and give a sense of your reality and importance, then blessings on you. Blessings on you anyway and in every way.

But I implore you on my knees to end this torture. To grant me, unworthy and guilty as I am (though improved if not purified by waiting), grant me a glimpse of your beautiful face again, of your sweet eyes and lips, of your wonderful Hand.

Your Hand (the left one, the master's hand) is always in front of my eyes. How I'd like to adore it as the living symbol of your power over me! I want to kiss it all over for hours at a time. I'd like you to put it over my face, like this. It's so big it covers my face up altogether. It's so strong it could kill me without any effort. It's so gentle that it alone could make me happy. I'd like you to lie down on the bed and, without taking any other notice of me, put your hand on my face and leave it

THE CAPRI LETTERS

279

there until I go to sleep. That will be the loveliest night of my life.

Often I've asked myself why I adore your Hand so. I've found no reason. It's a mystery. All I've thought of is: that dogs adore their masters' hands too.

Yes, I'd like to be your dog and nothing more. When you come (this is another thing I've thought of so often and for so long), you must put your belt around my neck. Then walk about the room holding me by it as if on a leash. And I'll go along on all fours. Are you laughing? Yes, of course, I'm ridiculous, I know. It'll be just a game to you, and to me a joy long desired and imagined, finally come true.

Thinking of your hand, for example, I've often wanted to give you a ring with a diamond on it, the most beautiful and expensive diamond I can afford, and for you to accept my present as a sign of my devotion. When I was in Paris, just after the war, I could not pass a jeweler's window without this thought occurring to me. Sometimes I was with my husband. I would stop in front of the window, and he'd think I wanted some jewel for myself. So he was pleased to stop too, sometimes for long periods, looking at the jewels without saying a word. He's such a good man. And he suspects nothing, absolutely nothing, about me. I might almost say that he doesn't know me.

But you, on the other hand, in the first five minutes of speaking to me, in that church in Naples—do you remember? —in the first five minutes you'd seen right down into my soul.

And do you remember our first kiss—between those two doors, when you suddenly took me in your arms and kissed me? If my words, and looks, and state of agitation hadn't made you understand what I was, that long kiss must have told you everything. What was I, really? What am I?

Everything passes. Nothing is important. Deep down, my real self is all love. Love for you. I'm your reflection. Inside me there is nothing except you. You fill me altogether. Do you understand?

But there are so many things that you don't know about me. How long, for instance, I've been living for you and on you. Even when I had no hope of seeing you again, I dedicated to you the most secret, the loveliest hours of my life. In America, for instance, while my husband was out lecturing (he was at the university then), I used to stay at home, alone, for entire afternoons. And I would bathe in perfumed bath essence and come out all fragrant, thinking of you, thinking that you were there waiting for me. But there was no one there. I would get into bed naked and smell my own perfume as if you were there to smell it, and squeeze my waist with my own poor hands as strongly as I could, as if it were your hands squeezing me. And gradually I'd become like a mad thing, tight in an embrace with you, who weren't there.

Here's a photograph of myself. I had it taken two days ago, at the Marina Piccola. I went down on purpose in a new bathing-dress I bought on Fifth Avenue in New York before leaving, for having photographs taken to send you, if you were delayed in coming to see me. You have been delayed, alas. You're not here yet. And don't even write to me. Of all the photographs, this was the only one like me. As you see, I'm still young. I've had a son. But I haven't changed very much. Do you still find me attractive?

My love, my sweet, my strength, my life and death, I kiss you, kiss you like that time between those two church doors in Naples, and more, more, much more.

YOUR JANE

THE CAPRI LETTERS

281

Capri, April 23

My Aldo:

Yesterday I went to Anacapri.

It wasn't just a sentimental trip for memory's sake. I went to see if the Danish *pension* was still there and if we could stay there this time without your having to come secretly, or climb up the bougainvillæa. . . .

Yes, it's still there. Everything just as it was. The Danish lady recognized me and gave me a warm greeting. All you need do, when you come, is stay with her. Take my old room. It's free. And I will be the one who will come and visit you this time.

You can't stay in my own house, you'll understand why.

You must come here once or twice and see the baby. But you won't be able to come very often, and we can't be together here.

My old room at the *pension* is just as it was. The same coverlet on the bed, the flowered cretonne curtains, the looking-glass on the dressing-table in the corner between the two windows. The shutters were half-shut. A ray of hot yellow sun was beating on the old tiled floor. Outside one could hear the chickens clucking. I felt a great peace, and a great joy thinking of you here. I remembered that time you stayed hidden all day long in the room. How frightened I was! But how sweet my fright was too! You were so sleepy. It was nights and nights since you'd had a good sleep. So that day, when the colonel wasn't in Capri and you were free, you hadn't the strength to get up at dawn, like the other times, and leave. And you fell asleep. You slept nearly the whole day, while I went round the room on tiptoe, never taking my eyes off you. You were sleeping on my bed. Almost naked. And how small my bed seemed! How big you were! You had one arm folded back with the hand under the pillow. But the other, the master's Hand, was hanging down on one side, asleep too. I remember going down on my knees and kissing it very gently, so as not to awake you. Then when you did wake up, you were hungry; do you remember how hungry you were? I locked you in and went down to the kitchen, to get you some bread and ham.

I came back here from Anacapri fuller of you than ever, if that were possible. I tried to remember, one by one, all the times we'd been together. First at Anacapri, and then in Rome. I don't think I was able to remember, exactly, every single time. But I did the places. The room at Anacapri. Then your room in Rome, in the Trastevere; then the next one in Prati; then the third, the last one, at Santa Maria Maggiore, when I came from France to visit you on Christmas Eve. . . . And the pinewood at Fregene, that September day when we went by bus, and I'd brought beer and sandwiches in a basket and we went on and on into the pinewood till we reached a completely deserted spot near the sea; and we were so happy.

I've never told you, but do you know what I thought of, almost every time, *immediately afterwards*? Lying on top of you, with my head in the "nest" (do you remember we used to call it the *nest*, that place between your shoulder and neck where I put my head?), lying on top of you, breathing with your own very breath, I thought, almost every time, I don't know why, of death. I had been so happy, I was so happy, that I wanted to die. And there was nothing more except to die. But no; that's true, but it's not exact. It was a more complex, a deeper sensation. The fullness of love which you gave me was fused with the idea of death. The love you gave me was certain, as death is certain. Nothing was more certain. I should never experience anything truer than your love—and death. And it seemed to me then, while I lay stretched on you, in silence, in peace, in infinite sad happiness, that I was already dead, already still, already certain of the only two certainties we can have, death and love. Love, which passes; death, which remains forever.

My Aldo! Do I need to tell you that I've felt nothing of the kind with any other man in the world? Before you, as I told you, I'd only had one or two silly flirtations with boys at college. And afterwards, my husband. Oh, I've never, never, not once thought of death after having been with my husband.

What is making love with my husband like? Fresh water. And with you it's like heady liquor. With him it's a willed, forced act; with you an uncontrollable abandon of my whole nature. With him it's a cold, bitter thought, conscious of itself at every second, and with you the transformation of all of me into feeling and sensation, like a flower in the wind, a stone in the sun, a fish in water.

When I was with you, sleep would come to me suddenly, neither desired nor foreseen. When with him it would hang back, be anxiously invoked, provoked, and eventually feigned as I waited. How often I've pretended to sleep, afterwards, with my husband! He always believed in my pretense. He hadn't the slightest suspicion. And if he'd left his arm under my back from tenderness (for he loves me more than anything else in the world), I wouldn't dare move it for fear of waking him up. Then I'd notice he was still awake and that the arm must be hurting him. . . . But I continued to feign sleep because he made me pity him, and I thought it would make him suffer much more to take the physical pain away and replace it by the moral pain of discovering my pretense and discontent. Very often, to avoid rejecting his embrace, I would think of you. I would close my eyes, sigh deeply, and imagine that it was you holding me. Was that bad? It was certainly bad. But what could I do? I was punished for my idiocy in having escaped from you as if you were a mistake, while you were, you are, the truth. My truth, my way, my life.

The mistake, on the other hand, was my husband. And gradually because of that I almost got to the point of hating him. Hating him, but not with my mind. He has always behaved perfectly to me. I've never had anything to complain of from him. He's always been full of attention and care and delicacy. It tortures me to have to watch him expressing his love for me without my being in the least moved.

No, I've never hated him with my mind. But I have with my senses and body. It's stronger than myself. Sometimes, at table, particularly when he chews celery, or a crust, or an apple, I feel an absurd impulse as if I wanted to kill him. And at those moments I feel I could do so without remorse.

I repeat, I have nothing against him. I can think and say nothing but good of him. He's intelligent, he's a hard worker, he's good, he loves no one in the world but me, our baby, and his work.

Yet, more and more every day, I see him as my mistake. And I hate him because he represents my mistake. If I hadn't married him, I would have married you.

This is the fourth letter I've written you, my love.

I hope and pray to God it may be the last.

I don't know how I have the strength to go on.

If you just can't come to Capri because of your work or

some other reason, write to me frankly and say so. I'll try to find an excuse to come to Rome. But tell me, in the name of Heaven!

Did you like my photograph? It wasn't a mistake sending it to you?

That's enough now, it's late. It's two in the morning. My hand is tired with all this writing. But I can do nothing else. It's the only way I live.

I've just broken off a moment and gone out on the terrace. The air is stifling, and that hot wind is blowing. I saw between the plants, beyond the black blobs of gardens and villas, the lights up there of the piazza and hotels. Suppose you'd already arrived, are there, and I know nothing of it. You weren't on the funicular this evening either, after the arrival of the boat. But you might have taken a car, or come up on foot. There, I'm thinking that if you were here on Capri, how different it would be, even if for some time and for some reason we couldn't see each other. Now, like this, without you, Capri—is a prison or a torture chamber. When will it end?

YOUR JANE

(5)

Capri, May 2

MY TREASURE AND MY LIFE:

I'm a fool, an idiot, I could hit myself, I'm so angry at my own thoughtlessness.

Last night—it's happened the last few nights—I couldn't sleep for spasms of desire for you.

Suddenly an idea came to me. I'm furious with myself that this hadn't occurred to me before.

Perhaps you don't come, I thought, because you're not sure

you have enough money, and don't want to tell me so. That's why you don't even write.

I enclose a check for a hundred thousand lire, in case that's true. Please, please cash it, and come at once. You can give it back to me when you're able to during one of your next films. In your letter you told me that you had hopes of a good job for this summer. So just consider that the producers have paid you something in advance.

Anyway, don't be offended. Try to understand the state of mind I'm in. I'd do any mad thing to see you here!

Now, every night before going to bed, I wind on my bare flesh a great rough cord, tight round my waist. And pretend it's your two hands gripping me tight. The rope hurts a lot. It scarcely allows me to breathe. In the morning, when I take it off, the skin round my waist is all red and livid. In the first few days the marks had gone by evening. But now they remain. I feel that if I don't do this, I would do other mad things. Hit the baby perhaps, or mistreat the nurse. So I persuade myself that this is the best thing to do. I'm the only one who suffers.

For some time I've been going for a long walk every morning toward the point of Tragara. I just go along paths and then turn into the short, hard grass, burned by the sun. The sun is already as hot as summer. I walk for an hour or more. Then lie down on one of those spiky porous rocks scattered over that part. And there I stay, motionless, with a straw hat over my eyes, until the rock begins to hurt me. And even after it begins hurting I still lie there. I lie there as long as I can without moving. Physical pain is the one thing that gives me any relief from this terrible desire for you. It was lying on these rocks the first time, in fact, that I realized this. And that night I had the idea of winding that rope tight around me.

When I can't bear it any longer, then I get up, aching all over. The blazing sunlight hurts me too. I look at the arid, exciting landscape, with rocks contorted and heaped up shapelessly as if flung there by an earthquake. I look at the dark-green, almost black sea at my feet. The *Faraglioni* standing out huge and rather absurd. I look at the distant, misty haze of the Amalfi coast, the ash-blue mountains scarcely visible; and glimmering white halfway up the cliffs the vague blobs of houses and villages. There's life over there too, I think. Tears and suffering and tortured desires like mine. And suddenly the whole world seems made of pain. Even in the depths of the sea below, which seems so smooth and gleaming, there must be crude, agonizing life, terrible struggles, deaths, disasters.

And yet I can't prevent myself imagining you may possibly be arriving at Capri this very moment. You've been to Don Raffaele. And Don Raffaele has shown you how to get to the villa. At the villa the nurse has told you I've gone out for a walk toward Tragara. And so you've come to find me. You're coming toward me now. Your steps are muffled by the grass. Or perhaps I hear them but don't dare to believe my ears. You see me, come up behind me, grasp me. . . .

JANE

(6)

May 6

ALDO:

This is the last letter I'll write you, if you don't reply or don't come. I fling myself at your feet. I want to be your servant. I'll arrange, if you require it, for my husband and child to be your servants too.

You can't ask more of me.

But perhaps you don't want to ask this or anything else of me. Perhaps you don't want to ask me for anything at all. You just don't want me.

And yet, I swear to you, if you wished me, I'd be ready to . . .

[*Here I must skip three pages so mad that I can't even copy them out. This is the end of the letter:*]

. . . This morning at dawn I was still awake. Like the other mornings, I began to hear, against the distant sound of surf, the calls of the swallows, strident, yet fresh and sweet. They grew, first gradually, then rapidly, till they filled the air, even blotted out the sound of the sea.

I rose up from my bed of torture and went out on the terrace. Everything was calm, still, and colorless in the cold blue light. Except for the black and white swallows, crisscrossing in all directions in front of me.

I went back to bed. Lying there, my eyes closed, I could still hear the happy screeching of the swallows. And then I thought, for the first time, of something I had known long ago. The noise swallows make is due to their clearing the air at high speed with beaks open to devour insects, which is the only purpose of their sudden twirls and curves and dips. They devour, they kill. In my imagination I saw their open beaks, their small, lively, rapacious, voracious eyes. And suddenly that screeching which I had so much liked seemed horrible to me. I shut the window and thrust my head under the pillow. But still I could hear, muffled, that atrocious screeching. Finally, as the sun rose, it gradually ceased and I fell asleep.

THE CAPRI LETTERS

I slept till midday. I haven't been to Tragara any more, of course.

Good-by, Aldo. Shall I still be waiting for you?

I'll be waiting for you all my life. You know that.

You're like the swallows too. Perhaps without knowing it, you're devouring me, killing me.

Yet I love you all the same. With all my soul and all my body, forever,

JANE

The very night I returned to Paris, I rang up Dorotea. The call came through at midnight. Dorotea, of course, was not at home.

"She's gone to the cinema," the landlady told me.

"Tell her I'm sorry to have left without being able to telephone her. Tell her I followed her advice and found what I was looking for. And thank her. And say everything's all right. And that we'll be meeting very soon."

My first, instinctive, unreasoning, uncontrollable reaction to reading the letters had been that: to telephone Dorotea. Why?

I asked myself if she had really gone to the cinema. Perhaps she had, perhaps she hadn't. But whom had she gone with? And at what time would she get home? And would she be alone? I couldn't sleep, thinking of her.

As I'd read the letters I had thought of her, only of her. Jane's feelings for Aldo reminded me of mine for Dorotea.

My last picture of Dorotea had been turned inside out at once while reading the first letter. Dorotea was no longer a housewife camouflaged as a prostitute; she was, instead, a prostitute camouflaged as a housewife. Her real nature was just the one I'd seen that very first instant I'd met her with Jane in that *trattoria*. Had I any doubt of that still? Why, even the phone call I'd just made . . . I couldn't get to sleep. Till, at three in the morning, I rang up again. And the landlady answered again. She'd been asleep and, with all her deference for me, was now angry. No, Dorotea hadn't yet returned.

Even so, the picture of the housewife was now superimposed and confused with that other picture, of a cold, vicious, energetic woman who thought nothing of sleeping with a different man every night for money. The picture of her, with an apron round her hips, her sleeves turned back over her strong arms, kneading the *scarcella* with those practiced ancient movements of hers, merged, ironically, sweetly, making her more of a temptress than ever, into the picture of the painted woman loaded with vulgar jewelry, still, at that moment perhaps, ogling passers-by from a café in Via Veneto, as at the period of the liberation and the *segnorine*. She was a *segnorina* of the Renaissance, that's what my Dorotea was. Her face with its olive skin and bluish tints, her luminous animal eyes, reminded me, as I've already observed, of the models of Sebastiano del Piombo. But when she was without make-up and dressed for housework, as I'd seen her the last time, her statuesque form, so solid and rounded even made me think of Piero della Francesca.

I looked again at the photograph of poor Jane in one of her letters. Her effort to transform herself into a vamp was painful. The bikini she'd bought on Fifth Avenue, the pose clumsily showing off her legs, the smile which was intended to be knowing and merely appeared hysterical; she *looked* like a respectable girl badly made up as a prostitute for amateur dramatics. My God! Was this the real Jane, then? Had she really become like that, never a real woman, in spite of producing children? Had she lost her soul because she'd never given it?

All this time I was lying on my bed, that bed of fear and anguish, in the little hotel in the rue des Saints-Pères. I saw Jane again as she'd been in my dream: grim and mute, her eyes, which had been gray and gentle, now glittering and almost black with despair, her cheeks, once so pale, now red with that peculiar redness. . . .

Was I, perhaps, condemned to the same end too?

I had recognized myself in every page, every line, of the letters; the same feelings, same desires, same follies.

And when we had stopped together at a jeweler's window and she had gazed at the gold and jewels there, symbols of money, she had thought of Aldo, and I had gazed too and thought of Dorotea.

In the last letter but one was the check for a hundred thousand lire. No one had cashed it. It had come back. Now it was in my hands. But what did they mean, that hysteria, those frenzies and transports?

I did not think God could be so hard on her. Jane was not in hell. She had suffered too much. She'd already been in hell here on earth. I wept for her, I still loved her tenderly, like a sister; more than a sister, I loved her as another self in female form, who when she went had left me those letters so that I should understand what to do.

23.

I went to Rome. I rented the studio in Via Margutta. I asked Dorotea to come and live with me. She hesitated, then accepted.

Every Monday morning I flew to Paris, and returned to Rome by night train every Friday. I spent only two days a week with Dorotea, Saturday and Sunday.

Why didn't I take her to Paris?

As I'd decided to live with her, why didn't I take that step too?

What prevented me was an instinct, obscure and contradictory, but very close to my deepest reason for loving her. If only I'd followed this instinct afterwards too, and not taken her to America! But there it is, everything that happens is fated and it's useless to complain and recriminate. I was afraid that, by taking her (she who had never even been to Milan) to a foreign city where I would have her all to myself, I would lose her; I mean, lose interest in her. For I loved her as she was, in her squalid independence, in her abject collusion with that old procuress of Via Boncompagni, in her mysterious nightly excursions.

Why on earth then, you'll say, did you take that studio in Via Margutta? Why did you bring her there? Wasn't that already a beginning of the disenchantment that you wanted to avoid by leaving her in Rome and not taking her to Paris?

Yet, it was. But my fear of not desiring her any more was hidden: it was a kind of unconscious force which, gradually and almost insensibly, through agonizing yet decreasing alternations of hope and disappointment, was urging me to the stage I have now reached, of not desiring her any more.

If I'd taken her to Paris, I should have speeded up this process. And that was, at heart, the one thing I wanted to avoid. For though we may have an urge for perdition, we want to move gradually, cowardly toward it, saying to ourselves as we go that we can still be saved.

Dorotea assured me that when I was in Paris she lived and slept at Via Boncompagni. But I suspected (and I cannot tell you now whether the suspicion gave me more pain or pleasure, because it may have given me both together), I suspected her of having her lovers at Via Margutta itself.

Certainly, from the moment I rented the studio in Via Margutta and spent every week-end there with Dorotea, thus officially, as it were, making her my mistress, I used to telephone from Paris many times during the week to find out what she was doing; and always, after the time agreed by me, half past twelve at night, I'd find her at home in Via Boncompagni.

But at other times or in other places, and in Via Margutta too, she could do exactly what she liked.

So each time I returned I made absurd scenes of jealousy; absurd because if I did not find, and in fact I never did find, some cigarette stump of a different brand from hers in an ashtray, I was disappointed.

"Who was here yesterday? I'll throw you out; I'll kill you!" I would shout, apparently tortured by jealousy. But if I'd been sincere (for I was tortured in fact by desire), I would have thrown myself on my knees in front of her and muttered: "Please, please tell me there was some man here yesterday; please tell me you made love with him here, in our bed! Tell me and I'll bless you and cover you with kisses!"

In other words, I had taken Dorotea to live with a prostitute, not to transform her into a wife. But I had not made this clear to her. She didn't understand it; or perhaps she understood only too well.

After some time, exasperated at never finding, on my return, any proof of her infidelity, I had her watched by a private detective agency. And each week the reports disappointed me and left no room for the smallest doubt. The man from the agency would smile with satisfaction as he handed me the report. I would smile too as I took it from him. So it went on; and I cannot say that, mingled with my disappointment, there might not also have been some satisfaction too. What did I want at heart? To be hurt. So there was always a part of me quite pleased to avoid that.

I had even told the agency that if Dorotea was seen entering the studio in Via Margutta or the flat in Via Boncompagni, or anywhere else, in the company of any man whatsoever, they were to send me an urgent cable. I would have jumped into the first available plane, perhaps surprised her, then afterwards . . .

Nothing like that happened at all. Shadowing her cost me a lot of money, and seeing it was pointless, I gave it up.

Finally I asked UNESCO for a month's leave, saying I wanted to visit my children in America, and went to Rome.

After spending the whole of that month, more or less night and day, with Dorotea, I found I could no longer tear myself away from her and return to Paris. I was being driven insane by that absurd jealousy, continually suspecting her of being unfaithful and never finding any proof.

Dorotea seemed to have understood it all: how my absence, before, for five days in every week, had been enough to throw me into this state of uncertainty every time I returned.

But how something more was needed to arouse it now: continual little pricks; telephone calls that I would interrupt on some unexpected return home and that I'd consider—and perhaps they really were—mysterious; prolonged absences; lateness at appointments; glances and smiles which, as we walked together through the streets of Rome, I would think, without ever being sure, she was giving other men.

I could never put my finger on any positive fact. She would elude my questions with an embrace, a caress, a declaration of faith; or sometimes with a vague reply in a muttered monosyllable, while a strange sly smile glinted in the corner of her eyes, a smile that I had never seen before; or sometimes even with a violent flash of rage and irritation, which stopped me, without, however, convincing me of her sincerity.

In fact, I was caught in her web and I felt I hadn't the strength to tear myself away and return to Paris, as I should have. I began to put off my departure from day to day. Then I told UNESCO headquarters that I was ill. So another month passed, perhaps more. Until one day some kind compatriot of mine, I never bothered to find out who, gave himself the job of informing my superiors that I'd not gone to the States at all as I'd declared in order to obtain leave, and what my illness really was.

Naturally, I knew nothing about this heroic espionage, until I was called urgently back to Paris. Guessing the truth, and weighing the possible consequences of my reply, I tried to play for time and did not move from Rome. Ten days later I was fired from UNESCO. That was early in January last year.

Then began a ghastly life with Dorotea. My financial resources had shrunk at a blow. Dorotea had incited me to give up UNESCO. Sometimes I'd told her that I would take her to

Paris with me, but Paris didn't interest her—I don't know why. She preferred to stay in Rome. Her obstinacy about this was inexplicable. I told myself that perhaps it was due to a sense of inferiority. She talked a little English, which she'd learned during the liberation in a way you can guess; but not a single word of French. And perhaps Paris, the city of smart sophisticated women, intimidated and frightened her. That's what I told myself. The truth I discovered later, and by degrees. For Dorotea had a great plan, and this plan was so important, so vital to her that she tried at all costs to avoid any opposition to it from me and was very cautious in revealing it to me.

Since the days of the liberation, and perhaps before, when as a child at home she had seen the emigrants leaving for America and heard of millionaires returning, she had dreamed of America as a paradise on earth. It was a fixed, deep-rooted idea, to which she clung stubbornly through any experience. Anyone who knows southern Italy will understand what I mean.

But if America hadn't been a paradise on earth, it would not be so difficult to get into. Even in the wild period of the liberation, to succeed in marrying a GI was always a great stroke of luck for an Italian girl, *segnorina* or not.

The American soldiers then seemed to her, and to all the others, angels who could, if fortune willed, open the gates of that paradise. And among these angels I, an officer, a major, was an absolute archangel. From this came her unshakable sweetness to me, her compliance with each of my whims, her patience at all my rudeness and insults. Superimposed on my figure she saw the Statue of Liberty, the entrance to New York. Even when I was at her feet, she couldn't see me otherwise. And she loved me for that, without making any distinctions, and quite disinterestedly. Even if, during the first period of our relationship, she might have had hopes of my taking her to America afterwards, when she heard that I was married and a father, she still continued, without mentioning it, to show herself as docile as ever to me. Oh, it was not self-interest! Her love for America was mystical; and I was part of that love, its living symbol.

Self-interest came in later. Wasn't it bound to?

When I took her to live in Via Margutta, when I began to show clear signs that I no longer needed only her body, but also her heart, when finally I gave up UNESCO in order to stay in Rome with her, then, naturally, she realized for the first time that the myth could suddenly become reality. I was no longer an archangel; I was a flesh-and-blood American citizen who could, must, marry her and take her there. Paris—what did Paris matter? To her it wasn't worth the smallest village in Arkansas. In Paris, she felt, and quite rightly, I would end by tiring of her and seeking other distractions. No, no, I must stay there with her in Via Margutta until the great moment came.

She played her hand just as she should—perfectly. After eleven months of being married to her, after ten of being together in America, I've only just seen Dorotea's cards. The final one I saw last night.

In Via Margutta I didn't understand.

Apart from America perhaps Dorotea also loved me for myself and perhaps not. But that wasn't the important thing, because in either case she didn't want to lose me and had realized that in order not to, there was only one path for her to follow, though it was a difficult and terribly exhausting one. She had to give me the daily suspicion, and never the certainty, of infidelity. This meant she had to be faithful to me in fact, in order not to run any risk whatever of being found out. Even if she did not love me, her aim was so big it was worth any sacrifice. For I did really want her to betray me. She could not help noticing this vicious desire of mine, from my ridiculous whims, my abject longing to be jealous. But that ancient good sense of hers, that peasant canniness, made her see what I did not see: the future; a very close one if she had given way to my whims and finally granted me the abjection I was longing for. "This man," Dorotea must have said to herself, judging me with that Roman simplicity of hers, "this man's aching for me to put the horns on him and give him definite proof of it, so he can quarrel with me, hit me, be hit by me, and finally make love. But I know, I know, how these things end. That will happen two or three times at the most, and then it will all blow over. He'll become a nice boy again, because he is a nice boy at heart. Then he'll hate me, and as I've been unfaithful (he has the proof!), he'll throw me out, and then it's good-by to America, I'll have done for myself with my own hands! No, no, the thing to do here is to go on being serious and good until he realizes too at a certain moment that it's all just nonsense."

The thing about this was that the same identical reasoning, or almost the same, could be made by a woman sincerely in love.

And anyway, what do I think about it now? Can I say, today that Dorotea has never loved me and doesn't love me?

Certainly not. Quite the contrary.

And even if she hasn't ever loved me and doesn't love me now with a real love, I must say that she's always been tender, respectful, and deeply grateful to me. With herself Dorotea is honest. There's no doubt about that. She has not forgotten what her life was like until the day when I changed it for her. The daily anxiety, the need to get hold of money every day for herself and her mother and an aunt, both old and ill, whom she kept back home. She had chosen the profession of prostitute. Perhaps she could and should have chosen another. But had she really *chosen*? To what point was she to blame? Life had led her to it. Anyway, she doesn't forget how much she owes me, and proves it by her affection, even after eleven months of marriage to me.

Why should I say that she doesn't love me?

When you, my dear Mario, saw me nearly a year ago in Via Margutta, Dorotea and I were, as perhaps you may have already realized, at the most critical point of our relationship.

Don't imagine I didn't notice that Dorotea attracted you too. I've a very lively memory of the trip we all made to Tor San Lorenzo, with Dorotea between us in the jeep. I saw, understood, felt everything. And you too, perhaps, realized that I'd noticed and that, alas, my jealousy was—how shall I put it?—rather ambiguous. Dorotea flirted with you. I am sure you tried your luck; I only wish you'd succeeded! But I am sure you didn't. Dorotea was an impregnable fortress. Stalingrad, my dear fellow.

And when, gradually, my money dwindled more and more and finally came to an end, then America, which I'd always talked about to Dorotea with academic languor, as a purely theoretical possibility, America seemed the only solution.

I could always apply to Loewen, with whom I still corresponded and for whom I did some little job now and then, taking a photograph, measuring a picture, checking a reference. I wrote to Loewen. And Loewen replied, by airmail, telling me to come at once. He didn't feel up to taking his usual autumn-session course at New York University. I could take his place. It was ideal for me, he said to me.

It was also ideal for Dorotea.

I married her a fortnight later. Her witnesses were her so-called brother-in-law, the one of the fireworks, and an old friend of the landlady's of Via Boncompagni, a seventy-year-old doctor, paunchy and in his second childhood; mine, Willy Osgood and Tem O'Rourke. I'd have liked to cable for you to come from Paris. But I knew that you wouldn't be able to; you were too busy with your films. And anyway I would have had too much to explain.

On the 29th day of July, Dorotea saw the Statue of Liberty with her own eyes. We went by boat. She was afraid of airplanes.

What had decided me to marry and return to America?

Lack of money? And the fear of having to abandon Dorotea because of that?

Was that so horrible that I couldn't face it?

No, my dear fellow, I married Dorotea and took her to America for quite a different reason, or at least on quite a different impulse. A secondary and transitory impulse. And yet without it I wouldn't have married her at all.

That evening that Loewen's letter arrived was the moment of decision. I had written to Loewen because Dorotea had urged me to. But I'd hoped for a negative reply, at least for the moment.

But when Loewen's letter arrived and it was clear that in America there was work and money waiting for me, and that it depended entirely on myself whether I took it or left it, whether I kept Dorotea and took her to America or stayed on in Europe alone, then I was faced for the first time with the thought of what would happen if I really did marry her and take her to the States. Would I introduce her to Jane's parents? To her brothers, her uncles? To my colleagues like the Pratts? And to so many others, worse, more conventional and hypocritical, than they? To all those people whom I hated deep in my heart? To that Philistine world which had been the first cause of my poor Jane's mistaken life, and of her death?

I imagined the puritan provincial reaction to Dorotea of those compatriots of mine. How I'd enjoy it all! This was a really fine revenge. To arrive among them and introduce my wife, a prostitute!

Was I profaning Jane's memory? I thought of the letters and told myself that, on the contrary, I was following her suggestion, carrying out her will and testament, doing with Dorotea what Jane blamed herself for not having done with Aldo. I was choosing for life, marrying the being with whom I'd thought I'd sinned most deeply, the being whom I despised yet desired more than any other in the world.

Yet deep in my heart I still had a hope that's almost unconfessable, a hope of desecration.

Dorotea would be acting as a mother to my children. This gift of their innocence, this contamination of my paternal affection offered to her impurity, this sacrilege—as soon as the idea occurred to me, I felt an instinctive revulsion. No, not that, I said to myself, that's too much; even if I marry Dorotea, even if I take her to America, we won't live with my children. Instincts made up of my physiological heredity, my education, tradition, religion, culture, my pity and my pride, rose up in protest.

And yet this, and this alone, was the spark, by promising

me a new pleasure in the holocaust of so many other dear old memories, that made me decide.

I'd found Loewen's letter in the studio in Via Margutta that evening, when I came home about nine. I read it, and translated it to Dorotea. She said nothing, but, as I read, went on coming and going between the little kitchen and the studio, preparing supper. When I'd finished reading, I said nothing either. I looked at the letter and at Dorotea every time she came back from the kitchen, looked at her, trying to discover on her face what she was thinking. Oh, I knew only too well what she was thinking. Then I tried to imagine what she would say to me when she decided to speak.

Finally she brought in a steaming bowl. She put it down in the center of the table, ladled out the portions, and sat down. Then she spoke.

"Come on," she said. "Eat up now. You can decide afterwards."

And I ate. And looked at her as I ate. And as I looked at her, thought of all I've told you. That is, I thought, for the first time, of the reality of marrying her and taking her to the States. And when the thought of the children occurred to me, I felt such a sharp stab of pain that I stopped eating, got up from the table, and couldn't return.

I went out on the terrace.

Dora had not said anything. Perhaps she understood. Perhaps she guessed.

I went out on the terrace above that little yard, among the squalid little houses, with the dark tall mass of the Pincio in front of me.

Up above, along the tree-lined avenue, at regular intervals, shone the lights of street lamps; and lower down, crisscrossing one another, the headlamps of cars. Couples were walking slowly along, or looking over the parapet in the darkness.

I was suffering at the thought of my children, Jane's and my children; suffering at the thought that I couldn't resist the temptation to give them a prostitute as a second mother; that, on the contrary, it was only the idea of this suffering, with its possibilities of pleasure, that decided me to take the great step.

If I were a man, I said to myself, looking up toward the black mass of the Pincio, if I were a man I would have the strength to marry Dora and take her to America, and resist this final contamination at the same time.

Or I'd realize that I would not have such strength and so renounce Dorotea completely and forever.

But I'm not a man. I'm an aging, selfish, complicated, cowardly adolescent, just sentimental enough to adore my children and follow all the tender traditions in which I've been brought up; cynical enough to put my own pleasure first, if my pleasure was to flout my children and tradition.

As if ignoring the final result of my internal debate, I went on saying to myself: "Why am I not a man? Why can't I have the strength to be one?" And I tried to imagine both the solutions that avoided the third, the only one I felt drawn toward. Abandon Dorotea? Or marry her and take her to the States, but not live with the children?

Naturally I inclined toward this last. Because, in spite of the solemn promise I'd made to myself, I pretended that, once in America, I could still change my mind.

I haven't been sincere, just now, in hinting that I realized then how things would end. To diminish our past sins, we always try to make them out as fated. We persuade ourselves that we had struggled against them from scruples or generosity or selfishness, while knowing from the first that there was nothing to be done, the temptation was too strong, the game was lost. And yet if we are honest, if we re-evoke those instants, sometimes, alas, so brief, in their tragic detail, we remember having been free, free to decide in one way or the other, by the sacrifice either of a pleasure or of a duty; and the remorse we feel now is due only to our certainty of having been free then.

I looked at the black mass of the Pincio and the headlights crisscrossing up there, among the trees of the avenue. I knew that behind me, beyond the open door, Dorotea was still sitting at the table looking at me. To stimulate this passion which had already reached its maximum and was therefore on the point of declining, would I have to sacrifice my tenderest, most deep-seated feelings?

The fresh voice of a girl called out, somewhere in the night: "Nando! Maria!"

A cat mewed.

Oh, God, my God, I must decide!

No, only about the *possibility* of making such a sacrifice, I told myself finally. Then sighed deeply. And turned round. Dorotea was sitting at the table. But she was not eating, or looking at me. She was reading an illustrated magazine.

I went inside and put a hand on her shoulder. She raised her eyes from the paper and fixed them on me.

"Well," she said calmly, "have you decided?"

Her yellow-green eyes filled with golden flecks, her mysterious eyes in which I had so often and for so long lost myself in dreams, said nothing more to me at that moment, no longer held any mystery. She was nothing in particular now, I saw. Not evil or even good. She was an ordinary human being, with her own problems which did not concern me.

"I've decided," I said, smiling; and it was like the leap in the void, into nothingness, of one committing suicide by flinging himself over a precipice.

24.

Once in America, as you'll have already understood from the letter I wrote you two months ago, everything went just opposite to what I'd thought. I'm still amazed by it all.

My course at New York University began in September. We arrived on July 29. So we had a whole month before us. The first week we spent in New York. Loewen, who knew my situation, was generous and kind; he was determined to compensate me for all the little jobs I had done for him in Italy, and begged me to accept two thousand dollars.

Then I dressed Dorotea in American style from head to foot. I made her cut her hair, shorten her nails, and so on. After a week I took her to Atlantic Highlands, where my in-laws were at a country place of theirs for the children's sea-bathing.

There wasn't even any initial difficulty. My in-laws greeted Dorotea, from the first moment, with calm, affectionate kindness; and it was they, even if I had not wished it, who insisted on the children getting to know her at once. My father-in-law, who had never looked kindly on my marriage to his daughter, now seemed satisfied for the first time.

"Poor Jane's death was certainly a terrible misfortune; but now everything has turned out for the best," he seemed to be thinking. I knew his hatred for Europe and Europeans, his age-old contempt for the Latin peoples, particularly for Italians. And I could not manage to understand the reason for his sympathetic attitude to Dorotea, his confidence in her.

With my mother-in-law, who had on the other hand adored Jane and approved every one of her decisions without reserve, it was even more surprising and less explicable.

It crossed my mind that, in spite of their affection for their little grandchildren, the explanation might be that the two old people had been put out by the shouts and vivacity of two small children in the house, and the responsibilities they brought with them. The children had turned their lives upside down, those ordered, methodical, selfish lives of all old people, particularly if rich. They must have longer to free themselves of the encumbrance. Dorotea was their salvation.

So, probably, there was no need to search for any other explanation, though I'm sure that if Dorotea had not made such a favorable impression on them, they would have had the honesty to continue looking after the children and sacrificing their comfort.

But Dorotea was perfect. In the first place, she very rarely said anything. In the second place, she concentrated, for the fortnight we were at Atlantic Highlands as guests of my in-laws, entirely on the kitchen.

Every day she made a new dish with her own hands, spaghetti, *ravioli, fettuccini, gnocchi;* she put my father- and mother-in-law through the whole repertoire of Italian cooking, and also the famous *scarcella*, which was not a great success, however, except with the children.

Dorotea is a great cook. Anyone who can cook these dishes, said my father- and mother-in-law to each other, and my brothers- and sisters-in-law too when they came over to Atlantic Highlands one Sunday, anyone who can cook those dishes must be a very nice woman. "From the people, of course." But decent, honest, and sympathetic. And anyway, even these most conservative and contrary to any breaking of social barriers do not bother overmuch when it's a question of foreigners, and when it suits their convenience. Dorotea was "from the people." But they scarcely noticed it because she was Italian and didn't speak English; so everything went perfectly.

In September we moved, with the babies, to Long Island. I had taken a charming little house, with a pretty garden around it. To get to the university, in Manhattan, was rather less than an hour by subway. But the air was good, with all that green around, and the water not far away. Just what was wanted for the children.

And what about Dorotea?

Dorotea is happy.

But Dorotea is nothing to me any more. That light I already saw fading in her eyes in the last second of liberty has not gone on again. My in-laws are quite right. Dorotea is now a really nice woman. She doesn't attract me any more. Every night it's as it was with Jane. A voluntary, desperate, considered act.

I still ask myself, ceaselessly, how this can be possible. How could what seemed a radioactive charge in her body have dissolved, consumed itself, and with it the spell that bound me?

Perhaps that's what I was wanting, without knowing it?

If it was, then I can say I have achieved my aim.

It's three o'clock at night. Dorotea and the children are sleeping on the floor above.

I'm writing these last pages in the house on Long Island, where we are still living, nearly a year later. My work is going well, the children are flourishing, Dorotea is getting fatter, everything's all right. Except with me, who feel I'm dying of boredom. Can't you possibly find me an excuse to come to Rome?

I think of that mysterious telephone call which we received, poor Jane and I, at the Grand Hotel. Who had telephoned us? Who was blackmailing us? A friend of Dorotea's? Or a friend of Aldo's? I'd like to come to Rome and meet this Aldo. Who knows?

Last night Dorotea showed her last card. She's pregnant. Do you realize what that means?

Well, about five this afternoon, when I finished my lectures, I rang her up to say I'd be very late getting home; not to expect me to dinner; and not to wait up for me, but go to bed. I had a headache and needed exercise. I wanted to do something idiotic, return home on foot. Idiotic because it's more than ten miles, nearly twenty kilometers.

I did it. I came home on foot. I crossed Brooklyn Bridge and then the whole of Brooklyn. The bridge and the East River were lovely. But then, horrors! All those streets, all those formless, characterless houses, groups of buildings that are useful and have no ambition beyond just that, being useful. A movie theater, a garage, a grocer's, an apartment house, another movie, another garage, another grocer's, another apartment house. And the colors and advertising signs, they're useful too. Of course, I agree that the cities of ancient times were also made to be useful. But now they're no longer ideal for that purpose. They're useless and impractical, and that very fact makes them almost beautiful.

And as I walked on, dusk gradually fell here too, in the streets of Brooklyn and Long Island, as in Paris, Capri, and Rome.

Interminable avenues of Long Island, houses surrounded by their grass and trees on each side, lighted windows, voices and music of television, decent American families at dinner. And every now and then the houses get closer. Shops, a drug-store, an undertaker, a movie. I stop, eat a sandwich, drink a sarsaparilla. Then I start walking again. It's warm. My feet begin to hurt. I take off my jacket, carry it on my arm. Against my forearm, in the inside of my coat, I feel the packet of Jane's letters, which I always carry with me, even if I'll never reread them.

I walk on; it's night now. Already some of the houses are dark and silent amid the green. On, on. My house is still far away. I stop and rest for ten minutes at a deserted cross-street; sit on the sidewalk, smoke a cigarette, and gaze at what I see in front of me. The night, three or four streets losing them-selves in the night, with their perspective of bluish lamps. Houses here and there among the trees. The clean, smooth asphalt, with its studs, its white lines. Some advertising bill-boards. The names of the streets, on other signboards, rectan-gular, clear, each carefully placed. Directing arrows, on other yellow signboards, to places near by.

In the middle of the cross-street a big blue lantern is wav-ing in the breeze just blowing up. The traffic lights, red and green, alternate at regular intervals. Occasionally a car passes, going very fast. If the lights are red, it arrives, stops, waits.

I look at that blue lantern waving against the black sky,

waving despairingly in the wind. My God, must I end my life here?

And yet these sights should be familiar. The landscape in which I spent my youth was the same, or very like it. Why do I think of Rome?

Finally I get up and start walking again.

Two hours ago, toward one in the morning, I came in sight of my home. *My* home. The home where Dorotea and my children are sleeping. I'm tired, I long to have a glass of whisky there, at home. And smoke a pipe. And finish my writing. But I pause and look at the house, a hundred yards away. The windows are dark. My heart shrinks at going back in there again. Suppose I run away. Just like that, without saying anything, vanish into the world. Where to—the Far West, Mexico?

No, no, I want to return to Rome.

I sit down again on the sidewalk, and take the packet of Jane's letters out of my pocket. I've been wanting to do this for a long time. I decide to burn them at once. I take them from their envelopes, one by one, keeping my eyes half-closed to avoid reading a phrase, a word, without wanting to. Slowly, very slowly, I tear them all up, every envelope, every sheet; then I look round and find a few dry sticks in a field near by. I break them up and make a sort of framework, leaning the sticks against the curb. Then, still keeping my eyes half-closed, I arrange the torn letters and envelopes over it. There's a wind. Two bits fly away. I have to thrust all the others into my pockets and run to catch them. Then I put everything back on the twigs, study the direction of the wind, and kneel down so as to shield them with my body. And light up. The letters burn quickly.

They're burned. I get to my feet.

A man comes up, a middle-aged man, unshaven, coarsely dressed, an Irish or German type. He looks at me in a hostile way. I think he's going to stop and ask for alms. But no, not at all. He gives me a malevolent glance of hatred, contempt, perhaps of indifference, and goes off into the night.

Now I'm standing still, in front of my home. I must make up my mind to enter it. The man who passed . . . I seem to have lived through this moment before. Perhaps one night at B—, when I was with Jane.

Now I must go inside. There, I'm moving. All I have to do is cross the street. I take the house keys out of my pocket.

I ask myself if I'll ever manage to escape again.

When, though?

When will you call me?

A NOTE ON THE TYPE

The text of this book was set on the Linotype in
JANSON, a recutting made direct from the type cast
from matrices made by Anton Janson. Whether or
not Janson was of Dutch ancestry is not known,
but it is known that he purchased a foundry and
was a practicing type-founder in Leipzig during
the years 1600 to 1687. Janson's first specimen sheet
was issued in 1675. His successor issued a specimen
sheet showing all of the Janson types in 1689.

His type is an excellent example of the influential
and sturdy Dutch types that prevailed in England
prior to the development by William Caslon of his
own incomparable designs, which he evolved from
these Dutch faces. The Dutch in their turn had
been influenced by Garamond in France. The general tone of Janson, however, is darker than Garamond and has a sturdiness and substance quite
different from its predecessors.

This book was composed, printed, and bound by
H. WOLFF, New York. Paper manufactured by
P. H. GLATFELTER CO., Spring Grove, Pennsylvania.